THE CONJUROR'S BIRD

Martin Davies

WINDSOR
PARAGON

First published 2005
by
Hodder and Stoughton
This Large Print edition published 2006
by
BBC Audiobooks Ltd by arrangement with
Hodder and Stoughton Ltd

Hardcover ISBN 10: 1 4056 1541 9
           ISBN 13: 978 1 405 61541 9
Softcover ISBN 10: 1 4056 1542 7
           ISBN 13: 978 1 405 61542 6

British Library Cataloguing in Publication Data available

Printed and bound in Great Britain by
Antony Rowe Ltd., Chippenham, Wiltshire

This book is dedicated to my mother—
for many more reasons than can be listed here

We are a careless species. We lose things without knowing. But sometimes they leave behind a tiny fragment of themselves that lets us guess at the original. For my grandfather it was a feather; for me, a face.

CHAPTER ONE

THURSDAY NIGHT AT THE TAXIDERMIST'S

That Thursday evening I was working late, removing the skull of a dead owl. It was December outside but at my workbench the heat from the lamp was making my fingers sweat. I was at the hardest part of the whole operation, the bit where you have to ease the skull very gently down the neck without damaging the skin, and as I began to work it loose I found my eyes were blinking with the concentration. But I could sense it was working, that I was doing it well, and when I heard the telephone grumbling at the back of the workshop I decided to let it ring. It was too late for a summons to the pub and even though I'd taken down the sign and removed myself from the Yellow Pages, the five-pint pranksters ('I've got this chicken that needs stuffing . . .') would still occasionally get through. This was their time to call but tonight I wasn't in the mood. Until I remembered Katya and changed my mind.

Katya was the latest student to rent the flat at the top of the house. It was always students because I kept the rent low to make up for any dead animals they might meet in the hallway. They were prepared to overlook a bit of that because the location was central and because my students in the Natural Sciences department were prepared to vouch for my character. Students will overlook a great deal if you have a reputation as a rebel and, in a painfully earnest, save-the-world department, I qualified by riding a motorbike and by refusing to toe the university line on current conservation theory. It was that easy.

The top-floor flat was self-contained. Katya and I had a front door and a staircase in common and very little else—in the couple of months since she'd moved in we'd exchanged some polite smiles and rather fewer words. Every ten days or so her mother would ring from Sweden and I'd dutifully take down a message on a yellow pad and leave it at the bottom of the stairs, along with the suggestion that Katya might give her mother the number of the upstairs phone. The next day the note would be gone but her mother would continue to ring downstairs. She was a polite woman, struggling slightly with her English, struggling not to let any anxiety show. I felt sorry for her. Which is why, even though the owl was just beginning to fall into line, I peeled off my gloves and answered the phone.

It wasn't Katya's mother.

It was a voice I hadn't heard for fifteen years. A scarcely remembered, totally familiar, soft, low voice.

'Fitz,' it asked, 'is that you?'

'Gabriella.' A rhetorical statement, if such a thing is possible.

'Yes, it's me. It's been a long time, Fitz.'

It wasn't clear if that was a reproach or an apology.

'Yes, a long time.' The words came out sounding defensive. 'Though I got your letters.'

'You didn't reply.'

'You know I'm not a great one for writing.'

2

She couldn't deny that. I was famous for it.

'Look, Fitz, I'm over in London for a few days and there's someone I want you to meet. He's a collector and he's got quite a good story to tell. I think you'll be interested. What are you doing tomorrow?'

I looked at the remains of the owl on the workbench. It would just have to take its chance in the freezer.

'I think tomorrow is reasonably free,' I concluded.

'Good. Can we say seven in the bar at the Mecklenburg? It's off Oxford Street, just by Selfridges.'

How like Gabby to realise that the Mecklenburg Hotel was not among my usual drinking venues.

'All right. Seven tomorrow . . .'

'It will be good to see you. I've told Karl that if anyone can help him you can.'

'Karl . . . ?'

'Karl Anderson.'

'Ah, yes. The collector. I've read about him. What sort of help would that be?'

She paused. She had never liked talking over the phone.

'Not now. Wait for tomorrow. But I promise you'll be interested, Fitz. It's about the Mysterious Bird of Ulieta.'

*   *   *

She was right, of course. I *was* interested. In all sorts of ways. Abandoning the owl to the darkness, I climbed the stairs to the room where I did most of my living. It was an untidy, comfortable room, warmly lit and smelling of old paper. The bed was permanently unmade and the desk was littered with notes for a book I wasn't really writing. Some of them were noticeably dusty. One whole wall was taken up with shelves of carefully ordered books but I didn't need to look anything up to know that Gabby wasn't being melodramatic. Despite its name the bird was real enough, or it had been once. I'd even made some notes about it for an article, back in the days when I was going to be famous.

And now, all these years later, she wanted to ask me about it. She and her friend Karl Anderson. I'd seen a picture of them together once, taken by a mutual friend about three years earlier at one of the big summer lectures in Salzburg. She was leaning very lightly on his arm, still dark and slim and calm, still with that familiar half-questioning smile.

I settled down on the bed and looked thoughtfully at the small trunk in the corner of the room. What they wanted to know was probably in there along with everything else—the dodo, the heath hen, the passenger pigeon, the lost and the forgotten, all mixed together—years of jotted notes and observations still waiting to be given a shape.

But instead of thinking about them, I thought about Gabby and the man she wanted me to meet. I'd read a lot about him over the years but everything I knew really came down to three things. That Karl Anderson was a man with a reputation for finding things. That he was used to getting what he wanted. And that nowadays he was far too successful to do his searching in person unless the stakes were very high indeed.

I wasn't sure I liked the sound of him.

I checked my watch and realised I could still just catch the pub.

Journeys begin in many different ways. It was Cook, a man experienced in preparations for a long sea expedition, who persuaded Joseph Banks to return to Revesby before they sailed; so that in the summer of 1768, two months before they were due to depart, he made the journey back to Lincolnshire; back to the woods and fields that for the next three years were what he thought of when he thought of home.

*　　　*　　　*

The summers before the *Endeavour* set sail seemed lonelier to her than the winters. Each summer day she spent alone was haunted by a sense of joy wasted. And against the uncertainty of her future she began to paint, as if she might trap and keep each day by its details. The transit of Venus, which he travelled so far to observe, was less to her than the passing of the seasons in the Revesby woods.

CHAPTER TWO

FRIDAY AT THE MECKLENBURG

It was raining heavily by the time I reached the Mecklenburg Hotel. By abandoning the bus at Oxford Circus I arrived wet and out of breath, but at least I was on time. The hotel turned out to be an ugly building, concrete on the outside and expensively mock Edwardian beyond the revolving doors. I stood for a moment in the lobby, dripping on the carpet, slightly disappointed. Then, suddenly self-conscious, I followed a sign to the gents where I dried my hair and pushed it into some sort of order. When I'd finished I looked better but still underdressed. Amongst academics I considered myself reasonably stylish. Here I just looked like someone who might steal the towels.

I paused in front of the mirror to collect my thoughts. It was hard to imagine what Anderson might want. The bird from Ulieta was an enigma, one of nature's conjuring tricks—a creature that had disappeared as if with a wave of the hand. But this disappearance had been final and there would be no coming back. The audience was left looking for feathers that had long ceased to exist. Not even Anderson could do much about that.

Upstairs, in the Rosebery Bar, despite the cigarette smoke there was a smell of perfume and leather. Not the sort of desiccated leather that featured in my jacket and parts of my shoes. This leather was new and expensive and smelled soft, if that's possible. Its effect was to make me aware of the smell of rain I'd brought in with me. Among these dry, groomed people it was the odour of not quite belonging.

Gabriella was easy to spot. She was sitting in a corner under a soft lamp, framed in best cinema style by a twisting curve of smoke. She was, as before, dark and slender, so neat as to seem flawless. She was wearing a slim black dress in a fifties style, but in her case there could be no question of being out of place. She had slipped into this time of Chanel and soft leather with the same maddening grace that she might slip into a taxi. Beside her, behind the smoke, was a tall, blond man in his early fifties, squarely Scandinavian, constructed in straight lines. A good-looking man. He was turned to Gabby and talking quite eagerly as I edged hesitantly towards them, past a group of pre-theatre Americans.

Then Gabby looked up and noticed me.

'Hello, Fitz,' she said quietly as I arrived at their table, and suddenly I was annoyed with her for not having changed and annoyed with myself for noticing. And annoyed that somewhere on my right an impeccably suited arm was being advanced to shake my hand.

'Fitz, this is Karl Anderson,' she said, as if that would make it all right.

I nodded at him, not caring much, and turned back to Gabriella. She was so startlingly familiar it was hard to breathe.

'Perhaps we should all sit down?' suggested Anderson calmly. 'I'm sure Mr Fitzgerald would like a drink.'

He was right. A drink was exactly what I wanted.

8

                    *   *   *

And so I sat down at the small round table and joined in a painfully well-mannered conversation that tiptoed carefully around any awkwardness. A waiter brought me a beer, and more drinks were ordered. I was aware of Gabby sitting next to me, close enough for my hand to fall on hers if I let it drop from the table. The new drinks arrived almost immediately—Anderson was drinking as quickly as I was and ordered deft refills whenever our glasses were nearly empty. I watched him while Gabriella told us about the lectures she was about to give in Edinburgh and Munich. A tall, well-proportioned man, seven or eight years older than me but not looking it—a maverick, a charmer, a big personality in a dusty discipline.

Beside him, Gabriella seemed tiny, like a bird. It was as if she'd slipped through the years without friction, her freshness and vitality untouched. She must have been ten years younger than the big man next to her, and yet they matched. They made a good-looking couple.

'So what are you doing with yourself these days, Mr Fitzgerald? Your withdrawal from field work is a great loss to us all.' He was a Norwegian by birth but his English was only very slightly accented and very perfectly pronounced.

'Oh, I keep myself busy. Teaching mostly. "Natural History: the historical context"—the Greeks and Romans, early naturalists, the Darwinian controversy. That sort of thing. It's a compulsory module, so the students have to turn up, even if I'm no good.'

'And are you good?'

9

'Well, I'm controversial, which is the next best thing. My first lecture is "The Taxidermist as Hero". I always enjoy that one.'

At that moment Anderson was diverted by the waiter and Gabby caught my eye.

'I'm glad you could come, Fitz,' she said, and she sounded as if she meant it. Personally, I was withholding judgement. It wasn't until the third drink was beginning to have an effect that Anderson turned to the subject we'd all been waiting for.

'You must be wondering why I'm here, Mr Fitzgerald, intruding on this meeting of old friends.'

I raised an eyebrow to acknowledge the question but didn't reply, so he carried on.

'I was lucky enough to hear Gabriella speak in Prague a few years ago and we have been friends ever since. She mentioned you to me as a man with a great deal of knowledge in one of the areas I am interested in. I am also, of course, aware of your grandfather's work.'

He paused to put his glass down neatly on its paper coaster. I waited for the commonplace compliment that usually came with any mention of my grandfather but none followed. Instead Anderson leaned forward and lowered his voice.

'I am a collector, Mr Fitzgerald. I am here because I am looking for something incredibly rare. Something that may not even exist any more. Gabriella thinks you may be able to help me. It is well known you are an authority on extinct birds.' His eyes lingered on my face for a moment. 'What do you know of the bird from the Society Islands, the one they call the Mysterious Bird of Ulieta?'

'Not much,' I told him calmly, truthfully. 'Rather a fanciful piece of naming, I've always thought.'

Again his intent, searching gaze.

'Not perhaps so fanciful.' He leaned back and rubbed the back of his neck with his fingertips. 'Let us talk about it a little.'

He finished rubbing and placed his fingertips softly on the edge of the table in front of him. His eyes met mine again.

'The rarest bird ever recorded, Mr Fitzgerald. Seen only once, in 1774, by Captain Cook's second expedition. A routine collecting party on a South Sea island known then as Ulieta. A single specimen captured, of a species never seen before. Preserved by Johann Forster and brought back to England. No bird like it ever found again, on Ulieta or anywhere else. Extinct before it was ever really discovered.'

He paused and his eyes dropped to the table top where he ran one fingertip across a drop of liquid, shaping it thoughtfully into the shape of an X.

'I'm sure none of that is new to you, Mr Fitzgerald. On his return Johann Forster gave away the preserved specimen. The *only* specimen. The only specimen ever found. Of course he had no way of knowing its rarity then. Nor did the young man he gave it to, the naturalist Joseph Banks.'

He looked up at me again and now there was an excitement in his eye that had not been there before.

'Yes, Mr Fitzgerald. It is two hundred years since that one specimen went missing from Banks's collection. No one knows what's happened to it. I think it's time it was found, don't you?'

11

He came to realise later that discovery was not a science. That summer his journey to Revesby was slow and troublesome, but despite the great heat his thoughts were of the southern ocean. The *Endeavour* was close to readiness and his mind turned easily to the voyage ahead. Yet gradually, as the miles passed, the shapes and shadows of his own country began to gather him back, until in the last few miles he found his heart began to beat a little faster and his eyes reached forward for a glimpse of home.

When it came, the old house was waiting for him, its arms spread wide as if to embrace a prodigal. At first the mellow stone against the trees seemed to exist quite on its own, but at the sound of his carriage people began to spill out in welcome: familiar, friendly faces whose greetings were already tinged with goodbyes. In the days that followed he found his journey was the subject of every conversation, and every person who spoke of it took care to speak confidently of his return. Revesby, it seemed, was proud and anxious in equal measure. That night there were lights and dancing. Gentlemen flushed by music and wine thumped his back and wished him luck and noticed how brightly his spirits shone. And they were right. He felt strong and vital and talked of great discoveries, and when the music played he danced wildly and often. The gentlemen's daughters were a blur to him: bright satins, soft hands, and always a hush of whispers behind him, speculating and excited. By day, while the house drowsed in the heat, he left the talk behind him and set out on foot for the cool of the woods.

12

*   *   *

He knew she was there, in the woods, before he saw her. At first she was only a movement, some way off, as if a deer had shadowed away from the corner of his vision. Later he found twigs broken and grass cushioned into a hollow. Then, on a day when the sun was bright, he saw her at a distance against the trees on the edge of a meadow, too far away for him to see her face. She moved easily and lightly through the long grasses, slipping between sun and shadow like a white thread stitching the trees to the meadow.

After that he asked about her and they told him her name. As he walked home that evening he thought again of the way she moved along the margin of the wood and felt his curiosity aroused. The night was warm around him, a cloak of heavy summer scent. He thought of her as he walked.

If she knew of his arrival she did not think of it. The woods were her summer and her escape. Each day with quick fingers she drew what she found in them, and in these little acts of salvage she gathered close to her the things she knew best. She did not expect to be noticed. Discovery is not a science; there is too much chance in it.

CHAPTER THREE

THE GENE ARK

Anderson had done his research. He knew all there was to know about the bird from Ulieta. Which frankly wasn't that much. In May 1774, Captain Cook had brought his ship, the *Resolution*, to the island of Ulieta. Ulieta was small, one of the spattering of islands in the blue Pacific that came to be known collectively as the Society Islands. Cook stayed there some days, to make repairs and trade with the local people. On June 1st, despite the enervating heat and a crew weakened by stomach disorders, Johann Forster, the ship's naturalist and a difficult man, insisted that an expedition be sent ashore to gather specimens. A number of birds were shot and killed that day but there was only one of them that Forster didn't recognise. After he had recorded his observations of it, the specimen was passed to his son, Georg, one of the ship's artists, who made and coloured a drawing of the bird. Immediately afterwards the bird was cleaned and its skin preserved for mounting.

It was not an unusual day's work for either father or son. There were many new specimens that voyage, many creatures to record, draw and preserve. That day in Ulieta would have been of no great interest to anyone if it hadn't been for one thing: that single specimen collected by Forster remains the only bird of its kind ever recorded, anywhere. Andrew Garrett went to Ulieta in the

1850s but could find no sign of it. Subsequently others tried and failed. We'll never know if the species was once widespread. We can't guess at its song or the shape of its nest or the mating rituals it acted out. We only know that the individual handled by Forster was one of the very last of its kind. If the expedition that morning had taken a different path, or if the aim of one sailor had been a little less precise, then the extinction of an entire species would have passed without us knowing. It would have vanished from the planet unmarked by humankind.

We can't even agree on its name. Forster named it *Turdus badius*, the bay thrush, a name that never fails to raise a smirk among my more scatologically minded students. Another naturalist, Latham, who studied the specimen back in London, named it more precisely and recorded it as *Turdus ulietensis*. James Greenway, writing nearly two hundred years later, wasn't even convinced that the bird was a kind of thrush. He listed it simply as 'the Mysterious Bird of Ulieta'. Which is as good a name as any.

When the Forsters returned to Britain the following year, the specimens they had collected on Cook's expedition were theirs to dispose of. Johann Forster was permanently in financial difficulties and he sought help from Joseph Banks, the naturalist on Cook's previous voyage. Banks was a young man with money and a future and he was generous towards Forster. In return Forster presented him with specimens. One was the bird from Ulieta—we know this because Latham saw the bird in Banks's collection at some point in the 1770s and recorded it in his book *A General*

15

Synopsis of Birds. It is as well that he did, because after that there is no further record of that specimen. The specimen, like the species itself, simply disappeared.

It would be tempting to question the evidence of Latham and Forster—to speculate that the bird they examined was just a variation on some other, more common species—but we can't argue it away so easily. Because Georg Forster's drawing still exists, safe in the hands of the Natural History Museum. It shows us exactly what the bird looked like. You can go there and see it for yourself if you like.

*   *   *

The Rosebery Bar was no less full when Anderson finally finished speaking but the atmosphere had begun to change. The after-work drinkers with trains to catch had moved on, while those who replaced them were relaxing into the evening. Somewhere out of sight a pianist had started to play and someone at the bar had dimmed the lights in sympathy. Suit jackets dropped on the backs of sofas, ties were looser and feet in black tights had crept from their shoes and were curled up discreetly on the red leather sofas.

I drained my drink slowly and looked at Gabriella, then at Anderson. Both were watching me but if they were looking for a reaction all they got was a raised eyebrow. I can't deny a little buzz of excitement at the story he was telling but I was puzzled. Anyone who was interested in extinct birds knew the only ever specimen of the Ulieta bird had disappeared in the eighteenth century.

16

People might even joke about finding it somewhere, like a lost Botticelli tucked away in an attic. But no one *seriously* imagined the specimen still existed. Taxidermy wasn't very advanced back then and birds were notoriously hard to preserve. Museum records are full of eighteenth-century specimens that simply fell apart after about seventy or eighty years. Every collection had its wastage. The bird from Ulieta was just one of thousands that didn't make it.

'Tell me, Anderson,' I asked, 'why would a man like you suddenly decide to look for something like that?'

'What if I told you I was an enthusiast?'

'I wouldn't believe you. You're a businessman. You find things on commission for the sort of people who can't enjoy anything unless they own it. Cash for dinosaur remains, endangered species on demand, that sort of thing. Why would you spend time looking for something that probably disintegrated two hundred years ago?'

He smiled to himself, a quiet, confident smile.

'It might have survived. Specimens of that age do exist.'

'Very, very few. How many? Perhaps a dozen. It's hard to imagine this was one of them. Joseph Banks was the pre-eminent scientist of his generation. He didn't just lose rare birds. If this one blipped off the radar at some point it's because it fell apart. And if it had survived, there'd be records. In two hundred years someone would have mentioned owning the rarest bird in the world.'

Anderson had caught the waiter's eye again and more drinks were arriving.

'You may be right, Mr Fitzgerald. And yet I intend to find it nevertheless. The rewards for doing so would be . . . considerable.'

'Yes?' It seemed unlikely. 'Who's interested in stuffed birds nowadays? Oh, I don't deny it would be quite a coup—the natural history establishment would be overjoyed. But there's no money in museums.'

'Sadly true, Mr Fitzgerald. But museums were not the market I had in mind.'

Anderson took another sip and sat back as if that was all he had to say on the subject. It was left to Gabby to explain.

'Fitz, have you ever heard of the Ark Project?'

For a moment I thought she was referring to something in our past and I had to blink away a glimpse of rainforest. But it was apparent from her tone and the focus of her eyes that her thoughts were very firmly in the present. Anderson, his legs now stretched out in front of him, pushed himself back into the conversation.

'The Gene Ark, to give it its full title. It was set up in Canada by Ted Staest. Have you heard of Staest?'

Only vaguely. A Canadian. A man famous for being rich. I passed.

'Ted Staest owns one of the big North American pharmaceutical companies—brands in every country, you know the sort of thing. Staest's big thing now is DNA. The Ark Project is basically his own personal DNA bank, Mr Fitzgerald. He collects genetic material from rare and vanishing species and stores it. The idea is to invest in rare DNA the way you or I might invest in art or antiques. He holds it against potential increases in

18

value.'

Gabby sensed my scorn.

'It's true, Fitz. I know it sounds crazy but there's a scramble going on to own genetic coding. Even the pharmaceutical companies aren't sure of its value but no one wants to let the others get it first, so they're spending now and they'll ask questions later. They keep the public interested with high-profile talk, rebreeding extinct species, that sort of thing. But it's the bioengineering possibilities that they're interested in.'

The Rosebery Bar began to seem a strangely foreign place. The crowd had started to thin slightly and the pianist had taken a break to the accompaniment of some pattering applause. I looked around at the people who remained—people in their twenties buying drinks I couldn't afford in a world I had no time for.

'But the Ulieta bird would be two hundred years old. It would just be a dried skin. There couldn't possibly be material of any value in that, could there?'

Gabby and Anderson looked at each other and Anderson shrugged.

'Who knows? Techniques develop all the time. And to be frank, Mr Fitzgerald, I don't think Ted Staest cares very much either way. He's a man who knows the value of publicity and he's very taken by the story of that missing bird, the rarest bird in history. "The Mysterious Bird of Ulieta" would make good headlines, wouldn't it? Turning up a specimen like that would help get the Ark Project in the news. The rarest bird in the world, patented by Ted Staest.'

'And he is paying you to find it?'

19

'He is paying me to find it *first*. It's hard to keep that sort of thing quiet. Where there's a market there are always others hoping to cash in.'

'OK,' I said carefully, trying to draw it all together, 'so a rich Canadian wants to find a nonexistent bird specimen because he thinks it will boost his share price. That's bizarre but I can just about get my head round it. What I can't see is why you're telling me about any of this.'

Again Anderson looked at me appraisingly. It was Gabby who answered.

'Karl won't be the only one to contact you, Fitz. People remember all the work you did on extinct birds. They'll want to know what you can tell them.'

Anderson nodded.

'Fifteen years ago, Mr Fitzgerald, your research into extinct birds was known to everyone in the field. We know you visited museums and collections all over the world, collections that no one else has ever properly studied. You collected maps, drawings, inventories, letters, all in your famous wooden chest. We all waited for you to publish but you never did. If anyone has any information that might lead to the Ulieta bird, it would be you.'

'So you think I might be able to help you find it?'

'You have contacts. You know the sort of people who might have heard rumours. I'm sure you could make some calls, see what you could find.'

'And if I can't find anything?'

He looked unconcerned, and took a slow, relaxed sip of his drink.

'To be honest, Mr Fitzgerald, I have a lead

already. But I thought you'd be interested in joining me in this. And if you can make the search quicker and easier for me, that's all to the good.'

'And why did you think I'd be interested in looking for it?'

He paused and looked me directly in the eye.

'Because you never found anything like the Ulieta bird, Mr Fitzgerald. All that time searching for specimens of extinct birds, but you never found one like this. Oh, you found some rare specimens all right, but never the specimen of a bird lost without trace. And to find the only ever specimen of a bird seen only once . . . Think of it! This is your chance, Mr Fitzgerald.' He sat back and let his words sink in. 'As long as I get the bird, I'm happy for you to have the headlines. And I would of course pay you for your time. Fifty thousand dollars was the sum I had in mind.'

If I felt incredulous, I tried not to show it. Instead I took a long swig of beer and did some rapid calculations. Fifty thousand dollars was a pretty significant sum to someone like me. If Anderson was prepared to send that sort of money in my direction, how much was he expecting to make? A hundred and fifty thousand dollars? Two hundred thousand? Too much, surely. No one would pay that. Stuffed birds weren't in fashion.

I lowered my glass and, to avoid Anderson's eye, I looked around for a waiter. Perhaps I was behind the times. After all, this specimen would be a one-off, a one-in-a-million curiosity . . .

'I don't get it,' I said. 'I figure for you to come all this way on the off chance that it might still exist, that must mean someone's offering some pretty weird money for it. How can it possibly be worth

21

that much?'

Anderson smiled and shook his head. 'Let us not exaggerate its importance. It would be an amazing find, yes, and Ted Staest would pay well for it. But I'm over here on a different piece of business and looking for the Ulieta bird is really just a favour for Ted Staest. As a client, he could mean a great deal to me in the long term. So if I can sort this for him without too much fuss, then that's good business. I'm not even too bothered about covering my costs.'

I watched him closely as he signalled for refills. He seemed relaxed enough, but I was still suspicious.

'What brings you here then if it's not the Ulieta bird?' I asked.

'Oh, various things. Botanical art, mainly. Do you know much about eighteenth-century botanical art, Mr Fitzgerald?'

'Not much.'

'There's something of a rage for it at the moment, particularly in the States. There are one or two pieces I'm hoping to pick up while I'm over here, which I suspect could be very valuable indeed. Very fashionable and extremely rare. The best possible combination.'

He spoke as if the paintings were completely without interest to him so long as a profit was assured. I looked across at Gabby and then looked back at him.

'What happened to you, Anderson?' I asked softly. 'Once upon a time you were a pioneer. I saw you interviewed when you found those plesiosaur remains. You *glowed* with pleasure. And it wasn't to do with money back then.'

For the first time that evening he looked a little annoyed, but his tone when he spoke was utterly unruffled.

'We all make our choices, Mr Fitzgerald. After all, you were a serious scientist once.'

He let his hand fall back to the table so that it rested against Gabriella's arm.

I'd like to say it was his first mistake, but even before his hand touched hers I knew I wasn't going to help him. That just made it easier. I stood up. For Gabby's sake I decided to be honest.

'Look, Anderson, there's nothing in my notes that will help you or anyone else. Even fifteen years ago a bit of a myth had built up around them, but it's all just paper, a lot of observations about some old specimens no one much cares about any more. I'd be taking your money under false pretences.'

I swallowed. I was trying hard to keep my voice low.

'There's another thing I should say,' I went on. 'I don't believe that bird still exists, but if by some miracle it *has* survived all this time, I shudder to think of it being pulled apart in a lab, tested and analysed and washed with chemicals in pursuit of some genetic conjuring trick.' I paused and met his eye as calmly as I could. 'I think it might be you who doesn't understand its value, Mr Anderson.'

I nodded to Gabby as I turned away, but I didn't look back. Fifteen years on, and she still had the same effect on me. As I walked away, the same old image went with me—a bare room and a crumpled bed, an electric fan churning the heat; and with it, always, unbidden but inescapable, the sound of Gabby's voice. Only now she was with Anderson.

23

And I was glad there was nothing I could do to help them.

Beyond the Mecklenburg's revolving doors the rain had almost stopped, leaving the roads shiny under the streetlamps. The buses were still running but I chose to walk, my mind turning over everything I'd heard since the start of the evening. Halfway home I stopped at a late-night coffee place. It was still empty, waiting for the post-pub crowd to pass through. In two hours it would be packed. I claimed a corner for myself and thought about Gabby—how she'd been, how she'd looked, how I felt. How Anderson had sat so comfortably beside her. Gradually, as the rain began to fall again, I began to think about the lost bird that had brought them here. Anderson's search seemed too bizarre to be true. A unique bird, an unexplained disappearance, an infinitesimal possibility that somewhere the sole specimen might still exist. It was an amazing thought, the sort of discovery I'd dreamed about once. But surely not possible? I should have been laughing at the idea—but Anderson wasn't the sort of man who inspired much humour.

My mind was still turning over that thought when I left the café and stepped out into the rain. It took me a little while to walk home and when I got there it took me a little longer to grasp the meaning of the broken front door that greeted me. Its small window pane had been smashed through to the hallway and beyond it Katya was sitting at the foot of the stairs, looking out over the shattered glass.

24

On first seeing her face, he decided that she was not, after all, beautiful.

She was, indeed, very much as the people of Revesby had described her—her hair brown, her figure slight, her features neat but ordinary.

His disappointment kept him on the edge of the clearing in the cool of the oak trees. Beyond their shade, where the woman sat drawing, he could smell the sun on the hot earth. The afternoon light showed her very clearly: a slim figure in white muslin, her skin slightly freckled, a frown of intense concentration deep on her forehead as she drew. Glimpsed through the trees, moving in and out of the shadow, her form had struck him as uniquely graceful, and more than once its promise had brought him back to the woods in the hope of satisfying his curiosity. But now with his wood nymph exposed as a sun-browned girl he hesitated, and he might have turned away into the shadow had she not at that moment looked directly at where he stood.

Her gaze embarrassed him. She was alone in the woods and he had been observing her quite openly. A gentleman, he thought, would bow and withdraw.

And yet he stepped out into the sunshine, clearing his throat and looking down as he did so to hide his confusion. When he looked up again she had risen to her feet and was facing him with her drawing book folded across her bosom.

'My apologies if I have disturbed you,' he said, advancing. 'I often walk this way and did not think to find this remote spot so happily tenanted.' He extended his hand. 'My name is Joseph Banks.'

She looked down at his hand but didn't take it.

25

When she spoke her voice was quiet.

'I know who you are, Mr Banks. Revesby is too small to permit otherwise. Even those who wish to avoid each other are not always able to do so.'

'Then I am pleased that is not the case today.' He smiled, and indicated her drawing book. 'I see you are an artist.'

For a moment she looked down and Banks studied her face. Then, when he realised that she intended to make no reply, he bowed and smiled into the silence she had left for him.

'I'm sure we shall meet again soon. Perhaps you will be at home when I call upon your father.'

Her eyes had remained lowered but now they moved sharply to his face. She spoke very clearly, her voice much harder.

'Perhaps you are mistaken as to *my* identity, sir. My family does not receive visitors. Our neighbours do not call on us and we do not expect them.'

He smiled and bowed again.

'I shall wish you goodbye,' he said. 'Until we meet again.'

*   *   *

She preyed upon his mind for reasons he didn't understand. Perhaps it was the unusual circumstance of her being alone, or perhaps her demeanour as she drew. But more than either of these was the impression of a person hidden, and he found himself speculating about the emotions beneath her shell.

*   *   *

Next morning Banks took his sister Sophia to pay

26

visits in the village. Ahead of them the sun was shining and the meadows were full of the scent of summer. Both air and sunshine felt fresh on his cheek. With the danger of his great voyage looming, he had never felt more aware of being alive.

The various calls were made with good humour. Banks was pleased to be with his sister and she was pleased to show him to their neighbours. Their summer mood lasted until the end of the village. There, when Sophia went to turn back, Banks stopped her and indicated a small stone-built house that lay ahead of them.

'I'm told the black sheep of the parish is unwell, Sophia. They say he is dying. I would like to call to find out how he fares.'

'No, really, Joseph!' She pulled on his arm and her face was suddenly serious. 'Since the *incident* it is not proper to call. And besides he has suffered a seizure that leaves him insensible to the world around. Even, one fears, insensible to his own disgrace.'

But he was not to be dissuaded. With a firm arm he continued to steer her towards the house until turning back would have seemed so deliberate a snub that it was not to be contemplated. The old woman who answered the door informed them that the daughter of the house was not at home and that the master was unable to receive.

'Do you think you might keep my card, nurse, so that he is aware of my visit?' Banks asked.

'I fear he will know nothing of it, sir.'

Banks nodded, his card still between his fingers. He might have spoken more but Sophia's pressure on his arm persuaded him to nod once more and move away.

The same morning, as they returned home through the place called Slipper Wood, Banks spied a

27

movement in the shadows. They watched for a moment until it became clear they were glimpsing the figure of a woman dressed in white. As they looked, the figure stopped by the trunk of a tree with her face turned towards it. For some seconds she was motionless, then she began to slip around the tree, her face still close to the bark. When her circuit was complete, she moved to a neighbouring trunk, and repeated the ritual.

'I fear that is the invalid's daughter,' Sophia told him. 'She is often to be seen alone in the woods. It does little to redeem her family's reputation in the eyes of the village.'

'How old is she?' he asked.

'She must now be sixteen or seventeen.'

He watched for a while longer, his face unreadable against the sunlight.

'What does she do in the woods?' he asked.

'Really, I have no idea. Perhaps she is hoping to catch the attention of a passing gentleman of susceptible disposition. Though her looks are sadly ordinary and she has no prospects whatsoever.'

That evening the party at the Abbey was joined by Dr Taylor from the village. Sophia related what they had seen in Slipper Wood and turned to the doctor to support her in her disapproval.

'Indeed. That young girl is most difficult,' he confirmed. 'Since her father's disgrace she shuns us all most markedly. It is as if misfortune has aged her and hardened her. She is alone a great deal too much, I fear.'

Banks nodded and the conversation turned to other subjects.

The next morning he took a magnifying glass from his study and returned to the place in Slipper Wood where he had seen her. So great was his absorption there that his business correspondence of the morning went unattended and a letter beginning '*My dearest H . . .*' was left unfinished on his desk.

CHAPTER FOUR

AFTER A BURGLARY

I was feeling distinctly uneasy as I sat in my small back kitchen and watched Katya make tea. Opposite me, across the table, a young policeman was asking the usual questions. No, nothing was missing. No sign of any disturbance at all. No damage, nothing.

'Passport, cheque book, post office book . . . All all right, sir?' He made me feel like somebody's grandfather.

'Yes, all still here.'

'Do you keep money on the premises?'

'I'd like to but I never seem to manage it.'

'Well, if you're really sure, sir.'

He made a note on his pad and looked up at Katya as she approached the table with three mugs of tea balanced on a dinner plate. 'I know this must be very disturbing for you both.'

The remark was intended entirely for her and it made me glance up at her as she turned for the sugar, my attention caught by the young man's interest. I hadn't seen much of Katya since she moved in and I'd never looked at her very carefully before. Now I found her taller and slimmer than I'd thought, attractive in a youthful, slightly angular way. She was wearing black and her hair was dark too, long and straight with a fringe that framed her face. Before then the small silver stud in her nose was the only thing I'd ever really taken in. A strange thing, I thought randomly, how little

I'd noticed her.

She answered the officer's questions with a faint accent, but she spoke English naturally, as if she'd grown up with it. Her story was very simple. She had returned a little before twelve and had found the glass in the door broken. She'd called the police immediately and waited on the stairs. She hadn't touched anything. She had lived here two months. She had never seen anyone acting suspiciously near the front door. She was from Sweden and was studying for a master's degree in history.

At this point something bleeped in the officer's pocket and he began to put away his notebook.

'There's nothing much else I can do here, sir,' he told me neutrally. 'Probably just kids. But I'm afraid you'll need to take steps to make these premises more secure. With a front door like that it's only surprising it didn't happen sooner.'

I got up to show him out but Katya rose too and, as she was nearer the door, I let them go with a nod. From the hallway I could hear a voice lowered confidentially.

'If you need me again, miss, here's the number to call. Any time. Just pick up the phone . . .'

Then the front door shut and Katya returned to the kitchen and the chair opposite me. The downstairs kitchen was my kitchen—Katya had her own—and it felt strange for us to be alone together there. Nevertheless, it was a good place to sit—an ageing boiler kept it warm at unlikely times and a quirk of the ventilation meant it always smelled of coffee from the offices next door. Even tonight it felt immune from the sense of intrusion that hung in the hallway and the rooms beyond. Most of the

31

space was taken up by an old wooden table and it was there that we sat, in the soft yellow light, neither of us speaking for a moment. When I looked up from my tea, she was watching me from under her fringe.

'Is it true?' she asked. 'Is there really nothing missing? You didn't seem sure.'

I paused before I replied, afraid of making a fool of myself.

'No, nothing missing. I just feel unsettled.'

Katya nodded. 'It's never nice to think of someone poking around. But at least they didn't take anything.'

That was what was worrying me. I could have understood theft.

'There's something I noticed,' I told her. 'Something a bit odd.'

She was looking at me carefully.

'What sort of thing?'

I didn't attempt to explain until she'd followed me upstairs and we were standing side by side facing the bookshelves that covered one wall of my bedroom.

'Have you ever seen any of those black-and-white films where the detective comes back to find his office has been ransacked? Well, this is exactly the opposite.'

She looked alarmed and slowly shook her head, not understanding. I wasn't quite sure how to explain.

'Here, run your finger along my desk. What happens?'

She picked up her finger and blew on it.

'Nothing happens. Just dust.'

'Exactly. Now do the same on the bookshelves.'

She didn't need to.

'Nothing. They've been dusted.'

'Take a look around. Do I look like a man who dusts?'

It wasn't hard to see what I meant. Everything in the room that wasn't in daily use was covered with a thin layer of dust—the chairs, the wooden chest, even the photograph by my bed. But the bookshelves were immaculate, beautifully and carefully wiped clean.

Someone had dusted my bookshelves.

It was really too absurd to believe. My first thought on finding it had been that something must be missing, that perhaps someone had wiped extravagantly for fingerprints after a theft. But there were no gaps between the crammed books to suggest an absence and I knew the contents of those shelves so well I could almost recite them. And besides, there was nothing worth stealing. No book in the whole collection of any real value.

To my surprise, Katya began to giggle.

'So,' she began, trying to restrain herself, 'you think someone would break in to do your cleaning? I mean, it isn't *that* messy.'

It was about then that I found myself liking her. I think it was her laughter, the way she kept things in proportion. The break-in was confusing, and the conversation with Anderson was still on my mind. I needed someone to listen while I tried to manufacture a little cosmos out of the chaos. So that she wouldn't go away I cleared her a seat and began to tell her about my evening at the Mecklenburg Hotel. But to make sense of that I found I had to tell her about the book I'd never written, the ultimate book about extinct birds. A book that was going to make each one, in a little way, live again. I told her about the discoveries I'd made in obscure collections and the unknown drawings found in the papers of dead travellers, and then about some of the birds themselves: the Stephen Island wren, entirely wiped out by a single domestic cat; the spectacled cormorant, eaten to the brink of extinction by Arctic explorers and finished off by a fleet of Russian whalers in the course of an afternoon.

Katya listened with her elbows on her knees and her hands around the tea she'd brought up with her. She didn't seem bored, and she prompted me when I hesitated. Once her tea was finished, I fetched two glasses and a bottle of Polish vodka from the freezer. When I went to close the curtains, the street outside lay in darkness, the night gathered thickly beyond the reach of the streetlamps. It had started to rain again.

'Why did you never finish it?' she asked as I filled the glasses.

It was hard to explain. I picked up the bottle and put it between us. It was still four-fifths full.

'Look,' I said, pointing to the empty fifth at the top of the bottle. 'When I set out I thought all I had to do was describe the gap here.' She looked at the empty part and nodded.

'But do you see? After three years I was further from finishing than when I started. The level in the bottle keeps falling and the rate it drops gets faster and faster. Each year there are more and more species on the brink, more empty space about to appear in the bottle. Sometimes they even discover new species, but they go straight onto the endangered lists too. And then there are the empty bottles we don't even know about, the birds extinct before we even noticed them. One day I suddenly realised that I'd never catch up. There's never going to be a definitive work about extinct birds. All we can do is record the handful we happen to know about. The rest are gone forever.'

She pursed her lips. 'I hadn't thought of it like that. But what has this got to do with the dust on your shelves?'

So I told her about my meeting with Anderson and his plan to hunt for the remains of the rarest bird in the world. The room got warmer as we talked. Every now and then Katya sipped at her drink, wrinkling her nose slightly at every sip. The idea of the lost specimen, the evidence of a whole vanished species, seemed to fascinate her.

'I can see why it's valuable,' she nodded as I tried to explain the DNA collectors, 'though fifty thousand dollars seems a huge amount for a dead bird.'

I shrugged. 'That depends on how you look at it. A great auk would be worth a fortune, and there are about twenty of them. And if you came across a preserved dodo you'd be able to retire for life. Seriously. You see, there's no such thing as a preserved dodo skin, only bones and beaks and things. So perhaps something genuinely unique does have a value.'

Katya looked unconvinced.

'It's got another sort of value too,' I went on. 'You see, for a species to officially exist, there has to be something called a *type*. That's a sample specimen, one that's held to be typical of the species. Without a specimen, there's no type, and without a type, science doesn't really recognise

35

that something exists. So if we're going to be strictly scientific about it, the Ulieta bird isn't even extinct. It just never happened. There's no physical evidence, no bones, no feathers, nothing. Just a drawing, a few lines of writing and one lost bird.'

Katya nodded slowly. 'But where do your books fit in?'

I looked at them.

'I've absolutely no idea. None of them are very special. Besides, if there was a clue somewhere, wouldn't whoever it was have taken it away?'

Katya turned and studied the wall of books thoughtfully. 'Perhaps they did. Perhaps there's a page torn out of one of them. You ought to check.'

'Let's see, a thousand books at three hundred pages per book . . .'

She turned back to me then and we both laughed, appalled at the thought of going through them.

'Perhaps another day,' she said.

'Perhaps another month.'

We stayed there drinking until the bottle was two-thirds empty. As we talked, I began to see her differently. Her face lit up when she spoke, and her vitality was infectious. Our conversation went from birds to history, and we rambled happily about the way things in the past come to be recorded, about the way time takes things away from us if we don't fight to keep them. It was common ground of sorts.

'My father teaches history at the university in Stockholm,' she told me. 'He used to be a real historian, the sort who went off and found things out. When he met my mother he was going to be the most brilliant historian in Sweden. Now he's never out of restaurants and TV studios and he writes the books the publishers tell him to write. He's too busy doing interviews to care any more.' She shrugged. 'We don't get on. That's why I came to England. I want to do it for myself.'

'And is that why you don't ring your mother?'

She paused, her face a half-frown. 'My father walked out on her when I was a teenager. She didn't even fight. Not even for my sake. She just let him go.'

It was too harsh a reason to reason against. She reached out and ran her finger down the spine of one of the volumes. We'd been talking for a long time now. It made questions easier. Now it was her turn.

'Why didn't you take the money you were offered?' she asked.

'If I wanted money I wouldn't be doing what I do. Besides, there was something about Anderson. I didn't like his suit.'

At that Katya spluttered on her vodka and began to laugh again and we were both still laughing as we swept up the glass in the hall and tried to seal up the broken windows with drawing pins and plastic bags.

Finally we stood by the semi-repaired door, facing each other, both smiling. Despite the break-in I felt oddly light-hearted.

'So many lost things,' she mused, her voice growing a little more serious. 'Why don't *you* go and look for it?'

I shook my head slowly.

'I wouldn't know where to start. The trail went cold two hundred years ago. And, besides, Anderson is a professional. He knows what he's doing.'

Those words ran through my mind again in the early hours of the morning when I finally reached my bed. It was an impossible task, surely. But Anderson's confidence disturbed me. Could he be right? Could it really be that the bird had survived in some unknown collection, untouched since the days of Cook and Joseph Banks? I tried to put the thought away, tried to remind myself that my life had moved on. But Anderson knew better than that. He understood that I'd left something unfinished, that I'd never made a find like the one he was intending. The bird of Ulieta. The lost bird. It would be the most remarkable find of all.

I knew I should sleep but my mind kept turning, and as the night began to change into the grey light of a winter dawn I realised I had one small, faint hope, something I knew that Anderson couldn't possibly know. A decision made, I felt able to swing myself into bed, and it was then I noticed that the photograph on my bedside table had fallen over, as if someone had knocked against the table. I stood it up carefully and looked at it for a moment. When I turned out the light the room didn't go dark.

Three days later she returned to the clearing where Banks had watched her sketch. It was a day to savour. The sky was an unblemished blue and the sun was hot on her skin. She found the fallen branch where she had been seated previously and fixed her attention on the ground before her. Without any great preparation she began to draw. As she worked, the silence of the woods turned to small noises—the water in the stream, the darting of unseen birds.

She had learned that only when she was in the woods could she be the person she knew herself to be. As her father's daughter she had needed to protect herself from the world she lived in. Here that world was no more than a fleeting odour on the breeze.

She didn't hear him approach. The sound of his voice, sudden in the quietness, made her start and turn.

'*Lichen pulmonarius*,' he said simply, and her eyes went to the place on the edge of the clearing where he stood. 'The name of the lichen on the trees in Slipper Wood,' he added.

With that he stepped forward into the sunlight and she saw he was smiling. Behind him the trees were deep green. Later she always remembered that moment, that smile.

'That *is* what you were looking at.' His voice betrayed no doubt. 'It grows only on the trees you were examining and on no others.'

He stood before her, his smile both a greeting and a challenge. His shirt was open at the neck, his hair unkempt. In one hand he swung a leather collecting bag. She had never seen anyone so alive.

'I don't know its Latin name,' she replied. 'They call

it tree lungwort. It's different from the lichens around it. But you're wrong to believe it grows nowhere else in these woods.'

'I am?' He placed his bag at his feet and looked at her again. She had remained seated, looking back at him. If she had flushed on his arrival there was no sign of it now. Yet he felt again that in the moment before his greeting he had glimpsed a person different from the one now before him. Now only the green eyes remained the same.

'I was sure I had examined each tree most particularly,' he said.

As he spoke he was wondering about that other person, the young girl alone, drawing so avidly. Later, in lands where people hadn't learned to hide their joy at living, he was to think of her again. But for now he was aware only that he was being studied by a cool and thoughtful face.

'It grows on just those twelve trees in Slipper Wood,' she stated. 'But you've certainly seen it elsewhere. You will find traces of it on nearly every tree in your home park.'

He shook his head in response, the naturalist in him reasserting himself.

'No, I had not observed it. Or rather, if I had, I had not noted it. Do you believe what they say, that it is a cure for sickness of the lungs?'

He began to feel embarrassed standing before her, as if his presence were an intrusion. And she was looking at him from where she sat with clear, calm eyes that neither welcomed him nor made him wish to depart.

'No, that's surely not true,' she said, her gaze turning for the moment to the trees all around them. 'They say so because of its appearance, like the texture of a lung. But that is coincidence, surely. I cannot believe that Providence felt it necessary to illustrate its workings in such literal ways.'

'I confess I am surprised. And overjoyed. I had no idea Revesby contained a fellow natural philosopher.'

Embarrassed at towering over her, yet unable to sit without being invited to do so, he instead sank to his haunches as though he wished to study something on the ground in front of him. It was, he knew, an assumption of informality.

To which she responded by rising to her feet and preparing to depart.

'I am hardly that, Mr Banks. I have no books to study and my tutor is no longer able to instruct me.'

'Your tutor?' he asked, rising hurriedly, caught off balance.

'My father, sir.'

'Of course. My apologies. I did not mean to pry.'

'And yet your presence here would suggest the opposite.'

It was not said coldly but with an air of detachment that made him step backwards.

'My apologies, madam. I had not realised my presence here was objectionable to you.' And as he spoke, she saw the sunlight go out of his face. The sight stopped her even as she began to move, though she had thought herself safe. She could feel it even then. She knew she should turn away and return to the village, past the low houses with their gazes averted as she passed. But she had not intended to wound, only to safeguard her own retreat. Around her the summer morning was still sweet. So, although she began to understand the risk, she turned back to him and met his eye.

'I am not used to company, Mr Banks. I have known these woods since I was a child and I was taught to notice what I saw around me. It would be a great luxury to talk about these things. But today I have this drawing to complete. Soon this flower's season will be past and my opportunity will be lost.'

He hesitated, concerned that her more curt response was the true one.

'Of course,' he responded. 'It was selfish of me to interrupt your work. Please be seated again,' and he gestured at the fallen branch. 'There are few here who share my interests.'

As she seated herself she took care that her dress fell properly to the ground. When he spoke again she had opened her book and was turning to the page of her unfinished drawing.

'I shall bid you farewell and leave you to your work . . .' he began.

But his sentence trailed away and she sensed no motion to withdraw. Instead she felt him move forward. When she looked up she saw his eyes fixed intently on the drawing in her hand and the expression on his face sent a flash of joy to her heart.

*   *   *

That day she stayed out late, until the light in the woods began to thicken into dusk. Then she returned home slowly along the fringes of the fields with the stars already showing above the trees. On reaching the house at the edge of the village, she paused with the door open, then let it close softly behind her, knowing that in the whole village on such an evening her door was the only one shut against the night air. Inside the house the shutters were fastened, trapping the heat of the day, and a candle burned in the dark. It was suffocatingly hot. She put her drawing book down on the bare table in front of her and listened. Upstairs her father was dying.

She stood listening for nearly a minute. She could hear the low whispering of Martha, the nurse, as she cleaned him. She had had so many months of practice now that it didn't take her long; even turning him barely made a sound. Beneath it all, regular and slow, his breath counted away the days and the hours. Finally, content from her place in the hallway that all was unchanged, she went to wash herself. Then with her hair still damp and loose she went upstairs.

Martha greeted her with a nod and a smile and briefly the two sat in silence on either side of the sleeping man.

'Thank you, Martha,' she said eventually. 'You can leave me for a while. You must get yourself some supper.'

The older woman began to stir herself then paused. 'Mr Ponsonby called again today, miss.'

The two exchanged a look.

'Then it's fortunate I was not at home, Martha.'

After another silence, Martha spoke again.

'He has not asked for rent these twelve months, miss.'

'I know he has not.' She lowered her head. 'There is nothing we can do about that.'

She might have said more but she was eager to be left alone that evening. When Martha had gone downstairs, she sat for a little, listening to her father's breathing. Sometimes at night its steady rise and fall crept into her dreams like the sighing of the sea. On other nights it fell quiet and then she would go to him and lean close, anxious, like a mother over a sleeping infant.

She had been upstairs, sleeping, that night they

brought him home. At first she thought it was drink that affected him and she had been ashamed. Then she saw that his hair was matted with blood and they told her how he had been found. He had been drunk, they said, and had interrupted the Ponsonbys at dinner. He'd been thrown out by the servants there and had wandered into the darkness. The men who found him had been returning horses to the stables at Highwold when they noticed him in a ditch, his head hard down on a stone.

She hurried them out as soon as they had carried him upstairs, hating them to see him so helpless. That night she tended him, mopping at the wound, an ache of anxiety deep in her stomach. The wound seemed clean. There was not much blood. Yet he would not stir. She tried to force a little brandy between his lips and then waited through the night for him to open his eyes.

The doctor came the next day even though she had not sent for him. He was a good man: there were few who would come willingly to their door.

'You must try to feed him,' he said. 'Anything he can be made to swallow without choking him. You need him to keep up his strength.'

The days that followed were suffused with half-light as the full daylight disturbed him. She found he would swallow what she could force between his lips but at other times he lay inert, unconscious of her touch. After a week Dr Taylor returned and brought with him Martha, a nurse. She was a woman from the next village who had once nursed his own children and at his request she was willing to accept work in the house of a sinner and a heathen.

'You must understand,' he said, when Martha had gone downstairs to store away her things, 'that the

44

longer he sleeps the less likely his waking.' She nodded at that but he could see she hadn't heard. It was a lesson he would have to repeat.

'Doctor,' she said when he came to leave, 'my father has debts. I have nothing to pay the nurse.'

He looked at the troubled green eyes.

'Martha will come to me for her wages,' he told her.

'But I cannot . . .'

She looked up at him, wordlessly asking him to understand. But he was a study of concentration fastening his glove and he paused only to add that he would call again when he could.

The day of his next visit he found her changed. She was neatly dressed and she did not smile as she greeted him. As she led him upstairs she explained there had been no change, that her father was still unaware of the world around him. But he could see for himself a change in the man's face, the grey pallor of his skin and a re-shaping of his cheeks, as though he was inching away from life. He knew she had seen it too; knew by the way she touched the patient as she tended him, softly now, like a caress. He had learned to recognise the way people begin to say goodbye.

'Doctor,' she whispered, 'it is possible that my father may not recover, is it not?'

'I fear that is possible,' he replied, wishing she had a mother to place an arm around her. 'The wound to his head is more profound than was apparent to the eye.'

'Will it be long?' Her voice was smaller than he had ever heard it.

'I cannot say. I have known men in his state survive for many weeks. Recover too, sometimes. You must tend him well and keep him comfortable.'

'I shall,' she said. 'And then . . .' But neither of

them cared to complete the sentence and after only a few words more the doctor withdrew.

She was already used to walking alone. The day after the doctor's visit she stood on the edge of the wood and let the sun warm her face as if its touch might smooth away every thought. She felt the roughness of the grass on her fingertips and let it fill her mind. She made herself memorise the pattern of leaves on the forest floor and the way the saplings turned and twisted towards the light. And to keep these things forever, to have them fill the emptiness inside her, she took up her pencil and drew.

CHAPTER FIVE

A PICTURE

It's a common thing for people to be fascinated by the ghosts that history leaves behind. Look in the public record offices on any Saturday and you'll find rows of people trying to summon up their ancestors, outlining with names and dates the shadows of people they can never truly find. Hans Michaels was like that, but for him it was birds, not people.

It was only by chance that I ever knew him. He wrote to me after reading an article I'd written about the spectacled cormorant and, as you don't generally get many letters about the spectacled cormorant, I wrote him quite a long reply. Some months later, after various letters had been exchanged, he invited me to visit him to look at some of the research he'd done. It was a humbling experience. I was the professional and he was the amateur but, when it came to the two or three species he had really concentrated on, he had found sources and references that were completely new to me. We spent the afternoon together, his wife bringing in tea from time to time, then leaving us alone. He offered me his research quite freely, quite openly, just happy to find someone who shared his interest. But by then I already knew I would never publish, and his generosity was wasted on me. I remember as I left that day he asked me about the Ulieta bird. I told him what I knew and he nodded and then said something about an idea

47

he'd been working on, something I didn't really listen to at the time. But it was that chance remark that now kept me awake in the dawn, wondering what it was he had found so promising.

I was up early the next morning. I'd slept for no more than an hour but my mind wouldn't rest and it was easier to get up and get on with things. After a shower and a cup of coffee I felt clear-headed and surprisingly vital. Outside it was a cold morning but the air felt fresh on my skin. The roads were already busy but I fired up my bike, then edged out against the traffic and headed south.

Hans Michaels lived in a red-brick villa in a village south of Guildford. Even allowing for a breakfast stop and some trouble finding the house, I was there ringing the bell at only a little after ten. At first his wife seemed exactly as I remembered her. Her voice from the hallway as she ordered me to wait had the same slightly curt edge and when she had undone the bolts on the door the face peering around it was still alert and intelligent.

'My name's Fitzgerald,' I told her. 'I was hoping to talk to your husband. It's about extinct birds.'

She looked at me evenly. 'My husband died five years ago, I'm afraid. But if you've called about his research, you'd better come in.' It was only as I followed her into the house that I noticed how slowly she moved ahead of me. And then there were the other things—the fraying hem on her skirt, a slight shake in her hand as she opened the living-room door, a button on her blouse not properly done up—little things that made me feel sad and guilty. It wouldn't have been difficult to stay in touch, I thought irrationally, as if somehow

48

my presence might have ameliorated the pain of ageing.

The living room was cluttered with furniture and objects. 'I still dust,' she told me, waving her hand airily around her front room, 'but there's a girl who comes in to do the rest. She isn't very good so my apologies if the place is not as clean as it should be. Please take a seat.' I sat down on one of the floral-print armchairs and she moved to the door and then paused. 'I do remember you, Mr Fitzgerald,' she told me. 'You're the expert. Hans used to talk about you. You came here to look at his work once.'

'That's right,' I replied. There didn't seem much else to say.

While she returned to the kitchen to make tea, I browsed amongst the books and pictures on her living-room walls. There was a small watercolour of a slim girl in an old-fashioned dress, her back turned and her head hidden beneath a parasol. Beyond her was a wash of pale sea.

'Me,' she explained when she came in and saw me looking. 'My sister painted it one summer. I was about fourteen, if I remember. She was always a romantic, my sister.'

Next to it was a black-and-white photograph of a smiling young man with a pipe. I recognised him immediately as the ordinary, inoffensive man I had met years before. I noticed it was the only picture with a frame that had no layer of dust.

While the tea was being poured I began to explain about the Ulieta bird. I told her I was after any information I could find and that I thought her husband might have been interested in the same area. In response to that she waved a small, brown

49

hand and gave a snort. 'If it was as obscure as you say, he probably did. He loved that sort of thing.'

'So tell me,' I asked, finally getting round to the question I'd been too polite to ask, 'do you still have his notes? Did you keep them?'

She looked at me for a moment and then leaned forward.

'Let me explain something. When you get to my age you have very few things left of those you love. You certainly hang on firmly to those you have.' She leaned back again in her armchair and pulled a paper tissue from the sleeve of her blouse. She dabbed carefully at her nose, then returned the tissue to her sleeve and looked at me again. 'The bird notes were the thing he was proudest of. Of course I kept them.'

'And may I see them?'

'Yes. I'm sure Hans would have liked that.'

The notes were kept in a room on the first floor. She climbed the stairs slowly and paused at the top before leading me into a large, book-lined room.

'Up there,' she said, pointing to the highest shelf. It ran all the way around the room and instead of books it carried a neat series of box files, each of them carefully labelled by hand. They stuck out above the books but it would have been easy not to notice them—compared to the smart leather volumes below, they looked old and faded and somehow very ordinary. Nevertheless, I could see at a glance the care that had been taken over them. There was one file per species and other files under subject headings, some of them named after various collectors or collections. It would have taken me a month to go through them all.

'Did he show them to many people?' I asked, my

eyes still wandering along the shelves.

'Just me,' she replied. 'And you.'

In my haste to scan the labels I nearly missed it. The one I was looking for wasn't a box file at all, just a folder placed between two boxes, and the ink on the cover was pale. Even here the Ulieta bird seemed determined to be elusive.

I paused beneath it and his wife nodded.

'Go on. You can stand on one of the chairs.'

I knew as soon as I lifted the folder down that it wasn't going to tell me the answer. It was too light—I thought for a moment that it was going to be completely empty. But I was wrong. Hans Michaels had done some research after all and what he'd discovered was there on a single sheet of paper. There was no text of any sort, no dates or references. Only a simple pencil sketch of a woman's face.

*   *   *

Looking at it again in the brighter light of the living room, I was still at a loss as to what it meant. She was a young woman, not beautiful, but noticeable, with eyes that caught your attention and then held it. There was something vivid in them that made the face memorable. And something knowing in them that made it sad.

'It's definitely by Hans,' my hostess told me. 'He was a good artist when he could be bothered. He'd often make a sketch of things if he wanted to remember them.'

I looked again at the face in the picture.

'You've no idea who she is?' I asked.

'Well, I don't *recognise* her, if that's what you

51

mean. But then I wouldn't really expect to. Don't you think there's something vaguely *period* about her? As if he's copied an old painting or a picture in an old book?'

'But who *is* she?' The question was more to myself than to her but she turned from the picture and looked at me.

'I rather think that is what you have to find out.'

Shortly after that she asked me to leave. She was getting tired and wanted to be alone. She wouldn't let me take the picture away and as I looked at it one final time I realised how little I had to go on. And it was that which started me thinking about my grandfather.

*   *   *

When my grandfather was a schoolboy he was once given a piece of Latin to translate. It was a passage written by a Roman historian and it described a tribute sent to a Roman general in North Africa by one of the great kingdoms of the south. The list of gifts was a traditional one, almost routine for the time: gold, silver, spices, precious stones, ivory, swords, peacocks. It was a straightforward bit of translation and my grandfather was about to move on when the last word made him pause. The word was an easy one—*pavus*, a peacock. Quite simple. But my grandfather knew a great deal more about ornithology than he did about Latin and he checked back again, for the first time taking an interest in the passage. There could be no doubt about it. The text said peacocks. The tribute was definitely from a great kingdom in the south. And it included peacocks. My grandfather read the passage again and wondered why no one else had noticed it. For one thing he knew for certain was that there was no such thing as an African peacock. There were blue peacocks from India and green peacocks from Java. But there were no peacocks in Africa.

My grandfather never seemed to have considered that the writer might have got it wrong or that he was using lazy, sloppy shorthand to describe the trappings of wealth. Instead the thought stayed in the back of his mind as an unresolved puzzle and when, as a postgraduate, he began collecting specimens in the field, he carried that puzzle with him. In his early twenties he was in the Caribbean and Central America, discovering some of the first physical remains of the Puerto Rican night hawk. Two years later he was in Africa on the trail of a rare fish-eating owl. In all that time he never seems to have mentioned his childhood suspicion that somewhere in Africa there were undiscovered peacocks. But the idea was there, waiting, and, when in 1913 an American called James Chapin emerged from the jungles of the Congo basin with a single feather that matched no known species, the suspicion bubbled over and an obsession was born.

*   *   *

I didn't go home until much later that day and by then it was raining and already dark. I'd arranged for someone to come and secure the broken front door and, in my absence, three temporary boards had been nailed across the window, giving the place a more neglected appearance than usual.

Nevertheless, there were lights on in Katya's room and, once inside, the hallway felt warm and lived in. I'd spent the whole afternoon in various libraries and I had a pile of books in my bag. The weight of them made me happy as I drew the curtains and shut out the night.

Rather to my surprise, I was interrupted at about seven o'clock by a knock on my bedroom door. Katya and I rarely bothered each other in our rooms. I could tell she was on her way out for the evening: her face was made up to accentuate the pale and her eyes were doubly dark. She didn't step in, just put her head and shoulders around the door and smiled. It was the sort of smile that follows an evening of confidences.

'There's something I wanted to show you,' she said. 'I went to the university library and got this.'

From behind the door she produced a hardback biography of Joseph Banks. It was the book I planned to read next.

'I like your Joseph Banks,' she said. 'He's an interesting man. And I've always liked a mystery.'

I held up the book I was reading and smiled. A different biography of the same man.

'Perhaps we should get together and compare notes.'

She gave me another little smile.

'Yes, that would be good,' she said, already beginning to go. 'I'm glad. I didn't like to think that your friend Anderson was going to get everything his own way.'

It was over an hour later when I was disturbed again, this time by the doorbell. I was slow rousing myself and before I reached the door the bell rang again, another long burst. The boarded-up window made it impossible to see who was outside so it wasn't until the door swung open and the light behind me touched the street that I realised it was Gabriella. Her eyes met mine and she smiled.

Her drawings amazed him and he marvelled at his discovery. It had been the habit of Banks's youth to sketch the samples he collected, part of the challenge of his calling. Yet he knew the drawings he had seen were far better than any he had ever achieved for himself. Not just artistically better—it was not a question of finer line or greater sensibility—but *scientifically* better, more closely observed and more scrupulous in their detail. Through each one he saw a flower or leaf anew, as if each had once been learned and then forgotten.

Because of her, the days before his departure from Revesby were filled with botanical fervour. He felt the sun on his back and inside him something of his first, violent passion for living things. Even the most familiar specimen was fascinating, each one miraculous. Soon, he knew, he would be many thousands of miles away, under tropical skies. It felt right that he should take with him these fresh memories of his home woods.

At first she had seemed reluctant for him to examine her work. When he glimpsed it, she pulled the book close to her and when their eyes met he understood instantly that there was nothing coquettish in her refusal. Her eyes held his and he thought she was about to speak; and then quite suddenly she yielded and the book was given up.

There in the woods, as the sun shone, she had watched him as he held her book for the first time, moving from one drawing to the next, his face full of wonder. It was then she felt the stirring wildness inside her that she didn't at the beginning understand. She knew about caution and guardedness, and in the freedom of the woods had found her own joy. But she knew nothing of the thing she felt that day and the shock of it made her silent. 'Remember this,' she told herself. 'Let me always remember this.' It was the first prayer she had uttered for a year that had not been for her father.

On each subsequent afternoon they had returned without prior arrangement to the same clearing. They worked through her drawing book page by page, discussing the nature and characteristics of each plant. Banks's pleasure in her company was instinctive and unthinking, and there was nothing in the calmness of the woods to make him pause and consider its implications. Even as she revelled in the sun full on her face, she marvelled at his blindness.

One afternoon he sat and watched her sketch. She had allowed it only after protest; she knew that he had no idea how much he asked of her. As she began to draw it felt like an unveiling and she was clumsy and tentative. But as she went on she felt a change inside her. As her concentration intensified, the turbulence within her calmed itself until soon she was unaware of his presence. He watched the familiar furrow appear and deepen in her brow and for a moment he wondered that he had ever considered her ordinary. When at last he disturbed her, the drawing was two-thirds complete.

'You have a gift,' he told her. 'A skill as great as any I know.'

She turned to him. 'When I draw I feel that drawing is all I have.'

'It is a special talent. I wish you could travel and paint the plants of the tropics. I can imagine you calm in the heat, drawing away, concentrating too hard to be concerned about the prowling tiger or the snake at your feet.'

He laughed and she smiled, even though his words made the walls that imprisoned her seem higher and closer.

So the afternoons passed as bright colours flecked with sadness. A week before his departure for London she pointed to one of the woodland birds in the trees around them and told him that small brown birds such as those were insufficient for him; his voyage was necessary so he could seek out birds of brighter colours and stranger shapes to satisfy him. Her seriousness was such that at first he felt wounded. Then when he began to defend himself he sensed a meaning in her words that moved him to meet her eyes and smile. He was still smiling later, as he said his farewell and left her to her drawing. As he approached the shadow of the trees, she called out to him.

'Mr Banks,' she called, so that he stopped and turned. 'Mr Banks, I'd like to thank you for the kindness you've shown me these few days.'

He shook his head, serious again.

'On the contrary, it is I who am in your debt. Your drawings have refreshed me in my calling. And the memory of these woodlands will sustain me when I am far at sea.'

She considered him carefully, her face made soft by the early-evening sun.

'I should like you to know I am grateful, all the same.'

He bowed and as he turned to leave he thought she would speak again. But when he paused she only nodded and with another smile he was gone.

On his return the following day he found the clearing empty. It was a surprise. The weather was fine and there remained in her book a dozen drawings he had yet to study. He had intended to ask her for one of them: he had a friend, Daniel Solander, a botanist, who was an excellent judge of such things. It saddened him that she was not there to hear his request. As he lay back on the grass, the scent of fresh summer turf was strong and glorious.

The afternoon was far advanced when he was awakened by the rustling of birds in the trees behind him. She had not come.

The next morning, in his hurry to return to the clearing in the woods, he almost missed the letter. The handwriting was unfamiliar but he knew at once it was hers.

'*Sir,*' she wrote, neatly and carefully. '*My father's health is declining and I must spend the days between now and your departure at his side. It would be a favour to us both if you did not call.*'

The letter was unsigned.

*　　　*　　　*

For all his entreaties, she would not see him. The day he received that note was a day of blue skies and as he strode into Revesby, her letter in his hand, there was already a heat haze between him and the horizon. At first he was inclined to take her decision lightly, a piece of coquetry perhaps, or at worst a temporary sadness at her father's health that would end when the crisis had passed. But at her door he was firmly turned back by the old woman who answered. The response was the same that afternoon: her mistress was indisposed and would not receive callers.

For some days he had planned, on his departure, to

present her with a book, a copy of Gerard's *Herbal*. Now he decided that she should have it early and he left it at her door with his compliments. Within an hour the gift had been returned. The next day he walked the woods restlessly, hurt by her coolness and angry at the hurt. Whatever direction he took, he found himself undecided at her door. On two or three occasions he advanced and was rebuffed; more often he cursed softly to himself and retreated to the Abbey deer park.

If the randomness of her sudden retreat irked him in the beginning, later he began to wonder at it. Dr Taylor insisted that her father's condition, although very poor, was neither better nor worse than before. Was it then some action on his part that had provoked this withdrawal? He remembered her last words and the slightly sad smile as she watched him turn away and he was sure it was not. He tried to condemn her for the inconsistency traditionally ascribed to her sex but found he could not. Even as he failed to understand what had occurred, he could not prevent himself from acknowledging that he had never met a woman less coquettish.

And yet in some way this knowledge increased his anger as if the things that made her different also made her culpable. On the fourth day he did not call.

In the darkened house she heard his footsteps come and go until they no longer came at all. Between his visits there was the steady breathing of her father and the creaking of the floorboards as they spread and contracted with the passage of the sun. The shutters let in little of the sunlight but trapped the heat at night so that her dampened handkerchief would sometimes dry before it had reached her father's brow. She seldom tried to look out but when she did she could glimpse the chestnut trees building like clouds above the meadow beyond the lane. And when a whisper of breeze slipped between the shutters and stirred up the dust, it smelled of fields and warm grass.

The cessation of his visits was a sorrow and a vindication. In a few summer days she had learned to fear hope in the way she had once feared despair. And so she cut herself away from him and hoped that when he was gone the woods would be hers again, at least until the day that gentle breathing stopped and everything would change.

In the evenings that followed she would take out her drawings and study each by lamplight. And at night, in the darkness, she held the thought of him so close that it seemed each new morning would not be enough to prise it from her grasp.

On the first day that Banks stopped calling at the house in Revesby he kept mostly to his room. The following morning he rose early and took a horse from the stables. He rode fast and dangerously to the house of Charles Cartwright, a neighbouring landowner with three unmarried daughters. There he flirted recklessly with each of them in turn and over dinner took more wine than was usual. He took his leave almost abruptly and rode back again, forcing the pace with whip and heels. He reached Revesby Abbey under a moon that was three-fifths full. Still in riding dress, he marched directly to his study. There he took clean paper and began to write without hesitation.

'*My dearest Harriet,*' he wrote. '*I return to London forthwith. Although I have been as always the worst of correspondents, my time here has made many things clear to me. I would wish to be allowed to call on you on my return to speak of certain matters that are better said than written . . .'*

CHAPTER SIX

SPIX'S MACAW

I had met Gabriella over the remains of a dead macaw. I was younger then and still an optimist, and the Brazilian rainforest was uncharted in all sorts of ways. I'd gone there with De Havilland's expedition, fresh from college and overconfident in my abilities. When De Havilland left, I stayed on, intending to join a group from Oxford which was due to arrive later that month. In fact the Oxford team took months to arrive as vital personnel fell sick or changed their minds and the funding kept falling through. But I was happy to wait. I was young and confident and there didn't seem to be any hurry. I had good contacts out there and through them I found a clean room with a desk and an electric fan. More importantly I had a chest full of jottings under my bed and an idea for a volume on lost avian species that would be my great work. It seemed a brilliant idea at the time.

I spent most of the days sleeping or moving with a glass in my hand through consular garden parties; my nights scribbling away with undisguised passion on the fate of the passenger pigeon or the great auk. My brain was clear and focused and I wrote page after page without crossings-out. I can be sure of that because the pages are still in the same chest, still under my bed.

It was one of the last days before the second expedition set out when Berkeley Harris, the quartermaster, came to find me.

'You free, Fitz?'

Harris never removed his pipe when he spoke. He was one of those men who wore long shorts all the time and did everything with a pipe in his mouth except eat, a breed that became extinct in Europe shortly after the war but in those days still lingered in small populations on the post-colonial fringes.

'I only ask because there's rather a pretty girl over at the bungalow who wants some help with a parrot. I said you were the man.'

Although he was never right about anything, he was right about Gabriella. She was leaning in the shade when Harris led me into the bungalow garden and all I could make out was a slim figure in the shadow. Then she stepped into the sunlight to meet us and I broke off from what I was saying and put out my hand. I'd met girls in the past who were considered beautiful and Gabriella was nothing like any of them. But there was something about her eyes and the way she held her head and crinkled her brow as she reached out her hand to shake mine.

'Miss Martinez, this is John Fitzgerald. I'm sure he'll be able to sort you out. Fitz, Miss Martinez works down at the zoo. Her parrot's died and she wants it stuffed.'

'Mounted. The term is mounted. We only say "stuffed" if we're trying to be crude.'

'I daresay. Anyway, I'll leave you to it. Got an expedition to mount, don't you know.'

She waited until he'd gone inside before she spoke. Her voice was the opposite of the giggling at consular garden parties.

'He's quite wrong, Mr Fitzgerald. It's not a zoo and it's not a parrot.'

I laughed.

'That's about average for Harris. Just what is it that I can help you with, Miss Martinez?'

She looked very earnestly into my eyes.

'I've just lost one of the rarest birds in the world.'

She could hardly have picked a better introduction.

*　　*　　*

The Gabriella who faced me now across the kitchen table had the same earnest eyes. She watched me with the same half-smile, studied my face with the same disarming care. As I opened a bottle of wine, it felt that the kitchen was too small for her, as if a dark forest animal had stepped by accident into a holding pen.

'To lost birds?' she suggested, raising her glass.

It wasn't my first choice but it would do.

'Lost birds.'

Our glasses met with a slightly plastic clunk.

'It's good to see you again, Fitz. We didn't get a chance to talk last night.'

'No, I noticed that.'

She cupped the glass in her hand and began to rock it gently so that the wine moved around in circles.

'I'd wanted to call before. You didn't reply to my letters though. I wasn't sure. Then when Karl asked about you it seemed a good excuse.'

She hadn't needed an excuse, but I didn't say so. We sat for a second or two and looked at each

65

other, not sure where to take up again. Eventually she began to talk, updating me on her project in the Amazon, how it had developed since we'd last seen each other, the sort of work she was doing there. Her eyes lit up as she talked about the successes, the little skirmishes won against a tide I knew would sweep her away. I'd kept up with my reading and I could see she was relieved that I could still talk about the latest science—island biogeography, conservation corridors—the sort of issues that her project was grappling with. By mutual consent we avoided the other stuff, the things we'd never talked about—those last days, the photograph by my bed, a life we'd left behind us. Instead we talked ratios and pie charts and variable extinction rates. Eventually, as I knew it would, the conversation edged round to the subject of the previous evening.

'There's something I wanted to ask you.' She put her glass down and put both hands behind her neck, flicking her hair outwards as if to free it from her collar. It was a gesture I recognised. 'You didn't like Karl very much, did you, John?'

'Was I supposed to?'

'Not really. I thought you'd be interested.'

'It was interesting that he wanted to give me fifty thousand dollars for making some phone calls.'

'I told him the money was a mistake. I said you'd either help him or you wouldn't.'

'You were right. I wouldn't.'

She looked at me with that familiar questioning intensity. It felt oddly normal to be talking to her, as though we were carrying on a conversation from the week before. She stood up and moved around the table to the chair next to mine.

'I want to tell you about Karl,' she said, leaning forward, her weight on the edge of her chair.

I turned to her and shook my head. Even though I was trying to keep my voice level, there was probably a trace of panic in it somewhere. 'I'm not sure I want to hear.'

'Let me tell you, Fitz. He isn't what you think. I could see in your eyes last night what you thought. I wondered if that was why you wouldn't help.'

'You can think what you like.'

She shook her head. 'You don't understand. Karl is an interesting man. He's a bit of a troublemaker, and you should like that. And he's always been given a rough time by the establishment. They won't take him seriously because he's not an academic, but he's still better at finding things than they are, and that makes them look stupid. You and he should be on the same side.' She paused, and looked down at her wine. 'But that's not why I introduced you. You know the sort of work I've always wanted to do, John. Well, now it's happening. Good work. Valuable work. It's making a difference to the whole way people think about conservation areas. And when I met Karl, the project was hanging in the balance. We're broke, Fitz. Everyone works for nothing and the grants we get from Europe don't even cover our computers. Karl pumped money in when we needed it and he's been doing it ever since.'

She lowered her voice and carried on.

'I thought like you did when I first met him. I thought he was the worst kind of charlatan—a collector, the sort of person we were protecting things *from*. But he hasn't asked for anything from

67

us. Anything from me. He meets the bills when things get particularly bad, that's all.'

'He isn't known for philanthropy.'

'Oh, I know he gets something in return. We give him stature and a way into the conservation world. I'm not so naïve to think it's purely for me. But I could do worse for a backer.'

'And in return you're going to help him find Joseph Banks's lost bird?'

'He doesn't need my help. He has a lead, something that tells him where to look. But he can't be sure it's going to work out and that's why he wants you on his side rather than on someone else's. You see, he's sure you know something. He says you'll have read the right books.'

'I don't know what he means, but it doesn't sound as though he really needs my help. And even if he did, I wouldn't help him.'

'Then help *me*.' Her hand moved on my arm and her grip was suddenly tight. 'If you won't help him, help me. I need to find this bird, Fitz. It means everything to the work we're doing.'

'I don't understand.'

She was still looking at me very hard, her head slightly tilted towards mine.

'This is my introduction to Ted Staest, Fitz. Karl is as generous as he can be, but Staest is in a different league. At the moment he's only interested in his DNA ark. But if we can help him with the bird, if I can get him to take an interest in the project . . . He gives out grants that would make your mouth water, Fitz. And without something like that I don't think we can keep going for long. The sort of money Staest could give us would keep the project going for years. Literally.

Five years of good work. It could mean the survival of a dozen species, Fitz. Think of that.'

The little kitchen suddenly seemed too hot. I moved from the table and walked around to the window. There I put my hands on the kitchen taps and tried to draw in their coolness. Helping her, helping Anderson, helping the project . . . I felt I was being drawn into a tangled, jangling net.

And then I remembered it was all built on a mistake.

'Gabby, there's a problem with all this. I don't know anything. There's no special key I can give you that might make a difference.'

'You have all the contacts. And your notes . . . I thought there must be something . . .'

I shook my head. However much I wanted there to be, there was nothing useful in my notes about the Ulieta bird.

'I'm sorry. If you have any sense, you'll go back to Anderson and be very nice to him until he finds the bird.'

It probably wasn't the most sensitive thing I've ever said. But I wasn't feeling very good about things just then.

Gabby stood up. I watched her reflection in the kitchen window. She wasn't looking at me.

'Tomorrow I fly to Germany,' she said, her voice neutral. 'I'll be back in a couple of weeks. I've promised I'll meet Karl then. He thinks he might be here for a month before it's all sorted.' She began to put on her jacket. 'If I find out anything useful in the meantime, I'll pass it on. You can choose what you want to do with it.'

She moved to the door but didn't go through it. I turned to look at her and found she was looking at me, her expression suddenly sad.

'Do you remember when we first met, John? The bird I brought you?'

'Yes, I remember. A Spix's macaw.'

'Do you know the latest?'

I nodded. The bird Gabby had found dying in a market cage had been one of the last of its kind. Ten years ago the total number of Spix's macaws in the wild was down to three. Eight years later there was only one, a single ageing male. The experts had expected it to succumb quite quickly to age or loneliness. But as far as we knew it was still there, alone, going steadfastly about the business of living. When it was gone, there would be thirty or so specimens left in captivity. None of them were breeding pairs.

Gabby and I looked at each other for a moment.

'I'll call you when I get back, John. I'd like to talk again.'

I waited by the taps until I heard her pull the front door behind her. It was only as I cleared up the glasses that I noticed her raincoat on the hook behind the door. Like a promise, I thought. Or just a careless goodbye.

*   *   *

That wasn't quite the end of my day, though it probably should have been. I needed to stop and go over things. And I needed some sleep. But the books on my wall wouldn't let me rest. What had Anderson said? Something about reading the right books. I tried to imagine I was finding out about the Ulieta bird for the first time. Where would I look? There were two books that would be the obvious places to start and I had them both, dust-free, in front of me. I took them down thoughtfully. The first was easily the most authoritative: *Extinct and Vanishing Birds of the World* by James Greenway. I opened it carefully and turned to the page about the Ulieta bird. The little that was known was laid out with admirable clarity. I studied the page very carefully, checking for markings on the paper, any sign that someone else might have been reading it the night before. But why should they? My edition was the most recent paperback. You could get hold of a copy tomorrow if you wanted one.

I turned to the second book, *Some Notes on Rare Avian Species* by R.A. Fosdyke. This one was quirky where Greenway was scientific, and slapdash where Greenway was rigorous. Fosdyke was an amateur in the sixties whose hobby had been to trace references to rare and extinct birds in old science journals. The book didn't pretend to be comprehensive but anyone who was serious about the subject had a copy because every now and then Fosdyke came up with a reference that no one else had.

I moved the book into the light and opened it carefully. Mine was a first edition, signed by Fosdyke himself shortly before he died. Was a signed first edition worth anything? Worth breaking in for? Apparently not, because this one was still here, clean but very unstolen. Inside, Fosdyke listed two references to the bird—both also listed in Greenway—and limited himself to the same conclusion: last seen in the collection of Sir Joseph Banks.

I closed the book wearily. Was that the clue

Anderson was so concerned about? If so, it was a disappointing one. Those two entries were the sum total of my knowledge and neither offered any help at all. Except, perhaps, a vague indication of where to start. And that was with Joseph Banks, the naturalist, sometime in the late 1700s.

London was stifling after the shady woods of Revesby but Banks was too intent on the actions ahead of him to stop and take note of it. His time was full of the practicalities surrounding his departure and so pressing were the demands that the breathless heat of the streets scarcely slowed him. During his days in Revesby some matters had not progressed in the manner he had wished and in addition there were bills to be paid, tradesmen to interview, provisions to be secured and innumerable letters to be written. His energy was fierce and unforgiving.

His engagement to Harriet Blosset was settled a few days after his return. He had met her only a few months earlier and his flirtation with her had not seemed beyond the commonplace. But on the day his place on Cook's expedition was first discussed seriously he was due to call on her guardian and, left alone with her in the garden, he found himself observing her in a different way. It was as if the prospect of his journey gave him a new perspective, as if he viewed everything more clearly. He watched her lean forward and was struck by the incredible beauty of a woman's form, by the perfect line that curved from her neck to her shoulder. When she walked ahead of him he marvelled at the narrowness of her waist and the delicacy of her arms and wrists as if he had never seen their like before. And then, when she looked at him, he saw in her eyes such pleading that he reached out and took her hand. That a creature so perfectly formed should look at him in that way seemed both astounding and wonderful.

He kissed her in the rose garden, as a lover should, and she flushed from her cheeks down to her shoulders. Then her hand tightened around his and *she* kissed *him*, harder and longer than before. Then she took his hand, suddenly full of laughter, and as she pulled him towards the house it seemed she might never let go of it. As he thought of her later, when he had returned to his rooms, he felt a surge of tenderness and a wonder at the happiness it was in his power to bestow.

He knew full well the expectations raised by his letter from Revesby. Finally, when the demands on his time allowed him to call, it was a short interview. She was flushed but contained, and in her kiss there was a girlish elation that touched him and sent him on his way feeling wise and a little paternal. No announcement was to be made until his return when such things could be done properly. Even so, those who saw them together thought her very much in love. Her fairness and her round blue eyes were of the kind that caught the eyes of strangers and she laughed gaily as she walked on his arm. If he moved away to talk to others she would quickly follow him, brighter and happier in his presence. Her pretty face at his shoulder made him feel strong and protective. Only when she talked of his return as if it was certain and imminent did his smile fade a little. And when he tried to speak of the dangers of the voyage, and of his hopes for it, she silenced him by taking his hand and kissing each of his fingers.

When he was not with Harriet Blosset, Banks sought the company of men. Cook was stern and practical in the last days before their departure and Banks warmed to him. His plainness and his sense stood out among the noise and excitement of the many, and as their journey grew closer Cook seemed to grow in stature, until in the final days he was the only person to whom Banks would defer. When the day finally came, Banks and Solander travelled together from London to Plymouth where they were to meet Cook and join the *Endeavour*. The journey took four days and in part it was a sombre one. Both now had to face the reality of the danger ahead of them. It was not until they were both on board, at anchor off Plymouth and looking out at the country they might never see again, that an inquiry from Solander made Banks think of Revesby.

'Things were well there,' he replied and looked out over the town where the docks were still busy. 'I was able to say my farewells to both the place and the people.' A smile crept into the corner of his mouth. 'And I was given a lesson in lichen by a student of the local flora.'

'Indeed?' Solander smiled. 'I had not realised that Revesby was such a centre of learning.'

'Oh, you underestimate Revesby at your peril, my friend. What would you say if I told you I discovered a botanical artist there whose skill is the equal of any of those who go with us?'

'I should say you exaggerate. Did you bring any examples of his work that might support such a claim?'

Banks's face suddenly grew serious again. 'No, I have none of that work to show you. And who knows? Perhaps I was mistaken.' He looked out to where the sun was low in the sky. 'It is time for us to go below, my friend. They will be waiting for us.'

*　　　*　　　*

In the house at the end of the village, the summer continued to beat on her door and every evening she would sit with her father until nightfall. Then she would tiptoe down the bare corridor to her bed and sit at the open shutter for a time, looking at the dark trees rippling in the breeze. She heard rumours of Banks's engagement only after the *Endeavour* had sailed; and in the hot, slow hours between sunset and dawn she would imagine him journeying with that unknown woman close to his heart. She thought of him standing on the edge of new worlds, hungry for life, drinking in the sights and the sounds as a gift to bring back for that one who was waiting for him.

She hadn't understood that without him the woods would be far emptier than before. Indeed the whole of Revesby seemed to shrink on his departure and suddenly people were once again as they had been before, mean-spirited or spiteful as the mood took them. She had known well that his presence that summer changed things for her. After he'd gone she paid the price she had expected to pay and her loneliness was barbed with jibes that he had never even guessed at.

To his own surprise he wrote her two letters in the first weeks of his voyage. The first was while the *Endeavour* was still at anchor, with Solander on deck overseeing their effects.

'*It was with great regret,*' he wrote, '*that I learned your father's condition was such that one who has only your interests at heart should be kept away from your door. I had some small items that I wished to leave with you for the duration of my journey, items I feel sure would have been of use to you in your studies. It is a matter of regret to me that these materials will now lie idle instead of fulfilling the use for which they were intended.*

'*In a few hours my voyage will begin in earnest and*

those of us who have chosen to embark on this venture are all too aware of the risks we undertake. It is therefore quite possible that we shall never meet again. I should like to thank you for the pleasure of your company during my last days in Revesby and to wish you well in the future.

'*I am yours, etc,*

Jo Banks'

Eighteen days later he found that letter still on the desk in his cabin and tore it sharply in two. It was the night when he felt that his voyage had truly begun. The sea was a deep blue and there was no scent of land on the breeze. But, most of all, the night was clear and when he stood near the prow of the ship he felt the huge arch of the sky embrace him. The air was warm against his skin and the stars were bright and as he stood there he felt a huge burden of responsibility fall from his shoulders. All at once he felt free to be happy.

Slowly the light faded and he watched until the blue was truly black and the sky and the sea merged seamlessly at the horizon. Then he went below and lit his lamp and wrote her a second letter.

'*The sea turned green today,*' he wrote, '*just for a moment in the morning light, a deep, deep green of the sort you never see from land. Above the sea, high above it, a single swift. I watched amazed to find it so far from solid earth. It seemed to wave a last farewell from all things to do with land.*

'*I have little time here to think of Revesby but when I do I am saddened at the manner of our parting. But most I am saddened that you cannot see this sky. The colours seem to change every instant as the clouds pass and the moon begins to rise. You would wish to paint this sky.'*

At that point there were sounds outside his cabin and he wrote no more that night. The letter was never finished.

CHAPTER SEVEN

IN THE MUSEUM

The following Monday Katya and I met in the café of the Natural History Museum to compare notes. Katya was neat in jeans and trainers with her hair pulled back. I was scruffy and slightly unkempt in an old jacket. The Natural History Museum welcomed both of us equally and, if anyone thought we made an odd couple, no one particularly showed it. Somewhere to our left the remains of a giant ground sloth towered silently over parties of schoolchildren. Many floors further up, safe in sepulchral darkness, the first-found archaeopteryx lay awkwardly in its bed of stone. We bent over our frothy cups of coffee and ignored them both.

I'd bumped into Katya that morning in the hallway as she was leaving for a lecture. Slightly to my surprise, I started telling her about Hans Michaels's widow. Up to that point I'd thought of that visit as my own secret, but on seeing Katya I changed my mind. I'd imagined the search for the Ulieta bird would be about checking records, following up on rumours, making phone calls. But Hans Michaels's sketch altered that. Now I was faced with a puzzle. I suppose I just wanted someone to help.

It was Katya who suggested meeting in the museum. I was pleased with the idea: it was one of my favourite places, elegant and airy and stuffed full of wonders. And the thought of talking things through with her made me feel better.

We began by sharing what we'd found out—the main facts of the case, if you like. As we didn't have many facts, we didn't expect to take too long. Nevertheless, we put our heads together and started off on the early life of Joseph Banks. He was a good subject—charming, dashing, good-looking and the leading natural scientist of his generation. Oh, and rich too. By the age of twenty-eight he'd been round the world with Captain Cook, established himself as the darling of society, been schemed after by various women with daughters, been painted by Joshua Reynolds and become one of the leading members of the Royal Society. I felt I'd got a good grasp on events; Katya had clearly done better on the people. After twenty minutes we'd come up with this:

1743		Joseph Banks born. Grew up in Lincolnshire (Revesby Abbey).
1760:	Age 17	At Oxford. An avid naturalist.
1766-7	Age 23	Expedition to Newfoundland with Daniel Solander.
1768	Age 25	Engaged to Harriet Blosset. Departed with Cook and Solander on the Endeavour. Gathered specimens. Observed the transit of Venus from Tahiti. Helped map coast of Australia. General hero and good companion.
1771	Age 28	Endeavour returns. Banks a huge hit in top social circles.
1772	Age 29	Cook's second voyage. Banks drops out at very last minute.

Replaced as ship's naturalist by Johann Forster.

1774   Age 31   Forster collects birds on island of Ulieta (now Raiatea).

1775   Age 32   Cook returns. Forster gives (only ever) specimen of Ulieta bird to Banks.

'How does that look for background?' I asked.

Katya nodded. 'It's good. We can call it "Events Leading up to the Crime".'

I looked at the list again.

'Actually, there are a couple of things in there I don't really understand. We've put down "*1768—Engaged to Harriet Blosset*". But he never married her, did he? What went wrong?'

Katya looked down at her notes again.

'Not sure. They'd met in London. Seems like the engagement was never announced—it was all arranged just before he sailed off with Cook. And it seems to have broken off again soon after he got back.'

'Do we know why?'

'Not really. But they'd had three years to go off the idea.'

Katya seemed to think this was a perfectly adequate reason in itself. Even so, I knew we were both thinking the same thing.

'Any pictures of her?' I wondered.

'Not in the books I've read so far.' Katya looked worried. 'We should be able to find one though, shouldn't we?'

I wasn't so sure. After some discussion we agreed to alter our list:

My other question was about Cook's second voyage a year later. Banks had been all set to go, with his provisions bought and his arrangements made, only to pull out on the very brink of departure over an argument with Cook about cabin space. It seemed a strangely petulant piece of behaviour from an otherwise good-natured man.

'Yes,' Katya agreed. 'You can tell it took people by surprise. Did you read about Mr Burnett?'

'Burnett?' The name didn't ring any bells.

Katya picked one of the books off the pile and leafed through it until she came to a page she'd already marked. It was the text of a letter from Captain Cook to the Admiralty, sent quite early on in his second voyage. The letter was quoted with Cook's original punctuation.

FROM CAPTAIN JAMES COOK OF THE
RESOLUTION TO THE SECRETARY OF THE
ADMIRALTY,
MADEIRA, 1ST AUGUST, 1772

. . . Three days before we arrived a person left the Island who went by the name of Burnett. He had been waiting for Mr Banks arrival about three months, at first he said he came here for the recovery of his health, but afterwards said his intention was to go with Mr Banks, to some he said he was unknown to this Gentleman, to others he said it was by his appointment he came here as he could not be receiv'd on board in England. At last when he heard that Mr Banks did not go with

82

us, he took the very first opportunity to get off the Island. He was in appearance rather ordinary than otherwise and employ'd his time in Botanizing &ca—Every part of Mr Burnetts behaviour and every action tended to prove that he was a Woman, I have not met with a person that entertains a doubt of a contrary nature. He brought letters of recommendation to an English House where he was accommodated during his stay. It must be observed that Mrs Burnett must have left England about the time we were first ready to sail . . .

Katya grinned as I finished reading.

'What do you think? A Joseph Banks groupie?'

I smiled. 'It could be. Or just gossip? Banks was a dashing young man with a bit of a reputation, so he was fair game for rumours. And the two men had fallen out. Perhaps Cook couldn't resist dishing a bit of dirt on Banks to the folks back home.'

Katya closed the book and put it back on the pile.

'Either way, it doesn't get us anywhere,' she said. 'The bird hadn't even been discovered then. But when Cook passed that way again at the end of his voyage he had the Ulieta bird on board. What do we know after that?'

It was an easy enough question because what we knew was virtually nil. It was like trying to read a murder mystery where all the pages describing the suspects had been torn out. And I had a nasty feeling that if we were to get as far as the denouement it would probably be Anderson revealing the answers. Nevertheless Anderson himself seemed to think we ought to know something, so we corralled our coffee cups and carried on looking.

The problem was clear enough. We knew that the bird had been given to Banks shortly after the *Resolution* returned to Britain. Latham saw it in Banks's collection in the couple of years that followed. But four years after Banks was given the bird a French ornithologist called Malbranque spent months studying the same collection and his catalogue made no mention of anything that might have been the Ulieta bird. After that it was never mentioned by anyone ever again.

That left a couple of years where we had nothing. Two blank years in which a specimen casually given had casually disappeared. Two years of London society tramping through Banks's house in Soho Square. Banks had kept records of any specimens presented to fellow collectors and scholars. The Ulieta bird wasn't listed. But at some point it was either destroyed or carried out of that house in Soho Square. And then, if Anderson was to be believed, it had spent the next two hundred years or so lying quietly, waiting to be discovered by someone who knew where to look.

As I jotted down the various dates, Katya began to check her watch. I remembered there were other things she was supposed to be doing.

'So what do we do next?' she asked.

I smiled and pulled out another blank sheet of paper.

'We play a game. According to Michaels's drawing there's a woman involved. Now what women were there in Banks's life at the time the bird disappeared? We write down all the ones we can think of here. They're all suspects. And if the bird was given to one of them we could check to see what happened to *their* collections. Assuming they had collections.'

Katya gave me a bright smile.

'I like it,' she said cheerfully, reaching for her notes. *'Cherchez la femme.* We're mad, of course, but I like it.'

For five minutes we tried to come up with names. The first three or four came quickly: Banks's mother, his sister Sophia, Harriet Blosset, one or two society hostesses whose names we had noted. Somewhere there would be portraits of them if we could be bothered to search. After that we paused.

'Anyone else?'

'There was a mistress,' Katya said at last. 'After his engagement. I read about her but I didn't write down her name.'

I nodded. I hadn't written it down either.

'Was she still around in 1775?'

Katya was packing up her things.

'I don't think so, but put her down if only to . . . What's the phrase?'

'Eliminate her from our inquiries?'

Katya stood up, smiling. 'That's the one. Then we go and find their portraits! Now, come on . . .' She jerked her head towards the museum's main hall. 'I want to have a look around.'

I glanced down at our list of suspects. In the space at the bottom of the list I added the words *Joseph Banks's mistress.* Then, as an afterthought, I added a question mark.

*   *   *

85

There was an irony to all this. My grandfather gave up the best part of his life in order to search for the African peacock—which is all the warning anyone should ever need about looking for things that might not exist and which you don't know where to find. And it might never have happened if it hadn't been for James Chapin's feather. Back in 1913, Chapin had been part of an expedition to the Congo basin in search of okapi, the mysterious jungle giraffe about which very little was known. One night towards the end of the expedition Chapin's party had been entertained by a group of local people and Chapin had admired the feathers worn by the group's leader. When he was allowed to take some of them away with him he found he could identify every feather except one. Puzzled, and interested to discover what bird it came from, he kept the feather with him, but by the end of the expedition the mystery remained. It was not a tail feather. There was nothing about it that guaranteed it came from a peacock. But it was enough for my grandfather. That single feather was the spark. And yet, though neither Chapin nor my grandfather could have believed it at the time, it was to be twenty-three years before a bird was found to match that feather.

*   *   *

Katya's guided tour of the Natural History Museum began where every tour of the Natural History Museum has to begin, in the main hall, under the skeleton of the giant diplodocus. It was a weekday morning in winter: quiet, no crowds, and long shafts of pale sunshine cutting diagonals across the hall.

We moved haphazardly from room to room, two small figures made tiny by the creatures around them, insignificant under the high ceilings; past fossil plates of great sea creatures and under the ribs of long extinct mammals, strange creatures from an improbable bestiary—ancient crocodiles, armadillos as big as ponies, sloths bigger than bears.

At one point Katya turned to me, curious.

'Have you always been the way you are? *Interested* in things, I mean.'

I looked at her, surprised by the question. A woman hurried past us, tugging along two small children.

'I suppose I have. In some things. I was always out in hedgerows, collecting. Started with beetles and tadpoles and worked my way up. Used to sneak off school to go and catch newts.'

'And what about later? When you were a teenager? Didn't you ever rebel? Take drugs and give up school?'

I laughed. 'At seventeen I spent my summer in Costa Rica cataloguing beetles.'

She laughed at that, but looked thoughtful.

'I did all those things,' she said. 'I mean drugs and things. It meant I never really . . .' She searched for the right word for a moment and then gave up. 'All the boyfriends I had back then were the ones who dropped out of school and smoked dope and lived in squats. I used to collect them.'

'How come?' I asked. 'It isn't how you strike me.'

She grimaced. 'Oh, you know. These things just happen. Come on.' She took my arm and led me on to the next gallery.

We wandered on in companionable silence for a little longer, until we came back to the main hall and the carefully reconstructed skeleton of a dodo.

'There you go. When people say "dead as a dodo", that's what they mean.'

'Three hundred years dead,' she nodded, reading the label.

'And speaking of dead birds . . .' I looked at my watch. 'We've got an appointment to keep.'

I led her to the small library at the back of the museum. Here, tucked away, is the museum's General Library where Geraldine, the long-serving librarian, was expecting me.

'They're just fetching it, Mr Fitzgerald,' she told me. 'Should be ready for you in a few minutes. And I've put out the Banks biographies you asked for on the table over there.'

'You'll see what in a moment,' I told Katya. 'In the meantime, let's look at these.'

We sat down next to each other and went through the pile of books, looking out for the name of Joseph Banks's mistress. Or at least that's what we tried to do. Instead we found that the more we looked for her, the less visible she became. No one even seemed to know her name. We'd made no progress at all by the time Geraldine returned with the object I'd requested. She left it on a table near us, covered only with a loose sheet of clear plastic.

It was a drawing of a bird, expertly done, its colours apparently as fresh as they had been on the June afternoon in 1774 when Georg Forster sat drawing in his cabin. Through the plastic sheet you could even glimpse traces of the artist at work—

the corrections to his original outlines, the places where his sweating hand had smudged his own pencil lines as he drew. Being face to face with the very paper he'd drawn on made that hot afternoon suddenly seemed very close, the bird in the picture very real.

'The bird itself . . .' Katya breathed.

'Yes, that's the one. The one they caught that day. The one that ended up in Joseph Banks's collection. We don't know how many of these there once were, or how they lived or anything. All we know of them is this one individual.'

We sat together in front of that picture, musing, until the room began to grow gloomy around us and Katya looked at her watch.

'I've got to go,' she said. 'I've got a tutorial.' She pulled on her coat. 'We should . . .' She trailed off. 'Well, whatever. I'll see you later.'

By the door she turned and waved.

After that I found it hard to settle again. I let Geraldine remove the picture and then returned to the reference books, still vaguely curious about the missing mistress. The next twenty minutes or so threw up a couple more mentions of her, which I photocopied for Katya before I went home. I still hadn't found out the mistress's name. And Katya didn't get to see the photocopies for quite a while, because when I got home I found a plain, unmarked envelope had been pushed through the door. Two things struck me about the document inside. The first was that it had been sent anonymously. The second was that it looked remarkably as though it might be Anderson's secret clue.

The measurement of time during a long sea voyage is a puzzle with more than one dimension. The question of longitude was left to Cook, a matter of sea clocks and dead reckoning, something recorded in logs and on the carved sticks of sailors when the breeze hung slack. To Banks, time was a mystery of a different sort. The days passed so fast that a year was gone before he knew it, and each passing day was simply piled in his memory onto the ones that had gone before, until the months of travel began to rise behind him like a ridge of mountains between him and home. And yet his last days in England, when he chose to think of them, remained vivid: the Revesby woods, Harriet's head on his shoulder, London left at dawn, Plymouth by sunset. It was as if each new adventure left these images sharper and they became his destination, the lights to navigate by if a night seemed starless. He felt that when the demands of the voyage were done, that world would be waiting for him just as it had always been, green and safe and ready for him.

In Revesby she measured time differently: by the leaves turning, by the lowering of the candles, by the slowing rhythm of her father's breath. While Banks's days passed quickly, hers did not pass at all; one grew into another imperceptibly until their combined mass began to press upon her memories. The sharp outlines of her days in the woods thickened under their weight and to preserve them she did two things. She continued to draw by day despite the shortening light, and with each line she felt she made the woods more real. Then by night, curled under her sheets, she did the same for her memories of him, reaching for them one by one, retouching the colour and lines of each until they became sunlit portraits hanging in the dark.

The autumn after Banks's departure was a short one and winter came early. But there was one day in October when the sun shone in a last reprise of summer and she left the house early to spend a final warm day in the woods. She hoped to slip through the village unseen but she quickly found she was not the only person drawn out of doors by the fine weather. In the meadow leading to the woods two figures stood on the path ahead of her, and when she came into view they hesitated. She recognised Banks's sister, Sophia, and Miss Taylor, the doctor's daughter, on the way from the Abbey into the village.

She noticed their hesitation even though she had become accustomed to it. It was something that had become automatic to the people of Revesby. This time she saw that if they wished to reach the village, they had no option but to continue towards her, and she felt a growing coldness inside as she prepared for the encounter. Ten yards before she came level with them she fixed her eyes on the trees ahead. *She* would not leave the path; she knew they would. There could be no collision, as a collision was something they could not ignore. She heard the rustle of skirts as the two women stepped from the path and began to point out an object in the distance. Knowing that her way was clear, she continued unchecked as she had done many times before. But this time as she drew level, in the rarest of lapses, she allowed her eyes to flicker from the trees to their faces. She saw Miss Taylor's chin lifted high and her face turned away, but with shock she realised that Miss Banks, like herself, had allowed her gaze to wander. Their eyes met for no more than a second, but before either could react she had passed by and, without a word, both parties continued on their way.

It was the first time she had encountered anyone from Revesby Abbey since the news of Banks's engagement. She found it hard to imagine him amongst his family, hard even to imagine him indoors, surrounded by china and the clutter of a drawing room. As she walked towards the woods she wished their eyes had not met.

Neither of the other two women referred to the meeting as they continued towards the village, although Miss Banks studied the face of her friend carefully, as if to divine what thoughts were unspoken there. After walking the length of Revesby, they came eventually to the house that stood with its shutters closed. The autumn light seemed to accentuate its shabbiness. Together they took in the sight, unafraid of being observed, until Miss Taylor sniffed.

'How good it will be when Mr Ponsonby is able to let that house to someone else!'

This caused the older woman to turn to her, puzzled.

'Mr Ponsonby? I had not realised he was the owner.'

'You have not heard?' It was a state of affairs Miss Taylor seemed eager to remedy. 'It falls to Mr Ponsonby because of the debts he holds. In the months since the *incident* there has been no money to pay the interest and the house is now all but owned by him. It is only through his goodwill that the family is allowed to remain.'

'His goodwill? Why should he feel any such thing? The man struck him at his own dinner table.'

'Mama says it is a truly Christian act as he seeks no credit for it. Only my father and Mr Burrows know of it.'

Sophia seemed thoughtful.

'And yet is it right that a young woman on her own should be placed so very much in his debt when her father dies? I think, if I were her, it is not a situation I should enjoy.'

Miss Taylor raised her eyebrows. 'Her family is not famous for its principles and she seems happy enough with the arrangement. We shall find out soon enough—Papa says her father cannot survive many more months. But let us not talk of such ugly things. The hedgerows are so pretty at this time of year, are they not, Sophia?'

And the two women stepped through the fields, the one chattering, the other unusually silent.

After that day, winter came on quickly. Dr Taylor called less frequently than before but he came early one morning in February when the village was still white with frost and there was ice on the path to their door. The cold made ordinary things look different and the doctor found himself noticing the footprints of birds on the pathway and a frozen spider's web, partly broken now, hanging uncleared across one window.

Inside he found the house cold, the fires small and newly lit. In the hallway, where he laid his hat and gloves, he could see his breath in short, white bursts in front of his face. He found that only the sickroom was truly warm and he could tell by the ash that the fire there had been tended through the night. His patient had, month by month, confounded the doctor's expectations, but today he saw at once that it could not be very much longer. For many months his visits had been for the sake of the daughter, not the father.

'What will you do?' he asked quietly, his examination complete. 'It will be soon now.'

'I will not think of it,' she said. 'I won't think him gone.' She reached out and took her father's hand.

The doctor nodded but after a short silence he spoke again. 'I have only a few connections but I know of someone . . . a family . . . children to teach . . .'

She looked up.

'You know what is said of me. They could not take me. They simply could not.' It was spoken quietly, without emotion.

The doctor nodded again.

'I'm sorry,' he said, although what aspect of the world he was regretting he did not say.

On his way out, the nurse, Martha, detained him at the front door with a hand on his arm and a gesture in the direction of the kitchen.

'I can borrow no more in the village on her father's name,' she said softly.

'I'm sorry,' he said again and hesitated. He was not a wealthy man and he had a family of his own. But he would not have her bury her father for want of food. And surely it could only be a few days more. 'Then you must borrow on my name,' he told her and stepped outside into the frozen morning.

*   *   *

That night she sat in the dark of her room and thought of the question the doctor had posed. She had opened the shutters and could feel the cold pressing in on her from the window. Beyond the glass a half-moon lit the meadow but left the great stand of trees in darkness. The grass was already sparkling with frost. She shivered and pulled her shawl closer to her neck. She knew there was only one answer to the doctor's question, one that many would think she was lucky to have. It didn't seem to matter to her so much now, as she sat there alone in the night with everything coming to an end.

For a moment she thought of Joseph Banks sailing through a southern summer and she was happy to think of it, happy that, unlike her, he was not straitjacketed by the cold and cramped by the long hours of darkness. And with the loss of her father now so close and so real, she found herself for the first time glad of Banks's engagement, glad he had found his happiness. It was then, as she looked out over the dark trees, that she understood the gift her father had given her by clinging so tenaciously to life. He had given her time. Time before their world fell apart for her to enjoy the woods and the summer; time to love a little; time to understand her loss so that the great, empty ache she would feel on his death was one she had already learned how to carry.

*   *   *

Winter in Lincolnshire was very far from Banks's mind. Among the smiling brown people of the southern seas he had found a new side to himself and a new value. Where others of the crew saw strangeness and barbarity he saw only men and women. And where the islanders found in Cook's officers an unnatural rigidity they saw in Banks an openness of heart that they recognised as something of themselves. Without ever underestimating the differences in education and experience, Banks soon realised that quickness of thought was not confined to the white faces around him; that the crew of the *Endeavour* had no monopoly on honour and strength of character. Fascinated and delighted, he gave himself

95

wholeheartedly to these people so different from him and so similar.

And as well as the people he encountered, there was a strange new world of jungle and reef to entrance him. He never tired of watching the light change on the water and marvelling at the colours and the sounds of the islands. The botanist in him was overwhelmed by the variety and abundance that crowded in on him. His collection of birds and plants and animals grew and grew until he began to realise that he had in his possession something unique and unprecedented.

He never told her of the night in Otaheite when she came so strongly into his thoughts. There had been a feast and dancing and he had been at the centre of both, laughing and shouting and clapping hands with every person there. Then, as he paused for breath, he caught a glimpse through the palms of moonlight on the sea and without a thought he slipped away to the water's edge. There he stood for a while, strangely detached from the noise behind him, suddenly aware of the night sounds: the wind in the trees, insect song, waves very far away breaking on rocks or a reef. And as he stood and absorbed the beauty of the place, he found himself all at once filled with an overwhelming sadness, an aching melancholy that flooded out of him until it seemed to fill the night.

At first he didn't understand. But as he waited in the shadow of the trees, he began to realise it was the moment itself he was grieving for, that whispering moonlit night that could never be his to keep. No matter how many birds and plants he gathered together in the hold of the *Endeavour*, he could never take back with him the perfection of that moment in that place. And it was then he thought of her and her drawing, and he knew that if she had been there, then this was the place he would have found her: curled by the shore, quietly storing away every nuance of the night.

*　　　*　　　*

As if to make up for the long summer, the winter held on in Revesby until March was almost gone. Lent came in with streams still frozen and the ground too hard to dig, and she waited tight-lipped for spring to lift the siege. Her father's breathing was quiet now but each breath was painfully fought for. She became determined that he should feel one last spring. As she cleaned him she would talk of the coming thaw, painting warm, bright pictures, as if her words could breathe into him the need to be alive. When she had finished washing him she would walk to the window and peep out at the dark skies and the trees still not in bud.

However, the first death in Revesby that year was not the one most expected. At the end of March, Dr Taylor died, outlived by the man he had paid to keep alive. The village was stricken by its loss and the funeral was attended by mourners from five parishes. She sat at home and grieved by the bedside where he had so often sat. The shock of his death brought a new dimension to her loneliness.

Martha looked at the pinched face of her patient and the ice on the windows and decided to stay. There was food in the larder now to last until spring and time then to see what could be done. Preoccupied by loss, her mistress thanked her with her eyes but said very little. She had begun to worry where the money would come from for the next funeral.

In London, Harriet Blosset was also waiting. In the

first months of Banks's absence she wore her situation like a mourning gown. At balls and dances she was fetching in her desolation and prettier than ever in all that it said and meant. She spent her days stitching him a great many waistcoats; but she found she was no Penelope and as the season progressed she proved too pretty a widow to remain in black forever. No one she danced with was quite like Banks, she told herself, but they were pressing and charming and a great deal closer. She began to suffer in her own way, a way no less painful for it being particular to her. As month followed month she was learning for herself about time and how to measure it. On the day when her closest friend's betrothal was announced she waited until she was alone and then she wept.

And in Revesby perhaps the dying man had listened to his daughter's exhortations. There were yellow crocuses outside his front door on the night when she woke at his bedside and found him gone.

CHAPTER EIGHT

A LETTER AND SOME LEAFLETS

It took me forty minutes to cancel three days' worth of university appointments and another twenty to get my bike tuned up ready for a journey. I was back in the kitchen boiling the kettle when Katya came in. I intercepted her in the hallway then made her a cup of tea before I pushed the envelope over to her. She opened it cautiously, not sure if it was good news or bad.

There were two photocopied sheets. The first showed the front of an envelope, grainily copied, the George V stamp clear, the postmark smudged and illegible. But the strong, sloping handwriting was easy to read.

> *Miss Martha Ainsby,*
> *The Old Manor,*
> *Stamford,*
> *Lincs*

The second sheet was a copy of a letter written in the same sloping hand.

> *The Savoy Hotel,*
> *17th January 1915*

> *My dear Martha,*
> *Colonel Winstanley was as good as his word and here I am in London. Sadly the arrangements were hasty*

and there was no time to write and warn you, still less time to visit. I have been here little more than eight hours but the papers are delivered to General Winters and at dawn tomorrow I set off to rejoin the regiment.

Your letter followed me around France and only caught up with me two days ago. What sad news! The old man was a great character and a good friend to us both. I'm glad the end was peaceful. He deserved as much.

It was great quick thinking to secure that precious bird of his. You know how I have always coveted it. Even without the connections to Cook and Banks, even without its subsequent history, it would still be the most remarkable and romantic object imaginable.

When I'm able to return for a proper visit, you and I shall record all its details and write to the Natural History Museum. It's only fair they are made aware of the survival of a specimen unique to science. Until then, guard it with your life—I don't want to return and find that young Vulpes of yours has snatched it from my grasp!

This brief glimpse of London has done me a power of good. My spirits *are high and I'm certain this job will be all done shortly so I can return to your side.*

Until then, remember me to everyone.

Your loving brother,

John

When Katya had finished reading we looked at each other across the table. She was sitting quite still but I could feel her suspense.

'The Ulieta bird,' she said quietly. 'That's what he's writing about, isn't it?' Her whole face asked the question.

'It could be.'

She made an impatient face and looked down at the letter.

'What do you mean, it *could* be? A specimen unique to science . . . connected to Cook, to Banks . . . It must be.'

'No, it just *could* be. And this letter *could* be the one that has got Anderson so excited. He'd be crazy looking for a stuffed bird that hasn't been seen for two hundred years, but a specimen that was safe and sound eighty years ago . . .'

'Then it *can* be found!' She clutched my arm. 'It means we've got as much chance as he has!'

I held up my hand. I wanted to keep things under some sort of control.

'Wait a minute, a lot has happened since 1914. The Blitz, death duties, an awful lot of rising damp. We can't be certain of anything.'

'But if it was still in one piece back then . . .'

'Yes, if it survived till then there's a chance it might still be around. Anderson obviously thinks

101

so. But if this is Anderson's big clue, who sent it to us? I can't imagine Anderson dropping it in just to make sure he doesn't have an unsporting advantage.'

Katya was still holding the photocopied sheets in front of her, as if they could ward off my doubts. 'I don't know.' She hesitated. 'Who else knew about it?'

I immediately thought of Gabby. She'd promised to pass on anything she found, and it looked as though she was keeping her word. By now she'd be somewhere in Germany but her raincoat was still behind my door. I reached over and took the papers out of Katya's hands.

'What are you going to do?' she asked.

'That's easy,' I told her. 'I'm going to Stamford to find out if these are real.'

'Very good,' she replied brightly. 'I'm coming too.'

*   *   *

We set out the next morning. Now that there were two of us travelling I had to leave the bike, but Geoff from the Hammer and Sickle had a car I often borrowed—a small rusty object the colour of a fading lemon. We packed a bag each while it was still dark and then we were off, nosing out into the London traffic just as the rush hour began.

It was a slow journey but we were childishly elated. The rain made it hard to see anything and the pained creaking of the windscreen wipers meant we had to shout to be heard. Inside the car, the radio didn't work and the heating only did enough to stop the windows from steaming up. On the outskirts of London we gave in, pulled over and put on our coats. Katya's was long and black, with the collar turned up around her face. Mine was old and tatty and made me look quite a lot like an extra from *Dr Zhivago*. Under the coat, inside me, there was a little pulse of optimism that refused to be dampened. What if that bird *had* survived all this time? It might. It just might. Coming suddenly to a stretch of open road, I plunged my foot down and the speedometer crept very slowly up to 65.

Outside London the rain began to ease and when I turned off the wipers the noise of the car settled to a low growl.

'You know this is crazy, don't you?' I asked her, my voice still a little raised.

'Of course.' She nodded with a smile. 'But it feels good, setting off in search of something.'

I smiled, partly at her, partly at the road ahead of me. 'That's what I always used to say to people. I spent six years in the rainforest, looking for things.'

'What sort of things?'

'Birds, plants. Connections. It was a genetic impulse. My grandfather was the same. And my father. Do you know, they both have beetles named after them? How could I possibly follow that?'

I laughed and Katya laughed with me.

'So what did *you* discover?'

I shrugged. 'Nothing much. When I was twenty-five I published a paper that showed how a certain species of tree frog was being badly affected by logging operations three hundred miles upstream. It was quite big news at the time—well, big news if you were into that sort of thing. I did some lectures about it. The thing is, they carried on logging anyway. When I next went back there were no frogs left.'

Katya looked at me not sure of my tone.

'But still, you'd done good work, hadn't you?'

'In an academic sense. But that didn't do the frogs much good.' I paused, uncertain how much else to say. 'I suppose that's when things began to go wrong between me and Gabriella. We'd met out there, you know. We ended up working together, setting up rainforest reserves. But after the frogs I began to wonder if we'd got it all wrong. All we were doing was treating the symptoms. The disease was so much bigger—population growth, consumer demand, that sort of thing. I began to tell people that reserves weren't the solution at all. They were just sticking plaster for our consciences. We should have been putting all that funding into tackling the causes.'

Katya was still looking at me from under her fringe. One hand held her coat closed at her neck, the other was hugged tight around her body.

'And that's why you two fell out? Weren't you really on the same side?'

'It wasn't only that. There were other things . . .' I thought of saying more but I was too slow or too shy, or too out of practice. 'There always are, aren't there?' I concluded lamely. 'Anyway, we went our separate ways. Gabby stayed in the rainforest and I set off with my notebooks to track down the surviving remains of all the birds that we'd already lost. I figured that if we were going to make things extinct, we owed it to the future to preserve the evidence, to show what they'd been like.' I smiled at her. 'I was a bit manic really. It was a difficult time. After a couple of years I calmed down and came back here to sort myself out. It was all a long time ago now. And another country.'

I smiled a little ruefully and then, before Katya could reply, the rain came on again and the wipers put an end to conversation.

A substantial bite had already been taken out of lunchtime by the time we found our way into the centre of Stamford. However, still fired with optimism, we found a pub near the station with a sign that read 'Bar Meals, Snacks, Bed and Breakfast'. The woman in the pub seemed mildly surprised when we asked for two rooms, but it was hard to tell if that was speculation about our relationship or just astonishment that anyone wanted to stay there at all. Leaving our bags still packed, we found a café for lunch and sat down to do some planning. Before eating I rang the university and told them where they could contact me in case Gabby tried to get in touch.

Still buoyed by a flood tide of confidence and by two strong cups of coffee, we agreed to split up. Katya would try the local record office while I'd see if the tourist information office could point us towards the Old Manor. It was at the tourist office that things first began to look a bit more difficult. It was the sort of place I'd expected—lots of fake pine and the smell of polish and cheap carpet. Along one wall was the usual rack of leaflets and brochures so I started there, half expecting to find the one I wanted straightaway. When my browsing failed to turn up anything useful, I waited politely until a would-be rail traveller finished monopolising the woman behind the counter. She looked up and caught my eye as he let the door bang behind him.

'I'm not supposed to do trains,' she said with a sad smile. 'I was only trying to help.'

She stopped smiling when I told her I was looking for a place called the Old Manor. Instead she looked at me as if I was trying to play some sort of trick on her.

'What *is* all this?' she asked. 'I had someone in here a couple of days ago asking about just the same place.'

I felt a slight stir of anxiety.

'And is that unusual?'

'Well, it wouldn't be,' she replied, still a little wary, 'except I'm not sure it exists.'

I don't know what disappointment she saw in my face but it was enough to persuade her to tell me about the previous visitor. She illustrated her story with a succession of leaflets, and soon I was holding a dozen different pieces of advertising for old houses in the surrounding area.

'This one seemed the best bet,' she told me, indicating one of them. 'The Old Grange. Tudor, mostly. It's just north of here.'

I nodded politely. 'And was this visitor a tall man? A Scandinavian?' I asked, pretty sure of the answer.

'No, not at all,' she replied, looking at me strangely again. 'He was an American. Very polite. Little round glasses. Getting on a bit. Now, are you going to tell me what all this is about?'

I explained I was trying to trace a family called Ainsby that had lived in the area in the early 1900s. The name didn't ring any bells with her but she

106

told me how to find the record office. Which, she said, was the same thing she'd told the polite American.

*   *   *

The rain continued for most of the day with only brief pauses to get its breath back. At six o'clock that evening Katya and I retreated to the bar at the Station Tavern. It looked better after dark, with a gas-flame fire and lots of small red lampshades making it harder to see the marks on the walls. But it was gloriously warm after the cold rain of a Lincolnshire evening and we even risked ordering food at the bar, then retired to the corner by the fire with a large glass of red wine and a pint of something dark and local.

The record office had told Katya what I'd already begun to fear. There was no trace of any family called Ainsby in or around Stamford in 1914 or, as far as they could see, at any other time. It had taken Katya three hours and the urgings of two different librarians to accept the fact. We had drawn the most emphatically featureless blank imaginable.

Even so, we ate our meal quite happily, speculating fu riously and trying to make things add up. Did this mean the letter we'd been sent was a fake? Neither of us wanted to believe that. Apart from Hans Michaels's drawing, it was the only clue we had. We decided to try again the next day, to dig a little deeper. After that we suddenly grew awkward with each other, and when Katya opted for an early night I stayed behind for another pint. I was contemplating the possibility of a third when an unpleasant breath of cold air made me look up. A small, round man had come into the pub and, judging from the state of his raincoat, the weather outside was getting worse. The bar of the Station Tavern was beginning to seem a better place by the minute and next to me the gas fire was still blazing away with a heart-warming hiss. I took out the collection of leaflets from the tourist office and spread them out across the table.

'No good, any of them,' said an American voice above me. The newcomer had made his way over to my table, where he was flapping the water off the sides of his coat.

'I'm sorry?' I replied, as coldly as a man can when he's just been caught reading a leaflet titled 'The Pixie Glen and Elves' Grotto, Fairbank'.

'None of them is the place you're looking for,' he replied, discarding his coat onto a neighbouring stool. 'You're Fitzgerald,' he added. 'Mind if I join you?'

He was already pulling up a chair. The removal of his coat revealed a woollen three-piece suit of the sort worn by country doctors in the 1930s. His hair was grey and slightly curly and he wore thick glasses in old-fashioned frames. He looked absurdly un-American.

'The name's Potts,' he said, holding out his hand. 'I called the university and they told me I'd find you here. I'm staying at the George on the High Street,' he added.

While I was still registering this, he reached into a pocket and pulled out a pile of leaflets similar to my own. These he began to count out onto the table with a twinkle in his eye.

'The Old Grange? No. Hawsley Manor? No.

Thurley Hall? Definitely not. Radnors? Jeez, that was the place that makes cheese. No way. Pulkington Hall? No. As for the Pixie Glen place'—he gave a shudder—'well, you can go there if you like, but don't say I didn't warn you.'

I dropped my leaflets on top of his.

'I think you'd better start again. Who are you?'

'I'm Potts.' He practically winked at me, like an uncle sharing a secret. 'I guess I'm here for the same reason you are.'

'You're looking for a lost bird?'

'That's the one.' He reached into his jacket and handed me a card. It didn't give much away.

Emeric Potts
Art, Antiques, Ephemera

'You're an art dealer?' I asked, looking at him more carefully.

He pursed his lips as if to blow the idea away.

'Not exactly. But you could say that art dealers are my business. I find the things they want to sell. Looking for a lost Van Dyck? Want a first-edition *Ulysses*? I'm your man.'

I gave him back his card.

'Isn't this a little outside your normal line of work?'

'Oh, I prefer to call it a natural diversification. After all, you could say taxidermy is just a continuation of sculpture by other means.'

'So you know someone who wants to buy the

Ulieta bird.'

Potts looked pained.

'Such directness, Mr Fitzgerald. Let's just say that I'm very interested in finding it. And people seem to think you're the best person to help. I rang you a few times in the last few days but I guess you were always out.'

I studied his face, not sure what to make of him.

'So what are you doing here in Stamford? Not just looking for me, surely?'

He reached into his pocket again and pulled out a folded piece of paper.

'You've seen this?' he asked.

'I'm not sure,' I lied, recognising instantly the photocopied sheet he placed in front of me. It was another copy of John Ainsby's letter.

'Of course you have.' He leaned back. 'I sent it to you myself.'

I admit that took me by surprise, and my face must have shown it.

'Who did you think sent it, Mr Fitzgerald? Karl Anderson?'

'No. Well, I mean . . .'

He chuckled softly to himself. 'Well, it's Anderson's letter, all right. This is what's brought him over here in a hurry to try to find the thing.'

'He told me he was coming over anyway. Something to do with botanical paintings. The Ulieta bird is just a sideline to him.'

Potts was still smiling affably, but I felt that he was studying me carefully from behind his glasses.

'He told you that, did he? Well, who's to say?' And with that he took his glasses off and began to polish them on his waistcoat, apparently with no further interest in Anderson and his motives. But I couldn't let him stop there.

'I'm sorry, this doesn't make sense. Why would *you* send me that letter?'

He shrugged in a way that suggested the answer was obvious.

'I thought I'd put it under your nose to see what happened. You're the expert, Mr Fitzgerald. And I'm told that finding something like this would mean a lot to you. So I reckoned that when you saw John Ainsby's letter, either you'd ignore it, in which case I'd know it's a dead end, or you'd come running up here, in which case we might be onto something. And here you are.'

He was clearly a man who liked to talk. As he warmed up in front of the fire, and with no prompting from me, he began to tell me a lot more about the Ainsby letter. Apparently Anderson had been put onto it by an academic doing research into the First World War. Extinct birds may not have been Anderson's main area of expertise, but he knew about the Ulieta bird, and he grasped the letter's significance at once. His first step was to take a copy to Ted Staest, and the two men came to some sort of agreement about the bird's value—though exactly what they agreed was something Potts seemed rather vague about. It wasn't until rumours about the bird began to leak out that Potts got hold of his own copy of the letter.

'Not through official channels, you understand, Mr Fitzgerald.'

'You mean you bribed someone?'

He looked offended. 'Please, Mr Fitzgerald, there's no need for us to go into the details. Suffice it to say that I have a copy. And now, so do you.'

He indicated the piece of paper in front of him.

111

'It's an intriguing letter, isn't it, Mr Fitzgerald? The references to Cook and Banks, the unique specimen . . . And of course it's addressed to Lincolnshire, Banks's own county. All very promising. There's one bit though . . . *"I don't want to return and find that young Vulpes of yours has snatched it from my grasp!"* What do you make of that? A rival for the bird?'

I shrugged. '*Vulpes* means fox, so I expect he means someone cunning and a bit predatory. The way he uses it sounds affectionate though, doesn't it? I wondered if it was a suitor of hers—someone prowling around while her brother's away.'

'A suitor. A lover . . .' He played with the idea. 'Yes, I can see that. Interesting . . .' Behind his glasses, his eyes seemed to cloud with thought, but a second later his unflappable exterior was back in place and he was telling me how the Ainsby letter had brought him first to London, and then to Stamford. But in Stamford he'd drawn a blank. No trace of the Ainsbys, no trace of the Old Manor, no stuffed bird. No trace of Anderson either.

'That was beginning to worry me most,' he confided. 'I figured if I wasn't where Anderson was, I was in the wrong place. Then on my fourth day here I noticed a guy in the George.' He took a card from his wallet. *Edward Smith, Discretion Guaranteed, 63 North Hill Road, London N17.*

'This guy Smith is working for Anderson. He admitted it quickly enough when pressed. He has a fairly confident air about him. Seemed to be hinting it was pretty much all over. Even so, I was happier once I'd found him. I'd be happier still if I knew where Anderson was.'

'What's Smith actually doing?' I asked.

112

Potts shrugged.

'Goes out early, comes back late. Takes his car. I tried tailing him one day but he must have spotted me. We drove around the county for six and a half hours. Jeez, the roads here are really something, you know that?'

He sat back in his seat and looked at me pleasantly.

'You know, if it wasn't for noticing Smith I'd have quit by now—if there's anything here to find, I can't find it, and the weather stinks. So that's where you come in. Listen, we may as well be straight with each other.' He leaned forward, almost self-consciously conspiratorial. 'You're right that this isn't my line, Mr Fitzgerald. But I'm very, very keen to find that bird before Anderson does. Here's the deal. You find me that bird and we can go to Staest together. You can deal with him direct. All I ask is a small cut, say five per cent. Call it an introduction fee, if you like.'

It was then I began to understand the real value of Potts's avuncular demeanour. For the next twenty minutes or so, very gently and with the greatest politeness, he interrogated me about the whereabouts of the Ulieta bird. Of course it shouldn't have taken him half that long but, like Anderson, he seemed reluctant to believe how little I knew. Even my empty glass wasn't enough to stop the questions, until finally I insisted on going to the bar to buy myself another pint. He declined a drink himself and when I came back he was squeezing himself into his raincoat. He paused to shake my hand.

'Remember what I've said tonight, Mr Fitzgerald. My job here is to find that bird before

Anderson. But if you get to it before either of us, remember that I'll be happy to help you get the best price for it.'

When he'd gone I drank my pint in silence, feeling sure there was something going on that I wasn't quite grasping. Potts seemed eager enough to get hold of the bird, but, like Anderson, he didn't seem too bothered about making money out of it. Was this really all about pleasing Ted Staest? How much is the goodwill of a Canadian billionaire worth? Or was that the wrong tack? Was the actual value of the bird so immense that they were happy to let me name my price, knowing that I'd never dream up a value even close to the real one? I examined that theory for a while and then discarded it. There was no way the bird could be worth that much. At least not unless this DNA business was a lot more lucrative than I imagined.

In front of me on the table were the two sets of tourist leaflets, Potts's and mine. Eventually I picked them up and began to go through them again. After all, I had no other clues to follow.

It was only much later, when I tried to put the leaflets back in my pocket, that I found the photocopies I'd made for Katya at the Natural History Museum, the two references to Joseph Banks's mistress. I looked around. The bar was still warm and still serving. It seemed a shame to go to bed. So I settled down again and started to read them properly for the first time.

Death seemed to stalk the *Endeavour* when she finally turned for home. After leaving Batavia the air seemed full of fever and they lost men almost daily. Banks himself was almost among them and Solander's health also suffered. Twenty-three men died between Batavia and the Cape: by the time the *Endeavour* reached Atlantic waters, Parkinson, Monkhouse and Molineux were all dead and about a third of the crew with them. The survivors turned their faces north and hoped for home.

But the last days of a journey can be the hardest. At sea every one of them had an order to live by and clear duties to perform. They knew their routine and their instructions and at all times they had a destination ahead of them. With the approach of land these certainties began to dissolve. As the Channel drew nearer, men would pause in their work to scan the horizon. Banks was one of them. He knew even then, long before they arrived in London, that their return would be momentous. They had seen and recorded things beyond the imaginations of the people who had sent them. He brought back with him a collection—specimens, plants and artefacts—that was unlike anything that had ever been seen before. He was too young not to enjoy the anticipation of triumph. And too human not to be a little changed by it.

Nevertheless, he was nervous and found himself envying Cook. Banks knew that the Yorkshireman's reputation was made, and he found that he envied him his wife at home and his sturdy sense of belonging. For himself, Banks discovered that the aspects of home he had cherished in the South Seas began to seem subtly different as he edged nearer to the reality.

He found it easy to imagine himself in the salons of London, recounting his voyage and meeting the great philosophers of the day on equal terms. It was perhaps an image he had carried with him all along, hidden deep so that not even he could look at it until he was sure of success. But when he tried to imagine Harriet with him in that world, the picture he formed would begin to fade. She seemed to him to sit uneasily beside those men of serious science and he was ashamed to find that when he remembered her, instead of recalling her face, he found his pulse quickening at the recollection of a neck as smooth as pale china, of his fingertips trailing gently down the line of her soft, bare shoulders. These images returned to him over and over, as he tried instead to remember her voice or her smile. Disconcerted, he swept such thoughts away until the time came when he would meet her in person.

When the *Endeavour* finally anchored in Deal they had been away almost three years.

Their return was an even greater sensation than he could possibly have expected, his reception in London beyond anything he had imagined. Within days of their arrival he had become the public face of the expedition, the young man who had combined daring and adventure with the most dedicated pursuit of knowledge. While Cook sank quietly into the routine debriefings of the Admiralty, Banks took the same message into polite society and opened a new world to its imaginings. If he had feared that the uniqueness of his experience would not be readily appreciated, he was quite wrong. And if the pictures and the paintings of the places discovered were not enough, the specimens acquired there were a wonder of their own. He had collected plant samples that would fascinate botanists for years to come and there were other, even more sensational things to describe. It was hard to talk of plants and propagation while your listeners wanted to marvel at the shape and habits of the kangaroo. Carried to fame by both the novelty and the daring of the tales he had to tell, Banks was rushed breathless through parlours and dining rooms, scarcely able to believe the honours paid him.

At first he rode this wave of celebrity as a small boat rides the storm, frantic in his activity yet lifted from wave to wave without control of his direction or his destiny. For five days after his return he did not visit Harriet Blosset until she sent him a hurt, reproachful letter complaining of his very public negligence. He went to see her then and each found the other altered, so that the interview was awkward and unsatisfying. She found him constrained and uncertain where before he had been easy and amusing, and his talk of distant islands was less interesting to her than talk of a future with her in London and the shires. She greeted him coldly, unaware how much of her attraction had been in the openness with which she showed her feelings for him. This proud, resentful Harriet was a stranger to him. As their interview progressed he found her less striking than he remembered, the creamy white of her skin less perfect and her gait less graceful and natural. He wanted to touch her, to feel the softness he remembered, but the formality in her manner gave him no encouragement. They had sat together for a painful, inconclusive half-hour and then he had excused himself. His time was not his own, he told her, and he was bound in a few days' time to return to Revesby to inquire into the management of his estates. On his return, he promised, he would call again and then there would be time to talk of the future.

Perhaps it was the excitements of London society or the rigours of his voyage that had affected him but as he journeyed back to Revesby he barely thought of his last visit there. His mind was on the improvements he might make and the decisions that needed to be taken about rents and rates. He was surprised on his arrival to be greeted by people and faces he hadn't thought of for over three years, each of them smiling and eager to make him welcome, their reserve quite blown away by the fame and fortune he had obtained for himself. Their effect was to make him pause and remember, and it was his welcome in Revesby that brought him properly home. Amid all the greetings there was a moment of sadness for him when he heard of Dr Taylor's death two years before. The doctor's family, he was told, had left Revesby shortly after, their circumstances much reduced. It was commonly known that they had gone to live with Mrs Taylor's family in Clerkenwell and Miss Taylor, the eldest of the daughters, had married a curate. Her younger sister, still only seventeen, had married a man of forty who owned a little property in the Fens.

Banks felt genuine sadness at the news but he comforted himself with the discovery that his estates had been well managed in his absence: after three days of accounts and rent books, he was satisfied that there were no dreadful acts of neglect that needed remedy. Much of his time at first was spent in the dimness of the Abbey with the ledgers but in the afternoons he would head into the sunshine with his steward, Nicholson, to see for himself how things stood. The tenant farms, the cottages, the deer park and gardens; each was inspected and found satisfactory.

It was on the afternoon of his sixth day that he and

Nicholson, returning on foot from one such expedition, turned their attention to the woods that lay between the Abbey and the village. It was a hot afternoon in late summer and the shade was welcomed by both of them. A few minutes into the trees Banks paused, as if surprised at where he stood. With Nicholson at his side his thoughts had been entirely on business and it came to him as a shock to recognise the place in which he found himself.

'This way, if you will,' he muttered to Nicholson, and struck off to his right. 'There is a little clearing this way, I believe.'

The steward followed him until both emerged into a space between the trees where the canopy parted and let in the sun. Banks was smiling quietly to himself.

'How little things change,' he murmured. 'After so many years away it is strange to find the paths, even the shape of particular trees, exactly as they were when I stood here last.'

Nicholson looked around him. 'There's no denying the woods change slowly, sir. I daresay your children will run down these paths and believe they're the first to discover them.'

Banks nodded. He liked Nicholson.

'Tell me,' he said, 'when I was here last there was a young lady who used to roam these woods as if they were her own. Her father had the house at the end of the village. He was something of a freethinker and there was always scandal attached to his name. And he was much given to drinking and insulting his neighbours.'

'Yes, sir, I know the gentleman you mean. He died a couple of years back, in the spring. An unpopular gentleman he was in these parts.'

'And the daughter? Where is she now? Is she

married?'

'She's gone, sir. I don't know where. Not married though, I'll warrant. Not if what they say is true.'

Banks had been looking around the clearing but at this he stopped and looked sharply at the man beside him.

'What do you mean by that?'

'Well, sir,' the steward began uncomfortably, 'I don't pretend to know anything for certain but the women in the village always held that being her father's daughter she was . . . Well, you know, sir. Coming from a family like that.'

If he hoped his employer would take pity on his embarrassment he was disappointed. Banks's questioning gaze forced him to continue.

'Well, there was a lot of talk, sir. About where she went and who she went with. There was no talk of her marrying, sir.'

'Really, Nicholson! That sounds like no more than common gossip.'

'I don't know to be sure. But I saw her for myself, sir, just once since she left here. It was up in Louth on market day. I don't usually go that far but there were some horses I wanted to see. I saw her quite plain up near the church and, well, she was very smartly dressed, sir. Not like we'd ever seen her here in Revesby when her father was alive.'

Banks looked down at his feet while he digested this.

'And she was alone?'

'With Martha, sir. The woman who used to look after her father.'

Banks looked up, his features firmly set and a little stern.

'Thank you, Nicholson. That is very interesting.

But of course it is taking us very far from a proper valuation of all this timber . . .'

With that the two men turned towards the Abbey and continued their inspection, leaving the clearing empty but for the sunshine and a pair of small birds that fluttered quickly to the forest floor when they were gone.

It was another three days before Banks was able to find the time to ride to Louth. During those days it occurred to him more than once that there was no reason for such a visit, yet he went anyway. The fortunes or otherwise of his former neighbours were, he knew, no concern of his; but his return to the woods had stirred memories and he was in a reflective mood as he guided his horse into Louth marketplace. He was frowning as he dismounted.

In Louth he called on friends and inquired after her by name. They were delighted to see him and insisted on his taking tea or wine or luncheon but none of them could help with his inquiry. Next he tried a friend of his father's, a local magistrate who knew the town and its surroundings better than anyone. He seemed puzzled by the request.

'Most likely she is married,' he concluded. 'I probably know her by a different name. You have been away too long, Joseph, to expect everything to stay the same. She is probably the mother of two strapping young boys by now.'

'Indeed.' Banks smiled, uncertain of himself. 'It was only a passing thought. If you had known her whereabouts I would have liked to offer my condolences for the loss of her father.'

'Yes, of course,' replied the older man. 'Very proper. Now why not step this way and sample some of the very excellent port wine that has been sent me by my nephew?'

It was another hour before Banks was once more at liberty. Uncertain how to proceed and feeling a little foolish at the rashness of his expedition, he made his way across the market square towards the church where Nicholson claimed to have seen her. It was late afternoon and the town smelled hot and airless; coming to the churchyard, Banks was happy to sit for a moment in the shade of the lych gate where the air seemed cooler. With the market over for the afternoon the whole town seemed to have fallen silent in the heat, and the churchyard promised shadow and solitude. The church was an old one with an impressive spire, the foot of its walls green-mossed by the passing years. He looked out across the gravestones of the parish and some were fallen into angles and near obliterated by lichen, others were clean and poignant. A private, hidden place. Leaving the shade, he began to make his way around the church, pausing at some of the stones to read their messages, pleased to be thinking of something other than his own foolishness. After a leisurely circling of the church he returned to a long green stone sunk into the grass near the lych gate. It seemed, if possible, even older than the rest but he was unable to decipher its inscription. Coming to it again, he lowered himself onto his haunches and began to scrape with his fingernails at the lichen that hid the names of the souls at rest there. Engrossed by the task, he worked quickly and the first name was almost legible when a voice spoke behind him.

'*Lichen pulmonarius*,' it said.

*   *   *

She often walked that way in the afternoon when the

heat in the little town was oppressive and the churchyard offered peace. It was always a quiet place at that hour and it was rare for her to encounter anyone else within its walls.

But then on that unremarkable August afternoon she turned into the lych gate and was confronted by a figure crouching by a gravestone. She recognised him instantly, from somewhere deep inside, and the shock of it disarmed her. In the days before her father's death she had often imagined how the moment would be if she were to meet him again. But that had been long ago, in Revesby, before her life changed. She had never imagined seeing him in Louth. Even when she had heard, fifth hand, that he had returned and was safe, she had put him out of her mind. It was easier that way.

On seeing him in the churchyard she could only stare. His back was turned. His hair was dressed differently. She must be mistaken. It was too unlikely, it was too impossible. In that hesitation any thought of escape was lost. He was no more than eight yards away from her and the urge to observe him was too strong for her. She heard Martha approaching from behind and held out a hand to make her stop. Then she stood in silence and watched as he worked at the green stone with his nail, until she realised with amazement that she knew what he was scraping at. The words escaped her before she'd even decided to speak.

*   *   *

He turned and looked up so abruptly at the sound of her voice that he almost lost his balance. She was standing at the lych gate, slight and straight, watching him. She was partly concealed by shadow but was instantly familiar, her figure and her face exactly as he remembered. A beautiful face, he thought suddenly, though he had not always thought so. Then she moved so that the light fell differently and in brighter sunshine he noticed differences. She was paler now, he decided, looking for the freckles he remembered and finding them fewer and less prominent. As if she has been too much indoors, he thought.

As he began to step towards her, she seemed to move back but then stopped and stood her ground, her face serious and her eyes meeting his. He opened his mouth to speak, to call her by her name, but as he began she shook her head and held up her hand.

'No, you must not call me by that name. I have a different name here.'

He stopped, no more than a pace away from her.

'Then you are married?'

The shake of her head was almost imperceptible.

'No, I'm not married. Here I am known as Miss Brown.' Her eyes were still meeting his. He looked around awkwardly, not sure what he planned to say or do. Then he met her eyes again.

'Our acquaintance was very short, Miss Brown. There are too few botanical artists in the world for me to neglect them when I meet them. Fewer now than when I saw you last. I would very much like to hear how things have been with you.'

She looked down for a second or so before speaking.

'Martha,' she said, indicating the seat near the lych gate. 'Please wait for me here. I have something to say to Mr Banks.'

He held his arm out to her. When she took it he paused at the touch of her hand and then she moved forward and they stepped out a little stiffly from the lych-gate shadows.

CHAPTER NINE

MYSTERIES

It wasn't until the following evening that Katya and I talked about Joseph Banks's mistress. We spent the day on the tourist trail, driving through weak sunshine from Tudor manor to Georgian pile, paying entry fees and asking questions. There is a part of us all that can rise to the challenge of a search and that day both Katya and I were full of energy and our spirits never flagged. Katya was particularly good. When we found the Old Grange closed for the season she stepped boldly up to the front door and roused a startled woman in pearls. At Pulkington Hall she discovered a bald, red-faced man who seemed so charmed by her interest that he insisted on showing us his greenhouse. Neither of them had ever heard of the Ainsbys.

Not everywhere was shut. We watched cheese being made at Radnors, and at Fairbank we made our own crop circles in the long grass by the Pixie Glen. We found one house that was liberally supplied with cases of stuffed birds, mostly Victorian, which to the surprise of the caretaker we studied with enormous care. By four o'clock the fields were turning grey. It was dark as we drove back to Stamford along unfamiliar roads, our world shrunk to the tunnel of light dug by our headlamps. Suddenly Katya began to laugh.

'Did you see the look on that woman's face when you congratulated her on her stuffed grouse?'

There was a low, happy chuckle in her voice that made me want to smile. But instead I rolled my eyes and grimaced. 'Well, what else could I say? She'd just caught me standing on an antique chair, peering at it.' I began to laugh too. 'Anyway,' I retaliated, 'at least I didn't flirt with anyone. You and that old man in the tea room . . . I thought he was going to insist on coming home with us.'

The oncoming headlights lit up her smile. 'I had to be nice. From the look of him he'd probably been around here in person since 1914. And since you mention it, the woman at the Old Grange definitely liked you. She went all giggly whenever you asked her anything.'

We parked the car near the station and found a dimly lit Italian restaurant where we settled down with a bottle of wine, still laughing at ourselves. After a couple of glasses I pushed the menus to one side and got out the photocopies I'd read the night before.

'You remember we noticed that Joseph Banks had a mistress soon after he came back from his voyage with Cook? Well, I looked her up and guess what I found out.'

'What?'

'Nothing. That's what's interesting. In all the books about him she only seems to exist between the lines. People refer to her but no one tells us anything. They don't even know her name. Here, read this.'

The first sheet was a page from an ageing biography of Banks by a man called Havelock. It was part of a chapter describing the couple of years after Banks's return from his round-the-world expedition with Cook. I'd marked the passage I was interested in.

Little is known about Banks's personal life after the end of his engagement to Miss Blosset. It seems he was content to postpone thoughts of matrimony and concentrate his energies on his scientific calling. However, it is unlikely that a young man of such wealth and good looks would have ignored the fairer sex entirely and it is perhaps unsurprising that there was talk of a mistress. The Town & Country Magazine, *a scurrilous publication that was always ready to lampoon men such as Banks, referred to her only as Miss B—n and suggested that Banks was sufficiently attached to her to install her in rooms in Orchard Street. But, whatever the gossip, it proved a transient affair and after 1774 she is not mentioned again. Happily adventures such as this one did not distract Banks from his scientific duties . . .*

'*Scientific duties* indeed! Patronising sod.' Katya narrowed her eyes and made a little growling sound at the back of her throat. 'I hope none of the fairer sex ever tried to distract Havelock from *his* work.'

'Unlikely, if his prose is anything to go by.'

She turned to the second sheet, a page from a more recent biography.

Although Banks died without children, his affair with Miss B—n seems to have resulted in a pregnancy, at least according to the gossip columnists of the time. On this occasion the gossip may not have been entirely malicious. In 1773 a letter to Banks from Johann Fabricius, who spent a lot of time studying Banks's collection in the 1770s, seems to confirm the rumours: 'My best compliments and wishes in Orchard Street. What has she brought you? Well, it is all the same, if a boy he will be clever and strong like his father, if a girl, she will be pretty and genteel like her mother.' *For all that, there is no further mention of either mother or child and, whether the affair was ended by mutual agreement or by death in childbirth, it is clear that by 1774 it was indeed over.*

*   *   *

Katya pushed the paper back to me and raised her eyebrows.

'Is there a picture of her anywhere?' she asked.

'I'm not sure. We should check it out.'

Katya seemed less sure. 'Sad story,' she said, 'though from a practical point of view we can cross her off our list of suspects if she was gone by 1774. The Ulieta bird didn't even arrive in the country until a year after that.'

I nodded, for a moment not really thinking about the bird; thinking instead of a life unrecorded, of the fragility of human tenderness. 'It *is* sad,' I agreed. 'Sad that no one even knows her name.'

Katya refilled our glasses and held up hers for a toast.

'To solving mysteries,' she said.

'And finding things,' I added, though I wasn't sure if the two were always the same.

That night we both got outrageously drunk. Around us the tables filled and candles were lit and a crackly recording of old Italian songs sobbed away somewhere in the darkness. The evening slipped by effortlessly. Towards the end of the first bottle Katya began to tell me about herself. She told me her family had spent eight years in London while her father taught here. She'd been fourteen when they went back to Sweden and her parents' marriage broke up on their return. She'd spent four or five years after that rebelling against both of them—dropping out of school, living in a squat, trying to do all the things that parents like least.

'So what changed?' I asked her.

'I did. When I was about nineteen.' She smiled a half-smile and gave a slight shrug. 'One day I realised that my life was just boring and miserable. I began to spend whole days in the library, reading. I pretended it was just a way of keeping warm when I had nowhere else to go, but then I found myself sneaking books out at night so that I could carry on. It made me stop and ask who I was trying to punish. A week later I signed up for school again. First, I wrote a long, angry letter to my father telling him it didn't mean I was forgiving him.'

After that the evening grew hazier. Tables began to empty but in our little pool of candlelight we scarcely noticed. We talked about history and politics and wondered aloud whether Joseph Banks had loved his mistress and whether she had loved him. At some point Katya leaned back and, eyeing me solemnly from under her fringe, asked me why I'd changed my mind about finding the bird.

'Who says I changed my mind?' I asked. I was vaguely aware that my thoughts weren't as clear as they had been.

'You *have* changed your mind. Definitely. The

night of the break-in you weren't very sure.'

She leaned forward now and deliberately dipped her head into my eye line so that I had to look at her.

'I suppose I thought Anderson would get there first.'

'And now you don't?'

'It's like he said. This sort of discovery was the one I was always looking for. All that time. I suppose I knew I had to give it another try.' I paused and thought for a moment. I'd reached that point in the evening where it didn't seem to matter if I was making sense or not. 'You know, sometimes someone's born and then they die and they're gone forever. I mean, however hard you try to remember them, you begin to lose them from that day. In the end you're left with something that's made up of fragments of them, little bits of memory and feelings.' I shrugged at her across the candlelight. 'And those are all we have and we should keep them.'

'People? Or do you mean birds?'

I shrugged again. 'Both, I suppose.'

She touched my hand then, but didn't say anything. She looked very lovely in the candlelight.

'And there's another reason for finding it, of course,' I went on solemnly.

She took her hand away and frowned. 'What's that?'

'Well, if that bird outlived Cook and Banks and survived all the wars and fires and floods since then, I'm damned if I'm going to let Anderson flog it off to somebody in a lab in the vague hope that by tearing it apart they may some day come up with a slightly modified chicken.'

She laughed at that and I laughed at myself, and I don't remember much after that, not even how we got back to our rooms, only a moment at the top of the stairs looking at Katya when it would have been easy to forget the photograph by my bedside and that bare room from so long ago with the crumpled bed and the electric fan. Easy to forget everything, in fact. A hazy, fleeting moment, gone before I even thought to grasp it.

A very few hours later I was woken by a series of painful raps on my bedroom door and by Potts's drawling American accent summoning me to breakfast. When I finally made it downstairs, dry-mouthed and a little croaky, Potts was settled neatly in the bit of the lounge bar where they served food. By daylight the bar seemed stained and tatty again and the air smelled of stale cigarette smoke.

'Over here, Mr Fitzgerald,' he said, beckoning me. 'I already checked out of the George. I thought I'd get these folks to cook me breakfast. I thought we could talk while we eat.'

He was as immaculate as before, this time in a suit of purple and green tweed, Santa Claus dressed for a grouse shoot. As he helped himself to coffee he explained that Smith, Anderson's detective, had left Stamford the night before. His departure meant there wasn't much reason to stay.

'That letter looks like a dead end,' he told me. 'I'm off to London to look for Anderson and to check out a couple of other little things too.'

I nibbled dully at a triangle of cold toast and couldn't think of anything useful to say. In front of me Potts demolished an enormous cooked breakfast.

'You know how old I am, Mr Fitzgerald?' he asked. 'I'm seventy years old next birthday. And do you know what I've learned in all those years? I've learned that breakfast is the only meal the British haven't managed to ruin. Jeez, some of the hotel dinners I've had in this country . . .'

He paused, dabbing at the corner of his mouth with a paper napkin. 'You know the other thing I've learned? I've learned to know when I'm wasting my time. And no matter how you look at it, neither of us is doing much good round here, peering into priest-holes and laughing at rare breeds of sheep. The answer's somewhere else.'

With that he settled to the remains of his breakfast and kept me busy with questions about what Katya and I had done the previous day. When he'd mopped the last traces of baked beans from his plate, he pulled a ten-pound note out of his wallet and pushed it under the salt pot.

'That should cover it,' he announced. Then he looked at me for a moment and pulled something else out of his wallet. 'Know who this is?' he asked.

I recognised her at once. Not a photograph, but a photocopy of an old print, the sort of cheap, printed portrait that was common in the eighteenth century—grainy, blurred and executed with no great finesse. It was a neat, pretty face, small-featured, unremarkable. And yet despite the journeyman haste of the work, the artist had caught something in the eyes that made the portrait oddly striking; something intelligent and compelling.

I looked up at Potts. 'Where did this come from?'

'It was lying around in Anderson's hotel room.'

'I didn't know you'd seen Anderson.'

'I haven't. I've no idea where he is. But I found out he'd kept his room at the Mecklenburg. So I went in and had a look through his papers.' Again that benign smile. 'Oh, don't look so shocked, Mr Fitzgerald. I just wandered around the corridor looking lost until a maid with a vacuum cleaner let me in.' He gave me a slightly rueful smile. 'There wasn't much to see. A copy of the letter we already have. Then a big bundle of photocopies of books and articles about Joseph Banks. Nothing very exciting. This picture was near the bottom and it kinda caught my eye. So I brought it with me.'

I gave him the picture back as coolly and as carelessly as I could manage. 'I'm sorry,' I said, 'I've no idea who she is.' And then I took a long, slow swig of tea. Because whoever she was, Hans Michaels had found her. And when Michaels sat down to make a sketch of her portrait, it was because she was the clue he thought would lead him to the Ulieta bird.

Potts shrugged and put the picture away, then stood up and shook my hand. As he headed for the door with his bags, I called after him.

'Mr Potts?' He turned back to me. 'That picture. Would you mind if I took a copy, just in case I come across it again?'

He put down his bags and took out the picture again, looking at it with new curiosity. 'Well, well,' he muttered. 'So it *is* important.'

'I don't know any more than you do,' I told him, almost truthfully. 'It just . . . Well, I don't have many leads.'

He regarded me briefly then placed the piece of paper on the table nearest him. 'It's yours. Keep it.' He picked up his bags again. 'I always keep copies.'

When he'd gone I stayed in the bar, smoking and drinking tea until Katya joined me. She helped herself to fruit juice and cereal and as she ate she studied the picture and listened to my account of breakfast with Potts. She looked amazingly fresh after her late night. I watched her eat with a sort of awe. Sometimes you forget how beautiful youth can be.

That afternoon in Louth the sun shone and the little churchyard seemed heavy with summer. No one else came to the lych gate and the high hedges muffled the sleepy movements of the town. Where the two figures sat side by side near the long grass there was only the noise of insects and the rustle of small birds foraging.

As she talked he looked ahead, at the moss on the gravestones or the honey stone of the church wall. From time to time she paused and studied his profile, still wondering at his being there, almost prepared to find herself mistaken.

'When we last met,' she began, 'my father was dying. He fell from the road when he was both drunk and angry. It's well known in Revesby that he attacked John Ponsonby at his own table, in front of his wife and daughters. You must have heard that. I believe he struck him with his fist as Mr Ponsonby rose to face him. Anyone in Revesby will tell you the details. It was what they expected of a man like my father: a non-believer, a man who let his daughter run wild in the woods. What they don't know is why my father went to the Ponsonby house that night. It was because everything he owned he'd sold to Ponsonby and that day he realised the sale included his own daughter.'

She let herself look at him. He was sitting leaning forwards, his forearms resting on his knees. She couldn't see his eyes but she could see the tension in the line of his jaw and the way he rubbed the knuckles of one hand with the fingers of the other. Sensing her hesitation, he turned and she found she could not read the expression in his eyes. Looking down, she continued.

'John Ponsonby is not all bad, though I have not

always thought so. If I tell you about him you must promise to take no action against him, must tell no one.'

Banks turned his head away again and ran his palm across the back of his neck. 'Of course,' he replied, flat-voiced. 'Please continue.'

*   *   *

She was nearly fourteen when Ponsonby first noticed her. He had seen her in the distance, early one summer evening as he approached Revesby on horseback. She was wearing white and she stood out against the green of the hedgerows in the late sunlight. Almost unthinkingly he found himself intrigued by the slim straight figure alone on the lane in front of him. By her carriage, a lady, he thought, although a lady would not be unaccompanied; yet surely too poised to be a village girl. As he drew nearer, he found himself stirred by the piquancy of that female neatness so alone; and he spurred his horse on at a trot.

Ponsonby was not by nature a libertine but his business took him well beyond the narrow morality of the village; and his indulgence in the habits of well-to-do young men had never quite ceased upon his marriage. There was nothing unusual in that, and in matters of personal conduct he did not feel himself any better or worse than his peers. Nevertheless, he had always conducted his liaisons at a discreet distance from his home. Indeed it had never occurred to him that Revesby itself could provide anyone to excite his amorous instincts. He therefore felt a slight shock when he came up to the figure in the lane and recognised the daughter of one of his debtors, a girl of no more than fourteen. He stopped beside her under the pretext of a greeting and took time to study her. She was, after all, nothing unusual, he thought: still little more than a girl, nothing striking or beautiful in her features. And yet he noticed her eyes, very deep and very green, and wondered if perhaps he had not been entirely mistaken.

From that day on he noticed her more and more. He would glimpse her in the woods or picking flowers in the hedgerows, always alone, supple and graceful, returning his gaze boldly with that clear, unafraid face. He took to calling on her father, something few in the village would do. When he called he would find the father either talkative or sullen, the daughter always short with him to the point of rudeness. Piqued by such unaccustomed treatment, his visits became more frequent.

She felt his interest in her from the first and instinctively sought to avoid him. Wherever they met she was aware of his gaze asking her questions and in company the smile he saved for her seemed to invite complicity as if they shared a secret. Worse, she knew that many of Ponsonby's visits involved the signing of papers. After those visits her father's spirits would rise and he would drink more freely. As his debts grew she felt the trap closing, yet even as she watched her father edging towards ruin she was aware of her love for him like a sharpening pain. The more fallible he revealed himself to be, the more she loved him. Even while she chafed at Ponsonby's attentions, part of her gave thanks for the money that allowed her father to buy his own sort of peace. And if Ponsonby's smile suggested a secret between them, perhaps she could not in truth deny it. They both watched her father and waited.

She was fifteen when the interview she had always imagined finally took place. It was late spring and there were still yellow crocuses at her door. That year Ponsonby had watched the girlishness grow out of her figure and, half believing her father's radical rhetoric, was afraid to wait longer lest he be forestalled. He wasn't proud of the suggestion he intended to make but she inspired a sort of desperation in him that he could neither understand nor escape. So he waited until he knew she was alone and then he called.

She knew at once that this visit was different. But he was her father's only friend and she was only fifteen; she could see no other course but to allow him inside. In the doorway of the small parlour he took her arm as she passed and drew her close to him so that she was only inches from his chest. At his touch she became suddenly quiescent, as if by standing very still she could be safe. She could smell the tobacco on his clothes, even the faint scent of sandalwood on his skin. They were smells that were always to remind her of him.

The sensation of her body so close to his shocked him with a sudden arousal and made him more decided. He had at first hesitated but now the thought that this soft, shivering creature should be anyone's but his filled him with an aching jealousy. He realised how much he wanted her.

'Please,' he said. 'I have things I must say to you.'

She stood, her head down, and gave no sign of understanding.

'I've watched you grow up unnoticed here,' he went on. 'I swear to you that you are worth more than anyone in this place will ever know. You have the sort of beauty they don't recognise, an intellect they cannot understand. You are different. And you're wasted here, with a father who doesn't think of you, in a house no one respectable will ever visit. There's no future for you here, no chance of an honest marriage because your father has delighted in making you unmarriageable. He boasts to anyone who'll listen that he has raised you a heathen, that you have learned no rules or religion to check your natural passions. The women here think you a wanton and the men know you to be a pauper. They forbid their daughters to speak to you lest your presence corrupt them.'

'I have no wish to speak to them,' she said quietly, her head still bowed.

'So what can the future hold for you here?' His tone was low, almost begging. 'It breaks my heart to see you here. There will be a time when your father will not be able to protect you. What then?'

Still she said nothing and suddenly his tone changed.

'Who knows? Perhaps what they say is true. Perhaps you already understand ways an attractive young girl with no money can hope to make a living? Perhaps if I were to scratch at the surface of your reserve, some of those natural passions would rise to the surface? Would they? Is that not the truth?' He tightened his grip and held her closer but she stayed limp and unresponsive, her eyes still turned away from his. With a half-sigh he let her go and took a step back from her. His voice was more controlled when he next spoke.

'I beg you, do not go wasting your virtue on some village boy, some clumsy farmer's son. You must believe me that you are too good for that.'

He paused and moved to the window, looked out over the lane. She remained where she had stood from the beginning, her eyes tracing meaningless patterns in the floorboards at her feet.

A silence ticked by between them and when he turned to her again his voice was strangely tender.

'When the time comes that you have nowhere else to go, come to me. I will take you away from this place, give you the books and clothes you cannot have here. You need a world beyond this place.'

She made no reply, no sign of having heard.

'The way you receive them makes my words sound like a threat. That is not how they are intended. Let me assure you I do not intend to coerce. I shall not make you return to this conversation unless you wish it. But I want you to understand that there is one person who appreciates your value. And if you are ever in need, I beg you to turn to me.'

When he left, she did not move to show him out. She simply remained where she was, her thoughts blank, until the light had faded, until the sound of her father's return forced her back to herself.

*   *   *

When she paused in her story there was silence in the little churchyard. Instead of responding, Banks stood up and took a few slow steps away from her, towards the corner of the church. He stayed there for a moment and she waited, watching him. When he turned and looked at her, she met his gaze with eyes that were clear and unafraid. Standing there in front of her in the silence of the summer evening, Banks knew he had to speak. But words wouldn't come. He found a pain and an anger inside him that seemed to make speech impossible.

'All those weeks in Revesby I was so blind,' he said at last. 'I should have seen, should have taken steps . . .'

She shook her head before he could finish. 'No, please do not say so. Those days in the woods . . . None of the rest of it seemed to matter. There were

141

only my drawings and the plants around us. Those days gave me more than you can know. They let me see that there will always be some things that are my own.'

And sitting there on the cold stone waiting for him to speak, she realised she had misunderstood. It was *he* who needed comforting. He who had travelled the whole world was the one lost, the one struggling to understand. She who had been nowhere knew so much more. So she rose and went to him and held out her hand.

'The afternoon is getting cooler. If you do not have to go, let us walk a little as we talk.'

He watched her approach and once again he found it difficult to speak. Instead, when she came level with him, he allowed her to take his arm and guide him slowly along the path around the sleeping church.

As they walked, she finished her story. Ponsonby had kept his word. After that visit he had seemed content to let the distance grow between them. His calls became less frequent and when he came it was usually at her father's invitation. Those discussions were always of money and left her father both excited and unsettled. He was drinking every evening now, alone in his study, and soon she began to fear for his physical health. She would often find him unconscious at his desk, brandy spilt over his papers and his breathing uneven. During the day he was flushed and unsteady and increasingly forgetful. He seemed to find it hard to concentrate. As the weeks passed she watched him slowly breaking down and the pain of her love for him grew sharper. She knew she would accept any suffering for his sake; but he was asking her to stand aside while he courted destruction. She held close to herself and tried to give him what he asked, knowing how forgetfulness eased his pain. But when she finally could take no more she chose the wrong words and the wrong time.

For some days previously he had been short-tempered and unable to rest. Finally one afternoon he scribbled a note and left the house in a hurry. She knew where he was going but said nothing. That evening Mr Ponsonby called and spent an hour with her father. When he was gone her father emerged from his study transformed, almost euphoric in his good humour.

'That man Ponsonby is a good fellow but a fool,' he declared. 'He has agreed to advance me a substantial sum against the sale of certain books in my library. Oh, I don't doubt the value of the volumes under discussion. I'm sure his money is secure. But in the matter of interest he is unnecessarily restrained. He says he does not wish to profit from a neighbour. And that must surely make him a fool.'

She listened to his words and felt sick inside. It was his blindness that hurt her most. Before she was able to pause and think, the words had escaped her.

'I'm sure Mr Ponsonby sees his interest paid in a different currency,' she said.

It was an ugly scene. At first he raged and she tried in vain to explain her words in any way other than the one she had intended. But there was no escaping what she'd said and her father was relentless. He pushed her and pushed her, drawing out the truth in tiny drops even as she begged him not to believe her. When he had heard everything, he turned his invective on his neighbour, repeating every word that had passed between them, finding betrayal in every smile, spluttering with rage at every mention of his name. It took her an hour to calm him. She swore herself false, promised him her suspicions were girlish fancy, praised

Ponsonby for a hundred qualities she had never before imagined; and she wept a little at her father's anger until eventually he became calmer.

'Leave me for a while,' he said at last. 'You have given me a great deal to think about.' And as he retired to his study she even dared to hope that her outburst might have done some good; that he might at least reconsider any further borrowing.

She did not hear him go out. She only became aware of his absence when she began to prepare for bed. Her knock on his door went unanswered and, afraid that he had drunk himself to sleep, she entered the study and found him gone. He had left behind him the smell of brandy and the start of a note that consisted only of her name. It was three hours later when the men brought him home and carried him to his room.

*   *   *

'And so,' she said, leaning a little more heavily on Banks's arm, 'I was to blame. And when you become accustomed to that, there is little else with the power to hurt.'

They walked on for a while. The sun was still warm but the shadows were longer now and she could feel a shiver growing inside her. She had never imagined telling him of this, never imagined walking with her arm through his. She found that the very fact of the moment, even though it seemed to her so desperate, made her in some way happy. But now she had reached the part of her story that could not be avoided. She waited for him to speak, to tell her to go on. She held her shoulders rigid to make sure the shiver could not happen.

'And so,' he began awkwardly, 'when your father died . . .'

'Yes,' she said simply, and waited for the meaning to be clear. 'There was nowhere else to turn.'

He paused again, his mind reeling, conflicting voices telling him to ask more, to ask nothing, to speak, to be silent.

'And?' He looked away as he asked the question.

'There was no money to pay for the funeral, so he provided it. Everything I thought of as mine was really his.'

'So he made you . . .?'

She stopped him then, pulling his arm so they came to a halt in front of the church door. She turned him to face her so that he had no choice but to look into her eyes.

'No,' she said, looking up at him. 'He would have allowed me to pursue any alternative had there been one. But there wasn't. I had nothing. A young woman with no money and no character, not brought up to serve, not fit to teach the children of decent people because she was raised with no religion and no morals. A woman known to meet a man in the woods and to return smiling each day. Do you see? Do you understand? He didn't make me. He didn't need to. I sent for him. All I asked was to live under a different name so that my father's critics would not hear of it and jeer.'

Her hand on his arm meant he could not move on and she was looking up at him with eyes full of fire. He had never before considered the price she might pay for their meetings, but he thought of it now. In his eyes she could see the pain and uncertainty but she carried on, relentless.

'He was gentle with me. Do you understand? He

145

did everything he could to make it right for me. His demands were never excessive. He has never alluded to my poverty, never reminded me of what I owe him. Never used it to humiliate me. He tries everything he knows to make me happy. And I let him try because it is all I can do in return.'

Still she looked at him and, as he looked down at her, the light in her eyes seemed to burn into him. He had never seen eyes so green, so bright; never seen eyes blaze as hers did.

The shadows were lengthening but the place where they stood remained in full sunlight. She saw the struggle in his face, saw words beginning to form on his lips, and she braced her shoulders tighter. When he spoke, his voice sounded raw.

'Come away with me,' he said. A blackbird flew from the undergrowth and passed by them with a cry. 'Come away with me,' he said again, more urgently. 'You have an alternative now.' Suddenly he smiled. 'I swear I will ask nothing of you but that you talk to me of lichen. And that you draw every day until your drawings astonish the world.'

As he spoke she felt such warmth rushing into her that she shivered. The fierce urging she had tried to forget was alive again, raging inside her. She knew that part of what he said was false; she knew that no one asked for nothing. But whatever the price to pay she would be alive again. She would be wondrously, wildly alive.

CHAPTER TEN

WORDS, PICTURES

It's an obvious thing to say, but journeys do not always lead where you expect. We'd been looking for a bird, but we'd found a face in a picture: the face of a woman with striking eyes and no name. For the next couple of days, pictures obsessed us. We began with the best portraits of the age, a morning in the National Portrait Gallery and a bizarre sort of identity parade. In the end it didn't take us long; there were many more portraits of men than women in the eighteenth-century galleries and after less than an hour we'd run out of suspects. So then we started again, this time looking at the men, in search of a family resemblance, enjoying ourselves and laughing until we found ourselves by accident in front of the portrait of Joseph Banks. While other visitors flowed past, we stood and looked at it in stillness, suddenly sober again.

It's a striking portrait. It shows Banks as a young man recently returned from his great voyage. He is seated in his study and there are papers on his desk, but his body is half turned away from them, engaging the painter directly with his eyes. His expression seems solemn at first but as you look properly you begin to detect the trace of a smile on his lips. It's the same with his eyes: behind the direct, neutral gaze there is a lightness that belies his gravity, a laughing young man peeping out from behind a serious façade. Of all the figures in the

147

paintings around him there is not one that looks so alive.

'Mmm,' murmured Katya, slightly salaciously. 'Attractive. Not handsome but definitely attractive. It's the good humour in his face. And the intelligence. You just know he was interested in things. The sort of man a girl could like.' And as we looked at him and he looked back, I knew she was right. The painting was by Reynolds and he had captured on the canvas an aura of youth and confidence and vitality that shone through the paint. It was hard to imagine that this man's company would ever be dull. Easy to imagine him living and loving. We stood and watched him with our shoulders touching until with a silent nod we agreed to go. As we walked down the main stairs I reached into my pocket and took out the other portrait we had, the photocopy Potts had given me. That picture had none of Reynolds's sumptuous paint to distinguish it. Just a woman's face, ordinary, unremarkable, anonymous. And yet, like Banks's, her smile caught your attention and reminded you this was a person too.

That afternoon we started in the British Library, working through every book of portraits we could find, scanning the faces of Georgian society in the hope that one would smile back at us with that slight, shy smile. It was mind-numbing work and the great hush of the library began to grow oppressive. I don't know how many women we looked at that day: the volumes of miniatures alone contained many hundreds of faces. By late afternoon we were shattered. A couple of suspects had been unearthed who bore a slight resemblance to the picture in front of us but neither was similar enough to lift our spirits. Instead our thoughts turned to food, and that night I cooked Katya dinner in the comforting warmth of my kitchen. We lit a candle and drank cold beer from the bottle and sat up late talking about sex and politics in the 1780s. At one point she sat back in her chair and smiled.

'What?' I asked. 'What's so funny?'

'We are,' she said. 'Come on, let's have another beer.'

The next day we returned to the British Library and carried on. By mid-morning we'd exhausted the books of portraits so we returned to biographies. After the biographies of Banks we began on the biographies of Banks's friends and associates—anything with pictures was good enough for us. Katya worked through the pile quicker than I did and eventually she came to an enticingly large volume in worn leather bindings.

'*Town & Country Magazine* for 1774 and 1775,' I explained in a whisper. 'Somewhere in there is the gossip item about Banks and his mistress. It's worth checking out.' She looked up at me and shrugged and then we both returned to the drudgery of searching.

It took me a little while to realise that Katya had stopped turning the pages. I looked up and saw she was sitting very still, her dark hair falling away from her face as she leaned over the book. Her eyes were full of something very like wonder.

'I've found her,' she said softly.

I got up and moved round the table to see what she was looking at. I could tell at once she was right. It was a small, grainy print, the sort of illustration churned out cheaply for the cheap press. There wasn't even any guarantee that it was an accurate likeness of the person it purported to be. But it was definitely the original of the grimy photocopy we had in front of us, definitely the same picture that Hans Michaels had once sketched.

'His mistress.' Katya was scarcely audible. 'Miss B. The one who disappears from the records.'

I had been looking at portraits of women for two days—the plain, the pretty, the wholesome, the lustrous. Many of them were people you'd notice quickly in a crowded room, but this woman's attractiveness wasn't like that. Her face was small, almost ordinary, but her eyes held you. Perhaps, in a crowded room, when you grew tired of the noise and the social trivialities, perhaps this was the woman you'd seek out.

'So we've found her,' I said, resting my hand on Katya's shoulder. 'Hans Michaels's woman. The clue to the bird. So tell me, now we've done that, what the hell do we do now?'

*　　　*　　　*

It wasn't until we'd left the British Library and stood facing each other in the courtyard outside it that Katya answered the question. 'I'll tell you what we do,' she began. 'We track her down. We find out who she really is and where she lived and what happened to her.'

The wind swirled around the courtyard and plucked Katya's scarf away from her face so that she had to pause to tuck it back in.

'And you have a plan for how we do that?' I wasn't feeling optimistic.

150

'No, but I will.' I could sense that her enthusiasm was burning bright again. 'Look, I have an idea. I'll see you at home this afternoon. By then I'll have worked it out.'

I was less convinced. We had found the original of Hans Michaels's sketch but we still didn't have any idea what linked her to the Ulieta bird. We didn't even know her name. Worse than that, *no one* seemed to know her name. She had appeared in 1773 as Joseph Banks's mistress. By the end of 1774 she'd disappeared. And there lay the catch. Because the bird from Ulieta didn't even arrive in Britain until 1775. I didn't like to say so but our prospects were looking pretty forlorn.

Katya and I said goodbye on the Euston Road and I watched her moving off towards St Pancras, her dark head bobbing along until I lost it in the eddying crowds. Then I thrust my hands a little deeper into my pockets and tried to refocus my thoughts. By rights I should have been going home to catch up on some work, but the idea never even occurred to me. Instead, I found myself a pub and a pint and settled down with the notes I'd made about the item in *Town & Country Magazine*.

As a bit of society gossip it was a surprisingly modern piece of work, all moral righteousness on the surface and sly innuendo underneath, and the more I looked at it, the more wary I became. Even so, it seemed a simple enough tale. Miss B—n was an orphan; Banks had known her when she was a girl, before his voyage on the *Endeavour*; on his return he had sought her out. There was no clue as to where he had sought her or where she had come from, nothing to suggest where she might suddenly have disappeared in the months after the magazine was published.

And this was all we had. Without this one piece of cheap, lazy writing there would be nothing to tell us that she had ever existed. It was the single feather hinting at the unknown bird. And that was not a comforting thought.

*   *   *

When James Chapin brought his mysterious feather back from the Congo it convinced my grandfather that his theories were true: an undiscovered peacock really *did* exist in Africa. Grimly, with a determination that defied logic, he set out to prove it. He began to plan an expedition to Africa that would search the jungles until specimens were found. All he needed were supplies, transport and the money to pay for them—and it was at that point that he began to encounter obstacles. Until then my grandfather's travels had been conducted largely at his own expense but now he found that his family fortunes were beginning to run a little thin. Even so, he had good connections, wealthy friends and no shortage of optimism. So he made the announcement that he intended to lead an expedition to the Congo to obtain specimens of a peacock previously unknown to western science—and waited for funds and support to come rolling in. It proved a long wait. To his amazement his theory was laughed at. A few lines of dubious Latin and a single feather did not strike the rest of the world as evidence of anything very much. It was made clear to him, painfully and repeatedly, that he would need much more by way of evidence before anyone would be disposed to hand over hard cash. Astonished at this lack of faith, he found himself alone and unsupported.

A different man might have accepted this setback and resolved to put it behind him but my grandfather's pride was hurt and he refused to give up. The more scepticism he encountered, the more evangelical he became, and years of frustration ensued while he became almost a laughing stock in scientific circles: the man people avoided at parties, the man who was unsound on peacocks.

Sitting by the Euston Road and looking at my notes about Miss B, I found myself feeling uneasy at the parallels. All I had was a picture and I didn't even know what it meant. Compared to that, my grandfather's case was positively watertight. A little unsettled, I headed home to look for Katya, but when I got there she'd already gone. The only sign of her was a note pinned by the stairs: *City of Westminster Archives, 10 St Ann's Street, SW1*.

*   *   *

We live in a society that is strangely superstitious about written records. Even while we're content to countenance the tearing down of rainforests and the destruction of countless unknown organisms every day, we hold on grimly to our documents and papers. Few of us are immune to this. I keep notes about dead birds for a book I won't write. Other people keep bills or bank statements or the unsolicited menus of long-closed takeaways. Our national archives bulge with ephemera that may one day transform themselves into history. The Victorian railway builders who demolished irreplaceable Tudor houses were careful to preserve for posterity the details of what they spent on iron and timber. And before that, when the enclosure of land was making an ancient landscape disappear without record, parish clerks were carefully detailing the beginnings and ends of lives that now exist only in their crumbling ledgers.

I found Katya in the research room of the Westminster archives, tucked away in a corner behind a large microfilm reader. At first I didn't recognise her. Her hair was tied up tightly and her brow was furrowed with lines of concentration that made me hesitate. Around her the room was warm and smelled very faintly of damp coats. Down one side of the room there were a couple of rows of filing cabinets and in its centre a cluster of terminals where a group of elderly women with handbags had congregated and were comparing notes.

Katya scarcely looked up when I walked over to her corner and didn't say hello. She just smiled and pointed to the chair next to her, then carried on, working rapidly with both hands on the reels of the microfilm viewer, spinning it deftly backwards and forwards.

'Am I interrupting something?' I asked, but she carried on turning, and pages of old copperplate handwriting skidded across the screen. I glimpsed names, dates, places.

'Shit!' she said suddenly and stopped turning the pages, her voice loud enough to make the elderly women turn and look. 'You've made me miss what I was looking for.'

'I'm sorry,' I said and our eyes met and held for a moment. Abruptly she turned back to the screen and smiled to herself.

'So you should be. Leaving me to do all the work.' She began to wind the handles back in the other direction, much slower now, until she found the place she was looking for. 'Here, look at this. Marylebone Parish rate books for 1774.'

Lit up in front of me were the pages of an old ledger, a photographic image of the time-stained, torn-edged original. The left-hand column was a list of addresses and next to each was a name, a date and a sum of money. Halfway down the page I saw the words *Orchard Street* and the date *April 30th 1774*. Each house number in the street had a name beside it except one. Next to Number 24 the space was blank.

'If the gossip is true, Orchard Street is where Miss B lived,' Katya reminded me, turning to see my reaction.

'So what does this mean?' I asked her, not sure of her point.

'24 Orchard Street is blank. That means the place was vacant when the collector called. Now look at this . . .'

She wound the microfilm through to the end, slid it out of the slot and dropped in a different film. She found the place she wanted with only a few turns of the wheel.

'Look. Orchard Street. Same set of addresses, one year earlier. This is 8th June 1773.'

The writing was clear:

24 Orchard Street Joseph Banks Esq

Katya turned to me again. 'I started in 1772, just to be safe. In '72 it was let to a Mr Metcalfe. In June 1773, the place was taken by Banks, just like

155

the gossip column said. And then by April 1774 the place is vacant.'

'So what does that mean?'

'It means the affair was over by then.'

'He could just have moved her somewhere else.'

Katya shook her head. 'She's never mentioned again, is she? All the books we've read agree on that. Perhaps she went to another man. Or Banks might have got bored of her and paid her to leave town.'

'There is another option, you know.'

Katya pulled a face. 'I know. And that one's the most likely. Death during childbirth. Or just after.'

'And her child. There's no mention of Banks having children, not even illegitimate ones.'

We looked at each other a little sombrely for a moment. Then Katya turned back to the screen and began to rewind the film. 'At least there's a way we can check.'

I raised an eyebrow. 'How?'

'Easy.' She finished winding and lifted the microfilm out of the reader. 'We check the Marylebone Parish registers of births and deaths. I can do it tomorrow. I just go through all the deaths in 1773 and 1774 and look for any woman whose name begins with B and ends in N.'

'But you might find dozens.'

'Well, at least that would give us some real names to check out, wouldn't it?'

I considered that. 'OK . . . So what if you don't find any names that fit? What then?'

She shrugged and looked me very firmly in the eye.

'Then we look somewhere else. If your friend Hans Michaels can find a connection, so can we.'

156

The next couple of days did very little to reward her optimism. Katya and I spent a morning up near Farringdon checking the parish registers but astonishingly there were no entries in the register of deaths that matched the name 'B—n'. Which, as Katya pointed out, could just mean she died somewhere else. But even though we'd run out of ideas about what to do next, neither of us seemed able to give up the chase. Anderson had been right: the Ulieta bird was the great discovery I never made, the event that some part of me still seemed to be waiting for; it was useless now to pretend I didn't care. I spent my time in the various London archives, flapping like a bird of ill omen over long lists of the dead. Katya would join me when she could, and we'd either squeeze together in front of one screen, or work side by side in companionable silence. But we still had no way of knowing how the picture of Miss B was linked with the bird, and there didn't seem any obvious way of finding out. As to the bird itself, we simply had no idea.

The Monday evening was stormy and the rain was lashing against the windows of my kitchen when I began to cook dinner. The ancient boiler was muttering throatily in response to the weather, making the kitchen warm and inviting. Katya came home just as the pans were beginning to bubble and we ate together with the lights low and the rain pleasingly impotent against the windows. Neither of us had anything to report so we opened a bottle of wine and didn't talk about the bird at all. The warmth and the wine perked us up and brought a sort of release; soon we were chatting happily, and when the bottle was finished, I got up to open a second. Instead of waiting, Katya came over and stood next to me.

'About the bird,' she began. 'You're going to have to do the searching without me for a day or two. I've got to go back to Sweden. Just for a few days. I won't be gone very long. There's a couple of things I need to do.' She took the bottle out of my hands and back to the table, where she started to pour.

'That's a bit sudden, isn't it?' I asked, watching her.

She glanced round at me. 'It's probably all a waste of time but it's stuff I've got to do. I'll tell you all about it when I get back.' I'd stayed standing, so she picked up both glasses and brought them over to me. 'Come on, another drink to see me off.'

I sipped the wine and said something that made her laugh, but although the rest of the evening went well, the kitchen seemed a slightly sadder place. Searching for the bird by myself didn't seem so appealing now. And when I woke up the next morning, Katya was already gone.

Richmond. Fashionable and discreet, where an orphaned young lady staying with a respectable old woman could live a quiet and genteel existence. Where, if she did not seek attention, she would remain unattended. Where, correctly chaperoned, she could walk on the hill or draw in the woods to her heart's content. Where an old friend from London could visit from time to time and take tea before returning home. Richmond, where in the summer of 1771 the arrival of quiet and unremarkable Miss Brown to live with elderly and deaf Mrs Jenkins, widow of a Revesby pensioner, went largely and happily unnoticed.

She took Martha with her as maid and attendant. Between them they set out to learn the things they had to learn: the conventions to respect, the rules to obey and the exercise of freedoms that neither had ever before encountered. They were given time to learn. Banks, determined to prove himself a disinterested benefactor, visited rarely but wrote often, anxious they should have all the things they needed. That was why, one morning three weeks after their arrival from Lincolnshire, five large packages arrived addressed to Miss Brown containing all manner of materials for drawing and painting. She spent a morning unpacking them, running her fingers over each one as it was removed from its paper, lost in awe that she should be the object of such fortune. Many years later, when she recalled those weeks, they always seemed to her to have happened to someone else, someone only a little like her. From the moment she stepped into the churchyard at Louth and saw him in front of her, the famous Joseph Banks kneeling as if she had somehow summoned him, none of it seemed quite real.

He had acted swiftly after their encounter in Lincolnshire, as if goaded by the thought of Ponsonby's visits to the house in Louth. In casting around for a family where she could stay respectably he had quickly thought of Mrs Jenkins, ageing widow of a long-serving steward to his father, whose small cottage on the edge of Richmond was paid for by the Revesby estate. She was neither a gossip nor a busybody and as an invalid was pleased to have genteel company. That settled, he set about arranging her carriage and funds for the journey. He spared neither time nor money, and Solander, who watched this act of philanthropy executed with the precision and urgency of a naval raid, began to wonder at the nature of its recipient. Within days Banks had sent word to Louth that all was arranged.

It was left to her to decide how she would manage her departure from the house where John Ponsonby had installed her. Unsure how to proceed, unsure what would happen, she decided to write to him, informing him that she was to leave for London. The tone of her note was formal but he arrived within hours to shred that formality, shouting, questioning, pacing, begging her to tell him what she planned. This she would not do; and, watching his angry gesticulations, she felt an overwhelming sadness at the thought of the intimacy she had shared with him—this flawed, confused stranger. Yes, she thought as she watched him, still a stranger despite everything, because a stranger was what she'd always needed him to be. She waited for him to threaten her, perhaps to forbid her to leave, to remind her of the debt she owed him. But after a time he became quiet and turned from her. She could hear him taking deep, slow breaths and she waited for him

160

to speak, as she had once waited before, when she was fifteen. Only this time, she realised, everything was changed.

'I have always told you that you are free to go,' he said at last. 'I will not break my word now. I would consider it a kindness if you were to tell me of any requirements you have, anything you need to ease your journey.'

Then his voice sank low, became a voice she scarcely recognised.

'To lose you so suddenly is hard to comprehend. But I have always been waiting for this. I have tried to pretend otherwise, for both our sakes, but I know you have never chosen to be here with me. I told you once you were wasted on Revesby; I never dared to tell you how much you were wasted on me. It was only a matter of time before someone saw that, as I once saw it. I hope he knows your worth. He should know that one day you might find someone more deserving of your attention than he.'

He turned and tried to smile but she saw he was not able. There were tears in his eyes as he spoke.

'You owe me nothing—and I owe you a great deal. Two years of your company I have never deserved and will not forget.'

She looked at him as he stood, suddenly small and unhappy in front of her, and part of the great barrier of reserve she had held so firmly between them began to tremble at its edges. Her body felt her own again. There were so many things for which she would never forgive him but, at the last, she felt so much more forgiveness than she had ever thought possible.

The next day she left Lincolnshire.

*   *   *

Banks saw her deliverance from Louth as something shining and noble that he had achieved. In the euphoria of those days of fame and advancement he was prepared to ignore the innuendoes of his friends in return for the knowledge that he had acted selflessly to right a wrong; and while he was busy on London business it was convenient to think of her as little more than a vehicle for his own good nature, a curiosity he had discovered and befriended. But when he was with her, that simplicity became a great deal more complicated.

Each time he visited Richmond he planned to play the part of the modest benefactor, cutting short with proper grace any unbecoming shows of gratitude. But that was never how things were. The second time he called on her, she had already been in Richmond seven weeks and a very young maid whom he didn't recognise answered the door and showed him into a small front parlour. There he waited, and he continued to wait for what seemed an unpardonable amount of time, his rehearsed speech of solicitude fading from his thoughts, until he heard the sound of female laughter from the corridor beyond. Just as he recognised her voice, the door opened enough for a head to fit around it.

'I'm afraid, sir, you are the victim of a misunderstanding,' she laughed. 'Have you been waiting here a *very* long time?'

He attempted to muster the dignity of a slighted benefactor. 'A full ten minutes, I believe.'

She laughed again, apparently unconcerned by his manner.

'That was stupid of me. I'm sorry. I told Jenny I was working and would be down shortly, and then I lost myself in what I was doing. I had intended her to tell you I was working.'

'And if she had?' he asked. 'Ten minutes would still be ten minutes.' By now they were looking each other in the eye and he was beginning to find his own stiffness ridiculous.

'Really, sir.' She came into the room properly now and he saw she was dressed formally in a way he had not yet grown to expect. Her hair was drawn up like that of every lady he knew and yet she still looked different. 'Really, if you were told I was working, I thought after a time you would find your way up. You have watched me draw before, as I recall. And I give you full licence to interrupt me without invitation.'

'I should never dream . . .'

'Of course not,' she interrupted him, laughter in her voice but her face formed into an expression of seriousness. 'That would be to take advantage of your position. I should have understood that you would never do that. But truly, sir'—her voice now bright again—'I release you from that scruple. If I am to draw well I cannot always be running down here to make conversation.'

He hesitated, the inner young man wrestling with the wise benefactor. Then he smiled and his whole face changed.

'I would very much like to see your work,' he said.

She seemed a whole new person to him, as if the shell he had once noticed about her had been dramatically cast off. Beneath he found laughter he had not seen before and a sort of wildness he had never guessed at.

She showed him the upstairs room where she had laid out her material. She explained that Mrs Jenkins used little more than one room at the back of the house where she very largely kept to her bed. 'Having me here gives her licence to be an invalid,' she said. 'I spend much of the morning sitting with her and running errands but she sleeps at this time of the afternoon so it is a good time to work. And she has no objection to my using this room. Which is good because it has by far the best light.'

That afternoon they discussed some drawings of oak leaves and acorns that she had been working on. The drawings seemed very fine to him: very fresh but very correct, intricate in their detail. But she kept pressing him to comment, as if she wanted him to go further. Finally she turned to him, her head angled as if in thought.

'But why do you think I have chosen this subject to draw?'

He hesitated, distracted by her face close to his and determined not to be distracted.

'The oak is a very good subject. And widespread in the park, of course.' He trailed off, aware of an impatient twitch in her eyebrow.

With a little skip she moved away from him, away from the picture, until she stood behind it.

'It is good of you to comment on my work,' she said, 'but if the work does not draw your attention to its subject then it is not a success.'

He looked again at the image she had created, his eyes flicking from the picture in front of him to the woman behind it.

'Very well. You have drawn a collection of oak leaves and acorns. The leaves and acorns are both brown but that is because they are last year's. Perhaps it is surprising to find a twig with both acorns and leaves still intact at this point in the year?'

She shook her head. 'No, there's still a lot of last

year's fall on the ground.'

'Well, then . . . Each leaf shows the standard indentations and each . . .' Suddenly he paused. 'I see,' he said. 'You are right to be impatient with me. The acorns have no stalks, they are connected directly to the twig. And the leaves have long stalks. This is a sessile oak, not an English oak. And found in the park, you say? I know of sessile oaks in Wales but I have never heard of them occurring here.'

She nodded, her eyes bright. 'It *is* interesting, is it not? In case you think my observation is at fault, the original sample is over there, by the window. You can see for yourself.'

From that conversation they moved on to other native trees and Banks talked of the variations on familiar themes that he had found in his travels. It was only when he had forgotten the mood of his arrival that she drew his mind back to it. They were discussing a study she had done of beech leaves when she suddenly turned to him and said, 'You must not think me ungrateful.'

For a moment he was unbalanced by her directness and unsure how to respond.

'All this, I mean.' She waved her hand as if to embrace the room, the house and everything around them. 'I thank you for it every day. More often than that. And I realise you scarcely know me. I must appear to you a random act of kindness.'

He was honest enough to nod at this.

'That is how I explain things to myself,' he replied. 'I call it a generous impulse, a making good of Revesby's faults. And I think myself a warm-hearted fellow.' He paused, still looking at her. 'And yet there is something in the time we spend together that marks it as different. I came here today to patronise you. I

165

know I did. But within moments of seeing you I remembered why it is not possible. You have never given me the opportunity.'

She smiled a little sadly.

'This place. My position here. It is the model of respectability. I look after an infirm old woman. I walk in the fresh air, properly accompanied. I draw a little. I dress respectably. Strangers might take me for a saint. But we both know that isn't true. There is something we have never spoken of . . .' She looked away, uncertain of her words. 'Of the fact that the object of your charity is no longer what they call a maiden.'

Suddenly the joy went out of him. 'Please,' he said, standing abruptly. 'We have no need to talk of it. It pains me to think of it.'

She moved a little further away from him.

'And yet,' she said softly, 'I cannot help but think that perhaps the pain is more mine than yours.' She paused a little while her words hung in the air between them. 'And you do me no favour by pretending I am what I am not.'

He rode back to London that evening a more thoughtful man than when he'd set out that morning with the sun still high.

*   *   *

Even though he was only three months returned from the *Endeavour*, he began to plan for his next long voyage. Cook had received word from the Admiralty to prepare for a second expedition and Banks was invited to go with him. The success of their first venture had been so spectacular that a second had never been in doubt; but he was surprised how quickly it was proposed, with less than a year between the date of their return and their next departure.

It never occurred to him to decline the opportunity. Before the first voyage he had almost had to beg before permission was granted for him to join the venture. This time there could be no choice but him. The public expected it, Cook spoke strongly in favour and the Royal Society supported him. The general assumption that it could be no one but Banks gave him tremendous satisfaction. It was not an assumption he felt inclined to dispute.

Nevertheless, it came too soon. There was much work to be done on the describing of his *Endeavour* collection and he was still revelling in the success of that voyage, still enjoying the high tide that swept him through London society. Introductions and invitations were reaching him from all quarters and he had begun to form the centre of a circle of eager young men who, he felt, could between them make a difference to the world they lived in. He believed that with another three years in London he could begin to shape the course of botany for a generation or more. At home his ideas seemed set to flourish and take root. At sea he would once again be no more than one part of the ship's complement, no more entitled than the ship's carpenters to decide what course should be set.

And then there was Harriet. Relations between them had never recovered from their three years apart. On his return from Lincolnshire he had called on her most promptly. He explained to her his plan to go abroad again, used it to show the impossibility of his ever making a proper husband. The news of a second expedition so quickly after the first was not well received. There were tears when he first spoke of it and reproaches that it was an excuse to break his promise. Finally, back in her guardian's rose garden, they began to address each other as they truly felt. She accused him of reneging on his promise, of making her an object of pity and ridicule. But, she said, it would be equally ridiculous for her to continue an understanding with a man who never intended to remain in London long enough to visit a church. On his part he pointed out that his ambitions to travel had never been a secret. He declared that on his return he had fully intended their nuptials to go ahead but he had found such a change in her that he had hardly felt it right to go on. An interview with her guardian followed, very tense and very formal. Banks regretted that he was not, as he had hoped, in a position to marry at this time; his travels prevented it. As he knew it was unreasonable to make the lady wait, he sought to be freed from his engagement. Frank words were exchanged. An agreement was reached. Banks left feeling guilty and miserable—and, to his own shame, greatly relieved.

One of the few places where his spirits were never low was the little house in Richmond. It seemed to exist on a different continent from his London life and the fears and concerns he took with him appeared petty and vain on his arrival there. She would listen to him quietly when he wanted to talk but more often he found himself dismissing it all from his mind and talking about science again, newly alive with ideas and optimism. It was as if he had discovered a world where only the elements of himself that felt pure and genuine were able to flourish. He took to sharing with her the botanical ideas he had only half formed and always when he left her they were a little more ordered, a fraction closer to being ready for the scrutiny of his peers. And yet despite these escapes to Richmond, his plans for a second voyage began of necessity to take shape.

One November morning, nearly three months after her arrival in Richmond, he had arranged to accompany her and Mrs Jenkins to Hampton Court. He called for them early in his carriage only to be greeted at the door with the news that Mrs Jenkins could not go. After an awkward few minutes of confusion, it was agreed that Martha should travel in her stead and, as the carriage rumbled along the banks of the Thames with Martha dozing in one corner, he found himself talking at length about his next voyage.

As always, he had underestimated her. He had expected her to ask about the effect of his absence on her own position, on the Richmond establishment, about the date of his likely return. Even about her position should he not return. Instead every step they took around the ancient palace was accompanied by questions about the details of the proposed expedition. She wanted to know everything: what orders Cook sailed under, what course was to be set, what his own hopes and aspirations were for the voyage. He found himself discussing at length the possibilities of new continents in the southern latitudes, what conditions could exist there, what life such land might support. And then she moved on to details of navigation—what instruments would be used, what equipment taken, what methods did he most trust for the calculation of longitude? And of design, would the vessel be another collier? Of mortality at sea, what could be done to reduce it? Of the crew, who would go? Who would be new, who tried and seasoned?

When the carriage rolled gently to a halt in Richmond their conversation was still far from flagging. She looked out of the window in dismay.

'Here so soon? And I still have questions to ask!' It

was agreed eventually that Martha, who was dozing again, would be allowed to get down and warn Mrs Jenkins of a delay in their return while the carriage took a turn around the park. As the carriage rolled forward again, she turned to him and said, 'One thing disappoints me. You seem too little excited at the prospect ahead of you. Were I a man there would be nothing else I could talk about.'

'Is that so? Yet when we first met in the Revesby woods, I was only a few weeks away from such an expedition and surely I remember that we scarcely talked of it. Our conversation was of lichen and woodland flowers.'

'Oh, but do not tell me you were not excited! You had a shine about you then that spoke of excitement in everything you did or saw or said.'

'And do I not have that shine now?'

She looked at him and her eyes were suddenly tender.

'You are different now. Making your way. It was new to you then. Now you have the world a little on your shoulders.'

It was a cue to pass to another subject but he felt a sadness at her words that seemed to prevent it.

'So I shine to you less?'

Although it was still bright outside, the inside of the carriage was in shadow. She wanted to reach out and take his hand and tell him that nothing shone in her life so brightly as he. But instead she searched for words that she was permitted to say.

'You shine with a different lustre now,' she said softly. 'You have less time for the things most real to you.'

'Yes,' he said after a moment's thought. 'I think that's true.'

And suddenly, looking at her, looking into her green eyes, without planning or reason, he went on, 'And I discover that one of the things most real is you.'

They were already seated close to each other and when he saw she was silent in surprise he wanted to reach out and touch her cheek and tell her gently, 'It's true, though I have only just known it.' And as she looked up at his troubled face she thought to run her fingers into his hair and tell him that all was well, that she knew, that even when he didn't know, she knew. And when she said nothing he wished they were back in the Revesby woods where it would have been very easy to lean forward, closer to her lips. And when he did move forward very slightly, her eyes opened wide and said 'yes.' So he reached across and let his fingers touch her cheek and a voice in his head he had never heard before told him, *this is what love is*, and he leaned forward and she saw the pleading in his face and as she felt the first, warm touch of his lips she found her own mouth moving softly under his and heard somewhere far removed the words '*I love you.*'

CHAPTER ELEVEN

IN LINCOLN

Katya flew out to Sweden and left me fretting behind her. Two days of desperate searching seemed to have got us nowhere. There were no archives left in the city that between us we hadn't covered, and there was still no clear indication that Miss B had died in London in 1774. But if she hadn't died, where had she gone? She could have moved anywhere in London, to another man, another name, another parish. Even if we knew what the B stood for, it would still be impossible to find her. So instead, after banging my head against the futility of the question, I decided to speculate a little. If it was impossible to find where she'd *gone*, perhaps we could at least find where she had come from. That prospect didn't seem so unlikely. According to the *Town & Country Magazine*, Banks had known her before he sailed with Cook, at a time when she was still of school age. Even though I was inclined to treat that account with caution, there must have been some core of truth behind it. Then, when Banks got back three years later, she was old enough to become his mistress. So that would make her between thirteen and sixteen when Banks sailed. So if I believed my own reasoning, she must have been born sometime between 1752 and 1755.

What else could I work out? When Banks returned, he had felt the need to rescue her from economic distress and restore her to some degree of social respectability, so her background, while impoverished, was not beyond the social pale. But where did the wealthy Joseph Banks meet someone of schoolgirl age from such an impoverished background? As a young man about town Banks would have had male friends with younger sisters but they were surely unlikely to die and leave their sisters destitute. And if they had, I was sure the gossip mongers would have referred to it. It didn't seem like the sort of connection that would have been easy to keep secret.

Of course she could have been a tradesman's daughter or the daughter of one of the professional men he met in his day-to-day affairs. But I wasn't completely convinced that young aristocrats formed relationships so easily with the daughters of their tradesmen. For now I was prepared to hope they didn't. The option I kept coming back to was very different: Lincolnshire.

Banks inherited Revesby Abbey when he was still a young man, and took his responsibilities seriously. He'd have been aware of the financial predicaments of the families around his estates, and it wouldn't be unconventional for a beneficent landowner to concern himself with the plight of an orphaned girl whose family had once been his neighbours. The village of Revesby would have been a relatively small place, after all. Small enough in fact to make a search of the parish records a reasonable idea. Even without a whole name to search for, it might be possible to turn something up.

Directory Enquiries gave me the number of the Lincolnshire County Archives and the woman I spoke to there couldn't have been more helpful.

Yes, she thought they had the parish records for Revesby. She'd check. After a pause she came back. Yes, the Revesby records were on microfilm. Yes, I could come in and check them any time during opening hours.

I think it was her helpfulness that decided me. She made it sound as though everything was possible. I had a couple of days ahead of me with no teaching to do and I still had keys to the rusty yellow car. I set off the following day.

                    *   *   *

Lincoln is a striking city. The hill it stands on lurches out of the surrounding flatness, topped by a cathedral that is all vertical lines reaching for the sky. The modern town is sprawled around its base and contains, along with a lot of shops, a labyrinthine one-way system that eventually led me to a long-stay car park. By then it was already after four and too late to begin at the archives, so instead I hauled my bag out of the car, slung it over my shoulder and set off up the hill to find myself somewhere to stay. It felt like a holiday and I was going to enjoy myself. Eventually I found a small, plush hotel near the top of the hill, tucked into the knot of old streets immediately below the cathedral. It was the sort of place where every room was different and the walls and floors did not always meet at right angles. The reception area was thickly carpeted in red and the desk was the old-fashioned type with a bell and a visitors' book instead of a computer. It felt warm and smelled of wood fires and somewhere out of sight there were bottles clinking gently as though someone was restocking the bar. It was also phenomenally expensive, but just then it didn't seem to matter. I was feeling reckless and, if this was all just folly, let it at least be folly on a noble scale.

That night I had dinner in a little restaurant close to the hotel and read a crumpled detective story from the hotel library. After dinner I sat up late by the fire in the hotel bar, drinking big glasses of brandy and feeling that all was well with the world. And it was—at least until the following morning, when I left my bag at reception and strode off to find the county archives. They turned out to be friendly and modern and every bit as helpful as they had promised to be. A pleasant-faced woman with glasses sorted out my reader's card and gave me a form to fill in about the records I was after.

'Revesby parish from 1750,' she read when I handed it back. 'No problem.' Then she paused and her pen hovered over the form. 'And what name is it you're looking for? It's just for our records really.'

She looked up when I hesitated. 'I really don't know,' I told her honestly. 'I only know it begins with B and ends in N. It might have five letters in it but I can't even be sure of that.'

She raised an eyebrow at that and I guessed she was relegating me from serious researcher to whimsical eccentric. Even so, she showed me where to find the relevant microfilms and then left me to get on with it.

I'd been right about Revesby being a small place. It was the record of births that I was interested in and it wasn't a long or difficult morning's work to list all the girls born between

175

1750 and 1760 or thereabouts whose names might fit the bill. My list for Revesby came out like this.

Jan 1st 1750	*Mary, bastard daughter of [blank]*
Sept 29th 1752	*Mary, daughter of Richard Burnett & Elizabeth his wife*
April 18th 1756	*Mary, daughter of James Browne & Susanna his wife*
Feb 20th 1757	*Mary, daughter of William Burton & Anne his wife*
Jan 18th 1761	*Elizabeth, daughter of James Browne & Susanna his wife*

When I sat back and looked at it I wasn't sure what I'd found, apart from a clear fondness among the Revesby parishioners for the name Mary. The name that leapt out at me was Burton, but there was a Browne there too and I wasn't too worried about the E on the end—spelling was fluid back then and the E might easily have got lost later. And although Mary Burton and Mary Browne were both on the young side, about twelve or thirteen when Banks set off on his voyage, either of them could have grown up to become Miss B. I realised as I wound back the microfilm that my fingers were trembling very slightly. I felt I was getting somewhere.

My next step was to run a check. I knew from *Town & Country Magazine* that Miss B had become an orphan while Banks was away, so I went back and looked at Revesby's record of deaths. This wasn't foolproof, of course. Miss B's father could have died somewhere quite different. But it was worth a try. A quick check of those years came up with the deaths of only four adult males, but

William Burton was one of them.

January 12th 1768   James Turner
Nov 7th 1768   William Burton
March 25th 1769   Dr Taylor
April 12th 1769   Richard Burnett

I noted the names down and looked at them, the grains of excitement beginning to grow inside me. James Browne, it seemed, had disqualified himself by living on for another eighteen years. But William Burton had died three months after Banks sailed, so his daughter Mary fitted on both counts ... It wasn't much to go on. Only a thread. But my hands were sweating a little as I noted down the dates. If I was right, if Mary Burton was the name of the woman in the picture, then finally I had something to go on. I could go back to London and try to trace her through the records. And if Hans Michaels was right, then finding her was the key to finding the Ulieta bird.

Carried away by the moment, I found myself scanning through the remaining records, my eyes still hungry for detail. And it was that careless impulse which brought my whole theory crashing to the ground. Around me, the same earnest faces were peering at the same screens, but now mine was just another one of them. The excitement was gone, blown out in an instant. Because Mary Burton had been buried in Revesby alongside her father—only six months after Joseph Banks returned to Britain.

I could have stayed longer and tried to think up some new theory to fit these facts, but I had a long drive home ahead of me so I took defeat on the chin. If Mary Burton wasn't Miss B, then the Revesby connection was probably just another blind alley. Perhaps, after all, the only way forward was to track down the Ainsby family. I stored the lists I'd made in my jacket pocket, thanked the librarian who'd helped me, and then set off back towards the cathedral in the mild, damp, deeply grey afternoon. It was three fifteen by the time I arrived back at the hotel to collect my bag. Three fifteen is a ghostly time in county town hotels. Lunches are over by two thirty and even the stragglers have gone by three. All the guests who plan to go out are out, and those who plan to stay in are probably snoozing in their rooms. A thick silence falls on everything except the clocks, which seize their moment and begin to tick louder.

It was just that sort of silence that greeted me when I reached the reception desk and my defiant striking of the bell did very little to dent it. I could see my bag behind the desk but it seemed hasty somehow to go behind and fetch it, so I waited, leaning on the dark oak counter, looking idly at the various leaflets and notices displayed there. After a few moments my eye fell on the guest register, still open at the page where I'd been the last person to sign it. I was about to turn away again when a familiar word caught my attention—*Mecklenburg*. My eye leapt back to it and my blood began to pump a little faster: *Mecklenburg Hotel*. The words were written under the column headed 'Address' and to their left, in beautiful handwriting, was the name *Karl Anderson*. I checked the dates. He'd arrived a week ago and hadn't yet checked out. This was the place where he'd come to find the bird.

178

It was late when I got home. The phone was ringing as I opened the front door, but by the time I'd closed it behind me the ringing had stopped. It left behind a silence that seemed unusually anxious, a stillness that seemed ill at ease. I knew from the moment the door closed behind me that something was wrong.

There was no mess this time, no broken window or shattered glass. Only a broken catch on a kitchen window where the ill-fitting frame had been levered open. Not even a footprint on the paintwork or a broken plate, knocked from the draining board. I took it in with a dull sense of incredulity: the window hanging open, the broken lock, the habitual warmth of the kitchen dispersed into the winter night. And suddenly I felt angry. Not shocked, not horrified, just full of choking rage at the effrontery of it all. I was cold and lonely and tired, and this place was my sanctuary. How *dare* someone come forcing their way in here? How *dare* they? Absurdly, the thing that seemed to anger me most was the open window. I'd been planning to wallow in the room's warmth, and the squandered heat was somehow more than I was prepared to put up with.

I pulled the window closed, and began a quick, clinical inspection, my brain racing. Whoever had done this, I was going to find them. I'd call the police, give them Anderson's name, get them to find out what was going on. And I wanted to tell him myself that there was nothing here to find. Because that was the other thing that made me angry—the pointlessness of it all. My notes held no secrets. I knew nothing and could help no one. And the thought only made me even madder.

There was no sign of any disturbance in the kitchen, and none in the hallway. My workshop seemed untouched too, the tools and chemicals still neat in their cupboards. My bedroom, then . . . I climbed the stairs two at a time, impatient to know the worst. But this time, there was to be no lucky escape, no cryptic overtidiness. The room had been ransacked.

The worst thing was the paper. My old trunk had been pulled into the centre of the room and the contents scattered over every surface. All those notes on extinct birds, most of them untouched for a dozen years, now sprawled in confusion. They had never been properly sorted, but they had been piled together with some rudiments of sense. Now they were flung in all directions, a random diaspora of lost species, a last, giddy flapping of flightless wings. No two consecutive pieces of paper seemed to have remained together. Someone had been through each one, and discarded each in different directions. And they had found nothing. I knew that. There was nothing to find.

As I gazed at them, I could feel my heart beating uncomfortably fast. The anger inside me had coiled into something tight and powerful. I'd ring the police right now, get them on the heels of whoever had been here. And I'd go back to Lincoln, find Anderson, show him what I thought of him. Was this the sort of thing his 'researchers' did? Well, we'd see. We'd see what a bit of police questioning would find out . . .

But I didn't move towards the phone. Instead I sat down on the edge of my bed and took a deep breath. It was impossible to be sure, but it occurred to me that despite the chaos there may actually be nothing missing. Nothing had been worth taking. So what would I report? Another theftless break-in. A window that didn't lock properly. An assurance from some tired young policeman that I'd been lucky. A warning to get some proper locks. Yes, I'd report it. But first I wanted to think.

Before that night, Anderson's story about the lost bird had stirred up some old emotions, emotions probably better left where I'd buried them. But now with my anger came an unwonted clarity. Looking around the overturned bedroom, I realised why finding the Ulieta bird was important to me. Not for posterity, not for science, not even for the fame of being its finder. But for myself, to fill a hollow of discontent that had lain inside me too long, studiously ignored for fifteen years, now washed into view by the flood tide of events. The same discontent I felt whenever I looked at the photograph by my bed or thought of my days in Brazil. Finding the bird—holding it in my hands in defiance of all logic—would be my proof that even the most fragile things can sometimes cheat oblivion.

I checked through the rest of the house perfunctorily, still busy with my thoughts. Only when that surge of emotion had begun to pass did some semblance of perspective return, and with it came the bald truth. The few clues I had led nowhere, and I had no idea where to go.

I was sitting in the kitchen, still in my coat, when the phone rang. The noise startled me, and there

181

was a temptation not to answer it, an urge to be left alone in contemplation of my own helplessness. But when I heard Katya's voice I felt strangely comforted. And there was an unfamiliar note in it. She sounded excited.

'Fitz?' she began. 'Listen, I think I may have found something.'

She didn't wait for me to ask questions, or give me any time to speak.

'I've been digging around,' she told me. 'In the Fabricius papers. You know, the naturalist who knew Banks. There's an archive of his stuff in Denmark—it's an easy journey from where my family live. I didn't say anything before, in case it was all a waste of time. Listen, it's about the bird.'

Hastily, her voice more accented than normal, she told me she'd gone to Sweden to see her father. 'He was *so* patronising,' she told me. 'He just loved the fact I'd come to him for help. But he *was* quite helpful. He arranged for me to get access to the Fabricius archive. I've been there all day today and I've only just started. There's a couple more days' work here at least. But I've found something. It was one of the first letters I looked at. I almost didn't notice it.'

'Go on. What have you found?' Suddenly, telling her about the burglary didn't seem so important.

'It's a letter to Fabricius from a man in France, dated 1778. Apparently Fabricius had tried to buy some drawings from him and this was a letter of refusal. There's a PS at the bottom. Here, I'll read it to you. *"I assume from your last letter that the picture of* Turdus ulietensis *you have received from Lincolnshire is by the same artist. I wish you joy of it. I'm sure it is fine work."* Do you see? *Turdus*

182

ulietensis—that's our bird, isn't it?'

But I could barely reply. Katya had stumbled across something amazing, something that would be meaningless to most people but which meant everything to us—proof that our lost bird had survived its time in Joseph Banks's collection. Because a year or so after it was last seen there, someone had been making a painting of it— someone somewhere in Lincolnshire.

*   *   *

Katya had used up her phonecard before I had a chance to tell her about my own discovery in Lincoln. That's why when the phone rang again later that night, I was quick to answer, hoping she'd found another opportunity to call. But it wasn't Katya this time; it was Gabby. Her lectures were over. She was flying back to London.

They lay in bed, naked together, long into the evening. After the urgency of their first passion came a long, slow time of discovery in which they lay and touched, hardly talking, each from time to time running their fingertips over the other as if to memorise an outline or reassure themselves that what they felt was real. The lines of an autumn sun edged slowly around the ceiling and he watched them lengthen and fade with his head on her shoulder, his cheek resting against the swell of her breast.

'When I saw you in the wood that day,' he said, his fingers running very slowly across the bare smoothness of her stomach, 'I didn't expect this.'

'Nor I,' she replied. 'I have never expected this.'

He smiled. 'I'm glad. I thought you might think . . .'

'No, I never thought that. I hoped but I didn't expect.'

At that he laughed and he raised his head and kissed her neck.

It was a small bedroom, low-ceilinged, hung in shades of green and russet; the light was fading quickly around them yet still touched her skin with the palest hint of gold. Before it was completely dark they slept a little and he woke to the touch of her lips moving slowly across his chest in small, pinching kisses. He could smell her hair close to his face and feel the warmth of her body slipping gently over his, and for a fragment of a moment he could scarcely believe that the happiness inside him was his own; then he felt her teeth nip teasingly at his skin and in an instant they were rolling and struggling in each other's arms.

When the day was quite gone she rose to light the lamp. He watched as she swung herself upright so that her back was towards him, long, straight, beautiful. Then she stood up, still naked, and moved soundlessly across the room, hair spilling over her shoulder, her pale skin still light in the darkness. When the lamp flared she saw him watching her, his eyes moving over her body.

'I never learned to be coy,' she said simply.

'I would not change the way you are,' he replied. Then he held out his hand and pulled her back under the sheets and into his arms.

'And what of Mrs Jenkins?' she asked, teasing. 'Do you not consider this an abuse of her hospitality?'

'Mrs Jenkins is an old friend,' he responded with a smile and a shrug. 'She will no doubt scold me for being alone with you but she will probably think the better of me.'

'She will do neither. She is asleep in her room and she won't emerge till morning. Martha told her we were taking tea in the drawing room.'

'What about Martha? Is she discreet?' he asked.

'Oh, yes. And she has been waiting for this for weeks. Your restraint has infuriated her.'

'But that's outrageous!'

When he'd finished laughing she shook her head reprovingly.

'You see, Martha has been hearing everything the gossips say about Joseph Banks, the great circumnavigator, and what he got up to in the South Seas. If half of what they say of you is true, you can hardly blame her for expecting a little more impatience and a little less scruple.'

He found himself blushing. It made her smile.

'They slander me abominably,' he said, 'but there *were* occasions . . . I'm prepared to admit I was not chaste for the entire duration of the voyage.'

'Ah . . .' She ran a hand across his chest. 'I'm glad you are prepared to admit that.' He waited for her to tease him but in the silence that followed he realised her mood had changed. 'After all,' she said quietly, almost to herself, 'I have already admitted the same.'

She felt him go silent, felt his body tensing. Then he rolled her off him and turned onto his side so that they lay facing each other, their heads on the same pillow.

'About what I said . . .' he began.

'I was harsh on you.'

'You were fair. I cannot imagine what it must be like knowing no alternative but to give yourself in that way.'

'No,' she said quietly. 'But people suffer much worse. I've been lucky.'

'Men place such great store on virtue,' he continued. 'When you told me what had happened . . .'

'Yes?' Their faces were only a few inches apart, their naked legs still entwined.

'It hurt me.'

'Yes, I saw. It surprised me. It wasn't what I expected.'

'Partly it was shock, I think. I'm not used to a woman talking frankly of such things.'

'And why did it hurt?'

'It's hard to say.'

'Say it anyway.'

He shook his head. 'What does it matter? I've found you now. The rest means nothing.'

She reached up and ran a finger down the ridge of his nose, then kissed his lips.

'That's how you feel now,' she said. 'Here with me. You may not always feel it.'

'When you told me about Ponsonby, I realised I was jealous.'

'Jealous of *him*?'

'Yes. I realised that I'd always thought of you as my discovery. Mine, not his.'

Her smile made him smile back. 'But must I always be someone's?' she asked.

'Of course not.'

She smiled again. 'Know this.' She took his hand and placed it against her naked breast. 'Here, now, for as long as this night lasts, I *am* yours. Totally yours.'

'And beyond that?'

She shook her head. 'I can't tell you what lies beyond tonight. Not out there beyond this room.'

He began to move his hand on her breast in an almost imperceptible caress. 'I wish the rest of the world would vanish and leave us here forever.'

She reached around him and ran the flat of her hand down his spine.

'None of it is there until you look at it,' she said, pulling him closer.

'I'll never look,' he said.

'You will,' she said, 'but kiss me first.'

'Always,' he whispered, and outside no wheels turned, no hooves rang out and they could almost believe the world had fallen still for them.

* * *

At nine o'clock they roused themselves from the warmth of the covers and began to dress. Before going downstairs Banks took one last look around the green-and-russet bedroom, the glowing lamp, the sheets in turmoil, the pillow still double-hollowed where their heads had rested. He waited as she tied her hair, looking at him instead of the glass so that a tendril of brown hair spilled out and hung down her cheek.

187

'It isn't just Martha,' he said. 'There are the other servants. Are you not afraid for your reputation?'

'I have no reputation,' she replied, simply. 'Are you not afraid for yours?'

'I have very little, either. They portray me as a tireless philanderer. And besides . . .'

'The world judges men differently?'

'Yes.'

She looked at him, her hands still moving deftly in her hair. 'I don't,' she said.

He watched as the stray tendril was chased and escaped again. 'If we are to be together as I would wish, you cannot stay living here. It is too far. I could take rooms for you in London. Somewhere discreet. You would be barely noticed among the crowds. I believe you would be happy there.'

She looked back at him and continued to pin her hair.

'As your mistress?'

He paused. 'As the woman I want to be with.'

She came to him then and placed her hands flat against his chest. 'You do not need to explain. I understand what I can and cannot be. But if I am ever to be with you as you suggest, there are certain things you must agree.'

He nodded, suddenly a little solemn.

'It is too soon for me to move now. Even Richmond is still strange to me and London will be yet stranger. And soon you will be gone. If I am to be left to wait for you, I would rather do it here where things are a little familiar, where the fields and trees are close at hand.'

He nodded. 'And the other things?'

'I will not use my father's name. When people talk of the mistress you keep, I want no one to think of that little girl from Revesby who used to go to you in the woods. I don't want them to have that satisfaction.'

'Of course, Miss Brown. So it shall be.' He touched the curl of loose hair. 'I like the name for you.'

She moved his hand away from her cheek and returned it to his side.

'The other thing is harder for you. Some day you will marry . . .'

'Why should I?'

'You will. You will have to. I won't remain as an encumbrance in your life when that happens. I have my pride. When the time comes that you no longer hold me the way you held me tonight, then I will take my leave and go.'

'It will not come. But of course you should be free to leave whatever happens. I would not wish you caged. I shall make sure you have the means to act as you choose.'

'And you will let me go? You will not pursue me, whatever your feelings?'

'I begin to think you plan to abandon me.'

'Perhaps,' she replied quietly. 'If there must come a time of parting then I want to prepare myself. That way it will hurt less. I have already hurt one man by leaving him; you encouraged me in that, urged me to put my own life to the fore. Perhaps one day one of us may have to apply that reasoning again.'

'Shhh,' he said and touched her lips very softly with the tip of his finger. Then, when she tried to speak again, he kissed her.

*　　　*　　　*

From the window she watched him step into the darkness, his stride as light as a boy's. Then she turned back to where Martha was waiting for her.

'Are you all right, miss?'

She blushed. 'Yes, Martha. Very right.'

'He's a very charming young man, miss.'

'He's more than that. When he talks about what he might do with the world, he has more new ideas in ten minutes than in all those books of my father's combined.'

'That's right, miss, it's his ideas you like. It seems we'll be in this house for a while then.'

'Yes, we'll be staying here for now, Martha.'

'It's no odds to me.'

'Is it not?' She hesitated, not sure what she wanted to say. 'There'll be a time when we go back, Martha. To Lincolnshire. You know that?'

Martha looked up to the window, the direction of Banks's departure.

'Yes, I know that, miss. And things will turn out right. Even then.'

That night she sat up until Martha had gone to bed, waiting so that she could go to her room alone. There she found everything just as she had left it, the air warm and scented, the lamp burning low, the bedclothes ploughed into wild furrows. As she undressed she let herself remember every moment and movement that had passed between them there; and when she finally lay under the sheets she found the scent of his body still lingered against hers.

*   *   *

Banks travelled back to London alive with excitement. He felt he had stumbled on something he had never imagined, someone who asked the questions he needed to answer and knew better than him whether

190

his answers were true. And now he found . . . He blushed to himself as he thought of how she had been with him that night, so alive and loving and challenging.

At New Burlington Street he got down from the carriage and walked the few streets to Solander's dwelling. There he shouted and knocked and rattled the locks in radiant humour until the door was opened for him and he could leap up the stairs three by three. As he burst into the study he was already rehearsing the phrases he would use to tell Solander of his good fortune.

When Banks tumbled through the door, Solander looked up from his desk and smiled as he had smiled more than once in the months before this one.

'Which is it this time, Joseph?' he asked, turning and putting down his pen. 'A new idea or a new woman? Whichever it is, it is a more than usually exciting one by the look of it.'

And then, looking at his most trusted friend, Banks felt a change in himself so sudden that it was like missing a step that has always been there. He could only shake his head and say, 'Solander, I'm the most confounded fellow and I find I have completely forgotten why I called. No, please don't move. I have drunk a good deal too much brandy. It is far, far better I should leave.'

And Solander, to his astonishment, found himself looking at a closing door and listening to the sound of running feet descending his stairs.

CHAPTER TWELVE

A NAME IN TWO PLACES

We arranged to meet the following afternoon in a café near Queensway.

Gabby's choice of café wasn't a random one. It was a place from our early days, back when we were setting up the project that later became *her* project. There was no denying that in those days we had been impossibly in love. Each step we took together seemed natural and automatic, from our very first meeting over the remains of the Spix's macaw, to our times in London, lobbying and fundraising and embracing a future together that even fifteen years later we had still not fully disentangled.

That life seemed hard to imagine now, I reflected, as I made my way up the Bayswater Road to meet her. When things went wrong between us we'd discovered the sort of differences that made all the good things unimportant. It had been me who walked away, but it was Gabby who had been most deceived: she thought she was linking her life to one like her own. She only found out the truth when she discovered, devastatingly and beyond all doubt, that I simply didn't share her single-mindedness. In fact I came to resent it with a fierce passion. I was emotional where she was professional, erratic where she was objective. By the time I began to question the work we were doing in the rainforest, the gap between us was already too wide to bridge.

Even so, we had never managed to cut our ties completely. Gabby still wrote. I still thought of her. And I was thinking of her that morning when I arrived, slightly late, at the café where we used to meet. I had spent the morning shovelling my notes back into the trunk and trying to fix the broken window-catch, and now I wanted to know why.

The café was a small place, a counter and a coffee machine and five or six tables tucked away from the door. She was sitting at the far end, where we used to sit, and when she saw me she stood up.

'Hello, John,' she said, and that was all, but when I made my way forward to where she was standing she reached up and pressed her cheek against mine. I caught the scent of her hair, familiar and slightly disorientating.

We ordered coffees and sat down, then looked at each other across the little round table. She was as neat as ever and today her hair was tied back, making her eyes seem bigger. When neither of us spoke she tilted her head a little to one side and gave me that familiar half-smile.

'It feels strange to see you again so soon. After so long not seeing each other.'

It didn't feel strange to me. If anything it seemed frighteningly *normal* to be sitting with her again. Everything had changed since the days we were together, but somehow there remained this instinctive, uninvited familiarity.

She looked well and I told her so, though what I really meant to say was that she hadn't changed.

Her eyes conducted a quick survey of my face. 'You look well too. More relaxed.'

'Well, I've had fifteen years to work out what I want from life.'

She nodded. I was glad she didn't ask me what.

In fact she didn't say anything for a second or two and when she looked up her expression had changed.

'I wanted to ask . . .' she began, and I could see her struggling for the right words. 'Do you still think of . . . ?'

It was the subject that was always between us. Would always be between us. The electric fan, the crumpled bed, Gabby's voice downstairs . . .

'Yes,' I said slowly. 'I think of her all the time.'

She looked away briefly. Outside I could see cars and buses splashing through the December gloom.

'I know how much she meant to you,' she said softly and we both paused awkwardly. 'It's been a long time since then, John. We should have sorted things out before this. You've never met anyone since then?'

'I suppose I haven't wanted to. What about you?'

She looked down at her coffee and shrugged. 'I've been busy.'

'Karl Anderson seems to like you.'

'He does.' Her voice was hard, defensive; but then she caught hold of herself and began to relax again. 'He's a good man, Fitz. Oh, I know he's gone commercial and that's unforgivable to some people. But they made that happen—all those academics who wouldn't give him a chance. Underneath he still cares. He just can't afford to let it show.'

'Does he want to marry you?'

She shrugged again. 'It isn't an issue.'

'For him?'

'For either of us.'

I put down my coffee cup and looked at her.

'Look, Gabby, I need you to tell me what's going on.'

'What do you mean? Between me and Karl?'

'I mean about the Ulieta bird. There's something you're not telling me.'

She blew onto the top of her coffee.

'I don't know what you mean. Karl just wants to find it.'

I stared at her hard.

'Someone broke into my house the night we met. And someone broke in again yesterday and riffled through my notes. Someone's going to a lot of trouble to find that bird. Why? What's it really worth? I can't work it out, but I'd be an idiot not to realise it's worth a lot more than anyone's telling me.'

Gabby shook her head, returning my gaze unwaveringly.

'No, Fitz. It's true what Karl told you. That specimen's worth a lot, but not much more than Karl offered you.'

'So why does everyone seem to want it so badly?' I could feel myself growing angry. 'Look, I'm not just going to sit here like a fool. I want to know what's going on. There *must* be something about that bird that makes it valuable and I want to know what. Otherwise . . .'

She raised her eyebrows, deliberately provocative.

'Otherwise I go to the papers. The scientific press. I can make sure everyone knows Anderson's hunting for the single specimen of the Ulieta bird. Then if the thing really does exist, he won't be selling it to anyone. Not for a long time, at any rate. They'll slap an export order on it before you can blink and it will be staying here for years while they wrangle over it. Something tells me that isn't part of Anderson's plan.'

I don't know how I'd expected Gabby to react to that, but, instead of anxiety or defiance, she leaned forward and touched my hand.

'Oh, Fitz, you really don't get it, do you?' She was shaking her head now. 'Can't you see? This is about more than just your precious bird. No one really cares about that. Oh, I know you do, and it's true that Ted Staest will pay a few thousand dollars for it. Perhaps more, who knows? It's a good enough news story. But Karl isn't stuck over here in the middle of winter for that. Don't you see? It isn't the bird he's after.'

'Then what . . .?' I was blinking at her now, feeling foolish, and embarrassed at showing it. 'What *is* he after?'

Gabby reached out and uncurled my fingers from my cup, then took them between hers. I thought about moving them away, but in the end I let them stay.

'I shouldn't tell you,' she said. 'I promised not to. Only Karl knows, and perhaps a couple of other people who've got wind of it.'

'What?' I tightened my fingers around hers.

'It's a bit of a tale. Have you ever heard of a French artist called Roitelet?'

Something stirred in my memory.

'Vaguely. It rings a bell.'

'Don't worry, no one knows much about him. He was a botanical artist in the last half of the eighteenth century, but that's about all anyone knows. He isn't recorded as being on any of the major expeditions, but we know he travelled because he came back with a collection of amazing botanical paintings. Twenty-four of them. Fruit, flowers. Brilliant, bright, wonderfully observed. Apparently they were something special. Just then botanical art was flourishing, but Roitelet's was the finest anywhere.'

'What do you mean, "apparently"? What happened?'

'The owner kept the collection in his town house in Paris, and the place was ransacked during one of the Paris uprisings. Only three paintings by Roitelet survived. They're incredibly sought after. One of them was auctioned last year in New York. It made over a hundred thousand dollars.'

It sounded like a healthy sum, but surely not one to get completely overexcited about.

'OK . . . So what's that got to do with the Ulieta bird?'

Gabby smiled.

'This is where it all gets complicated. You see, all through the nineteenth century there were rumours about another collection of Roitelet paintings, a whole second portfolio that had somehow ended up in England. There are various different sources for the rumours but the main one is a letter written by a man called Finchley in the middle of the century. This Finchley was a landed gentleman with estates in the Midlands, but he was also something of a scholar. In about 1850 he wrote a letter to a friend of his, a man who made a hobby of collecting botanical paintings.'

She paused and unlaced her fingers from mine so she could take a sip of coffee.

'Go on,' I said, still not sure where this was leading.

'It's a jokey letter about something that happened when he was touring Lincolnshire. He heard tell of a local man who was reputed to own a preserved specimen of a rare bird, and out of curiosity he made sure to find the man and see the specimen for himself. From his description, and from what he was told about it, it seems almost certain that this was the Ulieta bird—and still apparently in one piece. But that wasn't what the letter was really about. The incident that intrigued Finchley happened just as his inspection of the bird was drawing to an end. The owner of the specimen insisted on opening up the glass case the bird was kept in and showing Finchley a collection of papers that had been hidden under the green cloth the bird was standing on. To Finchley's amazement, the papers were a collection of paintings by Roitelet—twelve of them, pristine condition, all studies of English wildflowers. The man who owned them apparently had no idea what they were worth, and apparently wasn't very interested when Finchley told him. He insisted that the bird was a family heirloom, and the pictures with it, and they could happily stay where they'd been put. Judging by his letter, Finchley found the whole thing rather amusing, assuring his friend that the stubbornness of the old man had been more than a match for the generous offers he had made for the paintings, and stating pretty clearly that he thought it was unlikely any wealth in the world would be enough to move the pictures from the spot.'

'I see . . .' I murmured, but although she was

telling me what I wanted to know, I wasn't finding it very satisfying. 'But isn't that all too tenuous for words? Even if we believe in a collection of French paintings turning up in some backwoods part of Lincolnshire, surely there's no way they'd still be there? And not still with the bird. There's been generations of people since then who've had the opportunity to sell them off. Anything could have happened to them. Wouldn't someone who heard about them through Finchley have made sure they got their hands on them in the end?'

Gabby nodded, still cradling her coffee.

'You'd think so, wouldn't you? But the thing is that no other Roitelets have ever come to light. There are only the rumours. And if a collector had got hold of them, then the art world would expect to know about it. Also Finchley's letter gives no details of where he'd found the bird or who owned it. It's almost as if he was deliberately teasing his friend by not telling. So there's still the possibility that the paintings are out there somewhere. And one way of finding them would be to find the bird.'

'So they wanted to use me to find the pictures.' It made sense, and I didn't much like it.

'Not use you, Fitz. Karl knew you'd be interested in finding the bird and he was happy to let you have the money for it. He's found a clue that he thinks points him to where the bird might be.'

'I know. A letter.' I looked at her. 'All this stuff you've told me, these rumours of missing paintings, it's all a bit vague, isn't it? Anderson's a businessman. I can't see him spending money on something like that. His chances of finding anything at all must be tiny.'

'Twelve paintings by Roitelet, Fitz. If they were only half as good as the ones we know about, they'd still cause a sensation. And if each of them went for a hundred thousand dollars . . . Well, you can do the sums. And that portfolio together, as a collection, would probably be worth even more. There's just one snag.'

'What's that?'

'Karl's having problems finding the bird.'

My heart gave a little leap. 'What sort of problems?'

'He's having a few setbacks.' Gabby leaned a little closer to me, earnest and intense; beautiful in a way not usually found in Bayswater coffee shops. 'It was all to do with a house sale. Karl has traced the bird to a big house somewhere that was broken up after the war. He thought it was all sorted. But apparently the bird wasn't where he expected it to be. Now his people are going through all the sale records again, trying to find out what they've missed.'

'Interesting. Do you know where this house was?'

'No. Karl didn't say. But I know he's in Lincolnshire at the moment.' She paused, looking down at her hands on the table in front of her. 'Tell me, have you thought of anything at all that might help?'

I decided to trust her. 'Look, Gabby, I'm not pretending I know anything useful but I've got an idea I'm going to follow. It's about a woman Joseph Banks knew when he was young. I don't know what she's got to do with the bird but I think there's a connection. It may come to nothing but I'll see what happens.'

'And if you find it?'

I looked down for a moment. 'Let's find it first. We can talk about it then.'

She leaned back and raised an eyebrow. 'Who knows, John, perhaps there's a bit of your grandfather in you after all.' Then she reached behind her head and began to rearrange the pinning of her hair, flashing me a warm, affectionate smile. 'And seeing as there's no one in your life to be jealous, I think you could buy me dinner tonight.'

*   *   *

Gabby's attitude towards my grandfather had always in trigued me. On paper he was the sort of person she most despised, a wealthy, rather arrogant Anglo-Saxon who treated the rest of the world as an adventure park and plundered it for specimens as a kind of game. It's hard to imagine him having any time for Gabby's painstakingly correct brand of conservation. Yet I always sensed in Gabby a grudging respect for him. I suppose both of them were prepared to put aside their lives in pursuit of their dreams.

My grandfather, Hugh Fitzgerald, acquired a wife quite early in his career. The war had forced him to put his plans for the African peacock on hold and after surviving four years on the Western Front he met my grandmother, a rather shy seventeen-year-old, a dozen years his junior. If children did not follow as soon as was expected in those days, it's probably because he was largely an absentee husband. After the wedding he installed her in his mother's house in Devon and then went abroad almost immediately, part of an expedition to Central America that lasted nearly two years. When he came back he based himself in London, staying at his club, trying to arrange his next venture.

Unfortunately for him that routine began to change. During his spells in London he would talk long and often to anyone who would listen about his belief in the existence of African peacocks, and gradually he began to get something of a reputation. The establishment was wary of eccentrics but my grandfather couldn't see what he was becoming. The impression of fanaticism was strengthened in 1926 when he was asked to lead a party of mining engineers to West Africa. His main task was to escort them safely into the interior and out again and by all accounts he managed it competently enough. However, at the end of the expedition, instead of returning to London, he stayed on and retraced his steps into the jungle with only a couple of local guides as support. Even though he was hundreds of miles from where Chapin had found the mysterious feather, it seems his idea was to continue the search.

He remained out of contact for almost ten months and when he eventually emerged from the jungle he was ragged with fever. For a time it was doubtful if he'd live but he was brought home to Devon where his wife nursed him patiently. Under her care he pulled through the crisis though it's doubtful whether he ever fully recovered his strength. It was nearly three years before he was back in London again and by then things had changed significantly. His unplanned foray into the West African jungle was widely known about and was taken as proof that he was no longer reliable, and by then the rather gung-ho Victorian tradition of exploration which he represented was out of fashion.

If there were any lessons for me in all that, the prospect of an evening with Gabby was enough to push them to one side. We met in a smart French restaurant in Soho amid a lot of stripped pine where we sat behind some very large menus and talked about things that had nothing to do with Karl Anderson. Gabby had always been good company and that night she was at her most entertaining. We drank white wine and as the evening mellowed around us she became quite daring, telling me a series of scandalous and probably slanderous tales about acquaintances we had in common. Even when we talked about conservation the mood of the evening stayed the same. Gabby leaned forward and spun her dreams, and as she talked I found the sounds and the colours of the rainforest coming back to me. The wine must have made me sentimental and I found myself missing them.

Gabby shimmered that evening. There were still difficult things between us but that night they didn't seem to matter. The old warmth flowed between us without friction. At the end of the evening, outside the Mecklenburg Hotel, there was a moment as we said goodbye that I couldn't define, a pause when an unasked question seemed to pass between us. I hesitated, and Gabby smiled a little sadly, then reached up and kissed me on the cheek.

'Goodnight, Fitz,' she said, and stepped away. I stood in the dark and watched her disappear behind the inviting lights of the waiting hotel.

*　　　*　　　*

Katya came home the following day. She didn't
ring ahead, so I had no idea she was coming until
that evening, when I heard the key in the lock. She
looked tired and a little worn, and older, too—
dressed differently, in a skirt and blouse, with her
hair pinned up into a tight knot. She looked so
unlike the person I knew that I blinked when I saw
her.

'What?' she asked, looking up and seeing my
expression. 'Oh, these. My father thinks you're not
fit to be introduced to his friends unless you look
like this.'

'I'm sorry,' I said, a little embarrassed. 'Come
and sit down and I'll get you a beer.'

'That sounds good.' She reached up and untied
her hair so that it fell around her face. Then she
caught a few strands between her fingers and held
them up so she could peer at them. 'The clothes
were bad enough but I had to listen to him go on
about my hair. I colour it black. Really it's just a
very plain brown.'

In the kitchen she dropped into a chair and was
watching me open bottles of lager when she
noticed the twisted window-catch. She was on her
feet immediately, peering at it.

'What's happened?'

'Things have moved on a little. I'll tell you all
about it in a moment.'

'Someone's broken in again? Did they take
anything?'

I shook my head and smiled.

'Nothing to steal.'

'But why?'

'It turns out that finding our bird might be worth rather more than we thought. It's a long story. But don't worry. Everything's fine. First I want you to tell me what you've been up to. Here, drink this. Unless you're too smartly dressed to drink from the bottle.'

She laughed then, like the Katya I recognised.

'OK, I'll go first.' She stretched and looked happy. 'In fact you know the good bit already. The stuff I told you over the phone. After that I thought I'd find a lot more and I got really excited. But I don't think there's anything else in those papers we need to know. That's why I didn't ring again. I was waiting till I found something stupendous. But there was nothing.'

'I think what you've found *is* pretty stupendous. It proves the bird survived Banks's collection. *And* it gives us a good idea about where to look.'

She was keen to talk, and she told me all about Fabricius' papers. As she talked, the tiredness left her and she became animated. Most of the correspondence she'd been through had been about scientific issues. Very little of it concerned Fabricius' time in England—it seemed to be a part of his life he didn't much write about—and none of it mentioned Banks. As well as the letter referring to the Ulieta bird, there were two others from the same man, a Frenchman called Martin, both about drawings Fabricius wanted to buy, but neither of them mentioned the Ulieta bird.

'Do you mind me doing all that?' Katya asked when her account was over.

'No, of course not.'

205

'I felt a bit embarrassed about it. This is your search really. I felt as though I was barging in . . .' She looked at me for a moment. 'Anyway, tell me what's been going on here.'

'Hard to know where to start. I suppose the real discovery came yesterday, when I met up with Gabby.'

'Oh?' She took a swig from her beer but didn't look round.

'But before that I'd been up to Lincolnshire. And guess who I found there?'

Katya sat quietly while I told her how I'd ended up in Lincoln, and about my discovery of Karl Anderson's whereabouts. She listened politely, but she didn't seem as interested as I'd expected.

'Anyway,' I concluded, 'in the end I didn't come up with anything amazing . . .' I reached into the jacket on the back of my chair. 'But for a moment I thought I had. Here, take a look at these. They're the lists I made of women born in Revesby whose names began with B.'

I spread the papers on the table.

Jan 1st 1750	*Mary, bastard daughter of [blank]*
Sept 29th 1752	*Mary, daughter of Richard Burnett & Elizabeth his wife*
April 18th 1756	*Mary, daughter of James Browne & Susanna his wife*
Feb 20th 1757	*Mary, daughter of William Burton & Anne his wife*
Jan 18th 1761	*Elizabeth, daughter of James Browne & Susanna his wife*

'I got quite excited by Mary Burton, even though she was born a little later than I'd hoped. When I

206

found her father had died while Banks was away, I really thought I was onto something . . .'

I looked up and realised that Katya wasn't listening. Her air of detachment had evaporated and she was staring at the sheet of paper, her lips moving as if she were calculating something.

'Here, Fitz. Look here.' Her tone was urgent. She pointed at the second name on the list. 'That's roughly the right year, isn't it? That would make her about sixteen when Banks left, about nineteen when he got back?'

'Yes . . .' I wasn't sure where this was leading.

'*Mary Burnett*. You see?'

'But *Burnett* doesn't end in an N.'

'That letter . . .' She looked around helplessly. 'Which book was it in? The letter written by Captain Cook at the start of his second voyage. About a woman pretending to be a man. *Remember*?'

I remembered the letter but I still didn't see the connection.

'*Burnett*. I'm sure that's what the woman was calling herself. *Mr Burnett*.'

In the end we had to go upstairs and find the right book before I was convinced. But Katya was right.

Three days before we arrived a person left the Island who went by the name of Burnett. He had been waiting for Mr Banks arrival about three months, at first he said he came here for the recovery of his health, but afterwards said his intention was to go with Mr Banks, to some he said he was unknown to this Gentleman, to others he said it was by his appointment he came here as he could not be receiv'd on board in England. At last when he heard that Mr Banks did not go with us, he took the very first opportunity to get off the Island. He was in appearance rather ordinary than otherwise and employ'd his time in Botanizing &ca—Every part of Mr Burnetts behaviour and every action tended to prove that he was a Woman, I have not met with a person that entertains a doubt of a contrary nature.

'What do you think?' she asked triumphantly.

'It's hard to tell. It could just be a coincidence.'

'And look here.' Katya picked up the other paper that I'd laid out on the table. 'Her father died while Banks was abroad. What if she and Banks were being discreet when she became his mistress and used a name that wasn't hers? That would make sense. And Burnett isn't too far from Brown, is it? *Burnett, brunette, brune, brown . . .*'

I sat back and looked at her before replying. 'They're not going to like this at the university,' I told her. 'We need to go back to Lincoln. How soon can you leave?'

*   *   *

We drove northwards through the grey light of a day that never seemed to get started. The flat Lincolnshire plain slipped past in various shades of ochre and brown and for the most part we were silent beneath the throaty straining of the engine, comfortable enough with each other to retreat into separate places. As we drove, I wondered how much time there was before we'd have to give up this unlikely chase and go back to our real lives. I was already burning bridges that I'd probably need later but while this strange interlude lasted it was easier not to think about the practicalities I'd left behind. Katya must have been thinking something similar because at one point, after a long silence, she laughed and turned to me.

'It's quite hard to believe this is real, isn't it?'

'Yes,' I nodded. 'We're as mad as each other.'

She smiled in reply then reached out and touched my forearm. But when I turned and looked at her she was already back in her own thoughts, her head turned to the wide open fields.

We arrived in the middle of the afternoon but it felt later. The hotel lights were already on, and inside there was warmth and the immediate promise of comfort. A dreamy trickle of piano music came from the wood-panelled bar and somewhere close we could smell a wood fire. Katya looked around her. 'Wow,' she said. 'Very nice. And very English. Can I afford it?'

'On me,' I said. 'When we find the bird I'll dock it from your share.'

She looked at me but didn't argue. It was just another thing I was happy to let go, another reckoning to be dealt with later.

We checked in and dropped our bags in our rooms, then returned to the streets so Katya could get her bearings. It was a Sunday and the town was quiet but it was bitterly cold now that the light had faded. After the dreary winter daylight the encroaching darkness was almost a relief. Old-fashioned lamps lit the narrow streets around the cathedral and the places still open—a café, a bookshop, a restaurant—threw welcoming glances onto the cobbles. Looking up, we could see the cathedral outlined against the sky and behind it the clouds, now broken into fragments and giving way to stars. There would be a frost.

When we reached the cathedral close we could hear organ music.

'Do you want to go in and listen?' I asked Katya.

'Not my thing, I think.' Katya put her hand on my shoulder. 'But you go if you want to. I'll head back and have a shower to warm up. I'll meet you in the bar.'

So I went alone and sat in the shadows of the dimly lit cathedral and let the music envelop me. There was no service, just the organist practising for evensong. By the time I left I felt relaxed and soothed and found myself looking forward to a glass of wine in the hotel bar. What I wasn't anticipating though was what I found when I got there. In one corner, near the fireplace, Karl Anderson was lounging comfortably in one of the big leather armchairs. Opposite him, sleek and perfect in a slim red dress, was Gabby. And between them, almost casually, a bottle of champagne poking its head out of a large silver bucket.

It was a winter of dreams and forgetting. Snow fell in Richmond in late November and lingered until February, a white cloak drawn over their past and muffling the present. He would arrive on horseback, a dark figure against the white, the snow turning to ice in the folds of his cloak; inside he'd find the fires crackling noisily and the smell of hot wine and spices thick in the air. Even when he travelled at dusk he would find the lamps burning for him, the windows glowing red with welcome, and always in the green bedroom a single lamp and a fire that turned the russet drapes to amber. The place seemed timeless, wrapped in winter and wood smoke as if nothing that happened in the rest of the world would ever change it. The ride there from the city was slow, the roads deep, his hands numb on the reins, and yet it was a journey he relished. He would arrive feeling clean and pure, fit for the welcome that awaited him. When he travelled through days of sunshine and dazzling whiteness, he would see children skating on frozen ponds and old women collecting firewood and he would feel a sort of intoxication, as if every face he saw he loved a little.

She never looked out for his coming but came to recognise the sound of his approach. First the chimes of a harness, a boy running to take his horse, then footsteps, a firm knock and Jenny the maid scampering eagerly to answer it. Then she would hear his voice—always indistinct but low and merry. She would continue with what she was doing until that moment and then would begin to put down her things so that when he entered she was free to rise and welcome him. But best of all was his arrival in the winter darkness when the house had settled for the night.

Those were the times, always unexpected, when he had suddenly risen in the middle of a London evening and, making his excuses, had returned to his house, there to cause consternation amongst his ostlers by calling for a horse. Sometimes he reached Richmond to find the whole house asleep, her fire no more than an orange glow at the window. She would hear Martha plod to the door with grumbling reluctance and hush him when he tried to speak, and she would stir and smile at the sound, only to sleep again until she heard her bedroom door squeak open. Then, with her eyes still closed, she would pull back one corner of the blankets and wait half dreaming while he warmed his hands at the fire. Often on those occasions she would wake in the deep of the night to find him sleeping curled against her; and then she would sleep again, smiling, happy at the thought of waking.

When he arrived in daylight she put away all thoughts of her work and they spent the afternoons by the fire or walking through the frozen woods, talking of things that mattered less than the fact of their talking. Sometimes their conversation was brilliant—ideas imagined beyond every bound of reality. Sometimes they talked of things that made them laugh for reasons they could never afterwards explain. And as they talked, the trees and the fields around them, even the cart-pocked tracks, seemed to lie unconscious, waiting for spring to restart their clocks. In that solstitial pause she would forget the past that had brought her there and any fears for the future. The end of the week seemed an unimaginable distance.

For him the snow seemed to obliterate the stains of the past, all the things that marred his perfect happiness. At night they would lull themselves by the fire and dream of a world where everything, including themselves, could be anything they wished.

'You would stay here and grow plants,' she said, 'and devise a way to farm pineapples on your precious Fens.'

'Too cold,' he said.

'You would heat the water with underground pipes and people would come from Brazil to bathe there.'

He mused on the thought. 'In that case, you would tour the shires of England and produce the definitive work on mosses and lichen. And you would learn how to grow moss on the inside walls of all our great buildings so that it might be studied in greater comfort by all who visited. And for your pains, of course, you would be elected unanimously to the Royal Society.'

'Too young and a woman.'

'You would write under the name of Tom Brown the Elder.'

'Ah! And am I only ever to paint lichen?'

'Very well, you would travel with me around the world and you would draw while I collect. Between us we would create a collection that would be the wonder of the world.'

'A woman at sea?'

'I should disguise you as a boy.'

'For the sake of art only?' She reached her face up to his and very lightly brushed her lips against his neck.

'Well,' he mused, beginning to smile, 'perhaps not purely for your drawings.' And with a great tug he pulled her to him and kissed her while she laughed.

*　　*　　*

When February drew to a close the snow began to give way to water and his journey became slower and

213

less elating. Time had rediscovered them and the deepening mud was a warning. It was only four months until he was due to leave on the *Resolution*.

Their time together became quieter, parting more painful. Neither wanted to think of their days ending, but each day they did. It made both of them less playful. When they did laugh together there was a wildness about them, a desperation to seize the moment and hold it for as long as it could be held. Instead of walking, they took to sitting quietly together for long periods, touching more.

Finally they lay close to each other one night with only the fire lighting the room and he said, 'Come with me.'

She was lying half on him, her head on his chest, one leg between his. She might have been asleep but at his words she raised her head to look at him. Beyond her the fire still glowed dimly. He expected her to laugh, to tease him, but instead she held his gaze for a long time.

'I couldn't,' she replied at last.

'You could!' With sudden energy he rolled her onto her side, then moved to kneel beside her. 'De Commerson did it. His mistress travelled the world dressed as his page. She saw the East Indies, China, India—amazing, wonderful places!'

'And people know she did.' Her voice stayed calm. 'She was caught in the end.'

She kneeled up to face him. His energy was infectious.

'You could join the ship in Madeira,' he continued, 'away from prying eyes. I would tell Cook that one of my draughtsmen was joining us there.'

'Joseph! It isn't possible, a woman at sea pretending to be a man. The arrangements on board . . .'

'I will have more space for my party this time. It is already being arranged. I will demand an extra cabin, next to mine. They won't refuse me that.'

She looked away from him, trying to imagine herself cropped, tightly jacketed.

'Just think!' he cried. 'You could see the oceans and the tropics for yourself, see all the things we talk of with your very own eyes. You could stand with me on unmapped lands, pick out the Southern Cross in the night sky. You could smell the brine in the wind as we round the Cape. All those things you've imagined, you could see them for yourself! Think of it! Think what it could be!'

It was impossible, she knew, madness born of the long nights and the winter stars. Yet the firelight wove his words into bright images and her deepest-held dreams seemed for a moment close enough to reach. She would be prepared to risk a great deal to touch just one of them. And what did she have that she was putting at risk? Only him. And she would lose him anyway.

A week later a carriage rolled into the busy yard of the Bell Post, a crowded coaching inn some half a day's journey from London on the Bath road. It was an unremarkable carriage and the servant who leapt down to hand out its occupants wore no livery. The two figures that descended were well, if unobtrusively, dressed; minor gentry, thought the landlord who welcomed them and showed them to a private room; to him their clothes were more important than their faces. He was too busy to note the solicitousness of one and the paleness of the other. The woman who served them looked more closely but her attention was caught by the larger of the two. Handsome, she thought, with proper manners and nice eyes. Intent on him, she barely noticed his slight, tongue-tied companion; otherwise she might perhaps have wondered at the smallness of his features. The boy from the taproom who rushed to hold the door as they left the inn thought little about the varied travellers who passed by him each day but remembered for many months the shining gold coin pressed into his palm.

And no one much cared that when the carriage departed it turned back towards London, the direction from which it had come.

*   *   *

She knew from the first that they were deluding themselves. Their experiments were too easy, too dependent on the carelessness of others. Further outings followed the first but the results were always the same. She fooled nobody: she merely passed unnoticed. That might suffice for the passage to Madeira where a quiet traveller who kept to his cabin would not be unusual, would not be much noted among the many others. Apart from a few sentences to ask for food to be brought she would barely have to speak. And to those who served on busy ships, Banks assured her, even seasick passengers were too much routine to excite curiosity. As long as her passage was paid and she caused no trouble she would be largely ignored.

But on Madeira she knew it would be different. He would give her letters to an English household there and they couldn't fail to be interested in their guest. Even if she spent her days botanising in the hills, it would be impossible to avoid the speculation of others. In her heart she knew it could not work and she

216

trembled at the thought of shameful and humiliating discovery. Yet what form would that take? Protected by letters of introduction, she would surely not be publicly denounced. Those who guessed were more likely to say nothing to her, to talk instead amongst themselves. The thought of being the subject of such derision horrified her, yet what harm could it do? If she failed entirely she would return to London on the first ship, anonymous again. She would have done no harm to Banks. And by then she would already have seen new places and things, studied for herself a foreign flora, made drawings she could keep forever.

Even if she were not exposed on Madeira, discovery would come when the *Resolution* arrived. There would be no fooling Cook, she knew. Banks had always talked admiringly of his perspicacity. At some point he would know the truth and what then? If it was immediate, she could slink away blushing and leave Joseph to repair his fences and continue the journey. He would be able to laugh off the incident and at the end of a three-year voyage it would have been forgotten. But if it was later, after they had sailed, what then? Could she live with the thought of discovery at sea? The humiliation would be almost overwhelming and there could be no quick escape. And yet, however dreadful, she would still be on board when they crossed the Equator, when they put in to Rio de Janeiro. Even if Cook insisted on her leaving the ship there, she would already have lived dreams she had never dared to believe in.

And there was something else, something that gave her a thrill of excitement that she didn't attempt to explain to Banks. From London to Madeira, and on the island itself, she would be travelling *alone*. With no attendant and no companions. She would be forced to rely on herself for everything. It was a vision of independence that could never be contemplated in her own world and just a glimpse of it stirred her. Mockery, derision, contempt, even disgust—these might cause her pain but not damage. On her return those things would wash away and leave only those things she had reached out and seized for herself.

Banks thought less of these things. It can be dangerous to be in love and an optimist. He was still a little intoxicated by his own successes and he knew his plan would work because he would make it work. The realities were less important than his determination to overcome them. But even for him there were moments when he became suddenly uneasy. He began to find himself waking in the night when she was beside him, panicking as he woke that she was not there. Then he would lie and watch her sleep, cradled in blankets, her breathing so light she barely stirred. At those moments a huge tenderness would rise up to engulf him and the thought of what they had contemplated was nothing more than laughable. For her to set off alone would be unimaginable folly perpetrated at his command; it would demonstrate nothing but his own colossal selfishness. He vowed that in the morning he would call off their plans. But when sleep started to reclaim him and his fears were less important than the closeness of her body, he would remember how brave she was, how special in her daring, and he was proud of her as his thoughts lost their focus and dissolved into the surety of sleep.

With the arrival of spring his London world became harder to escape. The pressures of preparing for a second voyage were different. Last time he had not been burdened by experience, nor by the attentions of countless botanists, taxonomists, philosophers, priests, clockmakers, chandlers, inventors, artists, specu lators, merchants, tailors, beggars and optimistic younger sons. Everyone seemed eager to claim acquaintance, to hint at schemes, to offer advice, to detail their talents or to ask most blatantly for preferment. And worse, his plans for his party and their accommodation on board were not going as he had wished.

He felt strongly that the problem was Cook. For their first voyage, the captain had opted not for a ship of the line, but for a squat, round-bottomed Whitby collier, a boat as slow as it was stable. The *Endeavour* had served them well but such ships were small and cramped, and for the second voyage Banks's ambitions had outgrown them. This time the Admiralty was convinced of the value of the voyage and was prepared to offer Cook a larger vessel should he want it, one that would be large enough to accommodate Banks's plans both scientific and personal. Yet to his dismay, Cook refused a frigate and insisted on another collier, and his masters supported his choice. Banks's frustration at this decision began to manifest itself in increasingly peevish letters to the Admiralty arguing his need for an expanded entourage and the space to accommodate them. This time around Banks had influence and the Admiralty agreed to certain alterations and additions to the *Resolution* in order to increase the space available. Banks would, after all, have the accommodation he demanded.

The result was a victory of sorts but he still felt wounded that his recommendation of a larger vessel had not been given more weight. Worse than that, the whole issue had brought him into conflict with Cook, a man he respected and with whom previously he had always been in accord. This shook Banks's confidence a

219

little and made him wonder if Cook would be quite so quiescent in the matter of Banks's extra passenger as he had anticipated. Yet even as he paced the floors of his house in New Burlington Street he knew that a little of his anger had its source elsewhere. The strict, even-handed honesty that the Yorkshireman brought to the argument illustrated a great many of the virtues that Banks admired in him. The thought that he proposed at best to deceive Cook, at worst to place him in a position that would both embarrass and anger him, was not a pleasant one. In the company of his friends, Banks was daring and irreverent. By the firelight in Richmond, he was pure and passionate. But Cook inspired different ideals in him, those of leadership and honesty that Banks had always esteemed in the navigator. Smuggling his mistress on board ship was hardly a demonstration of such qualities. And the more guilt he felt about his own behaviour, the more Cook's virtues began to irritate him and the more their conflict rankled.

Strangely, as his doubts grew, she became more reckless. Summer came early and the days became hot, the nights short and breathless. Her passage to Madeira was confirmed, the arrangements made for money and accommodation. It was a fantasy that seemed to have its own life and logic. She began to rehearse in her mind every step of the journey: the carriage to Southampton, embarking on the *Robin*, her voice as she did so, her name, her manner, her conduct. She rehearsed her lines and stared down her fears before they grew tall enough to engulf her. During that period Banks needed to be so much in London that his visits became shorter and irregular. That made it easier to imagine how her Richmond refuge would be if he were gone and she remained. What had once appeared to be discretion would become isolation, what was secretive would become suffocating. The more she reflected, the more she knew she could not stay without him. It mattered to her less and less what happened next as long as it was not that.

A week before she was due to depart, she dressed in her new clothes and slipped out into the dusk. The streets were already quiet but there were still figures moving through the warm half-light, stirring up the dust. Lights burned in houses and in the taverns by the river. The Thames was a dark glass reflecting nothing. She walked the streets unnoticed for an hour or more, saying goodbye to the things she had come to know. As she walked, the wind got up and began to break open the overcast night. Eventually she came to the place where the last houses stopped and gave way to woodland and here she paused. She felt very small and very alone and scared to the very core of her soul. But when she looked up at the clouds rushing across the moon, her lungs filled with a deep shuddering breath; and when she breathed out it was as if the night sky embraced her.

*   *   *

By the time he rode to meet her three days later, he had made his decision. The excitement of the game had gone on long enough but now they could maintain it no longer. They had planned that night as their last together. The next day he was to see her on her way. Now he would tell her she must not go, forbid it if necessary. It had been a mirage of his creation and the fault lay at his door: he would beg her forgiveness and they would plan instead their lives on his return. His decision brought with it an

221

immeasurable relief.

On his arrival in Richmond, Martha met him solemn-faced and handed him a note written in a now familiar sloping hand.

'My darling,' it began. *'Forgive me. If I spend another night in your arms you will make me change my mind. It is too easy to be afraid when you are beside me. Alone, I have no choice but to be brave. And I know that when you hold me you will tell me not to go. So I have gone already. I know it is what I must do. I will wait for you in Madeira. Find me there.'*

There was no signature, but at the foot of the page there was one more line of writing which, at the last, she had added in small, less certain letters:

'It is dark now and there is something in the wind that makes me afraid. Whatever befalls us I will always think of you. If you can, think of me.'

CHAPTER THIRTEEN

GRAMOPHONES

By checking into the same hotel, I'd planned to disconcert Karl Anderson. I hoped that it might persuade him I was hot on the trail, perhaps fluster him into making a mistake. Instead, as things turned out, the confusion was all mine.

Anderson rose to his feet as soon as he saw me and then came forward with a smile, his hand extended to shake mine. He looked as he had before: all Nordic good health and self-confidence. His suit was impeccably cut and he wore it well. An annoyingly attractive man.

'Ah, Mr Fitzgerald! We saw from the book that you had checked in. Welcome.' He might have owned the place. His grip was firm and suitably proprietorial.

'Hello, Fitz. I thought I might see you here.' Gabby was also on her feet.

'I thought you were in London,' I replied, trying to sound casual and almost certainly failing.

Anderson was quick to ooze unction over any trace of awkwardness.

'I rang Gabriella today and urged her to join me here to celebrate. I have a feeling that this may be a good week.'

Gabby rested her hand on his elbow.

'Karl thinks he may have found the bird.' Her eyes met mine. Beautiful eyes. But hard to read.

Anderson signalled for an extra glass, then put his hand on the back of my shoulder and guided me over to where they'd been sitting. 'Come and drink. You have to admit that the recovery of such a rare specimen is something worth celebrating.'

'You've actually seen it?' I asked, still standing.

'Not yet.' The smile didn't flicker. 'But I expect to.'

'I see.' I dropped into the leather vastness of the armchair. 'Then there's still hope.'

'Hope?' Anderson feigned surprise. 'Ah, of course! A few minutes ago I was lucky enough to bump into your charming companion. Katya, I believe her name is. I understand that you have been making certain investigations of your own.'

'I have one or two ideas,' I told him.

'Ideas about the Fabricius papers?'

That caught me off-balance. It hadn't occurred to me that Katya would tell him about her trip to Denmark. Though, of course, Anderson's charm was legendary.

'I can assure you that trail doesn't lead anywhere,' he went on. 'Joseph Banks's mistress and all that. I've been down all those alleys and they're all dead ends. If you'd told me, I could have saved you some trouble. You see, I know exactly where the bird was at the turn of the century and I think I know where it went after that. Remember, I've had a team of researchers working on this for months, Mr Fitzgerald. Today my team spoke to someone, a farmer whose family once lived near here. Soon I may be able to show you the bird itself.'

'And the pictures?' I asked, watching him closely.

'Pictures?' He looked calmly across at Gabby. 'Ah, yes. The paintings by Roitelet. You will forgive me for not mentioning them earlier, I'm sure. They are likely to be worth a very, very large sum of money indeed, and in such situations a degree of discretion is always sensible.'

'And you think you'll find them when you find the bird?'

'It seems a reasonable hope. Remember, they have never come up for sale, and no one has ever recorded seeing them. That means there is a very good chance they are still where they were before, still in the same case as the bird. Finchley, who saw them in the nineteenth century, says they were well hidden. Of course, they may not be by Roitelet at all. But the rumours are most persistent and Finchley is a reliable witness. And tomorrow I hope to know for certain. I have a very good feeling.'

'Just one thing,' I said, reaching out and stopping his arm as he tried to drink. 'Why did you break into my house?'

In that polite atmosphere, the rawness of my tone jarred, and left him in no doubt about how I was feeling. His eyes flicked quickly to my face and he seemed about to speak, but I carried on regardless.

'Or if not you, one of your people. I'm sure you don't do that sort of thing yourself. You might have asked them to leave things neater. They didn't need to throw the notes everywhere.'

He blinked at that.

'Someone has been through your notes?'

'You know it.'

He looked down at my hand on his arm, then up again and met my gaze directly.

'I can give you my word, Mr Fitzgerald, that was

nothing to do with me. I promise you that.'

We looked each other in the eye for a few seconds more, and then I took my hand away.

'Then who?'

It was Gabby who replied.

'Karl told you there'd be other people interested in the bird. Perhaps one of them . . .'

At that point a movement behind me caught Anderson's eye and he rose to his feet again. I turned round to see Katya hesitating at the door of the bar, all in black, her hair very dark. Anderson called out to her, something in Norwegian or Swedish, and beckoned her over. 'Join us,' he said in English. 'We'll open another bottle.'

I can't say it was the easiest of evenings, though Anderson seemed completely relaxed. He was careful to keep the conversation away from the Ulieta bird, telling us instead about his time as a young palaeontologist in America. The stories sounded well practised but they were good ones and I noticed they made Katya laugh. When the conversation became more general, Anderson turned to her and asked something about Sweden, which left Gabby and me to face each other. There, in Anderson's presence, the closeness I'd felt at our previous meeting seemed changed, and we chatted rather stiltedly, aware of the proximity of the others. From time to time Gabby's glance flicked over to Katya, slightly curious, not sure where she fitted in.

When Anderson began to make arrangements for the four of us to eat together I'd had enough, and I was quick to tell him that Katya and I had booked a table somewhere else. Outside, when we'd both found our coats, I had to admit to Katya

226

that it wasn't true.

'I just didn't want to spend the evening with Anderson,' I told her.

She looked at me a little strangely. 'He seems very friendly. And he's very entertaining too.'

'You like him?'

'He's an interesting man. Not how I imagined at all.' She put her hand on my arm and squeezed it slightly, guiding me down the narrow street. 'But he's very used to winning,' she said. 'I'm not sure that's something I like.'

For a moment we walked in silence but there was something else I had to say.

'I didn't think you'd tell him all about your Fabricius research. I thought that was between us.'

She looked hurt. 'Of course it is. I only told him I'd been looking at those papers. I didn't tell him what I'd found.'

'He seemed to know all about it. He said it was a dead end.'

She stopped me then, in the middle of the empty street, and looked up at me. 'Did you tell Gabriella about it?'

'Gabby?' I felt myself blushing. That night in the restaurant when the wine was flowing . . .

Katya watched me for a moment, then shrugged and walked on. Dinner that night wasn't a great success.

*   *   *

The next day we were in the county archives practically as soon as they opened. The librarian with the nice face recognised me again.

'People beginning with B, isn't it?' she asked

227

with a smile as we began to move towards the microfilm readers.

'Not this time,' I told her. 'This time it's only people called Burnett.'

She nodded at that. 'Did you have a particular one you're looking for?'

'Not really. We're going to start off with a Mary Burnett. After that we'll take any we can find.'

That rather casual summary was pretty much all we had by way of a plan. It didn't seem much, especially given Anderson's display of confidence the night before, but I was living in hope that his plan might go wrong, that something in all his relentless research might prove flawed.

Next to me Katya was all bristling efficiency, but somehow the night before had broken the flow of our understanding. In an attempt to get us back on track I showed her what I'd found on my previous visit.

'OK,' she said briskly, 'if this Mary Burnett is the one we're looking for, then she should have been an orphan by the time Banks got back. You've already found out that her father died, but what about her mother?'

We found the relevant rolls of film and checked them intently, edging slowly down the parish lists.

'Nothing,' Katya concluded eventually. 'Does that mean we're wrong?'

'Not necessarily. Perhap she died somewhere else. There are loads of reasons why she may not have been buried in Revesby.'

'Well, if our mystery woman really was this Mary Burnett and she came from Revesby in the first place, might she have come back here at some point? After her affair with Banks?'

I nodded. 'I suppose so. It's a long shot but it's possible. She might have married here. Or died here.' So that set us off on a desperately long search. We checked all the records of marriages in Revesby for the next forty years. We checked all the deaths for the next hundred. There was no further mention of Mary Burnett. Then, still hoping for a miracle, we began to check the records of neighbouring parishes. We broke for sandwiches at lunchtime, then carried on. At three o'clock we paused. On one wall of the library there was a map of the county.

'Lincolnshire's an incredibly large place,' I said.

'A lot of parishes,' Katya agreed.

'And why stop there? She might have settled in Norfolk. Or Yorkshire. There's plenty of parishes in Yorkshire.'

By four o'clock our eyes were aching from the screens, and the list of Burnetts we'd found was becoming increasingly meaningless. And we still hadn't found any other references to Mary Burnett. At four thirty we called it a day and packed up our notes. While Katya disappeared to find the ladies, I lingered by the main desk where the library staff were beginning to pack up. The librarian we'd spoken to earlier clearly thought I looked downcast.

'No luck?' she asked.

'I'm afraid not. We found some Burnetts but none of them are the ones we really wanted.'

She looked around the reading room. 'There's a gentleman who comes in here to do his family tree. We see a lot of him. He was telling me the other day that he was looking for Burnetts. It struck me this morning, as soon as you said the name. I was

229

going to point you out to him if he came in. He's here quite often, so perhaps if you come back tomorrow . . . His name's Bert. Most of the regulars can point him out to you.'

Before we left the building, Katya and I agreed to split up and meet again at seven to go through our notes. That arrangement made, she didn't wait for me: I watched her step out into the gathering gloom, her face buried deeply in the collar of her coat. Twenty yards down the road she turned and saw I was still watching her. A moment later she was out of sight, hidden behind the evening traffic; but before she turned away she'd raised her hand and given me the shyest of waves.

It lifted my spirits, and I was about to follow her into the dark when the friendly librarian called out to me.

'Excuse me, sir. I thought this might help.' She pushed a scrap of paper into my hand and gave me a rather surprising wink before bustling off in the other direction. The paper, when I unfolded it, had the name *Bert Fox* written on it, and next to it, in very neat handwriting, a phone number.

*   *   *

The piece of luck my grandfather had prayed for arrived so late that he'd almost given up waiting for it. Kicking around London with a diminishing reputation and nothing much to do with his time, the wait had turned him into a stubborn, angry man. When he welcomed in the New Year of 1933 at the Explorers' Club it was already twenty years since Chapin had found that single feather and through every one of those years my grandfather

230

had lived in permanent dread of hearing that the bird itself was discovered. And then, one day at the same club, he was introduced quite by chance to a South African called Myerson. Myerson had made a lot of money in mining—and, as my grandfather discovered, he was an avid collector of rare birds.

*   *   *

I hadn't anything better to do, so I decided to call the number I'd been given. After three or four rings a male voice answered.

'Excuse me,' I began, realising I hadn't worked out what to say. 'Is that Bert Fox?'

'Yeah.' His voice was gruff but not unfriendly.

'Look, you don't know me. My name's Fitzgerald. I've spent all day in the county archives and the librarian there said you might be able to help me. I'm trying to trace someone called Burnett.'

'That would've been Tina. In the library, I mean, I always tell her what I'm working on. Which one are you looking for?'

I told him I was looking for a woman who'd lived in London in the 1770s, someone who might be the Mary Burnett born in Revesby in 1752. He listened politely enough, but when I'd finished he grunted an apology.

'Don't think I can help you with her,' he muttered. 'I'm afraid Revesby isn't really my area.'

'Well, anything you know about Burnetts in Lincolnshire would be helpful, wherever they were.'

He thought about it. 'Sure, why not? If you want to talk family trees come round. I'm in all evening.'

He lived a bus ride away, in a street of red-brick Edwardian villas, three floors high. The front gardens were bounded by dark hedges spotted with laburnum trees or yews, still dripping arrhythmically after the last shower of rain. The house I was looking for had an old Ford Anglia parked in the driveway and another standing on bricks in the open garage. When I rang the bell, my host turned out to be someone quite unexpected. He was tall and wiry but slightly stooped, and the little hair he still had was tied back in a long silver ponytail. He was wearing a white, baggy, collarless shirt and a brown suede waistcoat, and his face was creased with lines that suggested both smiles and frowns. I noticed his hands were covered in dark stains: ink, perhaps, or oil.

'You're the Burnett man?' he asked and beckoned me indoors. 'Come on in. I'm working, but I can talk.'

At first glance, the room he showed me into seemed to be in chaos. There were shelves and tables everywhere, each one densely packed with ancient, wind-up gramophones. Scattered everywhere, on the tables and on the floor, were screws and levers and moulded chunks of metal in weird shapes. Near the middle of the room were three old, low sofas covered with more parts, surrounded by tottering piles of old gramophone records in white paper covers. Most of the room was in shadow but an enormous Anglepoise lamp shone brilliantly onto the table in the centre of the room where a gramophone appeared to lie in a thousand pieces.

'This is what I do,' he said. 'Gramophones. You'd be surprised how much work there is.' He

232

indicated the pieces on the table. 'Some gent brought this one up from Kent. Here, take a seat.'

I found an empty patch of sofa large enough to sit on and perched myself there. A record tipped from the arm of the chair and slid into my lap.

'A seventy-eight,' I commented, peering at it.

He waved his hand around the room. 'All of them are. Great sound. The only way you can hear them properly is on one of these.'

I waited patiently while he gave me an impassioned speech about the glories of early sound recording, smoking continuously as he talked and occasionally poking the metal pieces scattered in front of him.

'So tell me,' I said, eventually changing the subject, 'you're working on a family tree?'

He nodded, cigarette clutched firmly in the corner of his mouth. 'Yeah. I do it for my mum. She loves that kind of stuff. She's well into her nineties. Still lively though.' I made a hasty recalculation of his age. I'd taken him for about sixty but now I could see he was older, late sixties, seventy perhaps. 'Can't say I don't enjoy it, though,' he went on. 'It's a bit like one of these things.' He indicated the work in front of him. 'Putting bits together in the right order. Finding what you need to fill the gaps.'

'So what's your interest in people called Burnett?'

'There's Burnetts on my dad's side.' He began rooting around among the bits on the table in front of him. 'I did my mum's side first. That was quite easy. They were local gentry really. Easy to follow. Not that you ever really finish something like that, do you? You can always go further back. Or wider.

There's always someone you haven't found.'

That seemed a good cue to tell him the little I knew about Mary Burnett of Revesby, and about our failed attempts to find any other references to her. Eventually he shook his head.

'Don't think I can help you with her. She's earlier than the ones I'm interested in, and Revesby isn't really my bit of the county. My family all come from further north, the other side of Lincoln. And I've never come across any Mary Burnett.'

'So it was your grandfather who married a Burnett?'

'Nah.' He took a swift drag at his cigarette. 'Goes back much further than that.' He got up and came back with a scrap of paper. 'Look. This is me, at the top of the list, born 1925. Then there's my dad, then my granddad. He was Matthew Fox, born 1856. He didn't have my dad until he was forty-odd, so that leaps us back quite a long way. Then there's my great-granddad. He was another one who married late. Then my granddad's granddad, another Matthew. He was the one that married a Burnett.'

Albert Fox b.1925
Henry Fox b.1896
Matthew Fox b.1856
Joseph Fox b.1804
Matthew Fox b.1764

I watched him write, impressed. 'It must have taken some work to go back that far.'

'Nah, it wasn't too hard. Fox is an easy name, and I like to do a couple of afternoons a week. Get out of the house, you know. It's their wives that cause me problems, finding out about them. My grandfather married twice, a Smith and a Jones. Would you believe that?'

'You follow back all the wives as well?'

'I do what I can.' He shuffled more metal pieces on the table.

'And that last one on the list. You say he married a Burnett?'

'Yeah, though not yours.' He took a long draw on his cigarette, clearly not very interested in any Burnetts beyond his own family. Then he looked down and tapped the list. 'Those first three were all married in the same church. Makes them easy to trace. It was my father who broke the trend, married my mother in Cornwall. She was living with a cousin down there. That sort of thing is a pain for people trying to track you down later on.' He gave a dry chuckle as he contemplated the plight of future genealogists. 'Me, I was married in Finsbury Park registry office, so I guess I can't complain. But generally speaking it's one thing that makes the Foxes easy to track—they didn't move around much. Tenant farmers or the like. All in the Ainsby area.'

He was looking down again as he spoke so he didn't see me start forward.

'Hang on, hang on.' My tone of voice made him look up. 'Did you say *Ainsby*?'

'Yeah, that's right. Ainsby.'

'You mean Ainsby is a *place*, not a person?'

He looked at me as though I was either strange or simple. 'Yeah. North-west of here. Small village. Not much of a place now.'

I stood up quickly. 'I don't want to be rude, Mr

235

Fox, but do you mind if I rush off? There's something I really need to check. I think you might have told me something really, really important.'

If he was surprised at my sudden exit he didn't show it. He came to the door with me and then watched as I hurried out into the night. It was all I could do to stop myself from running.

Banks's emotions on the day he found her gone were a surprise to him. He expected to be angry. He expected to be hurt by her deception, pained by her stupidity, guilty at his part in such folly. He felt none of those things.

His first thought was to stop her. He demanded of Martha the time of her departure, did rapid calculations of how and where he could intercept her. If he returned directly to London, set off at once, he could surely be in Southampton before she sailed. But the *Resolution* was ready to sail and he was needed in London. To disappear now would throw the expedition into disarray, draw every attention to the reasons for his absence. More than anything she would hate that. And he had alternatives. He knew the ship she sailed on and the name she travelled under. A messenger would reach her in time. He would write to her now, beg her to return, promise her . . . Promise her what? The question stilled him and for half an hour or more he considered it as thoughts of pursuit were made to wait.

At the end of that time he crumpled her letter in his hand. She had gone. He unclenched his hand and balanced the ball of paper on his palm. She had gone, and for reasons that no arguments of his would alter. It was not for him but for herself, because she needed to go. He could persuade her to stay, perhaps. The cage-reared bird will always partly fear the sky. But in that small drawing room he felt something of the confines of her life, confines he would never know and perhaps would never understand again as clearly as he did at that moment.

He had ridden to Richmond determined to stop

her. That evening, as he drew nearer the lights of London, he began to see what the independence of thought that had always intrigued him really meant. It made her different from other women, but he had always tended to think of it as something external, like a bird's plumage. Now he could see it was more than that. It was something deep inside her, part of that essence that made her what she was. Perhaps there was an unusual clarity in the air that night. Perhaps being in love had sown seeds that grew and budded in that evening's starlight. He rode with a serenity inside him and a sense of understanding that he thought would remain with him forever.

It made him determined to live up to her example. In the last months he had begun to fear the condemnation of society, the disapproval of Cook, and perhaps most of all the possible ruin of his own ambitions. To avoid these things he had been prepared to disappoint the hopes he himself had nurtured in her. Now, as he pushed his horse into a canter, it seemed clear to him that her judgement of him was the only one that mattered. If their scheme failed now it would not be through his cowardice. He would make it work.

In New Burlington Street that night he listened to the hours strike and thought of her. It was a night they had planned to spend together and, finding himself alone, he slept poorly. In the ragged margin between sleep and wakefulness, images of her at sea swayed in and out of his mind: first on deck, held straight by her male clothing, rain and salt water lashing her face; then in the darkness of her cabin, undressing by candlelight, button by button. The thought of her arriving in Madeira and waiting for him there in the lush tropic heat began to stir him. The thought of greeting the quiet male figure in a public place, of going through the rituals of reacquaintance, of agreeing to share a bottle somewhere private, in her room perhaps, where with the door closed he would hold a finger to his lips then linger over each button and lace until he felt her skin naked under his fingers. He thought of the cabin reserved for her on board the *Resolution* and vowed again to make it work.

But with the morning came word that changed the course of his life. The Navy Board had challenged the seaworthiness of the *Resolution*. The pilot charged with taking her out of the Thames had been so alarmed at her handling he had refused to take her beyond the Nore. She was branded crank and unseaworthy and the Admiralty had accepted those claims. The changes made to accommodate Banks's party were to be reversed. The extra cabins were to be ripped out. His dreams of the night before were shown in daylight to be the fantasies they were. By the time he next saw the *Resolution*, the dark cabin of which he had thought so often was no more than frayed timber piled untidily on an estuary dock.

*　　　*　　　*

Nothing had prepared her for the strangeness of it. She knew nothing of the sea, nothing of ships and very little of the men who crewed them. Worse, she realised, she knew nothing of the way men were with other men. Their manners were rougher and their language coarser, but it was the physicality that alarmed her. It was as if an invisible cordon that had surrounded her all her life had been torn away, allowing strangers to brush against her or to touch her as a matter of course. The bumping and barging as she

239

made her way aboard seemed a deliberate provocation and it was all she could do to fight back a wave of panic. It was only when she observed the same men step wide around a woman that she began to understand.

She was certain it was only the pressures of departure that saved her from discovery. No one on board the *Robin* had time for her, no one cared. She was able to flee to her cabin like a rabbit to earth and once there she stayed, heart racing, her panic turning to despair and desolation. The shock of it all inflicted on her a sort of paralysis and for a full eight hours she clung to her refuge, declining the calls for food and jumping at every footstep that approached her door. She wanted only to be left alone and for the journey she had so coveted to be over. She longed for land.

As a prisoner in her own cabin she saw nothing of their departure but she felt it and heard it and knew there was no escape. The thought made her want to weep. The sounds of the ship were totally foreign to her. Even the language spoken there was unfamiliar and threatening. That first night she lay unable to sleep as boards groaned and creaked and the shouts of men were answered with other shouts, none of which she understood in either tone or meaning. She fell asleep still dressed, curled tightly under a blanket. Her last waking emotion was a longing for him to come.

When she awoke it seemed the vessel was in trouble. All around her the ship moaned and grunted and planks squealed under pressure of the sea. Her wooden walls tilted dangerously, then paused, and rolled back with a sickening lurch. A new panic surged up inside her and she was out from under her blanket in a moment, just as the cabin began to pitch again, faster and further than before. This new fear was enough to force her from her burrow. Opening the door enough to peer outside, she expected to hear the cries of a panicked crew but there was no rushing and no cries, nothing but the creaking of the ship. Slipping out and venturing a little further, she met a small boy carrying a huge bucket and she inquired faintly as to how the ship fared.

'First time at sea, is it?' he replied with a knowing grin. 'You're the third to ask me that this last half-hour. These waves is nothing, sir. Just a breeze in the Channel. Gets worse than this for sure.'

Reassured more by his calm than by his grim prophecy, she reached into an unfamiliar pocket and gave him a coin, asking if he would be able to find her some food. Looking at the coin, he almost dropped the bucket and promised not only food but his attention for the duration of the journey.

'I shall keep to my cabin a great deal,' she told him.

'There's many that do, sir, though you may like some air perhaps when the wind gets up.'

Both his first and second predictions were proved true only three days out to sea. By then she had come through the darkness of that first evening and was beginning to feel, if not confidence, at least a little pride in her achievement. She had come thus far largely unnoticed, had a willing servant to see to any needs and was now more at ease in her clothes, partly because she had not yet removed any. Yet when the *Robin* met rough seas for the first time, her instinct again was to fear imminent disaster. This time she succeeded in damping down her panic only to have it replaced by a dull churning in the pit of her stomach. After a few minutes of musing on this she suddenly straightened, reached for her cloak and stumbled outside. Her voyage was commencing in earnest.

*   *   *

The days before the *Resolution* sailed were among the worst of Banks's life. They seemed to pass in staccato bursts, time accelerating in the daylight hours while he cried out for a pause, then hanging heavy as he paced whole nights away, too fraught and frustrated for sleep. He blamed a host of different people for the ruin of his plans and bitterness began to consume him. Cook had been against him from the start, he decided. The Navy Board was made up of his enemies, people jealous of his success and resentful that a civilian should have any say in maritime matters. Lord Sandwich at the Admiralty was stubborn or misguided or ill-advised. All his raging seemed unable to sway them. Nevertheless, he spent those days restating his case in the strongest terms. Indeed his temper became so out of check that each interview, each letter, began to teeter on the brink of angry confrontation.

Unsurprisingly, Cook's views prevailed. Banks was rich, famous and well-connected, with prominent friends and a good deal of influence, all things that undoubtedly had weight with the Admiralty. But when it came to dispatching an expensive expedition to the other side of the world, the opinions of the professional seafarer held sway. Banks fumed.

Later—many years later—he was better able to understand the emotions that gripped him in those few days. At the time, however, nothing was clear. Banks had spent *his* money and *his* time putting together a team of unparalleled talents to advance the course of human learning and now he was to be thwarted by stubbornness and ignorance. He felt deeply let down, hurt on the most personal level that

242

his opinion had been so easily set aside. And when he thought of how this slight would appear to others—so blatant, so public—the humiliation of it boiled into rage and threatened to overwhelm him. He could never again sail with Cook after such an act of perfidy.

And underneath it all was the thought of that slim figure sailing to Madeira. How could he arrive and tell her she was to return alone while he went on? How admit to her that he had been so publicly humiliated in his attempt to secure her quarters? And what would it say of him if he were to accept his disappointment and meekly sail regardless? Their meeting in Madeira had been one he anticipated with a sensual thrill. Now it simply tasted bitter.

He continued to reason and rage right to the brink of departure but there were to be no more changes of heart. A letter to the Admiralty from the Navy Board dismissed his objections out of hand. It implied that Banks was not fit to comment on naval matters. Furthermore, the Board argued, even after the alterations had been reversed, Banks's accommodation on the *Resolution* was very nearly everything he had asked for. The only changes were a small reduction of the Great Cabin and the loss of one other small cabin.

One cabin! Banks found it impossible to describe his emotions. That cabin meant everything. White-faced with anger, he wrote to the Admiralty. The treatment he had received made it impossible for him to achieve the goals he had set himself. He had no alternative but to withdraw. At the same time he wrote to Cook and asked that all his equipment and effects be removed from the ship.

The letters dispatched, Banks remained in his study, still quivering with anger. There he paced in short, uneven lines until finally he came to a stop facing the window. He had been humiliated. He had had no alternative. It was a matter of honour. She would understand. He thought of her at sea, travelling ahead of him. She would arrive there soon. God, how happy that arrival would make her! He remained at the window until the light faded from the room and the papers on his desk became meaningless in the darkness.

*　　　*　　　*

The storm that lashed the *Robin* lasted through the night. When she first stepped out on the open deck there was a violet light in the sky above the horizon and the rain was driving horizontally on the wind, but she had no thoughts for the storm. Reaching the rail, she leaned out and vomited uncontrollably, one pulse of nausea following another until her stomach clenched with pain. She seemed to be there forever, utterly unconcerned about anything but the feelings inside her. At one point, waiting to retch, she looked along the rail and saw other passengers similarly affected, but then her stomach began to contract again and she leaned forward, not caring.

After twenty minutes she was cold and sodden but found she felt a little better. The strange light in the sky began to deepen into black and the ship seemed to roll less. Returning to her cabin to wash and change, she found she missed the wind on her face and after a few minutes she returned to the deck. It seemed deserted now. She stepped away from the hatch and looked around. The rain had stopped and the storm was dying away. The wind against her skin was cold but fresh and she felt better. More than that. She felt well. And happy. Yes, she was happy, there on the cold empty deck. Behind her the dawn was beginning to re-colour the sky. Pulling her dry cloak tight, she smiled in greeting. She had survived the night. In little more than a week she would reach Madeira.

CHAPTER FOURTEEN

METHOD

Most successful expeditions get lucky at some point and that night, on the bus back to the centre of Lincoln, I wondered if Bert Fox was my bit of luck. If so, there seemed a nasty possibility that he'd arrived rather late in the day. Which on reflection shouldn't have been a surprise—it was a feeling my grandfather would have recognised, too.

It isn't clear why Myerson was prepared to believe in the African peacock when no one else would but it seems he was willing to sink a considerable amount of cash into an expedition to the Congo. Whatever Myerson's reasoning, my grandfather's life was transformed by it, and he rediscovered energy that had seemed lost since his long illness. Myerson's offer didn't cover all the costs, so with a determination that verged on desperation my grandfather set about raising the rest. By the time he had mortgaged his house and borrowed against his wife's inheritance, he had enough to get his expedition off the ground.

At some point around that time, possibly carried there by his new euphoria, my grandfather visited Devon and by the time he set sail his wife was pregnant. It isn't clear if he knew this. It isn't clear if knowing it would have made much difference. However, it does seem pretty obvious from most contemporary accounts that he wasn't in the best state to lead an expedition: his objectivity was down to zero and his goal had become an obsession. In mountaineers they call it summit fever. It is something I've felt myself.

The bus got me back to the centre of Lincoln a little after seven, and Katya was already waiting for me in the hotel bar. I'd dreaded finding Anderson there too, but the room was nearly empty: only Katya in one corner and an elderly couple quarrelling in undertones. I think Katya knew something had happened when I didn't even stop at the bar, just went straight to her and sat down, placing two pieces of paper in front of her.

'We've been very stupid,' I said.

She peered forward to look at the things I'd brought, then she looked up, her eyes bright with curiosity.

'These are the photocopies we were sent,' she said. 'The letter to the woman in Stamford.'

'That's right. And where does it say in the letter that she was living in Stamford?'

She scanned the paper again. I could sense her mind already working, leaping ahead. 'Nothing in the letter,' she concluded. 'Only on the envelope.'

'Exactly.' I pushed forward the photocopy of the envelope that had arrived at the same time.

Miss Martha Ainsby,
The Old Manor,
Stamford,
Lincs

'We never saw the original,' I went on. 'The document Potts found was a photocopy. Now what if I tell you there's a *place* called Ainsby in Lincolnshire?'

247

She hesitated for a moment. 'You mean it's a local name? I don't see . . .' She carried on peering at the envelope as if for inspiration, and then suddenly it seemed to fall into place. 'Of course! Someone swapped the names!' She looked across at the paper again, her mind still working through it. 'The writing on the envelope looks genuine because it *is* genuine—it just had two words changed around. That would be easy to do. Just a bit of cutting and pasting. Especially if you knew that people were only going to see photocopies.'

She was looking at me, her eyes wide with discovery.

'And both of them are really grey, grainy copies that would hide a lot of mischief,' I agreed.

Katya looked back at the papers. 'So we were looking for the wrong person in the wrong place. We should have been asking about a family called Stamford that lived in Ainsby.'

'That's right. That's why there was nowhere called the Old Manor in Stamford. But I bet you anything you like that we'll find one in Ainsby.'

'I'm afraid not, Mr Fitzgerald.' The voice came from behind me. 'The Old Manor in Ainsby burned down during the last war.'

We'd been too engrossed in the papers in front of us to notice anyone else come into the bar. Now I looked up to see the rotund figure of Potts approaching us. His voice as he introduced himself to Katya was full of its usual lazy drawl.

'I'm Potts,' he told her, offering his hand. 'We didn't meet before but I saw you around the place in Stamford. When we were all being made fools of.'

Katya told him her name and he twinkled back

248

merrily, a slightly flirtatious favourite uncle. He was still wearing tweeds, still looked like a 1930s country doctor, and was still rather beguiling.

'I didn't mean to overhear,' he told us, 'but I take it you two have just got as far as working out about Ainsby village. Give me a moment to go to the bar and we'll drink to that.' We watched him patter to the bar and return with a bottle of red wine and three glasses. 'Now don't get the idea I'm ahead of you,' he explained mildly as he poured the drinks. 'I only sussed it out yesterday. Do you believe in coincidence? I'd been sitting around in London for a couple of days with no ideas and no inspiration. Then just as I was about to pack it in and go back to the States I found myself outside a shop in your Covent Garden district that sells maps and stuff. It's called Stamford's. You know it?'

I nodded. 'It's quite a famous shop. It's called *Stanfords*. With an N.'

'It is? Well, it was close enough to give me the prod I needed. There I was with people pushing by me wondering why this fat old American was standing in the street slapping his forehead. You see, as soon as I saw the name above the shop I realised what a fool I was. I blushed, I can tell you. It must be time for me to retire.'

He raised his drink to us and smiled over the top of his glasses. 'Anyway, since it happened to be a map shop I went in and checked some maps. Sure enough, there it was: Ainsby, Lincolnshire.' He shook his head ruefully. 'Anderson must still be laughing.'

I watched him for a moment, not sure how much of what he said I should believe. 'So what brought you to this hotel?' I asked. 'You're not telling us

249

that's coincidence too?'

'Oh, no. Not at all. I know Anderson's taste in hotels. I just phoned around all the most expensive ones in Lincolnshire until I found him. Does he know that you two are here as well?'

'We met him last night. He expects to have the bird in his hands sometime today.'

'Does he indeed?' Potts looked a little pensive at this. 'Well, we can ask him all about it in a moment. I called him late last night and arranged to meet him here at 8 p.m.' He pulled a fob watch out of his waistcoat pocket and flicked it open. 'While we wait for him, we can all have another drink and you can tell me about this place. This must be where the Lincoln green comes from, I guess . . .'

*   *   *

It was another strange evening. Anderson arrived twenty minutes later with Gabby in tow and I think they were both a little surprised at the committee assembled to greet them. Anderson responded with typical unruffled ease and insisted on ordering more wine—French and expensive. Gabby and I exchanged smiles but I found it difficult to catch her eye as the conversation circulated around the table.

We were a curious group. First there was Anderson, finely honed and immaculately dressed, and next to him Gabby, who couldn't help but challenge the popular image of a conservationist. She was too perfectly at home in a cocktail dress, too instinctively chic, to be imagined sweating and dirty in a makeshift field lab; and she'd always been that way, even in the hottest and dirtiest of times, always somehow cooler and neater than the rest of us. I knew at least one researcher who had stuck with her even when the salaries weren't being paid, purely because of the whiff of glamour she brought to the work. Next to those two, Katya looked younger and less confident. Potts, sitting beside her, looked vaguely cherubic. What people would have made of me, I couldn't guess. I wasn't sure I knew myself.

It was Potts who began the real business of the evening, leaning back and pushing his thumbs very firmly into his waistcoat pockets.

'We've just been admiring your handiwork, Mr Anderson.' He indicated the photocopied sheet that was still lying on the table. 'You used the Stamford letter to get Ted Staest interested in your little expedition, but you wanted to make sure he couldn't leak the information to anyone else. So you moved the names around on the envelope. Very neat. Simple, clever, effective. You must have had a good laugh at our expense.'

Anderson looked at the paper and smiled, but when he spoke it was with his usual calm politeness.

'On the contrary, I wouldn't dream of laughing. It never pays to belittle the competition. But you're right about me moving the names, even though it wasn't as carefully planned as you seem to think. I knew Staest would be interested in the bird, but he knew the story about the pictures too, and I couldn't be sure he'd keep quiet about it. It's amazing what you can do with tracing paper, an eraser and a hotel photocopier. And then, when I heard someone had got hold of the photocopy I'd

251

left with Staest . . .' He tailed off and gave us an apologetic shrug, leaving Potts to finish the sentence for him.

'When you heard that, you sent a man to Stamford so that I had someone to follow around. Nice touch.'

Anderson graced us all with his most charming smile. 'Not strictly necessary, I think. By then I was already six months ahead of you.'

Potts was looking a little rueful, like an elderly chess player just beaten by his favourite grandson. He leaned back in his chair and raised his glass.

'I guess you're right at that. To the victor the spoils.' He took a generous swig of red wine. 'May I ask if you actually *have* the spoils yet?'

'Not today. But I've got a meeting tomorrow. I'm confident I'll have the bird soon.'

'Pah! The bird. No one cares about the bird.' He looked up and corrected himself. 'Excepting Mr Fitzgerald here, of course. Now what about the pictures? Have you found them?'

'The man I'm meeting tomorrow doesn't know anything about the pictures. All he knows is that he has a very old stuffed bird. I know from my research that there's a good chance it's the right one.'

'So you haven't mentioned to this guy that his bird might be sitting on a million dollars' worth of art?'

Anderson clearly thought the question in poor taste and he looked up at the clock above the bar.

'Was there anything in particular you wanted to see me about tonight, Mr Potts? Because if not . . .'

The American nodded.

'Sure. No need to get touchy. Look, Anderson,

252

if you find those pictures, who will you sell them to?'

'Twelve paintings by Roitelet? I don't expect to be short of offers.'

'If you go public with them over here, you'll find yourself in a lot of trouble. You may be an expert in your own area, but I know about art. Trust me, they'll ban the export of those paintings quicker than you can dial a lawyer. But if you had someone to deal with the formalities . . . Look, Anderson, I could get those pictures to the States in no time, complete with all the documents you need to show that they've been in an attic somewhere in Pennsylvania all these years. No costs to you, no delays, no lawyers' fees. Only a modest commission.'

'I see.' Anderson exchanged a glance with Gabby. 'But your offer's premature. I'd like to wait until I actually have them in my hands before discussing anything like that.'

I watched them watching each other across the table, two men enjoying the games they played, and suddenly I felt weary. I looked over to Katya, but she wasn't looking back. From her I turned to Gabby, but she was watching Anderson, her face strangely serene. A silence had fallen but I couldn't think of anything to say. I wasn't even sure what I was feeling.

I was seized then by an urge to get away from them all for a few hours, out of the hotel, out of Lincoln. Like my grandfather, I'd plunged into something without really understanding what I was doing and now I was getting lost in it. It was time to get out. Anderson would get his pictures; Gabby would get the money to keep her project going for a few more years, would carry on fighting a war she could only lose. Katya would go back to college and get on with things, and for her all this would become an intriguing anecdote. And the Ulieta bird—what would happen to that? It was an afterthought now, destined to end its story in a freezer in Ted Staest's lab.

'There's one thing I'd like to ask,' I said before I got up to go. 'Finding the bird after all those years is quite an achievement. You could at least tell us how you did it.'

The warmth with which Anderson greeted the question surprised me. Beneath his smooth exterior, I could see he was excited by it, pleased at his own detective work. So while the remainder of the red wine was poured and drunk, Anderson told us what he'd been doing for the last six months. It was simplicity itself really; all he needed was patience and money and, of course, the necessary luck. Most of it he'd done from the States, paying researchers over here to do his work for him. He'd quickly found out about the Stamford family.

'John Stamford was killed on the Western Front in 1917,' he told us. 'He never had the homecoming he'd looked forward to. And by the end of the war, the family's fortunes had collapsed. The house had to be broken up into lots and sold off, and that was the end of the Stamfords. It's not clear what happened to his sister—probably she married and moved away. All we know for sure is that the contents of the Old Manor ended up under the auctioneer's hammer.'

That sale had been Anderson's real starting point. He obtained the catalogue listing the various lots, and concentrated on all the ones

254

including mounted birds and animals. From there he began to narrow down his search to the lots that could have contained the bird he wanted. The catalogue recorded the purchaser of each lot and Anderson set about tracing them. The trail could have gone cold at any time—*should* have gone cold by rights. But somehow, miraculously, it hadn't. With Anderson still in New York, his people over here managed to track the history of each of the lots he was interested in.

'The listings in the ledger weren't scientific,' he explained. 'It just gave descriptions. Things like "a collection of songbirds" or "four doves and pigeons". Even so, once I'd discounted the items it *couldn't* have been, I was left with seven items. Gradually we've tracked them down to where they are now. All seven of them. Can you imagine the odds against that? That's when I decided to come over. My only concern then was that someone might beat me to it, someone who had already done some of the work before.' He looked across the table at me. 'But it seems I needn't have worried.'

There was a general rearranging of focus as everyone looked at me but I just looked back at Anderson and nodded and let the attention swing back to him. He paused briefly, like a magician waiting for his moment.

'Now we've seen six of them, and none of them is the bird we're looking for. Tomorrow I'm getting photographs of the final one. I'll have an answer then.'

'Photographs?' Potts sounded wounded. '*Photographs?* Why not the real thing?'

Anderson raised an eyebrow.

'The last specimen has ended up quite a long way from Lincolnshire. My researcher saw it today and he's bringing over the Polaroids tomorrow.'

Potts frowned. 'With all due respect, Mr Anderson, it seems to me that you're not much better off than the rest of us. You can't be sure the bird was ever in that sale.'

Anderson nodded but there was no anxiety in his face. 'The war left the Stamford family in very great debt, Mr Potts, and their creditors were extremely demanding. Martha Stamford was allowed to retain only her personal effects. The legal documents are very clear about it. Everything else was sold.'

'But it could easily have been given away before that. Couldn't it?'

'Of course,' Anderson replied. 'But I'm looking at the percentages. She *might* have given it away, but why would she? She *might* have sold it privately but it would have been hard for her to get away with that and there's no record of such a sale. There's a *possibility* the bird disappeared from the Old Manor before the sale. But there's a greater probability it did not. And if it did not, and if I've found it . . . Well, we all know that those paintings by Roitelet have never been found.'

'And if the photos you see tomorrow are *not* the Ulieta bird?' I asked.

He looked at me steadily. 'Then it *is* lost. Searching any further would be impractical. Random search of the nation's attics is not an economically viable option, Mr Fitzgerald. Unless you have any ideas how to narrow the search?'

Everyone looked at me again. I turned to Katya and found her eyes on mine. I looked down at my

256

lap where my fingers were laced around each other.

'No,' I concluded. 'You're right. If it wasn't part of the sale it could be anywhere.'

And for some reason that thought made me feel much happier.

Even more than she feared the storm, she feared the ordeal of arriving. Yet when it came she found such beauty there that fear was impossible. From her first glimpse of land, from the first scent of it unannounced on the breeze, the sheer wonder of it entranced her. As the *Robin* drew nearer and she began to make out the details of trees and farms, an unfamiliar joy seized her. She knew as she looked that she was being touched by something so profound that she would never be the same again.

For the last mile or so, the *Robin* hugged the coast and she let the parade of shore and straggling houses roll past her, always with green, sloping mountains behind them. On reaching port she expected to be overwhelmed with panic. Instead, she disembarked almost in a trance, the bustling crowds barely noticed as she looked beyond them to the places from where they had appeared. The town seemed to her brilliant and exhilarating, though the accounts she'd read had called it neither. The houses that clustered around the harbour were either bright white squares or haphazard compilations of weather-worn timber. The sounds of the town were completely new, and even familiar noises were accompanied by exhortations in tumbling, foreign tongues. She had read of the dirt and squalor of foreign ports but the smell that reached her as the harbour enclosed them seemed right for the place—tar and heat and humans mixed with the stench of mud and floating waste. She watched a fellow passenger put a handkerchief to his nose but she was happy to breathe in the smell, to catch it and record it in her memory. The hills above the town, still green and hazy, were a promise of freshness that made her smile again.

The boy from the *Robin* saw her bags unloaded and another boy, from the house where she was to stay, was there to greet her. '*Senhor* Burnett?' he asked, looking not at her face but at her bags. 'You are to come.' He led her through the crowd to a waiting carriage then leapt up behind her. 'Your bags, they come,' he told her very earnestly before the driver picked up the reins and began to manoeuvre them through the chaotic traffic of the port.

The driver was a man of around fifty, his face creased by the sun into a smile. Did he look at her too carefully? Was there a flash of curiosity in his eyes as he nodded his greeting? Did anyone note the slimness of her figure? She didn't care. She simply didn't care. She was busy taking in a whole new world.

As they left the waterfront the driver began to point out sights in broken words of English. '*Igreja*,' he told her. 'Church. Santa Clara.' Following the line of his arm, she glimpsed roofs and a tower between trees and then the carriage moved forward and the sight was lost. As they drew away from the sea, buildings became fewer and she was lost in the lush greenery of an unfamiliar landscape. There seemed to be trees everywhere of every kind, and above them, clearer now, she could see the mountains. With a surge of exhilaration she realised that tomorrow she could walk among them. It seemed miraculous.

This daze of wonder and excitement helped her through the arrival at the English house where she was to stay. Long before they had reached the house, the road had become rutted and uneven, and she was alarmed when the driver pulled sharply off it, down a narrower track to where a neat stone villa stood shaded by trees. In front of it a plump woman was waiting, wiping her hands on her apron, before bobbing a quick salute and advancing with a smile. This was Mrs Drake, the widow of a Bristol wine agent, her hostess during her stay on the island. Still wiping her hands, Mrs Drake launched into a complicated speech of welcome as the carriage drew to a halt. When she saw the face of the figure that was handed down to greet her, she seemed to pause for a moment.

* * *

Banks's decision to withdraw from Cook's expedition caused a sensation. On hearing it, his entire party—Solander, Zoffany and the rest—had little alternative but to stand down too. What had promised to become the greatest scientific expedition ever mounted was suddenly reduced to a series of empty berths. Not even the hasty recruitment of a replacement naturalist called Forster and his son, an artist, was sufficient to disguise the fact that things had changed considerably from the original conception. To Banks's critics it was confirmation of something they had begun to maintain—that Banks was overconfident in his opinions and had too little respect for his seniors. For his friends it was baffling. They knew Banks could be volatile but they also knew of his determination and ambition, of the towering hopes he had for the voyage of the *Resolution*. It seemed inexplicable that he would sacrifice it entirely over a few feet of cabin space. Even if the issue had become a matter of pride, it seemed unlike him to be so deadly inflexible. For all of those who were due to go with him the decision meant the forfeiture of valuable future income, and for many there was the prospect of considerable financial loss. They met in low-voiced groups and shook their heads.

They were equally confused by Banks's reaction to

his own decision. They had expected him to be defiant, resilient, full of alternative schemes. The stores and equipment were all assembled and ready to go. Surely something could yet be salvaged? Instead Banks seemed lifeless and enervated. He was bitter towards the Admiralty and vengeful towards the Navy Board but at all other times he seemed subdued and detached. As his associates waited for him to outline a plan for the future of his party, he seemed reluctant to think about alternatives.

Eventually it was Solander who challenged him and insisted that he act. He found Banks in the study at New Burlington Street, looking silently out of the window. It was only by stubborn persistence that Solander persuaded him to pay attention.

'Come, Joseph, these last weeks have seen great setbacks to your plans but it is unbecoming to let them affect you so. The South Seas are not the only places of interest in the world. You have an expedition ready to depart, your equipment assembled at considerable expense. Many of your friends have made a great sacrifice to stand beside you in this matter. They are asking what you intend to do.'

'Do?' The word seemed to puzzle him.

'For instance, Wainwright tells me of a ship available to us bound for the West Indies. There is a great deal of work still to be done in collecting and identifying the flora and fauna there. You might consider that a possibility.'

'The West Indies?' Banks looked away as if unable to concentrate on his friend's words. 'No, it's not to be thought of. For it to be of any value we would be away a year.'

'We had planned to be away three.'

'I'm sorry, Solander, it's out of the question.'

Solander paused and seemed at a loss.

'The Royal Society will think it most surprising if after all your promises, and with a party assembled, you choose to do nothing at all.'

Banks turned and looked at him.

'The Royal Society be damned. I shall do as I please.'

Solander tried another tack. 'Inactivity at this time is going to invite a great deal of speculation. A lot of people will wonder what it is that keeps you here, what is more important to you than the increase in knowledge which you have made such a public show of advocating.'

The two men watched each other. Eventually Solander continued.

'The important thing is to do *something*, Joseph. You have to prove that this dispute with the Admiralty is their loss, not yours. To divert the resources you have assembled into an expedition of your own will underline your own seriousness.'

Banks nodded slowly. 'Yes, I can see that. Even so . . .'

'Such an expedition need not be a long one. I can understand that there may be matters here that require your attention. Perhaps just a few months away.'

'You have somewhere in mind?'

'If a short expedition is the thing, one could do worse than Iceland. It's a comparatively short voyage yet the island still demands considerable study. It would be a fitting object for your attentions.'

Banks turned back to the window. 'When would we depart?'

'As soon as we could. The Icelandic winter arrives early. We should try to move things along as quickly as we can.'

Banks began to calculate. It would take perhaps twenty days for his letter to reach Madeira. What would she do then? She would have to make arrangements, book a passage back to England. Then another twenty days before she could reach London. He must be waiting for her on her arrival. He must, or never look her in the eye again.

He turned back to Solander. 'Two months,' he said.

'Impossible. Our supplies are ready now. If we wait two months we may as well not go at all. There are men here who have given up the opportunity of a lifetime out of loyalty to you. You have a duty to them, Joseph.'

Banks flinched at the word.

'Besides,' Solander continued, 'it will smack of vacillation to delay that long and you must avoid that at all costs. If we go now, quickly, we can be back in three months' time. Whatever business it is that has arisen to unsettle you will have to wait that extra month or you will fail the friends who have trusted you. On my honour, you have no choice.'

Banks listened in silence and when Solander finished speaking he remained quiet, his eyes shut. The moments ticked away between them and Solander was about to speak again when Banks looked up at his friend and grimaced.

'Honour, is it? That is to be the banner under which I sail? Very well. I thank you for your concern and I own the truth in what you say. Let me know what needs to be done.'

And Solander departed hastily, before whatever anguish gripped his friend could return to change his mind.

*   *   *

At dinner on that first night in Madeira, Mrs Drake introduced her new lodger to the two other English visitors. The introductions were made in the villa's long dining room, a room lined with green paper and pale English prints, where the heat and the foliage pressed against the windows with equal urgency. The light was still bright when they took their places so all three could examine each other with ease. Of the two, Mr Dunivant was a loud, ruddy man in his fifties, a Bristol merchant with interests in Madeira wine. He talked more than he listened and did not seem unduly curious when Mrs Drake introduced him to his new dining companion. The second guest, Mr Maddox, was a much younger man, slim and handsome with inquiring eyes. Those eyes seemed to linger on their new acquaintance and when he spoke he smiled lazily.

'Welcome to Madeira, Mr Burnett. I understand you are a botanist,' he began.

'An amateur, sir. I am here to draw and paint some of the island's flora.'

'It amazes me where you find the interest in that,' Mr Dunivant interrupted. 'A good many young fellows seem interested in that sort of thing but I can't see what it profits them.'

Mr Maddox smiled politely. 'Yet does not the successful cultivation of your vines owe a great deal to the observations of those who have studied them over the years, sir?'

'Oh, yes. Well, I daresay. I have nothing against study when it is *applied*, you understand. But digging around amongst the things that grow in hedgerows and the like, that is surely not adding a great deal to human progress, Mr Burnett?'

In response she hesitated and Mr Maddox answered

264

for her.

'Are not a great many of our common medicines the result of just such digging around, sir?'

Dunivant pondered this, nodding, his mouth full of bread.

'I daresay you have a point,' he acknowledged before pausing to swallow. Maddox seized the opportunity to turn to the newcomer.

'Mrs Drake tells us that you are to join Mr Banks's party and go with Cook to the South Seas, Mr Burnett?'

'That is my intention, yes.'

Maddox pondered. 'I confess that I am a little surprised. My cousin is a friend of Banks and I understood that his whole party was assembled in London. Perhaps you are replacing one of the original party?'

She could feel herself blushing.

'Perhaps I gave you the wrong impression, Mr Maddox. I said it is my intention to join his party but perhaps I should better have described it as a hope. I am only a little acquainted with Mr Banks and yet I am hoping that an opportunity might arise when he arrives at Madeira for me to offer my services.'

Maddox paused again before replying. When he did, his tone was light and careless. 'I see. It's no matter. Mrs Drake must have been mistaken. She told me that you were a good friend of Banks. I wondered that I had never met you before for I have been often in his company.'

'I fear she has been very much mistaken. Indeed I hardly know him. He has in the past been good enough to compliment my work, that is all.'

Before Maddox could reply, Dunivant interrupted. 'I hear that fellow is one for the ladies. I hope neither

265

of you have joined him in that, eh?'

His roar of laughter allowed her a moment to recover and, before the conversation could resume, Mrs Drake bustled in with three servants behind her to serve the first course. Dunivant, delighted to be ceded the floor, began a series of anecdotes about the laziness of the islanders that lasted almost as long as the meal. By the time he fell quiet to apply himself to a glass of malmsey, the night had fallen and the table was lit by candles. A warm draught from the window licked across the table from time to time and made the flames flicker. It was in this uncertain light that Maddox turned to her again.

'I understand, Mr Burnett, that Mrs Drake's boy is engaged to guide you into the mountains tomorrow.'

'That is true, sir. In time I hope I shall need no guide.'

'Perhaps we shall meet. I am here to look after some of my father's interests on the island but I confess I am a lazy fellow. I frequently ignore my father's business and take a stroll in the hills instead.'

'Perhaps we shall,' she replied, making a note to herself to walk far and high.

'I should like that,' he replied quietly. 'You see I should very much like to see you draw.' And before she had a chance to reply to that, Mrs Drake reappeared to draw the meal to a close. That night, exhausted, she slept heavily. When she woke it was with a vague anxiety playing on her mind.

*   *   *

The plans for Iceland developed despite him. The charter of a ship, the *Sir Lawrence*, was negotiated largely by Solander; the itinerary was decided almost

266

without Banks noticing; and the movement of supplies on board began while he still watched the calendar and waited, hoping she would arrive. His occasional bursts of energy were enough to convince the public that his zeal for exploration was undiminished and in his letters he roused himself to a fitting show of enthusiasm. But to those closest to him he still seemed lost and without purpose.

Those days taught him for the first time what it was to wait. His thoughts were constantly at sea, travelling with his letter to Madeira, searching for a wind to speed her return. If the passage had been smooth his letter could be with her now. Or now. Or now. He tried to imagine what she would feel when she broke the seal and read his words. What would she think of him then? How could she respect him when he had failed her so? And sailing to Iceland before her return merely compounded his sin a hundred times over. Part of him longed for her to reach London before he sailed. Another part seized gladly at the idea of escape.

So instead of planning, he listened to the entreaties of his boyhood companions, the ones who knew the town and the town's clubs. When Solander next called on Banks he was not at home, nor had he been seen since the previous evening. The reason for his absence became clear later that afternoon when Banks arrived at his own door suspended between two footmen, almost insensible, and for the first time in weeks not caring where he was or why he was there.

*   *   *

Her first days in Madeira passed largely in a state of wonder. Rising early, she would leave the villa at dawn and head for the mountains. There she would follow

267

the *levadas*, the ancient irrigation channels that snaked around the contours of the hills, until she found the place where she had been working the previous day. On the first two mornings, the house-boy had shown her certain paths but thereafter she found her own way, under cinnamon trees, amid mangoes or bananas. She sketched flowers and leaves she had never seen before and, after a long morning of walking and drawing, she would settle in the shade and look out over the sea and eat the food she had brought with her. By then the sun was up and she would often doze for a little, lulled by the heavy scent of the afternoon and the music of the goat-bells above her as the drowsy animals browsed fitfully on the mountainsides.

On the fifth morning, she ventured into the town while it was barely awake, the air still cool but the sun already warm when it touched her. The quiet of the streets filled her with calm. As she made her way, she passed a carpenter's house where a man was already at work, singing a song apparently without words, almost tuneless, but sad and vital at the same time. Further on, under the window of a large house, she heard chords being played on a violin as if a child was practising. Like the song, the sounds seemed fitted to the empty streets and the morning's coolness.

If her days seemed perfect they were doomed to end with the ordeal of the dinner table. As well as Maddox and Dunivant, she met others there, members of the English fraternity who came to pay their respects to the new visitor. All asked about Banks and in her confusion she began to contradict herself. Some came away believing that awkward Mr Burnett was already assured a place with Banks, others that he scarcely knew him. And as she struggled, Maddox watched her, half amused, intervening from time to

268

time and deftly turning the conversation in different channels.

Then came the day when she was interrupted in her drawing. She had returned to a favourite place and was making a study of guava leaves. It was late morning and the air was already still and weighty with heat. Beyond the shade the light was dazzling and where she sat seemed a sanctuary. She could hear water flowing through a nearby stream and into a stone tank cut into the hillside. Engrossed in her work, she did not hear anyone approaching, and the first she knew of Maddox's arrival was the sound of his footsteps close behind her.

'I confess I owe you an apology,' he said, stepping out of the shadow and into the sun. 'I was inclined to disbelieve your claims to be a draughtsman. There are so many who believe they can draw, I find, and I thought you would be one of those. But without pretending to be an expert I can see that you really are an artist. Perhaps you really do plan to join Banks's party after all.'

Once again in his presence she felt the heat in her cheeks.

'As I told you, sir . . .'

'Oh, I don't mind very much what you told me.'

He threw himself down on the bank beside her, so close that she drew away from him.

'So this is where you pass your time. I admit that I bribed the boy to point me in the right direction. I find you a most interesting character, Mr Burnett.'

She ignored him, apparently intent on her work.

'It is getting hot, is it not?' Maddox continued. 'Are you not warm in that jacket?'

'I am very comfortable, thank you.'

'Really?' He pondered this. 'I know . . .' He

pointed to the water tank, cool and green in the shade. 'Do you swim?'

She carried on drawing. 'No. I have never learned.'

'Come!' He reached out and took her by the elbow. 'The tanks are not deep and are wonderfully cooling. And there are no peasant girls here for us to shock, are there?'

She shook him away. 'No, really, Mr Maddox. I don't care to swim.'

He smiled back at her, amused.

'You surprise me. Perhaps you will object to my carrying on without you?'

She looked at him steadily, not prepared to blink. 'Why should I object? You may do as you please.'

He jumped to his feet and, standing in front of her, began to unbutton his shirt. 'It will not disturb you at all?'

She returned his gaze. 'Of course not. Why should it?'

He continued to tug at his buttons, then dropped his shirt to the ground and began to undo his boots. 'You see, there's something about you,' he said as he undressed. 'Something intriguing. I guessed you might shy away from joining me. Perhaps you find the thought of such physical exertions . . . distasteful?'

She looked at him carefully. 'No, not distasteful. But hardly inspiring.'

He raised an eyebrow at that and continued to undress. When he was naked, he turned his back to her and walked slowly to the water's edge, then lowered himself in. As he bathed she returned to her drawing, unsettled but determined not to show it. When Maddox emerged from the water he took his clothes and retired a discreet distance to dry himself and dress. When he'd finished he returned to where

270

she sat and resumed his position on the bank beside
her. She carried on drawing as if he wasn't there and
for a while there was silence between them. When he
spoke his mocking tone was gone.

'Who are you?' he asked quietly.

'My name is Burnett,' she replied.

'I thought you would scream and run away,' he said,
smiling a little to himself. 'You called my bluff.'

'Why should I run?'

He looked at her carefully. 'I took you for a lady.'

She already knew he had guessed. But the words
still made her tremble inside. She succeeded in keeping
her voice low and steady.

'Well, you were wrong. It's obvious that I am not.'

He raised his eyebrow again. 'No, it is clear you are
quite another sort of woman. I find that even more
intriguing, I confess. If not a lady, you did not strike
me as . . . as that other thing. I find the fact that you
are not a lady rather stimulating.'

For a moment she wanted to strike him, to deliver
with all her strength a blow across his face that she
knew he deserved. But there was a calmness deep
inside her now. She would not break. She would not
run.

'I think, sir, it would be better if you were to leave
me now. I have work to complete.'

To her surprise he rose to his feet. 'Very well, *Mr*
Burnett.' He seemed about to go but he hesitated.
'Mrs Drake knows. They've all guessed. Are you aware
of that?'

She continued to draw, the blood hot in her cheeks,
her eyes very firmly fixed ahead of her.

'Oh, one other thing, Miss Burnett.' Maddox
reached into his jacket. 'A letter. For you. It arrived
this morning. From Mr Banks. About plants, no

doubt.'

He dropped the letter onto the grass in front of her and she left it there until she had watched him out of sight around the curve of the mountain. Then, still shaking, she reached down and opened it.

After reading its contents she sat for a long time, very still inside. She would finish her drawing before dusk, she decided. The next day she would look for a passage to England.

CHAPTER FIFTEEN

DISCOVERIES

I woke up next morning still determined to get away from Lincoln. After hearing Anderson's logic of the night before, I had absolutely no desire to hang around and witness his triumph. And although it was true that something could still go wrong for him, that was hardly a help to me. The Stamford letter was the best chance any of us had of finding the bird. If it proved a dead end, then we were all back where we started. The bird would stay hidden, if it had even survived this long.

When I was dressed, I set out to look for Katya. I wasn't sure what she'd say when I told her I was going back to London, but I expected her to be disappointed. The night before, working out the name switch on the Stamford letter, she'd been glowing with excitement. Even Anderson's confidence hadn't seemed to daunt her.

But tracking her down the next morning proved difficult. The woman at the reception desk told me she had gone out early without leaving a message, and so I went looking for her. I tried the country archives and the public library, and then a couple of cafés we'd been to. Not finding her left me at a loss. I was anxious not to hang around Lincoln, but I couldn't go without Katya, and I hadn't a clue where she was. For want of a better plan I began to wander the streets, studying faces and peering into shops.

In the end, I found Gabby, not Katya. I saw her

through the window of an old bookshop and, after a moment's hesitation, I went in. She was leaning elegantly against the shelves in the antiquarian book section, looking through a very old copy of Gerard's *Herbal*. She smiled when I joined her, but now there seemed to have grown up between us a distance that for some reason hadn't been there when we met in London.

'I thought you'd be out looking for the bird,' I told her, aware as I said it that I sounded slightly bitter, like a poor loser pretending not to be.

'Not yet.' With great care she placed the book back on the shelf. 'I'm meeting Karl at lunchtime to see the photos.'

'You must be feeling good. Even if there are no pictures, it looks like you'll get your introduction to Ted Staest.'

If there was anything amiss in my tone, she pretended not to hear it.

'I hope so.' She paused. 'I wanted to ask you, Fitz. Last night . . . Do you see what I mean about Karl now? Deep down, he's like you. Can't you see? I mean, he loves the search. The mechanics of it. The detective work. Part of him knows that those pictures could be total moonshine. Perhaps they never existed in the first place. Or perhaps they're not by Roitelet. Or they might be damaged, or just not any good. But they just *might* be everything we hope for, and it's the thought of them out there, waiting, that drives Karl on.'

That and a million dollars, I thought, but decided not to say so.

'So what do you think?' she went on. 'Will he find the bird?'

'If it was part of that sale he'll probably find it.'

274

'And if it wasn't part of that sale you think no one will find it?'

I met her eyes. 'Oh, if it exists someone will find it. Sometime. But not one of us. That sort of find comes about when someone gets curious about the things in their attic and takes them to an expert. If the Ulieta bird is ever seen again that'll be how it happens.'

Outside in the street, glimpsed through rows of books, shoppers were passing. I checked their faces idly.

'I fly back to Rio at the weekend,' Gabby said, and hesitated. 'Look, I've been thinking about you, that photograph by your bed . . . I know you won't forget her, John, but you have to move on. Don't wait until it's too late.'

*   *   *

That afternoon I drove out to Revesby. I set off in the fraying light of a winter afternoon, edging out of Lincoln cautiously, not sure what I was going to do. It crossed my mind to go to Ainsby, but Ainsby was all about the bird's recent history, and Anderson had reduced that to a piece of forensic analysis, a sort of relentless square search that would either succeed or fail. I was prepared to leave it to him. It was the bird's distant past that interested me now, the half-glimpsed story in the background—the one that Hans Michaels had had in mind when he made his drawing of the woman with no name. What was the story there? How had the Ulieta bird become a part of it? These things were interesting in a way Anderson's search would never be, and when I came to the road that led to

275

Ainsby I ignored it and drove south, towards Revesby.

As I drove, I found myself thinking of my grandfather again. When I was a young naturalist it had been easy to criticise him for his old-fashioned values and his poor planning, his lack of any scientific rigour. For the way he sacrificed his family to his own ambitions. But I knew there was a part of me that resembled him too. There had been a time in my life when I'd been the same, slogging around the world from collection to collection, squandering money I couldn't pay back and friendships that deserved better; a time when the only thing that seemed real was the dream of the great discovery, the one that would change my life. That time felt like madness now, and I wondered if my grandfather had ever come to that understanding. Was there a day out there in the jungle when he paused and promised himself that the future would be different? If there was, he ignored it and pressed on regardless.

My grandfather's party on that expedition was a small one: a young naturalist called Barnes, an experienced guide and four local men to carry and cook, each bribed with promises of unimaginable plenty if they could find a peacock in the African jungle. They travelled upcountry by river to Matadi and then by railway and barge to Stanleyville, but after that they were on foot. For eight weeks they headed northwards and then, perhaps a sign of indecision, they cut sharply to the north-east and carried on.

If you haven't been to the rainforests of the Congo it's hard to imagine the effect of the heat and humidity. It's unforgiving country and my

276

grandfather did nothing to seek its forgiveness. He met it head on, as if sheer strength of will was all he needed. Within four months Barnes had taken a fever, and within a few days more he was too weak to continue. After just 120 days my grandfather's plans of over twenty years had collapsed in confusion. In the end the party split so that Barnes could be carried home. It's telling that the invalid was accompanied by the guide and three of the four porters. Only one man chose to stay with my grandfather, who by now was eating virtually nothing and living on hydrochloride of quinine. Shouldering packs that were treble weight, the two men set off north again, beginning a trek that, in the passing fashion of the times, was to make them both quite famous. Neither of them could have known that the first formal identification of an African peacock was only a few months away.

*   *   *

I drove south towards Revesby, where the rolling hills of the Wolds gave way to the Lincolnshire Fens. I reached the village some time after three, with the sun already low in the sky so that the church stretched a long shadow over the corner where I parked my car. Revesby was a small, not very significant sort of place: no pub to offer welcome from the creeping shadows, no shop that I could see, just silence and a large, square green area, and houses hiding behind hedges. Not really a village green as such—Revesby is too disparate for that. If anything the space in the centre divides one side of the village from the other, leaving—at least on a winter's afternoon—a sense of emptiness. On one side of the grass square was a long row of single-storey cottages—almshouses, judging by their shape and design. On a stone set above one of the doors I could make out the name *Banks* and a date. I did a quick calculation. My man's grandfather, perhaps.

There was no real reason for my visit, only a curiosity to see where the lives I'd read about had once been lived. Revesby Abbey lay outside the village: the house where Joseph Banks had lived had burned down in the 1840s and its replacement was still a private house, aggressively signed as such. Instead I turned to the village church as a focus for my musings. Even that turned out to be a different building from the one Banks had known. His church had been torn down in the nineteenth century to make way for something more spacious, and now, like the Abbey, there was nothing left to see, only in one dark corner a model of the old church as it would have looked—small, irregular and appealing. In the years since, the new church had mellowed and become an old one in its turn but it didn't feel like the place I'd come looking for. That was all gone. I was a hundred years too late.

Outside the light was dying quietly, without fanfare. The graveyard around the church was older than the building it surrounded and I made my way through it, walking between gravestones that had been there when Banks was alive. Even in the gloom I could still make out names and dates where the moss had not yet overwritten them. Soon they would be gone. Eventually the brambles and the darkness combined against me and forced me to step away. My visit had told me nothing.

278

Or perhaps it had. As I got into the car I thought of the old gravestones sitting comfortably around the new church, their past reconciled to the present. Was there a lesson for me in that? After all, I reflected, my grandfather's was not the only expedition in history to carry on disastrously simply because the people involved had neither the vision to change nor the courage to give up.

*   *   *

The quietness of the afternoon had put me in the mood for company and, four or five miles along the Lincoln road when my headlights picked out the sign of a roadside pub, I pulled in, aware of the cold in my fingers and toes. Inside it was too early for more than a couple of drinkers to have gathered at the bar but there was already a good fire going and I settled myself pleasantly into a corner seat with a pint of beer. It was an old-fashioned, ungentrified country pub with no make-over and no menu. This was fox-hunting country and the walls were decorated with the remains of various creatures that had fallen foul of the fact. Most prominent was a glass case above the bar where a young vixen was carrying off a tatty, slightly greying hen. The case for the prosecution, I punned to myself. Around it, on the other walls, were the usual array of horse brasses and faded prints of Edwardian hunting scenes, testimonies to the age-old conflict between the Lincolnshire farmer and *Vulpes vulpes*, the red fox.

Vulpes vulpes, the red fox.

For a moment I was completely still, working it out in my head, and then came a rush of amazement at my own stupidity. When I did move, I was clumsy with haste. That letter, did I still have it with me? I groped in my pocket for the photocopied sheet. It was badly crumpled now. Where was that line I'd talked about with Potts? That throwaway line that I'd taken as nothing more important than a casual quip. There it was . . .

Until then, guard it with your life—I don't want to return and find that young Vulpes of yours has snatched it from my grasp!

I'd thought he meant it loosely, a jocular reference to a suitor at his sister's door. But what if he hadn't? A young *Vulpes*. A young Fox.

At first I couldn't find the number I wanted and then I couldn't find the phone. I misdialled twice before I got it right. And I almost punched the air when I heard his voice at the end of the line.

'Hello? Bert? It's John Fitzgerald here. I came round yesterday about your family tree.' In the background I could hear the crackling sob of a dimly remembered tenor as I raced on. 'I know it's an odd question, but in your time in the archives have you come across the name Martha Stamford anywhere?'

There was a pause. I thought I heard him chuckle.

'Yeah, you could say I've come across it.' He spoke very deliberately, as if he was amused by something. 'Martha Stamford's my mother.'

July was a month of winds. On the Thames, white water and ships uneasy on the swell. In Lincolnshire, floods. In the Bay of Biscay, bound for Portsmouth, a small ship, the *Saffron*, driven off course and forced to hug the coast. On board the *Saffron*, tired and sick, a small figure watching the sea-flecked wind and longing for home. But summer remained tightly furled and a three-week voyage turned to four. By the time she reached England he was already gone.

She had always imagined her return in bright colours. She had seen people in summer clothes waving on the docks, sunlight on the roofs, white sails and green sea lapping at the harbour walls. But she came ashore in Portsmouth under grey skies with rain in the air and the night already falling. The town looked drab, the streets dirty and there was no welcome. Standing unsteady on firm land, she felt the emptiness of the dusk eddying around her. She had measured out her strength in grains, like hour-glass sand; now she found it at an end. She needed a smile to welcome her. More than that. She wanted to be held very tightly, silently, without questions or conditions. But instead she stood unnoticed in the rain looking at the impartial faces of strangers. She had not written ahead to advise of her coming but even knowing he couldn't be there, she looked for him.

That night, restless in a cheap inn, she thought of the nights in Revesby when her father lay dying, nights when she would open the shutters and watch the trees tossing in the wind. She had thought then the trees were questions, not answers. Sometimes it is not until the end of a journey that you begin to say goodbye.

*　　　*　　　*

He sailed on a grey morning tide when the wind dropped long enough for the *Sir Lawrence* to creep out to sea. Most of his last hours in England had been spent either drunk or ashamed and he had begun to blame both on her. By running off ahead of him she had placed him in an impossible position and as a result he had been forced to give up his greatest adventure. If he had sailed with Cook, he reasoned, all would be well. But her rashness had made it impossible. It was intolerable and it was not of his making. And now he must sail if he was not to betray his companions; must stay if he was not to abandon her a second time. The misery of it all confounded him and it seemed to him that the intimacy of their Richmond winter had been blown away forever. It was easier to drink and forget. And when the wind dropped they sailed for Iceland.

In a sense the wind was his salvation. All the way to the Lizard and then up the Irish Sea it fought against the *Sir Lawrence*. Those on board were forced to focus on the struggles of the ship and Banks, the great circumnavigator, was wretchedly seasick. A landing on the Isle of Man had to be abandoned because of the rough seas. It was not until they neared the Hebrides that the weather relented and Banks, after the darkest month of his life, found the sun shining again.

*　　　*　　　*

She arrived in Richmond in late evening sunlight and found the place unchanged. In the time she had been away England had drifted into the folds of full

282

summer. The fields were higher, the hedges less kempt and the fresh playbills on the tavern door had begun to peel from their moorings. But nothing else seemed different. She had sailed through storms and seen places that those around her would never see; and in the time she had been away Richmond had done no more than stretch itself in the sun. Startled by the familiarity around her, avoiding the riverside, she made her way up the hill in the fading light to the discreet place where Martha, forewarned of her arrival, was waiting to greet her. There was nothing to draw attention to their meeting but anyone who chanced to be watching would have noticed, after a warm clasp of hands and some indistinct words, that the larger figure produced a letter and passed it to her companion who, after a pause, broke it open and began to read.

'*My dearest,*' she said aloud. '*Writing this causes me great distress. I have had no choice but to undertake another voyage . . .*' She read no further then, but held the letter for a moment before folding it into her pocket.

'Come, Martha,' she said, 'the letter will wait and I need more than anything to wash. And when I am clean and fed we have a great deal to talk about.' As the two dark figures turned to go, no moon rose above the trees behind them, no wind stirred the trees with a sigh.

There followed some months in which the two women in Richmond heard nothing of Banks. In August, arrived in Iceland, glorying in the air and exercise and in the uncomplicated spaces of an empty country, Banks thought of England only with a sense of release. In September he and Solander climbed Hekla and there was a moment when the sunlight flashed on the deep blue melt-water many feet below when he thought of how she would marvel at the colours. By late September the Icelandic autumn was advancing and, looking out over a treeless landscape, he more than once imagined the browns and golds of his home woods. From there, unless he took care, it was easy to imagine the russet hangings of that firelit bedroom. October brought the expedition to an end and carried him to Scotland where he chose to linger. He was no longer afraid to think of her but now he did it with regret, as if for something irretrievably lost. And he was in no hurry to reach London and look again at the damage he had done there.

By November, when word reached her that Banks was in Edinburgh, her hair was growing long again and the notes and sketches she had made in Madeira were being transformed into colour. Even then he did not write and if she thought of him at all it did not seem to unsteady her hand or distract her from her strict regime of work.

*   *   *

He reached London in early December and was glad to find that in his absence the acrimony of his departure had largely been forgotten. A friendly letter from Cook awaited him. Lord Sandwich called on him and the two got drunk together. But he made no attempt to write to her. By now she must know of his arrival, he reasoned. If she chose to ignore him, it told him what he needed to know. If she wrote, her letter would tell him how he stood. And if it proved she harboured no grudge, he would call when his business in London allowed it.

After two weeks of hearing nothing, he rose one morning, called for his horse and set out for Richmond.

284

There was a light fall of snow on the ground that reminded him of the same journey at other times; but for the most part he was too intent on his own thoughts to see the beauty of it. It wasn't until the last half-mile that he became fully aware of his surroundings and felt a stirring of familiarity. When the door was opened it was by a servant he did not recognise.

'Miss Brown's at home, sir,' she told him. 'If you'll wait here, sir.'

The same girl returned a moment later.

'Miss Brown says you're to go up, sir. She's painting, sir.'

So, heavy-footed, he made his way upstairs to the room where she painted, rehearsing his words as he went. When he came to her door it was open and he saw the room flooded with sunlight. She was standing near the window with her back to him, intent on the picture before her. She was dressed in green and her brown hair, loosely pinned, tumbled over her collar in places. He barely had time to note the slimness of her figure before she turned and the light fell golden on her face.

'Hello, Joseph,' she said and he saw a light in her eyes that made him cross the room in two strides and take her in his arms.

*　　　*　　　*

'How is it that you are able to forgive me?'

They lay again in the green bedroom, little more than a year since the first time. Outside, the afternoon sun glowed against the windows, and threw ripples of light onto the bedclothes. They had barely spoken as they tugged and hurried each other out of their clothes but when their eyes met they laughed and paused to kiss. When they stumbled to the bed their bodies found a dialogue of their own and their whispered endearments were broken and half formed. Only when they had fallen still in each other's arms did the time for talking arrive.

'Forgive you for what?' she asked.

'For letting you go to Madeira. For failing to join you there because I was too proud and too angry to sail.'

'I understand. I know what happened. The hard part was coming back and finding you gone.'

His arms tightened a little around her. 'I was ashamed to see you. And I had to go. They were waiting for me to do something.'

'I know. I guessed. But by then I was tired of being a boy. I wanted to be a woman again.'

'And did you make a good boy?'

Her head lay on his shoulder and he could feel her smile.

'Not really. I was good at not attracting attention. Anyone who bothered to look seemed to guess. But not many looked. In a crowd I was quite anonymous.'

He tightened his arms a little more and bent his head to kiss her. He felt he had come home.

*　　　*　　　*

And yet it was not quite the same. While Cook was abroad with the *Resolution* Banks found it hard to settle, as if part of him had not been able to disembark and walk away. In response he began to plan more journeys, to Wales and to Holland. His career in London continued to take up a good deal of his time, building his influence in philosophical circles, establishing his reputation with the Royal Society. There were fewer spontaneous visits to Richmond and now there was no sense when they were together that time was standing still.

Their time apart seemed to have changed her. The wildness in her feeling for him seemed gone and he began to sense a doubt in her that had not been there before. At night she held him no less tenderly, but when mention was made of the future, he thought he saw a hesitation in her eyes. Then he would laugh and take her in his arms and tell her that she must never leave him, that he was only happy when she was with him: things that were both true and untrue.

When he asked her how she spent her time when he was in Iceland, she would answer with a shrug and say, 'I painted.'

By the early days of the New Year, Richmond had become impractical. To keep her close to him while he continued his work he persuaded her to move to London. She made the move amid the January mud to rooms above Orchard Street where she could hear the street criers on Oxford Street and the bells of fifty churches and where, when the wind blew from the west, she could think she caught the scent of open fields. The rooms were new and slightly grand and the day she looked at them for the first time was the day she first felt she'd become his mistress. She had made a great point of protecting her family name but here her caution seemed unnecessary: she had no name. She was Joseph Banks's mistress. The tradesmen who called knew it and the women in the street knew it and neither her name nor her past mattered to them. When she was gone, she knew, another woman would live there, visited by another man, and she too would not matter to anyone except perhaps to the man who kept

287

her.

Yet London had its compensations. Joseph was growing into his new life. His house in New Burlington Street was becoming a focus for all London's thinkers and philosophers and his collection there drew people from across Europe. And all day, from breakfast till nightfall, there was talk. Ideas whirled around him like a rising tide, each wave rolling over another and building on the one before. He shared it all with her, the two lying together at night forgetting to sleep, discussing and disputing, until they would notice the fire burning low and would roll contentedly into each other's arms.

She knew to count these days as precious. Then, in February and March, he travelled to Holland and left her alone in Orchard Street. Knowing that she was there made it easier for him to go; he knew that when he returned she would be there still, wise and lovely in equal measure. After two months of male companionship nothing could be better than returning to her. And in a different way his being gone was good for her. Not many months earlier she had felt that life without him would be an empty place but her Madeira paintings had changed all that. They gave her open space and brilliant horizons, and made walls fall away. She felt strong as she painted and that strength seemed boundless. When he departed, her world changed, and she took out her materials and painted.

*   *   *

He returned at the end of March, playful and loving, younger than ever in his energy and affection. He was to go to North Wales in the summer, he told her, to stay with Pennant and to tour the country there. He would bring her back tales of the dark Welsh mountains. And then next time, if the place did not prove impossible, they would go there together and she would see the wild moors and the famous Mount Snowdon. In the meantime he had someone she must meet, a Dane, a student of insects called Johann Fabricius who would be spending the summer studying his collection.

If she was a little more serious than usual on his return, he did not mark it and she waited until the first bustle of his arrival had subsided before she told him. By then she was already three months pregnant.

CHAPTER SIXTEEN

LEAVING LINCOLN

It was two in the morning before I returned to the hotel. On the fringes of the town there were cars on the roads but up on the hill there was only silence and starlight. I left the car and walked the final part of the way. The frost had begun to lay intricate patterns on the cobbles.

Inside the hotel a small lamp still lit the reception desk but left the rest of the room in shadow. The hotel's warmth wrapped itself around me and I paused for a moment to enjoy it, rubbing my hands together and loosening my scarf. Until then, I hadn't really noticed the cold, such was the excitement running through me. I felt *alive*, more vibrant and more joyful than for many years.

In my euphoria, it would have been easy to miss the figure in the darkness, but a movement in the shadow caught my eye as I was heading towards the stairs. Through a doorway to my left lay the hotel bar and in that patch of blackness I saw a small pinprick of light rise and glow brightly, then fall back out of sight. Someone was sitting there, smoking in the dark.

I moved forward to the doorway. 'Katya?' I asked, but the reply came in Potts's American drawl.

'She's gone to bed, Mr Fitzgerald. A couple of hours ago.' The red eye of the cigarette rose again and pulsed brighter, a lingering drag that was followed by the soft hush of smoke being sighed into the darkness.

'What about the other two?' I asked, pausing in the doorway, wondering where the light switch was, trying to make out his outline and failing.

'Anderson and your Gabriella? He's not here. He's driven up to Durham. She went to bed early. They've had a long day.'

'No news on the bird then?' I tried to keep my voice calm.

'Apparently not. You want to hear what happened?'

'Go on.' I could still make out nothing but the tip of his cigarette.

'Well, at one o'clock they left here in Anderson's car. They drove to a village called Storeby where they had lunch in a pub called the Bell. They ordered red wine but they didn't drink much of it. Anderson held her hand between courses and kissed her quite a bit. I've seen a lot of that sort of stuff over the years, Mr Fitzgerald, believe me. You'd be amazed at some of the things I've had to sit through.' Potts sighed and raised his cigarette back to his invisible lips. 'At twenty to three they were joined by two men, both of them people who've worked for Anderson before. I know that because I've made it my business to know it. You can take my word for it.'

'You've been following him?'

'Of course I have.' There was a very faint trace of impatience in his voice. 'That's what I do. Do you want to hear the rest of it?'

I said nothing so he carried on.

'One of the two men produced a pile of photographs and the four of them spent half an hour going through them. Anderson got quite excitable and began slapping the table, but not in a happy way. At the end of that time he got up and walked into the village and smoked a whole lot of cigarettes.' A little chuckle came from the darkness in front of me. 'Between you and me, Mr Fitzgerald, I'd say he was mightily pissed.'

'You think it was the wrong bird, then?'

'You can be damned sure it was.'

I let out a long breath.

'Just think of that. All that research, and nothing to show for it.'

'That's right. No bird, no paintings, nothing. He and Gabriella spent the rest of the afternoon in the pub, just talking. There was a lot of hand-holding and a lot of shrugging and every now and then he'd pick up one of the Polaroids and look annoyed.'

I watched the tip of the unseen cigarette flare brightly again. By now I could make out the shape of Potts's body, very faint in a deep armchair, and a glimmer of light reflected from the rim of his glasses.

'I spoke to one of the guys working for him, got the full story. It turns out the Polaroids came from a big house near Durham, where they've got quite a few things that came from Ainsby Manor. And they've got paintings too, quite a few botanical drawings. That's why Anderson was so keen. But according to the photos, none of the birds is *the* bird, and the paintings aren't right either. Anderson's driven up there to check them out for himself, but he's wasting his time. I got a look at the Polaroids and they're definitely not by Roitelet. But then Anderson doesn't know much about art. That's why he should have agreed to work with me.'

'So the stuffed bird's still out there.' I pondered for a moment. 'And what about you now, Mr Potts? Why are you sitting in the dark?'

It seemed an obvious question but Potts didn't seem bothered by it.

'I was waiting for you, Mr Fitzgerald. I was interested to know just when you'd come home. And I guess I'd like to know where you've been. Jeez, all that business of the Stamford letter has led us precisely nowhere. And I guess that means you're about our best hope for finding those pictures. You're the one who knows about stuffed birds. Perhaps you know more than you say.'

I was about to reply when a cigarette lighter clicked open and lit up Potts's face. I realised it wasn't a random act. He was using it to study mine.

'Who knows?' I turned away. 'I'm going to bed.'

I left Potts sitting in the dark but as I climbed the stairs I could still feel him watching me. It would be easy to underestimate Potts, I thought. Even so, it was all I could do that night not to run up the stairs. The adrenaline was still flowing and the strain of maintaining a calm exterior was almost more than I could bear. And all the time my brain was racing. I needed a *plan*. But more than that, I needed to talk.

On reaching my room I washed in cold water, waited five minutes, then turned off the lights. Then, without undressing, I sat down with my back against the door and waited some more. It was forty-five long, cold minutes before I heard Potts come upstairs. Even then I made myself wait another hour before I dared move. Then I washed again—in warm water this time to stop me shivering—and picked up the bedside phone. I rang Katya's number and let it ring for a fraction of a second before I hung up. Then I waited a few seconds and did it again, then a third time, each time just a fragment of a ring. On the sixth attempt, Katya answered, sleepy and confused.

'Don't say anything,' I whispered to her. 'Just get dressed as quietly as you can. We're going to London.'

*　　　*　　　*

At four thirty in the morning the roads were empty and the frost was white between the carriageways. The cold seemed to have a razor edge to it and the air rushing against the windscreen was flecked with ice. We drove with our coats on and our scarves pulled tight around our necks. Katya had taken an old blanket from the back seat and tucked it around her.

'So what's going on?' she asked when we'd successfully negotiated the outskirts of the town.

'Not yet,' I told her. 'Wait till we're warmer. I'm still piecing it all together.'

She thought for a moment. 'So tell me about Gabriella then.'

'Gabby? You know most of it already.'

'So tell me the rest.' She turned to look at me. 'I can't tell what you feel about her.'

I didn't answer for a few seconds, waiting while a fat Mercedes rushed past us faster than I'd expected.

'I suppose it took me a while to work it out myself.'

'And?'

I hesitated. 'I think I needed to see her again

before I really knew. So many things that mean a lot to me are tied up with her. That makes it hard to just let go.'

'Do you want to let go?'

'Yes. It's time.' My eyes were still on the road ahead.

'Because you found out she's with Anderson?'

'No, that's not why.' There was a firmness in my voice that seemed to surprise her. 'I knew before then. I was just scared to believe it.'

She considered that, her face turned forward now as she watched the road. 'And what about Gabby? Has she moved on?'

'In one way. She still has her work though. That doesn't change. It's what really matters to her. More than people do.'

'You sound quite harsh.'

'I don't mean to. Gabby really loved me once, I know that. But it was when I was part of her work. When I stepped away from it I stopped being part of her world. She couldn't understand that I had feelings more important to me than the whole bloody rainforest.'

After that Katya seemed content to huddle under her blanket and watch the night. I think she slept. Gradually, as the miles clicked by, the car grew warmer.

We'd been driving for more than an hour when Katya stirred and asked the time and said she was hungry. A little after that we pulled into a Little Chef for coffee and breakfast. Katya waited until the coffees were steaming in front of us before she placed her chin on her hands and raised her eyebrows at me. 'So?' she asked, and waited.

We talked for nearly an hour. By the time we'd

finished, the night sky was liquefying at the edges, its colour draining into the fields below. When we climbed back into the car Katya understood the bargain I had struck that evening in Lincolnshire and knew I had no more than a couple of days to come up with what I'd promised. Neither of us had any time to waste.

We drove in silence after that. When we reached the edge of London a rush of extra traffic signalled the dawn. We picked our way through it and arrived home. When I turned the engine off, Katya didn't move.

'What?' I asked.

'I was thinking about Karl Anderson. I think it's real, what he feels about Gabby. The way he looks at her.'

I thought about it. 'I'm not sure. I can't see their lives fitting together very well.'

Katya shrugged. 'Perhaps she's changed. Perhaps she's ready to do something different. Perhaps she'll marry Karl Anderson and settle down.'

I shook my head. 'Gabby won't change. What she does now is too much a part of her.' I paused. 'And with Anderson's money behind her, who knows, perhaps she'll save the planet after all. But she won't marry him. At least not for a while.'

'How can you be so sure?'

I kept my eyes very firmly ahead of me. 'Because at the moment she's still married to me,' I said.

*   *   *

I've often wondered if my grandfather's life would have been different if he'd ever met a woman he

296

loved. Whatever made him marry, it wasn't love. From the diaries he left behind you can see how little time he spent with his wife. They don't even explain why he married her. It's as if his proposal just bubbled to the surface one day to the equal surprise of them both. By the time either of them had the chance to wonder why, it was too late: my grandfather was back in the jungle and the pattern of their lives was established beyond hope of alteration.

The day in the Congo when my grandfather separated from the bulk of his party was a final chance to send back letters. He knew that the next opportunity would be many months away. And yet he didn't write to his wife or send back any message. Instead he and his remaining companion simply shouldered their burdens and set off into the silent crescendo of the forest.

Neither of them knew the terrain. Neither really knew where they were going. Their ignorance made easy things ten times more difficult than they should have been, and difficult things became impossible. They deliberately avoided the local people—who could have helped them—and seemed to seek out the most impenetrable tracts of forest for their path. In their first month they travelled a hundred miles but it's clear from my grandfather's log that their route was serpentine, their progress achieved at massive expense of energy. They pushed forwards into unmapped areas of jungle, my grandfather's positional reports becoming sketchier with every day that passed. They reached a river and misidentified it, then followed its course through dense undergrowth for three weeks. Then, when the quinine began to run low, they left the water and struck out for higher ground. For another month they continued in that way. In that time my grandfather gave up keeping his log book, as if he already knew the worst. It isn't even clear whether their increasingly circuitous route was an attempt to push on or a desperate effort to retreat the way they'd come. Either way it made no odds. They were lost and exhausted. Their supplies were almost gone. My grandfather's fever had returned. And nowhere they went was there any sign of peacocks.

* * *

When we went inside I showed Katya the photograph on my bedside table.

'My daughter,' I told her. 'She was just under a year old then. She died a few weeks after this was taken.'

We were sitting on the bed in my crumpled, comfortable little room, our knees and elbows touching.

'I'm so sorry,' she said. She held the picture gently between her fingertips.

'There are hundreds of things in Brazil that can kill a child. It's a fact of life out there. But it was more than that to me. It just changed everything.'

She touched my hand so I carried on. 'I wanted us to leave, to come back here. I couldn't bear just going on as if nothing had changed. But Gabby's work was a place for her to hide. She needed it more than ever then, I suppose, just when I stopped caring about it completely.'

For a moment I found myself there again: that plain room, its window half covered by a dirty net, an electric fan turning endlessly, achieving nothing. The stench of sweat. The small bed, empty; the blankets still curved into a child's shape. And Gabby downstairs, her voice flat, making the arrangements that had to be made.

'So you left her?'

'I was in her way. Everything she did I held against her as a sign of her not caring enough. It wasn't fair, but that's how it was. We were in danger of hating each other. In the end we agreed I had to go.' I looked at the picture in front of me, feeling the emptiness all over again. 'We called her Celeste, after Gabby's mother. This photograph is all there is of her now. Only this and the things we remember. When Gabby and I are gone, there's just the photograph. After that, nothing.'

We both sat silently for a little before Katya spoke. 'So that was when you started tracking down extinct birds?'

'That's right.' I gave a sort of off-beam smile. 'It all seems a bit obvious now, doesn't it? Hanging on to things. Refusing to let things go. But it didn't at the time.'

'And Gabby?'

'She got on with her work. She dealt with it like a grown-up, I suppose. While I was just angry about everything. I was like that for three years. In the end I was too exhausted to feel angry any longer so I came here and started stuffing birds.' I pointed to the corner of the room. 'I put all the papers for the book away in that trunk and began a different life. Now I don't feel angry any more. I don't think I even feel pain. I just feel so incredibly *sorry* that she never had a chance to grow up. There's so much that's wonderful in the world that she'll never see.'

'And you and Gabby never saw each other until this month?'

'It sounds ridiculous, doesn't it? I suppose I was angry with her. But she'd write to me and I'd read the letters and keep them. And while she was writing and I was reading there was still a link. She'd write about her work mostly. Never anything personal. That would have been too dangerous. And I knew there were men sometimes but while she was still writing that didn't seem to matter.'

'Because you still loved her.'

'No.' Again my voice was firm. 'That vanished somewhere. But she was the only other person who remembered Celeste. That was what mattered.'

Katya was looking away. We sat in silence for another moment before I spoke again.

'I wasn't trying to hide being married to Gabby. It just didn't seem to matter. It sounds stupid, but I find myself forgetting.'

Katya was looking out of the window, her face turned away from me. I thought at first she wasn't going to reply but then she turned and squeezed my hand.

'OK,' she said.

We didn't say much more after that, but Katya's hand stayed in mine. And when the silence was over we got up and set about getting hold of the Ulieta bird.

Pregnancy suited her. Even in the early months, before it showed, before Banks left for North Wales, she was aware of a warmth within her as if the life stirring there was already part of her future. She found herself more vital than before and her body seemed to find a new equilibrium and a new harmony. The collection of watercolours from her Madeira sketches grew rapidly. She knew she must finish them that summer and she painted with a passion inside her that showed itself only as a shining freshness in the meticulous detail of her work. She worked from early each morning until the heat of the afternoon, often dressed in nothing more than her nightdress, sometimes with a jacket of Banks's wrapped around her, its sleeves hanging loosely at her sides. In the afternoon, when the heat became unbearable, she rested quietly in the shaded drawing room. Martha would often find her at the window with the shutters a little open, watching the crowds of strangers below her, a calm, contented smile on her lips.

When the evening began to lift the heat from the streets, she would take up her paints again with a freedom in her heart that she had never before experienced. Even when Banks left for Wales her life felt no less complete. His absence was a relief, a chance to work uninterrupted. She had been very quickly aware of how her announcement had affected him. She had seen him touched with wonder, moved by both pride and excitement; and she had seen those things fade as he began to ponder what it meant and how things would change. She watched the explorer and the statesman struggle inside him.

That conflict pained her more for his sake than her

own. For her it made things easier. His departure for Wales was both a confirmation and a release.

And then there was Fabricius. He first came to the rooms in Orchard Street soon after she moved there, a pale, shy, slightly serious young man. She sensed he came reluctantly and at Banks's insistence. At first he seemed loath to notice her, his attention directed at Banks, his only interest apparently the taxonomy of insects. Then one afternoon he called at Orchard Street in search of Banks and found only her. She was painting, her hair loose around her shoulders. He attempted to withdraw. Amused by his embarrassment, she insisted that he wait. She settled him in a chair and while she worked she asked him questions that required him to talk. He answered carefully and precisely and eventually with growing animation, surprised to find that the slight figure in front of him understood the basic anatomy of insects and seemed to know a good deal about Linnaean principles. Lulled by the fact that her back was turned, he found himself talking at length, explaining to her about his life in Denmark and about his aspirations and hopes. When Banks's return interrupted him he grew confused and the formality of his farewell made her smile.

After that he began to call more often, always in the afternoons when the heat made it difficult for either of them to work. He would usually find her alone, as Banks was seldom there at that time of day. When Banks departed for Wales, Fabricius became her only visitor.

At first this dedication amused her and the shyness of the Dane made her mischievous. He hovered a little awkwardly in the background while she painted and she would tease him with personal questions and smile to herself at his attempts to answer. But gradually she began to find his presence restful, part of her daily routine, and she listened to the descriptions of his studies with only half her attention, intent on the detail of a leaf or the precise shade of a flower. She found that she began to listen for his arrival.

Her work fascinated him. When introduced to the mistress of the famous Joseph Banks he had expected studied coyness or the arch femininity of the professionally alluring. But what he saw on her easel astounded him. He had seen the work of Parkinson and Masson, of all the botanical artists of the day, but hers stood out. Her subjects seemed to live on the page as if they were still growing, still stirred by the breeze or freshened by dew. He would watch her paint, her body now curved with child, her small face furrowed with concentration, and feel intensely moved by what he saw. As June turned into July his visits grew longer.

They began to laugh together: uncertainly at first, then more often and more comfortably. It marked a new easiness between them. She began to call him by his first name and he found that when he took his leave in the evenings his mind was no longer disposed to study.

One day, as he admired her work, she turned to him. 'Do you know that this one is the last?' she asked. 'After this the work from Madeira is complete.'

'I had not realised,' he replied solemnly, his eyes still on the painting in front of him. 'It is the very finest body of work. It will grace the collection of botanical paintings that Mr Banks is assembling.'

She looked at him carefully then and shook her head slightly. 'We have not talked of that,' she said.

'But surely? Where else would it go? It must certainly be displayed.'

She began to put away her brushes, her back turned to him so that he could not see her face.

'Tell me, Johann, have you ever heard of a Frenchman called Martin? He is in London quite often.'

'I have met Monsieur Martin,' he replied. 'He is in London at the moment.'

'I have met him too,' she said. 'Joseph brought him here once.'

'And what of him?' His tone was short and suspicious.

'I don't know yet,' she replied and continued to put away her things.

That day Fabricius began to feel a disquiet that marred his time with her. Outside, the summer was still growing to its height but he found himself gripped by a sense of ending. Banks would return from Wales soon and here in London the companion of his summer was finishing her paintings. She was seven months pregnant. Soon she would be a mother, Banks a father. And he would be returning to Denmark and his studies.

Before departing that day he decided to speak. They were sitting in the drawing room, high above street level. The room was shaded against the heat and at the hour when he usually took his leave they were sitting together quietly in the shadow. Instead of rising and making his farewells, he prolonged their conversation hesitantly, aware of her hand on the cushion beside him, delicate and graceful next to his own. Finally, spurred more by impulse than calculation, he reached out and took it, gripping it much harder than he intended.

'I need to know,' he said simply. 'When your child is born, what will happen then?'

Very gently she detached her hand from his but she smiled as she returned his look.

'What usually happens will happen. I shall become a mother and do the things that mothers do.'

'And Banks? What will he do?'

'He is generous with his feelings. It is a good quality in a father.'

'And will you stay here? In Denmark it is one thing for a man to maintain a mistress, another to raise a family under the noses of his peers.'

She looked down.

'Things will be different in the future, yes.'

'You will leave London?'

'Yes, I will leave London.'

'And raise his child somewhere more discreet. I see. It is not uncommon for a young man in that position to . . .' He tailed off, suddenly embarrassed.

'To find companionship with another?' She was still looking down. 'A woman unencumbered with the cares of motherhood, perhaps?'

'Forgive me,' he said and took her hand again. This time she let him retain it. 'I should not have spoken in that way.'

She looked up and smiled again, her eyes slightly misted. 'You must understand. In the future his life is going to be very full of people and plans and social niceties that he will have no choice but to observe. But I also know there will never be a time when he does not think of us, of his child and me. Wherever his life takes him, that care will always be there, somewhere, underneath.'

It was Fabricius' turn to bow his head.

'Of course. How could it be otherwise? He is a lucky man. Though I hope he understands his good fortune. If I were he, I would not leave you alone at a

305

time such as this.'

'I am not alone, am I?' She pressed his hand a little tighter then rose and moved away from him. He saw she was smiling to herself, a sad, uncertain smile.

'Forgive me,' she explained, realising he was observing her. 'I was thinking of something someone once said to me. A gentleman. He told me that one day Joseph would lose me to someone who would value me more highly. I have thought of it often these last few months.'

'And you smile because you think he was mistaken?'

'No, Johann. I smile because once I chose to disbelieve him. Now I know that what he said was true.'

*   *   *

There is a hill in North Wales that the people there call Pen-y-Cloddiau, the hill of the ditches. It rises hunched from the Vale of Clwyd, a crooked vertebra in the spine of hills that runs northwards to the sea. Below it the whole vale is spread out like a map and the clusters of farms are reduced to no more than a cartographer's shading. The hill is so named because its summit is ringed by three mighty earthworks, the ancient, overgrown walls of a fortress whose very name is now lost, buried beneath the heather that has overrun its defences.

On a warm day in July Banks made the expedition there alone. His tour of Wales was almost complete and it had brought neither the escape he sought nor the clarity he needed. Now he stood on the curved ridge of the highest earthwork and looked out at the sun-bathed world of farms and forests below him. Above him there were skylarks. Beyond the vale the land rose again and he could pick out the blue ridges of Snowdonia, distant and slightly mysterious. The solitude of the place suited him.

As always in those months, when left alone he would think of her. The news that she was pregnant had shaken him. It was a change to the order of things that somehow he had never contemplated and it threw him off balance. At first he felt only amazement and a sense of wonder. But then there came doubt, a long slow tide of uncertainty that crept closer each day, tugging at the sands beneath his feet. It was on this stealth tide that he had travelled to Wales, guilty for going, resentful that his life had been taken from his control.

The sun was high above him as he stood on the empty hillside but it was cooler there than down in the vale. When he shut his eyes he could smell heather and hear bees. Stronger than either, he could feel how much he missed her. He wanted her with him there and then. He wanted her to run her fingers across his lips and smile at his seriousness, to feel her body curved against his. He wanted her to make sense of it all in the way he knew she would. But her body was a different shape now. Their world had changed. He had never imagined losing her undivided love. Now he knew he had been wrong. She would have a child to love. She would never be purely his again.

The advice of his friends was clear. A discreet establishment at a discreet distance, a generous allowance and a settlement to secure the child's future. Then he would be free to start afresh with someone sleek and pretty who would understand that their union should not result in lasting consequences. But he didn't want the future they described. He wanted the closeness that he had shared with her, he wanted her eyes when he couldn't see things clearly. But if she were to be occupied with a child . . . Standing there in the sunlight, wanting her more than he had ever done, he blamed her for everything he longed for but couldn't have.

*   *   *

Fabricius began to make plans for his departure: he would leave London before the autumn. His visits to Orchard Street had a different feel to them now. The painting was finished and her afternoons seemed busy with quite different things. On one occasion he arrived and found her sitting with Monsieur Martin, the Frenchman. The two seemed at ease together and Martin was elaborately polite and solicitous of her comfort. Fabricius had the feeling he had interrupted two people who shared an understanding. On another occasion his visit was interrupted by the arrival of a gentleman announced as Mr Parker from Lincoln. Fabricius took his leave discreetly, but not before he had caught a glimpse of a small, dry-looking man with a country appearance and an inscrutable expression. The following day he called and found the Frenchman there again, taking his leave. Hurt and suspicious, he waited until they were alone before he demanded a reason for the visits.

'Monsieur Martin is an admirer of my paintings,' she replied and offered no other explanation. Instead she came up to him and slipped her arm through his.

'Do not be anxious for me, my friend. A woman in my position needs friends. The gentlemen you have met are people who will help me.'

'If you need assistance . . .' he replied.

'Oh, I know you would help me. But you have

your studies. And I am not really a part of your life, though I have helped you to pass the dreariness of a hot summer in London.'

'Dreariness? You have done much more than that. You have . . .'

'No, do not say it. You will be gone from London soon. Joseph will be back. Let us leave these strange summer afternoons as they have always been, something gentle and good and not quite real. That is how we should remember them when we journey in our different directions. It's a consolation that I shall be able to follow your career from a distance. I know it will be distinguished.'

He cast his eyes down at that. A small part of him that had started to bloom seemed to shiver in the cold.

'I see. And I of course shall follow your future path. I'm sure Mr Banks will keep me informed of how you fare.'

Still with her arm in his, she led him across the room to the window. Looking out, her eyes on the people below, she spoke to him softly.

'It may be that these are the last moments we spend together. Whatever happens, promise not to be sad for me.'

'The thought of you suffering any hurt does more than sadden me. It leaves me desolate.'

'Do not let it. You must believe that I intend to be happy.'

He said nothing for a long time. 'I shall try,' he said at last and for a while longer they stood at the window while the sun lit their faces and sent the shadows long across the room.

CHAPTER SEVENTEEN

IN LONDON

Time was tight. I reckoned I had two days at the most before Potts and Anderson decided something was up and came looking for me. And I couldn't afford to have them on my back while I was desperately trying to call in favours and scrape together what I needed. The plan was for Katya to be back in Lincoln by evening to make sure they stayed there—we'd worked out what tale she'd spin—but we both had other things to do before then. First, still a bit groggy from lack of sleep, we went back to the Natural History Museum. I wanted Katya there with me as a second set of eyes so that between us we would be quite sure what we were looking for.

We had to wait about half an hour before Geraldine the librarian brought the picture to our table—the mysterious bird of Ulieta, drawn on the day it was last seen alive, still fresh and striking, utterly oblivious of its curious place in history. Katya studied the picture again then looked up at me.

'It's so *plain*, isn't it? When you first told me about it, I expected something really exotic. You know, bright colours and fancy feathers.'

'I know. Just a small, brown bird. There's nothing very striking about it, is there? But when you look at it closely, it changes. See? The beauty's all in the detail. Things you only notice when you look properly.' We let our eyes wander over all the tiny vagaries of shape and markings that made the bird beautiful and unique, and then we set about memorising them. I attempted a sketch; we both took notes, describing the tones of each shade of colour so we could remember them later. We did everything we could to burn the image into our minds: we measured and memorised and then we shut our eyes and tried to recall.

'Would you recognise the real thing if you saw it now?' I asked when our note-taking was over.

Katya nodded solemnly.

'Yes, I'm sure I would.'

'Of course, the colours would fade over time. We have to allow for that. Imagine those chestnut browns much paler, imagine the wings bleached where the sunlight has touched them. And the eyes won't look like that. The eyes will be eighteenth-century glass gone cloudy with time.'

'What about you? Is it clear in your mind?'

'As clear as it will ever be. Come on, let's go.'

Outside the museum we went our separate ways. We parted in wintry sunshine, the buses on the Cromwell Road swirling urgent eddies of late leaves around our feet.

'Good luck.' Katya smiled.

'Thank you.' I smiled back, awkwardly, not really sure what we did at moments of parting. In the end I just nodded a little foolishly and waved as I walked away.

My plan was to spend the rest of the day on the phone asking favours, but first I needed money. So when I found a cashpoint, I took out all the cash it would let me have. This was going to be an expensive business.

Katya's first action was to pay another visit to

the London archives. She was back on the trail of Miss B but this time she knew the names we were looking for. Even so, it wasn't easy. When she rang me at midday she'd found absolutely nothing.

'It doesn't matter,' I reminded her. 'It's just for neatness really, just to tie up the loose ends. What's really important is that you get back to Lincoln in time to stop the rest of them from getting too curious.'

She called again two hours later and this time her voice was clipped, a flood of excitement held back by crisp efficiency.

'I've found them,' she said. 'She went south of the river for the baptism. To be discreet, perhaps.'

'What does it say?'

'Sophia, daughter of the late Joseph Burnett and his wife Mary. September 1773.'

'So she pretended the father was dead? That would be so the real Joseph wasn't implicated.'

'What about you? How are you doing?'

I considered the question. 'I think I'll be able to get most of what I need. It's outrageous, really. I'm trying people I haven't seen for years. But most of them are being very generous. The trouble is that I'll have to spend most of tomorrow driving round to collect. Bristol, then Dorset, then a couple of places on the way back.'

'Will you have enough time?'

'I don't know. And if I don't pull it off Anderson is going to get wind of what's going on and blast us out of the water. You've got to get up to Lincoln quickly to keep his nose out of things.'

'I'm going there now,' she promised.

*　　*　　*

312

By a miracle of public transport, Katya was back in Lincoln in time for a pre-dinner drink. Before visiting the bar, however, she stopped at reception and told them I'd been called away suddenly but was keeping on my room for at least the next couple of days. Then she went upstairs, found Anderson's door and knocked on it.

The previous twenty-four hours hadn't been Anderson's best. He'd been forced to accept that his research had led to nothing, that the Ulieta bird hadn't been part of the sale at the Ainsby manor. That being the case, he knew there could be no quick win, no short cut to the bird or the pictures; not even any guarantee they still existed. By the time Katya arrived in Lincoln, he and Gabby were beginning to pack their bags. His urbane charm was wearing a little thin.

But all that changed when he opened his door and found Katya standing in front of him.

'How much will you pay for the bird?' she asked.

*   *   *

Half an hour later she found Potts in the bar.

'Ah, greetings.' He beamed and bobbed to his feet. 'You and Mr Fitzgerald made a very early start this morning. I've been looking for you.'

'And here I am.' Katya smiled brightly.

'And Mr Fitzgerald? Is he here?'

'He's been held up. He'll be back later, I think.'

'I see. Back from *where*, I wonder.'

'You'll have to ask him that.'

'You don't know?'

'I promised not to say.'

313

'I see. Well, in that case I have all evening to persuade you otherwise.'

Katya raised an eyebrow and looked deliberately enigmatic. 'There was something else I promised not to say too,' she teased.

'Is it very pointless to ask what?'

'That depends.' She studied him for a moment. 'Are you likely to pay more for the Ulieta bird than Karl Anderson will?'

*   *   *

That night I managed to snatch a few hours' sleep. It was my first for forty hours and I knew I was going to need it. The next day would be long and difficult. I wasn't sure how it would turn out.

It began at 6 a.m. and I was out of the house by seven, heading west towards Bristol. The morning was a bright one but when I got beyond the London sprawl there was frost on the fields and the branches of the bare trees were white. With the sun shining and the sky a very pure blue, it felt like a good day for driving and I sensed my tiredness slipping away. As the last remnants of the city were left behind I began to feel a deep stirring of exhilaration. I knew what I was doing and where I was going. And that morning when I thought of the face looking out of the photograph, I thought perhaps it wasn't wrong to smile back.

Luck went my way that day, and yet I shouldn't have been surprised—the discovery of most things is down to luck. People often feel uncomfortable about that. They want discovery to be driven by something more meaningful than coincidence. But they're wrong. It's the discovery itself that matters.

And if anything ever proved how important luck is, it was the discovery of the African peacock.

While my grandfather made his way on foot through the heat of the Congo forest, James Chapin, the American natu ralist, was visiting Belgium, making one of his periodic visits to the old Colonial Museum in Tervuren. It's a magnificent building, the Belgian rival to Versailles, and it houses an amazing number of artefacts and items of general clutter that over the years found their way there from the Belgian Congo. It was twenty-three years since Chapin had found that single feather, so it was hardly at the front of his mind. But while he was browsing through some of the less prominent items on display he came across two stuffed birds pushed away into a corner. No one appeared to have paid them any attention for a great many years. They were both described as Indian peacocks—juveniles, the label said, but Chapin knew at once they were not. Neither of them were young birds—the spurs on the male, for instance, were thick with age. Whatever they were, they were not juveniles. They certainly looked like peacocks, but not the sort of peacocks he had ever seen before.

Inquiries showed that the specimens had been donated, along with other exhibits, by a Belgian Congo trading company. Further inquiries by Chapin established precisely where in the Congo they had been collected. Armed with that information, Chapin arranged a new trip to Africa. It wasn't a difficult expedition because he knew exactly where to go. Within a few weeks he had collected a dozen or more live specimens of the Congo peacock, the only bird of its kind in the whole of Africa.

Yes, that's how it happened. While my grandfather hacked desperately into the heart of the Congo, the first African peacocks were found on a dusty shelf in a Belgian museum. They had been there all along.

*   *   *

That day I covered a lot of miles in the rusty lemon car and called in more favours than I had ever earned. I visited squat Victorian suburbs and villages with frosty village greens and ice-fringed ponds. I met one man in a betting shop and another in a rambling country vicarage. Some were able to offer me material assistance, others had nothing to give but advice on how an eighteenth-century specimen would be preserved and about what state it would be in now; about the sort of care I would need to exercise and the kinds of chemicals I might need to use if I wanted to carry the thing off. I listened to it all, and when there were no more donations to be collected and nothing more I could possibly learn, I drove home.

I didn't reach London until about ten o'clock, but instead of feeling tired my mind was alert and full of restless energy. I knew I should try to sleep so that I could start the next day fresh, but time was so critical that the idea of sleep seemed laughable; instead I dug out the keys and opened up my workshop. There, in the bright pool of light that flooded my workbench, I let my fingers lead me, until the restlessness in my brain gave way to the ferocious concentration of the taxidermist. The longer I worked, the more settled I became and

316

the clearer the path ahead of me appeared. It was going to be all right.

In the end I worked long, long into the night. Reviewing it the next day, it was some of the best work I'd ever done.

After that everything seemed to go right. I set out for Lincoln later that day.

Her child was born early, kicking and coughing amid the dust and heat of late August. The birth was a difficult one and for a month after it she was too weak to leave the house, too exhausted to go on with the plans she had laid. Instead she nursed her baby and herself through long, breathless days when the stench of London seemed to boil up to their windows; through floundering nights of sleeplessness.

Banks had returned from Wales barely three weeks before his daughter was born. On his arrival he found the rooms in Orchard Street changed. Her artist's clutter was all tidied away and in the places where four of her first Madeira paintings had hung there were now bare walls. The sole example of her work that remained in view was the collection of brown oak leaves and acorns that she had painted in her first months in Richmond. For all its plainness, it was her favourite: the first she had framed, the first she had hung on arriving in Orchard Street.

'The Madeira work is put away,' she explained. 'It felt right that it should all be kept together and I don't want to be distracted by it. You would not have me neglect our child for thoughts of line and shading?' He concurred, but her words saddened him and the removal of her paintings left the rooms subdued and empty. Even the arrival of a new life, for all the noise it brought, never seemed to Banks to fill the rooms as they once had been filled. Perhaps because of that his daughter failed to move him in the way he had expected to be moved. He found the little distance that had come to exist between father and mother came also between father and child. He willed her well from his very heart but it was as if the knot of

318

uncertainty that twisted inside him prevented him from loving. He was a man who found it easiest to love when he was loved and this was a time of doubt. They named her Sophia after his sister.

As she began to recover her health he would watch her laughing with the small bundle on her lap and at first he was jealous. He tried to shorten his visits, to entertain himself elsewhere, telling himself that her fascination with the child would dwindle with time. But the memory of the look on her face as she smiled down would often bring him back. For all his confusion, she was still a miracle to him. He wanted to take her in his arms and tell her so but found he didn't know how. And though she would often give him a look both tender and searching, she seemed unwilling to help him.

Eventually there came a day when he found her alone arranging flowers in a bowl, her hair neatly tied up and her dress crisp and fresh. She looked as she had looked in their first days in Richmond and a rush of tenderness carried him across the room until he stood behind her, his hands resting gently on her waist. She finished positioning a particular stalk then laid the other flowers down and turned her head so she could look at him over her shoulder. He met her gaze and remembered how green her eyes were, how soft the smile at the corner of her lips. He moved his hands further around her and pulled her to him. He could smell the familiar scent of her hair.

'It has been a long time since we were alone,' he whispered.

She leaned back then so that her cheek was touching his. 'Things are changed,' she said.

'You are not changed. You are still more special and more lovely than I can ever tell you.'

'We are both changed, Joseph. It is just that sometimes we forget.'

'Shut your eyes. Do I *feel* changed?'

'Do you remember how you used to hold me, at night in our little room with russet hangings?'

'That's how I'm holding you now.'

She moved her cheek from his and twisted around within his embrace until she was facing him. 'No, that was different.'

'How was it different?'

'You had no doubts then.'

For a moment he held her gaze and then he looked down. 'I don't doubt you,' he told her very quietly. 'I know that I love you. But I don't know what happens next.'

She leaned closer to him so that her cheek touched his and her lips almost touched his ear.

'You have things to do, Joseph. A world to change. You have to do all the things we have talked about.'

'But how?'

'You grow respectable. You set an example. You marry. You produce an heir.'

'No.'

'Yes.' She moved her cheek gently against his. 'I like to think I was a help to you once. Now, with Sophia, I'm in the way.'

'It isn't true.'

'And I must do my best for her.'

'Meaning?'

She broke away from his embrace and turned away from him. 'Have you thought how it will be for her to be known as your daughter?'

There was a sharpness in her tone that surprised him.

'I cannot believe that being my daughter is a

320

disadvantage,' he replied. 'She will not want, I can promise that.'

'She will be the daughter of your mistress. The daughter of a kept woman. Some people will never forgive her for that. It will be used against her for the rest of her life.'

'And the alternative?'

She came back into his arms and held him tightly before she answered. 'The alternative is that you let us go,' she said.

*   *   *

He vowed he would never let it happen. He swore that his life meant nothing without them. He refused to believe that his daughter's life could not be lived in London, discreetly, acknowledged by him, unseen by others. But she knew he was wrong. She looked at the small, perfect little creature that she had brought into the world and then thought of her own childhood. Her family had always been marked by disapproval and laden with shame. She had been shunned and scorned for being her father's daughter, had been cut in the streets of Louth for being John Ponsonby's mistress. And now she was Joseph Banks's mistress, seduced by that notorious adventurer. She held the tiny Sophia close to her and promised her that in her whole life she would never be scorned or shamed by anyone.

*   *   *

Fabricius left London shortly after Banks returned there. He went back to Denmark where the air was clean and the light shone off water that dazzled with its clarity. In London he had missed the great arching

321

Danish sky and now he found himself frequently looking up or stopping to scan the horizon with a sense of simple joy.

The close, confined afternoons in Orchard Street began to seem to him increasingly unbelievable, an episode in life that had come from nowhere and led him nowhere and left him back where he had begun. It seemed remarkable that he had somehow fallen into that quiet, unspoken partnership; remarkable that he had felt so much and been prepared to show his feelings. He thought of her often. Sometimes, when he was concentrating on a difficult piece of work, a word or a phrase would come into his head and he would pause and smile.

'*The thing about beetles,*' she had once teased him, '*is that however dull you become studying them, at least you will never run out of new ones to look at.*' For many years after his return, at the end of long days of study, he would sometimes sit back and address his students very solemnly. 'Gentlemen,' he would say, 'let us at least console ourselves with the one great certainty about beetles.'

'What certainty is that, sir?' they would always reply and then their rather serious mentor would surprise them with a smile and repeat her words; and for the briefest of moments he would be back in London where a slender young woman stood before him, painting.

Banks had been generous with access to his collection, and the examination of it that summer had left Fabricius with a great deal of work to do and much to ponder. Nevertheless he found himself shy of Banks now, as if his visits to Orchard Street had been an undiscovered betrayal. Perhaps that was why he waited until November of that year to write to Banks, and even then he had to re-work the letter several times. '*My best compliments and wishes in Orchard Street,*' he wrote. '*What has she brought you? Well, it is all the same, if a boy he will be clever and strong like his father, if a girl she will be pretty and genteel like her mother.*'

Banks's reply was short. He was the father of a daughter. Both mother and child were well.

When Banks next wrote to him it was February and the sky over Denmark was low and heavy with snow clouds. Banks's letter said nothing of Orchard Street, nothing of either mother or child. When Fabricius made his own discreet inquiries, he learned Banks had been deserted by his mistress. Miss Brown and her daughter had disappeared.

*   *   *

In January of 1774, four months after her daughter's birth, she left her rooms to walk in the nearby gardens. It was cold and the ground held a stiff frost but she was accompanied by Martha and, despite the chill, the two were talking comfortably when she heard her name spoken. Her true name. Not since the day she left Revesby to become John Ponsonby's mistress had anyone addressed her by that name. She had thought it a secret and she treasured it, the only way she could think of to protect her father's reputation. So the shock was a great one when a voice called out to her.

'Miss Burnett, I believe.' It was a man's voice and there was something in the way it lingered over the word *Miss* that made her turn sharply.

At first she didn't recognise him in his heavy winter coat but when she thought of Madeira she could see his face laughing at her in the candlelight.

'Mr Maddox,' she replied instinctively, surprise

making her incautious.

'So you remember me?' He smiled that lazy, confident smile. 'As I recall, I am dressed rather differently today from our last meeting. But then I would have to remark that the same is equally true of you.'

She felt herself blushing, suddenly aware of people within earshot, of the clarity of his voice.

'I'm afraid, sir, that Burnett is only the name under which I travelled,' she said quietly. 'Now if you will excuse me . . .'

He kept pace with her effortlessly. 'Such haste to be gone is most unflattering. The time was when you were not so shy. I feel it would be quite wrong to end our acquaintance so soon after rediscovering it, Miss Burnett. Especially under such *different* circumstances. And as you see, I have no alternative but to call you by that name until you furnish me with another.'

'My name can be of no interest to you, sir.'

'On the contrary, I find you most intriguing. I have often regretted that I never had the opportunity of coming to know you in quite the same way as you came to know me. Perhaps now that we are both in London we may be able to make good that omission.'

'I hardly think so, sir.'

He was still walking alongside her and in her hurry to get away from him she had left Martha slightly behind.

'Really?' She could hear the mocking smile in his voice. 'I wonder if your current gentleman knows of your former exploits? Perhaps you do not care for him to know. After all he may not wish to think he is in the company of a former ship's boy?'

'Sir!' She stopped walking and Martha came up puffing to her side. He paused too and eyed them both with his easy, unruffled smile. 'Come now, you must admit that good reasons for your extraordinary behaviour are hard to come by. I'm sure your current protector would not enjoy trying to discover them.'

She spoke as slowly and calmly as she was able.

'Sir, I would ask that you leave us at once. I'm sure you have business to attend to elsewhere.'

His smile widened and he gave a little nod of approval. 'I'm pleased to see that your spirit has not been diminished by your abandonment of male clothing. It was your spirit I admired that day you watched me bathe. I was convinced you would blush and run away.' He smiled broadly and made a little bow. 'As you have asked me to leave you, I shall leave you. But I can assure you that none of my business affairs are nearly so interesting as the surprising Miss Burnett. I shall be looking out for you. For a great city, London is surprisingly poor at keeping its secrets.'

At that, with another bow, he turned and walked away, leaving the two women silent behind him.

*   *   *

She tried to warn Joseph. She wrote him a note telling him of her encounter, telling him that she feared a scandal if Maddox told the story of her journey to Madeira. She begged him to visit so that she could explain the danger. And then she waited. For five days he did not come. He had been out of town, he explained, when he finally appeared. He had not been aware of her note. He stood in front of her like a sulking adolescent, deliberately late, petulant at being summoned but embarrassed at his petulance. When she saw how he carried himself she turned away and tried to leave the room but this dismissal piqued him further

325

and he caught her before she reached the door.

'I am here because you wished to talk to me.'

'There is no point,' she replied. 'I can see you are not to be talked to.'

'That is insulting. I have come away from the household of very good friends. They do not value my conversation so lightly.'

'Oh, Joseph!' She looked him in the eye and shook her head, suddenly weary. 'Then go and talk to them. We would both prefer it. Once you gave me your word that you would never hold me against my will. This is the night I remind you of it.'

The sharpness of her words shocked them both into stillness. In the silence that followed he stood aside so that she was free to pass out of the room.

'You are right,' he murmured. 'I will not detain you against your will.'

At that moment, in the sadness of his face, she saw clearly and for the last time the young man she loved; saw him hurt and confused and uncertain of her. For that brief moment she felt her resolution waver and she reached up and touched his face.

'My love,' she said, 'this isn't how it should be.'

He took her hand in his and pushed it to his lips, his eyes shut. They stood like that until she freed her hand.

'How has it come to this?' he asked. 'I know I love you now as much as I have ever loved you. Sometimes I forget that. I blame you because things are not as they used to be. I can feel such resentment. But even as I do another part of me thinks of you with such pride and such longing that I end up hating myself.'

'Perhaps love is always honest in the end.'

'Is that true?'

'I don't know,' she said. 'I would like it to be.'

'I seem always so weighed down by the world. There is so much to do that it seems I can do none of it well. And it feels there is no space for you. Yet sometimes, when I feel tired and alone, I don't understand why I am not with you.'

'And yet you are here less and less.'

He looked away and then turned back to her. 'There are so many things I want to be. Sometimes it is easier to pretend those things when I am not with you. You know me too well.'

'You can be anything. I've always told you that.'

'Yes, I can be anything. You make me believe that. But it comes at a price.'

She leaned against him then, her forehead resting lightly on his chest.

'Yes,' she said. 'It all comes at a price.'

*   *   *

That night he slept with his body pressed close to her. She slept too, but intermittently, woken from time to time by the presence of him so near her or by his arm reaching for her in his sleep. His sleep was peaceful and even, and in sleep he seemed young again, his face as uncreased as in the Revesby woods. As she lay there she felt again the warmth that always filled her when they were together at night. And when it came, the dawn on her skin was like an icy breath.

As the sun rose higher she fell eventually into a deeper sleep. He woke and watched her sleeping. He began to reach to wake her but her sleep seemed too perfect to disturb. If he had known it was the last time he would ever see her sleeping, he would never have left that room. But the night spent with her had reassured him and the morning was a bright one. A new day beckoned. He hurried to meet it. When she woke the room was full of light and he was gone.

*   *   *

Her letter reached him three days after that, in his house in New Burlington Street.

'*My love,*' she wrote, the words pressed deep into the paper. '*I have sold my Madeira paintings. I did it while you were away and didn't tell you. They are gone abroad. They are signed with a name that is not mine so they will never reappear to embarrass you. The terms were generous and I have commissions for more—I cannot help but be a little proud of it. With the money, I have prepared a home for our daughter. A quiet place where she will grow and be loved. All her life she will be loved. That is my promise.*
'*Goodbye, Joseph. I will love you forever.*'

When he reached the house in Orchard Street he found she had left everything. She and Martha were gone and Sophia's cot was empty but not even her clothes had been taken. The servants were as surprised and mystified as he. Only later, when the light was fading, did he notice that where her painting of oak leaves had once hung, there was now an empty space.

328

CHAPTER EIGHTEEN

A BROWN BIRD

The journey to Lincolnshire felt like a fresh start. In the end, not wanting to arrive early, I took a circuitous route and when I reached Lincoln I called in on Bert Fox to make arrangements. We agreed that he would deliver to the hotel at seven o'clock that evening, and then we fell to chatting, so that I didn't make it to the hotel until six. By that time another cold evening had settled on the streets and the hotel fires were stoked up high. I arrived on foot in the darkness and stepped quietly into the light of the lobby, my big overcoat still hunched around me, its collar high around my face. I found Potts sitting there reading a Raymond Chandler novel and watching the door. His eyes ran quickly over me when I came in, but I carried nothing and had no one with me. He looked disappointed, but when he rose to his feet to greet me he was all old-world charm in a new-world accent.

'Mr Fitzgerald! How very mysterious you're getting to be. Do you know, if there's one thing I didn't expect from you it was mystery?'

'Is that meant to be a compliment?'

'It's whatever you'd like it to be.' He waved in the direction of the reception desk. 'I guess you'll want to freshen up after your journey. After that I'd very much like to have a word with you alone.'

'I could meet you in the bar in half an hour.'

'Perhaps somewhere with a little more privacy?'

'No, I like the bar. That's about as private as I want to be.'

He nodded, accepting my terms. 'Sure. The bar then, in half an hour.' He pottered back to his sofa, for all the world a kindly old gent with nothing on his mind but his book.

I told the woman at reception that I was expecting someone to arrive with a parcel for me.

'When he comes,' I asked her, 'could you let him drop it off in my room, please? His name's Fox.'

When I got to my room I rang Katya and Anderson, in that order. Five minutes before I was due in the bar, Katya knocked at my door and let herself in.

'Phew!' she gasped when the door was shut, then flopped dramatically onto the bed in mock exhaustion. 'I'm so tired. They've been on at me all day, trying to persuade me to put in a word for them. The bidding is ferocious. And one of them always seems to be watching me whenever I leave my room.' She pushed herself upright. 'Did everything go all right?'

I sat down next to her. 'It went well. Look at this.' I pulled a piece of paper out of my pocket. 'It's my receipt. I'll only show it to them if they demand to see one. I don't want them tracking down Bert Fox and giving him hassle about any of this.'

Katya looked down at it and laughed. 'Five thousand pounds! That's going to make them *so* mad.' We both laughed then and with the laughter returned that warm thrill of complicity. 'Where is it now?' she asked.

'With Fox. I didn't want to bring it with me while they were all watching. He's going to bring it

330

around later.'

'And you're sure he won't change his mind?'

'Yes, I'm sure. Bert is an odd one. He's his own man with his own ideas. I always thought he might see things my way. I'm sure I can trust him.'

'What about the pictures?'

'The case is all sealed up. You can't tell if there are any paintings in there until it's opened.'

Katya looked at her watch. 'We should go down. The others are in the bar. Except Potts. He's hanging around at the end of the corridor, seeing who comes in and who goes out.'

'OK, then.' I stood up and gave her my hand to help her up. 'Let's collect him on our way.'

Potts showed no surprise when he found Anderson and Gabby waiting for us in the bar. He merely took off his little round glasses and rubbed them vigorously on his waistcoat.

'I see.' He smiled affably. 'You'd have been much better to talk to me by myself, Mr Fitzgerald. But, hey, let's see what happens.'

The room was empty apart from Anderson and Gabby, but the fire was already blazing. Behind the bar a slightly lugubrious barman was reading a book, which he pushed hastily out of sight when we came in. As if to compensate for the lack of drinkers, the music had been turned up. Someone was singing 'Fly Me to the Moon' with slightly too much feeling.

We gathered around the same table as before, but this time everyone was looking at me, not Anderson. I looked back at them, one by one: Anderson expectant, Katya happy and excited, Potts restless, darting swift glances to the door of the bar. And Gabby. Gabby was watching me

331

anxiously, and I wondered what she made of what she saw.

For once Anderson didn't wait for the drinks to be ordered before getting down to business. He wanted to know about the Ulieta bird. Was it true? Did I have it?

'Yes,' I told him. 'It's true. I bought it this afternoon for five thousand pounds. The owner was quite happy with the deal.'

'Who was the owner?' That was Potts cutting in but Anderson waved the question away impatiently.

'Did he have the pictures too?'

'No, he'd never heard of the pictures. But the seal of the case hasn't been broken for years. Probably not since the last century.'

'And you're sure it's the real thing?' he asked.

'You'll have to make up your own mind on that,' I told him. Then I turned back to Potts. 'As for the owner, it doesn't matter. I own it now.'

'And what will you do with it?' Gabby's voice was calmer than the men's and almost sultry in its softness. 'You can see why I'm curious, Fitz.'

They all stopped at that and waited for me to answer. Anderson cast a swift glance at Katya but she was looking at me too, an easy, contented smile on her face.

'Well,' I began, 'that's one of the things I thought we'd talk about this evening. But first there's a couple of questions I wanted to ask.'

'Such as?' Anderson was finally signalling to the barman.

'Such as, which one of you broke into my house?' I turned to Potts. 'Was it you?'

He was leaning back in his chair, his hands

332

joined over the generous curve of his stomach.

'Ah, Mr Fitzgerald! Just a little research. I would have liked to have things tidy but you'll understand that I wasn't keen to linger. It was important for me to check your notes, to see what you really knew about the Ulieta bird.'

'Why didn't you do that the first time? What was all that stuff about dusting the bookshelves?'

He looked back at me blankly.

'I don't think he can answer that.' Anderson sounded his usual calm self.

'It was *you*?'

'That's right.' He seemed amused by my surprise. 'Remember, Mr Fitzgerald, we're talking about something that could be worth a million dollars. That night, after you left the Mecklenburg, I tried to catch up with you. But when I reached your house no one was in. And your front door was practically inviting me to look around.'

'But what were you looking for? What was all that stuff with my bookshelves?'

Anderson stared at me as if he was seeing me clearly for the first time. And then he leaned back from the table and began to laugh: big, genuine gusts of laughter that rose from his diaphragm and made his whole ribcage heave. When the laughter subsided, he shook his head.

'You really *don't* know, do you? The famous John Fitzgerald, world authority on extinct birds, and somehow you still don't know, even though it's in the most obvious textbook.'

'Know what?' At that particular moment I disliked him more than ever. And his laughter was having an effect. Although they had no idea what he was laughing at, Gabby and Potts, even Katya,

333

were beginning to smile.

He gave a few more shakes of his head and then sat upright again, composing himself.

'OK, I'll start at the beginning. When we met at the hotel you said you knew nothing about the Ulieta bird—but I didn't believe you. There was one basic thing that you *had* to know, and when you pretended not to, I just assumed you knew a lot more besides.'

I was completely confused now and my expression made Anderson laugh some more.

'When I found you weren't there that evening, I thought I'd go in and try to take a look at your famous notes. But when I got to your room something on the bookcase caught my eye. You see, Mr Fitzgerald, an academic has to keep his library up to date. Fosdyke's *Notes on Avian Species*—you have the wrong edition.' He paused to let the comment sink in. 'I was pretty sure from the cover that yours was the first edition but I needed to take it down and look at it, just to check. Perhaps you stayed with that edition because it was signed by the author. I don't know. But then it suddenly dawned on me that perhaps you hadn't been pretending after all. Perhaps you really didn't know anything.'

I shrugged, still not comprehending.

'You see,' he went on, 'Fosdyke brought out a second edition a few years after the first. He'd added one or two new bits of information, including one about the Ulieta bird.' He turned now and looked at Katya. 'Fosdyke had found that letter, the one you saw in the Fabricius archives. The letter mentions a drawing of the Ulieta bird made in Lincolnshire and Fosdyke made a Latin joke about it. I can't quote it exactly but it's something like this: "*the specimen of* Turdus ulietensis *once owned by Joseph Banks seems likely to be the* Turdus lindensis *mentioned later by Fabricius*". Lindum is the Roman name for Lincoln,' he explained, looking around us, assuming ignorance. 'So that's why the letter sent to Martha Stamford was so exciting. Because it fitted with what we already knew—that the bird had somehow ended up in Lincolnshire.'

'So you put the book back, dusted the shelves so I didn't know which book you'd looked at, and left me to wallow in my ignorance?'

'More or less. I didn't think it would take you long to find out about the Lincolnshire reference but I wasn't going to point it out to you.' He turned to Katya. 'Considering you hadn't read Fosdyke, I was very impressed by the way you found it for yourself. Of course your friend here could have saved you all that trouble if he'd bothered to visit a decent reference library. Now, tell me, Mr Fitzgerald, what was the other question you wanted to ask?'

I reached into my pocket and pulled out the crumpled picture of Miss B that Potts had removed from Anderson's room.

'Do you know who this is?' I asked.

Anderson barely glanced at it. 'Joseph Banks's mistress. His first mistress. He went on to have others, of course.'

'Why did you have her picture in your room?'

'I have all sorts of stuff in my files. I brought it all with me. Does it matter?'

'You didn't think she was important in some way?'

'In finding the bird?' He breathed out a little impatiently. 'No, of course not. I had someone research Joseph Banks for me, so I knew all about the mistress. She was interesting because she knew Fabricius, and Fabricius knew something about the bird. But she's a dead end. No one can even say who she was.'

I looked across at Katya.

'No, I suppose no one will ever know who she really was.' Before Anderson could reply, one of the women from the reception desk appeared at our table.

'The gentleman has been and gone, sir,' she explained. 'He's left it in your room as you said.'

'Thank you.' I smiled, and turned to the others. 'What do you think? Is it time for us to go upstairs and inspect the merchandise?'

*   *   *

I'd left one small lamp on in my bedroom, so when we all filed in, the room was washed with a low, reddish light. It was a small room and the double bed where Katya had flopped earlier filled the centre of it. Otherwise there was only a small desk and wardrobe, a couple of chairs and just about enough space for the five of us to stand in.

Bert Fox had left his parcel in the centre of the bed and we instinctively spread out around it, Katya on my left, Anderson on my right with Gabby next to him and Potts a little apart, watching us all.

The parcel on the bed was a couple of feet tall and about the same across. It was wrapped in brown paper under a layer of bubble wrap and had

336

been crisscrossed with belts of heavy-duty pink tape. No one spoke at first but Anderson gave a little sigh on seeing it. It was a sigh that told me something. Before then I'd taken him for the ultimate professional, a man who looked for rare things purely for profit. But now I wondered if Gabby might have been right. Perhaps behind it all there really was a man who just loved the search. In a little way I found myself liking him more.

'You might need this.' Potts had taken a penknife out of his pocket. 'Come on. We're waiting.'

I started forward, suddenly full of doubt about the whole enterprise. But now I had no choice but to show them what was in the package. Slowly, with careful movements of the knife, I cut away the tape, then the plastic, until there was only the brown paper left. Suddenly impatient, I tore it away with two sweeps of my hands, leaving the object below uncovered.

The case was built of old, dark wood with a glass pane set into each side. One of the panes of glass was cracked and another was misted with a haze of tiny flaws so that it was almost opaque. Inside, crudely perched on a wooden branch, was a small, brown bird, its head cocked slightly towards us as if in surprise. A very *ordinary* bird, very like a thrush or a blackbird or something in between. It could have landed in a suburban garden without exciting much notice.

'Jeez!' exclaimed Potts. 'Is that it? All this fuss for that?'

But Anderson and Gabby were both crouching down, studying it intently through the two clear panes. I took a deep breath and turned on the overhead light so they could see it properly. And that made a difference.

It was easy to see the bird wasn't in a good state. It was a little shapeless, as if its body had begun to sag with gravity, and the harsher light showed that the once rufous feathers had faded to a stale grey in places. There was a patch on its neck where the feathers seemed to have been torn away from the skin and now stood up in an undignified tuft. But the better light also showed the shadings of colour that distinguished it, the tiny markings that made it neither a blackbird nor an ordinary thrush but something different and unknown.

Anderson turned to me, his eyes shining. 'What do you think? Is it the one?'

I shrugged. I wasn't enjoying this as much as I'd hoped. 'It certainly could be.'

He turned back and began to point out the details to Gabby. She was nodding, scrutinising it minutely. Neither of them were specialists but they both knew about birds and about preserved specimens, and they knew what they were looking for. Potts watched them both, observing their reactions. Katya took my arm and leaned against me slightly. I shut my eyes and waited. I could hear Anderson murmuring under his breath, repeating the description made by Forster over two hundred years ago: 'Head dusky marked with brown . . . Wing dusky, primaries edged with brown . . . Twelve tail feathers . . .' Eventually he stood up: I heard the click of his knees as he straightened. Something of his usual manner had returned.

'Of course it's nothing without provenance,' he said.

'I know that.'

338

He looked at me, surprised at my confidence. 'There would need to be tests done.'

'Of course. The lab people will want to do their bit of poking around.'

He bent down and looked at it again. 'It's a miracle that it's survived.'

'A miracle? Perhaps. It's certainly an amazing piece of luck.'

'Jeez!' Potts snorted. 'Are we doing business here or not? You two can compare bird-spotting notes later, because the most you're going to get for that is a few thousand dollars. What about the pictures? We need to open the case.'

'No.' I held out my hand to keep him away from the bed, and the authority in my voice seemed to surprise him. 'You two are interested in the pictures, I'm interested in the bird. So nobody's opening up the case until we have the right conditions, the right humidity, the full works. That's part of the deal—whatever happens, the bird is dealt with properly. Now, let's go back downstairs and talk figures.'

I leaned forward and replaced the brown-paper wrapper around the case to protect the bird from the light. When we left the room I took good care to lock the door behind me.

Back in the bar I watched Anderson settle back into one of the hotel sofas. When I'd met him at the Mecklenburg he had spoken in quite an offhand way about my grandfather. At the time I'd thought it was the contempt of the natural winner for the habitual loser. But perhaps I had it wrong. Like my grandfather, he'd begun this expedition feeling he had something within his grasp that only he believed in. Perhaps he was afraid that like my

339

grandfather he would be forestalled by some unforeseeable freak of chance. And now, the chance had happened, the lightning had struck. It was me who ended up with the bird.

Even so, it left him considerably better off than it had left my grandfather. By the time Chapin made his successful foray into the Congo basin and emerged with those living specimens of the Congo peacock, my grandfather and his companion had probably already come to the end of their journey. The remains of their equipment were found two years later by a pair of French surveyors, many miles east of where Chapin found his peacocks. The few rather pathetic objects that the Frenchmen retrieved included my grandfather's journal, the prose brittle with determination even while the logic and sense were draining from his words. The last entries were almost meaningless and nearly illegible. They contained no message for his wife or son, my father, a child he may not even have known existed.

The bodies were never found. When news of the expedition's demise reached Britain, a small memorial service was held. *The Times* praised his courage and endurance. My grandmother never remarried.

Unlike the two men who lost their lives in the jungle, Anderson would prosper. I watched as Gabby settled beside him on the bar's big velvet sofa. They sat close to each other, almost touching, as they had at the Mecklenburg. This time I didn't resent it. I just sat quietly and waited for someone to speak.

'Well, Mr Fitzgerald,' Potts began, 'what's the deal here? Are you selling the bird now and the paintings later, if they turn out to be there? I'm not prepared to bid blind.'

'I don't care about the pictures. Like I said, it's the bird that counts. I'm prepared to sell the bird to either of you, but these are my terms: as soon as we agree a price, we take the bird to the Natural History Museum, and the case is opened there, in proper conditions. The bird itself is donated to the Natural History Museum, but you get to keep the case and anything in it. And if the pictures are there, one per cent of anything you get for them goes to the museum for the upkeep of the bird.'

Potts snorted. 'You're joking, Mr Fitzgerald. No one can do business on those terms. There may not *be* any pictures! Or you might already have opened the case and taken them out for all we know.'

I looked at him steadily. 'I guess that's the risk you have to take.'

'You're living in dreamland if you think anyone will touch a deal like that. It stinks.'

But Anderson was watching Potts and smiling.

'Oh, I don't know,' he mused. 'I like what you're saying, Mr Fitzgerald. You're right to want to safeguard the bird. So let's see. Let's say I promise to make a donation to the Natural History Museum to cover all the costs incurred in restoring the bird and in keeping it on display in proper conditions, plus fifty grand more for the upkeep of other rare specimens. No Canadian millionaires, no laboratories, no DNA experiments. In return, if the pictures are there, I get to keep them. The risk is all mine.'

I nodded and turned to Potts.

'Frankly, this is all bullshit,' he told me, taking off his glasses and rubbing them on his waistcoat.

341

For all the innocence of the gesture, I could tell he was getting increasingly agitated. 'Look, Mr Fitzgerald, here's my offer. You open up the case. If the pictures are there, I look after the business of getting them over to the States nice and quiet. I take a ten per cent cut, but I promise you'll make a darn sight more this way than you will if you take them off to Sotheby's. I'm talking private sale here, Mr Fitzgerald. Discreet, tax-free. No questions, no red tape, no mark-ups to anyone else. Plus you get to keep the bird. If they're not there, we go our separate ways and you can give the bird to who the hell you like. Think of it, Mr Fitzgerald. Ninety per cent of a million dollars is going to pay for some pretty good bird preservation. And what's he offering you? Not a dime.'

'My offer's on the table, Mr Fitzgerald,' Anderson said evenly.

I turned back to Potts. 'He's guaranteeing the future of the bird, pictures or no pictures. I need you to do the same.'

'Oh, for chrissake!' He stood up, very clearly agitated now. 'This is crazy. Give me ten minutes. I need to think.'

We watched him stalk out of the bar, a slightly absurd figure, too rotund and genial for his anger to be taken very seriously. When he was out of sight, Anderson chuckled.

'I guess I've just matched his highest bid,' he remarked with a smile.

I looked over at Katya who raised her eyebrows at me questioningly. I answered her with a nod and then turned back to Anderson.

'Let's have another drink.'

'Yes, of course.' He sat forward and reached

342

into his jacket pocket for his wallet.

'Assuming Mr Potts doesn't change his mind, we'll need something in writing about all this,' he said.

'OK, start writing. Put down exactly what you've just said. Tomorrow I'll get it checked over by a solicitor.'

He produced a sheet of paper from his briefcase and began writing.

'It's amazing,' he mused as he wrote. 'Seeing that bird. Who would have believed it? Even if we don't find Roitelet's paintings, it was worth coming over just for that. I really mean it.'

He wrote in silence for a while, then pushed the paper over to me and looked round contentedly.

'Where's Potts?' he wondered idly. 'He's taking his time.'

For three or four seconds that statement hung in the air before anyone reacted. Then we all moved at once. Anderson was first to his feet and first to the door of the bar. I was a couple of yards behind him as he barged across the lobby and launched himself up the hotel stairs. And I was still behind him when he reached my room and found the lock forced, the bed empty, the bird gone.

In the years after her departure, Banks pursued both his work and his pleasures with a grim vehemence. His scientific projects enveloped him, and he laboured tirelessly at them, impressing all who met him with his fierce commitment to the advancement of knowledge. His standing grew and his career flourished. His reputation spread. His correspondence alone was enough to fill three days of the week, and a man so busy can allow himself little time for introspection. And he had little need for it. In his own mind he had already answered the question that so beset him in the days after her departure: the two of them, he knew, would never meet again.

But in that he was wrong. He was to see her one more time, some three years later, on a bright morning in spring. It was one of the last days he spent in the house on New Burlington Street, and his mind was fixed on the many matters squabbling for his attention. There were arrangements to be made, papers to be signed and formalities to be overcome. As a result, his temper was short that day and he had no intention of receiving callers. It was only by chance that he appeared on the stairs at the moment the front door was opened to her. She did not see him for that first moment, intent as she was on asking for him, but he saw her, and the sight made him stop abruptly. With the shock came a tightness in his lungs and he felt the blood running to his cheeks. Then she looked up and their eyes met again.

He brought her into the house himself, all the anger he had manufactured in the years since she'd left suddenly dissipated by the touch of her gloved fingers on his hand. All the recriminations he had rehearsed were replaced by speechlessness; all the coldness he carried in him changed to raw feeling.

She had prepared herself for that day, so the shock of meeting was less for her. But when she looked into his face she saw lines there she did not recognise and furrows where no frown had been. The sight of them touched her in a way she had not anticipated.

To him she seemed unchanged. As graceful and neat as that time he had come upon her arranging flowers. As poised behind her defences as that day a lifetime earlier when he had first spoken to her in the Revesby woods.

'I was in London,' she said. 'I came to thank you.'

He looked beyond her, into the street where a carriage was waiting.

'To thank me?' he asked, still confused by her presence.

'For not following us.'

The plural noun caught his attention.

'You mean . . .?'

'Sophia and I.'

'I see. I'd promised I would not.' Then he shook his head and found he could smile. 'In truth I was too resentful. I wanted you to return unbidden.'

She looked up and he could no longer avoid her eyes.

'You knew I would not.'

'Yes. I think I knew that.'

She saw the smile, but also the tension in his body, and she reproached herself for the visit, the lack of warning she had given him.

'I would not have come, but I had need to be in London and I wanted to tell you that Sophia is well and happy. Only that.'

'As you promised.'

'Yes, as I promised.'

He nodded.

'I think of her more often than you would believe.'

She shook her head. 'No, I would believe it.'

They stood still and looked at each other then. From outside, the bright spring day cast a silver light in the space between them.

'Do you blame me for what I did?' she asked.

'I try to.'

'Do you succeed?'

'For three years I have succeeded. But I was not then looking at your face.'

'Then I am glad that I came.'

*   *   *

They passed an hour together that morning, surrounded by his collection, the great magazine of curiosities that had filled his house and become the wonder of Europe. In the wide, light-filled rooms the size of the collection seemed to dwarf them and they drifted almost in silence from exhibit to exhibit, each more aware of the other than of the marvels before them. Sometimes she would pause to study an object and as she did so he would step back and watch her— until he realised that her concentration was too intense, that in truth she was tangled in her own thoughts. Then he would speak blithely of the first object to catch his eye and she would follow him to it, and for a little while they would discuss it brightly before again falling silent.

They moved from room to room, from the great display of human implements and the memorabilia of his days in the South Seas to the herbarium, where they flitted from plant to plant and back again. There

346

were the pictures too, wild landscapes and the faces of strange men and women; but most of all the botanical works, the incomparable collection of drawings made by Parkinson before his death on the *Endeavour*. She studied them most closely, not in admiration, but as one workman observes another to see what can be learned. From time to time she would nod as if acknowledging a particular touch of his brush.

Finally they came to the room of animal specimens, some mounted, many of them only skins stored flat. He showed her the greatest curiosities, the novelties that had become the talking point of his museum. As they browsed he paused for a moment and looked at her directly again.

'One thing I should tell you . . . Do you remember Lysart, the geologist? He has a daughter who is . . . who is like Sophia. She grows up in Kensington and he visits her often. But I can see it is difficult for her. Society is hard on such a woman.' He turned back to the drawing in front of him. 'It is only just that I should tell you as much.'

She nodded, scarcely looking at him, and their inspection moved on.

Towards the end of the final room she came upon a mounted bird of no great distinction. He studied the label. From the South Seas, he said, from an island near Otaheite.

'Such a plain bird to be so displayed,' she said.

'Indeed. I don't know why Forster mounted it. I remember he talked of some new practice in preservation that he wished to try. Perhaps he chose something unexceptional lest the experiment failed.'

She was still looking at the bird.

'But I like it,' she said. 'A plain, brown bird amongst all this glory. It has its own beauty, I think.'

347

'Take it,' he said urgently, seized with the desire that she should have an object to remind her of that day. 'Or I can have it sent to you.'

'But that would diminish your collection,' she replied.

'By a fraction. Who will notice?'

In the end he insisted and she gave him an address in Soho where it could be sent.

'It is the house of Monsieur Martin,' she told him. 'It is he who buys my work.'

And so, when she had gone, when their last words had been spoken and he had handed her into her carriage, the bird was taken down and prepared for dispatch.

For a few weeks its place in the rooms on New Burlington Street stood empty. But in the summer of that year his collection moved to Soho Square and the brown bird was forgotten.

CHAPTER NINETEEN

CONCLUSIONS

The day after Potts's theft from my hotel room saw the first snow of the year. Katya and I had been up half the night, calming Anderson and shaking our heads while the police were called, the hotel roused, details explained and a great deal of swearing done. When it was clear the bird had gone, I tore up my agreement with Anderson and gave the pieces back to him. I had sufficient respect for Potts by then to know it was highly unlikely that we would ever see either the bird or its case again. He certainly wasn't going to be stupid enough to stumble into the arms of the police with a stuffed bird in his possession. At about three o'clock, groggy from lack of sleep, Katya and I left Gabby and Anderson in the hotel bar and went to bed. I can't speak for the rest of them but that night I didn't even dream.

The next day we checked out of the hotel as the snow was beginning to fall. There was too little of it to turn the world white but the drift of snowflakes onto the cobbles was strangely soothing. I think we both felt the same. Katya put her arm through mine as we walked to the car.

'What will Potts do with it?' she asked.

'I don't know. When he finds there are no pictures, he might just dump it in the river. Or he might leave it dormant somewhere until things calm down, then sneak it to America to see what Ted Staest will pay for it.'

'And Anderson?'

'He'll write it off as a business loss, I guess. He'll soon find another project to replace it. And something tells me that, bird or no bird, he'll find the money to make sure Gabby's project carries on. I don't think that's a business thing for him.' I smiled at my own contradictions. 'They make a good couple,' I said.

'Seeing that bird last night mattered to him, didn't it?'

'I know. It makes me feel bad.'

Katya still had her arm in mine and she gave it a little squeeze. 'Do you think he'll ever find out?' she asked.

'Perhaps. In time. In a way I hope not.'

'Yes.' She nodded, understanding. 'He'd be happier not knowing. Tell me, did you really need to go to such trouble? All that work . . .'

'I think so. Otherwise Potts and Anderson would never have stopped looking. This way they can forget about it and leave us all in peace.'

Tiny flakes of snow were lingering in her hair as we talked and she pulled the collar of her coat around her face.

'And Gabby?' she asked. 'Did you say goodbye to her?'

'Sort of. I don't think she minded.'

'Didn't mind you keeping Anderson from the bird?'

'That too.'

We reached the car and found its windscreen wipers edged with a delicate line of snow.

'What would you have done if Potts hadn't stolen it?' she wondered.

'I've no idea. But I was sure he'd try something.

350

He's that sort of guy.'

We got in and began the practised routine of buttoning our coats and pulling our scarves tighter. It felt familiar and comfortable.

'Is it far?'

'About forty minutes in this thing.' I grinned, patting the steering wheel affectionately. 'Come on, let's get moving and see if we can get some heat in here.'

As we nudged our way out of Lincoln into the countryside, we were caught in an unannounced flurry of proper snow, thick flakes falling heavily and making the windscreen wipers do their job. Then almost as suddenly we drove out the other side and into sunshine. Around us, patchy white furrows scored the fields.

We talked as we drove, light-hearted now, taking our time to understand everything Bert Fox had told me about his family history.

'So Bert Fox's great-grandfather married a Sophia Burnett?'

'Yes, except it was his great-great-grandfather. Bert told me about it when I went to see him the first time, but I got so excited when he mentioned Ainsby that I never asked myself if his Burnett and our Burnett might be related.'

'So Mary Burnett brought her daughter to Lincolnshire. I wonder what became of her after that?'

'I don't suppose we'll ever know. But we know Sophia married Matthew Fox. He was a small-time farmer. Guess what their son was called?'

'Not . . . ?'

'Yup. Joseph. Joseph Fox's son was another Matthew Fox and he ended up as steward to the

Stamford family at the turn of this century. That Matthew Fox had a son called Henry, who grew up with the Stamford children. They all knew the stories about the stuffed bird Matthew had in his cottage. And Matthew Fox is the old man John Stamford was talking about in his letter. He died while Stamford was at the front.'

'And Martha Stamford grabbed the bird for safekeeping?'

'That's right. She already had an attachment to Henry Fox, the old man's son. The two of them had grown up together. He's the "young *Vulpes*" mentioned at the end of the letter.'

'A young Fox . . .' Katya smiled. 'You think John Stamford was worried about him prowling around his sister?'

'I don't think he sounds disapproving in his letter. But it's hard to tell.'

'And at the end of the war?'

'Martha gave the bird back. Henry Fox had been in France when his father died. But it was his bird. And that's why it missed the sale of everything in the Old Manor. When the dust settled after the war, Henry and Martha married. She'd moved to Cornwall to live with a cousin when the house was sold and he went to find her there. In a way the loss of all the family money must have helped them. If it hadn't been for the war they'd probably have been kept apart.'

We sat in silence then, pondering the vagaries of chance. Gradually the fields were left behind and we began to pick our way through the outskirts of the next town. A few minutes later I pulled up outside a terrace of smart Georgian houses three storeys high, tucked away down a quiet street a

352

short walk from the town centre.

'This is it. Where the last of the Stamfords ended up.'

On the pavement in front of the house a figure I recognised was lurking slightly disreputably, smoking a roll-up. Bert Fox's response to the weather had been to pull on a faded baseball cap and a grey, slightly saggy overcoat. He wore the coat unbuttoned so it hung open and I could see a T-shirt and a leather waistcoat underneath. His silver ponytail was squashed down by the cap and hidden under the collar of his coat.

'Just having a fag,' he explained when I introduced him to Katya. 'Mum doesn't like me smoking at her place.' He dropped the cigarette onto the pavement and pressed it with his toe. 'You'll like my mum,' he told Katya. 'She's a laugh.'

We went inside. The hallway had been built to feel spacious but the effect was undermined by the mass of objects squeezed into it. An umbrella stand by the door sprouted walking sticks and old-fashioned canes and two very long African spears. Next to it, a small table was covered with smaller objects—a cigar box, an ashtray-with-lighter, a porcelain bowl, a gold photograph frame, an ebony camel. And the walls were studded with pictures from waist height upwards so that the wallpaper beneath them was all but obscured—watercolours, miniatures, framed photographs and a couple of large portraits in oil, clumsy amongst their neighbours like ocean liners amidst a flotilla of small boats.

'Mum!' Fox shouted as he closed the door behind us. 'John's here again. Remember? To see the bird. Got a friend with him.'

We hung our coats above the walking sticks and were shown into the front room. Like the hallway, it was packed with objects but the effect was somehow more harmonious. Amidst the clutter, tiny under a pink blanket in a large green chair, sat the woman whose letter had first made us believe in the Ulieta bird. She was old now—so old that it had occurred to none of us that she might still be alive—but Martha Stamford had aged into a happy, laughing old lady. All around her were the mementoes of another age, but she herself was so alert it seemed impossible to believe that she had danced and flirted with men on leave from Passchendaele.

She greeted Katya with a nod and made her stand close so she could see her face.

'Albert says you're from Sweden,' she informed her.

'Yes, that's right. From near Stockholm.'

'Well, you're very welcome,' she replied. 'You must like it a lot to come here in winter,' she added, following a thought of her own. Then she looked up at me.

'So you've come for another look? It's a dull old thing, that bird, but I'm not surprised it's valuable. We've always treasured it in our family. It's part of our history, you know.'

And she began to tell me again how old Matthew Fox had called it his grandmother's most precious possession.

'She loved it because it was *her* mother's, you see. Her mother had been given it by a lover—at least that's what Matthew used to say. That was rather shocking, of course, but we all thought it

354

was terribly romantic. I remember old Matthew telling me how his grandmother took him by his hand when he was a boy and showed him all her treasures, and when she came to that bird she told him it was her mother's, and even though it was so plain her mother had always treasured it more than anything she owned because it was given to her by someone she loved. And I remember Henry—that's Albert's father—telling me how it was so valuable because of Captain Cook finding it. But none of them would ever sell it because it was a love gift.'

'And what about the pictures, Mum? Tell them about the pictures again.'

'Ah, yes. Those. Henry found them, not long after we were married. Beautiful things they were. All local wildflowers. There were harebells and bluebells and all sorts. So bright, they were. Lovely things. Henry had them all framed and we had them on the walls. But when we moved here there was no room so he sold them to the family that had bought the Old Manor. Got a few pounds for them, he did.'

Katya turned to me breathlessly.

'So they could still be there now?'

I shook my head and looked across at Bert Fox.

'The Old Manor burned down during the war,' he said. 'I suppose the flower pictures went with it.'

'Lovely things, they were,' his mother went on. 'Lovely bright colours. Better than having fresh flowers in the house, I used to say . . . But of course you don't want to listen to me going on. It's the bird you're interested in. Go on up and take a look at it.'

However, I hadn't quite finished with her

355

reminiscences. 'Tell me, do you know anything else about old Matthew's great-grandmother, the one who first owned the bird?'

'Oh, I don't think there's much to know. It's all too long ago now. Old Matthew must have heard tales about her but I don't think he told me.'

Bert Fox coughed quietly. 'She might be buried in the churchyard in Ainsby. I can't tell for sure because there's a gap in the records. It's a bit overgrown up in the old part but the stones are still there.'

'You mean we might be able to find her headstone?'

'Nah, not now. They're too far gone. You can't make 'em out now for all the moss and stuff grown over them.'

'Better than the crematorium,' chipped in his mother. 'That's what Albert says he wants.'

He winked at me. 'And that's where you'll be too, Mum, if they ask me to decide.'

At which she laughed happily and slapped him on the arm.

*　　　*　　　*

She didn't come with us to see the bird. She couldn't climb the stairs now and, as she put it, she already knew what it looked like. Before we left her I felt obliged to stop and tell her again what I'd told her when we first met, that someone would probably pay very good money for the specimen she had upstairs.

'Money?' she muttered, just as she had before. 'I've got what I need. It will be Bert's soon and then he can decide.' Bert looked across at me and gave a little shrug. Then he led us upstairs to the first-floor landing and the strange little room they called the Book Room.

It had been created years ago, probably soon after the house was built, when someone decided to alter the layout of the first-floor bedrooms. The construction of a new wall had created a strange, awkward room sandwiched between the main bedrooms. It had probably been used as a linen room then, but for as long as Bert Fox remembered it had been the Book Room, where the family books were kept. He showed us in and turned on the overhead light from the switch by the door. The room was narrow, about five feet wide but perhaps fifteen feet long. Both long walls had been covered with bookshelves, which meant only the far wall and the area above the door had any space for decoration. Here the temptation to hang too much had been resisted. The far wall was empty but for a rather drab study of dead oak leaves, but that was not the wall attracting our attention. Above the door, in a clear glass case, quiet master of the stillness below, stood the lost bird of Ulieta.

It wasn't unlike the bird I'd made in its image but it was far, far better preserved. To create mine I had been forced to beg and buy very old specimens of thrush and blackbird and it had taken all my skill to combine them believably into a counterfeit bird: where things proved difficult, I had simulated decrepitude to mask my failings. But this specimen had none of the torn feathers, none of the shapelessness. It was in a remarkable, almost incredible, state of preservation. To anyone who had seen Georg Forster's picture there could be no doubting that this was the original.

Katya and I both stood and wondered.

'How can it be so perfect?' she said at last.

'I don't know. It must be the most amazing fluke.'

But Bert Fox pointed around him. 'No outside walls to this room, you see. My father kept it in here with the books because this room never gets damp. And the temperature is always the same. Always cold.'

'But what about before then? All those years in a steward's cottage. It's amazing it survived.'

'My father said they'd been told to treat it with arsenic,' he said. 'I think each generation did what they could to look after it.'

'So that's why,' said Katya as if a missing piece of understanding had just fallen into place. 'That's why this one's still here when all those other specimens fell apart.'

She paused and looked up at the bird again before she realised we were both watching her, waiting for her to explain.

'Because of all that love,' she said simply.

*   *   *

When we went downstairs again we found Martha Stamford asleep under her pink blanket, surrounded by the multitude of objects that her life had touched with meaning. Above us Joseph Banks's bird had been restored to the stillness and the darkness of its sealed room. There seemed no reason to disturb either.

Before stepping out into the street, Katya and I stood in the doorway, trying to gauge the temperature. I waited while she buttoned up her coat and pulled her collar up to her nose, and then we stood close to each other for a second or two, looking up at the sky. Then we stepped out together into the winter sunshine.

Three days before his death at the age of seventy-six, Joseph Banks called for pen and ink and began a letter to his old travelling companion, Daniel Solander, a man who at that date had been dead for almost forty years.

'*My dear Solander,*' it began in a shaky hand, '*You once told me the past casts a shadow. You saw much I couldn't see. But I see now that beyond the shadow there is sunlight and trees and leaves.*

'*She has such green eyes, Solander—it is well that we are about to depart.*'

HISTORICAL NOTE

The Conjuror's Bird takes as its starting point a number of historical facts, the three most significant—and intriguing—being these:

The Mysterious Bird of Ulieta was first recorded in 1774, by Cook's expedition to the South Seas. No subsequent specimens were ever discovered.

In 1772 Sir Joseph Banks, the eminent naturalist, broke off his engagement and began an affair with one Miss B. Her identity and history remain unknown.

The search for the African peacock began early in the twentieth century with the discovery of a single feather. It took twenty-three years of searching before the first actual specimen was found.

The Mysterious Bird of Ulieta

I am indebted to James Greenway and his excellent book *Extinct and Vanishing Birds of the World* for the name 'Mysterious Bird of Ulieta' to describe the thrush-like bird *Turdus ulietensis*. The bird's history is very much as described in the novel. It was collected on Cook's second voyage of discovery, and was described by the naturalist on that voyage, Johann Forster.

Forster was a good scientist and the bird's details were well recorded. In addition, it was drawn by his son, Georg. The description given by Forster makes it hard to be certain what sort of bird it was. It appears to be a type of thrush (*turdus*) but certain details (concerning its tongue, for instance) cast some doubt on this. That mystery will never be resolved because, despite diligent searching, no other specimen of this bird has ever been found. If it were not for Forster's account and his son's drawing—still viewable at the Natural History Museum—there would be nothing to say it had ever existed.

As for the specimen itself, this was presented by Forster to Joseph Banks at the end of the voyage. It was recorded in his collection by Latham but, like many specimens from that time, its precise fate remains unknown.

Joseph Banks

The young naturalist Joseph Banks rose to public prominence as a result of his participation in Cook's first voyage of discovery. He went on to become a commanding figure in the Royal Society, its president for forty-two years and the unofficial scientific advisor to George III. But there are a couple of questions about his early life that remain unanswered.

Shortly before leaving with Cook he became engaged (at least informally) to Harriet Blosset. Shortly after his return this engagement was broken off—and at the same time we learn from the gossip magazine of the day—*Town & Country Magazine*—that Banks had begun an affair with a young girl known only as Miss B—n. That account, and the letter to Banks from Fabricius, both suggest a warm relationship and the birth of a child. But they throw no light on the lady's identity.

The affair must have begun very quickly after Banks's return (the timings are tight) but what happened to end the affair—and the fate of Miss B and her child—are still mysteries.

Shortly after *Town & Country Magazine* published its article, Banks was due to embark with Cook on a second great voyage of discovery. His quibbling over the extent of his accommodation and his sudden, last-minute refusal to partici pate are well documented but never fully explained. A letter from the Navy Board to the Admiralty concluded in the end that Banks had only one small cabin less than he had requested.

It is tempting to form a view about why this particular issue may have been so important to Banks if you read Cook's letter to the Admiralty from Madeira about the mysterious 'Mr Burnett' who was, apparently, a woman. The letter is often quoted but as far as I'm aware has never been properly explained.

My own researches into Miss B and her whereabouts followed much the same course as that ascribed to Fitz and Katya in the novel— including a visit to the archives in Lincoln, where I first found the name of Mary Burnett—born at just the right place and the right time to have been known to the young Joseph Banks.

The Congo Peacock

The story of James Chapin's discovery of the

Congo peacock is a true one. Chapin found a single feather early in the century but the bird itself was not actually found until twenty-three years later when he found two preserved specimens in a Belgian Museum. This discovery led directly to the successful search by Chapin for the birds themselves—a find that caused something of a sensation in the world of ornithology.

MD

ACKNOWLEDGEMENTS

Many people have helped me with the writing of this book. In particular I'd like to thank all those who have helped with comments, advice and exhortations to take a break and come and have a drink; Professor Mark Seaward for his wonderful knowledge of Lincolnshire lichens; Jo and Sam, for the Goat House; Jane, for her patience; my fellow toilers at the Café Rapallo; my parents, for the continual flow of cuttings, clippings and comments about Sir Joseph Banks; Yranie, as always, for her critical eye and uncritical support; and Margaret Lovegrove, for her enthusiasm just when I needed it.

Perhaps most importantly of all, I should acknowledge the many scholars, past and present, in particular Averil Lysaght and James C. Greenway, without whose work this book would never have happened.